WORLD DIVIDED

Book Two of the
SECRET WORLD CHRONICLE

BAEN BOOKS by MERCEDES LACKEY

BARDIC VOICES
The Lark and the Wren
The Robin and the Kestrel
The Eagle and the Nightingales
The Free Bards
Four & Twenty Blackbirds
Bardic Choices: A Cast of Corbies (with Josepha Sherman)

The Fire Rose

The Wizard of Karres (with Eric Flint & Dave Freer)

Werehunter

Fiddler Fair

Brain Ships (with Anne McCaffrey & Margaret Ball)
The Sword of Knowledge (with C.J. Cherryh, Leslie Fish, & Nancy Asire)

Bedlam's Bard (with Ellen Guon)
Beyond World's End (with Rosemary Edghill)
Spirits White as Lightning (with Rosemary Edghill)
Mad Maudlin (with Rosemary Edghill)
Music to My Sorrow (with Rosemary Edghill)
Bedlam's Edge (ed. with Rosemary Edghill)

THE SERRATED EDGE
Chrome Circle (with Larry Dixon)
The Chrome Borne (with Larry Dixon)
The Otherworld (with Larry Dixon & Mark Shepherd)

HISTORICAL FANTASIES WITH ROBERTA GELLIS
This Scepter'd Isle
Ill Met by Moonlight
By Slanderous Tongues
And Less Than Kind

HEIRS OF ALEXANDRIA SERIES
by Mercedes Lackey, Eric Flint & Dave Freer
The Shadow of the Lion
This Rough Magic
Much Fall of Blood

THE SECRET WORLD CHRONICLE
Invasion (with Steve Libbey, Cody Martin & Dennis Lee)
World Divided (with Cody Martin, Dennis Lee & Veronica Giguere)

To purchase these and all other Baen Book titles
in e-book format, please go to www.baen.com.

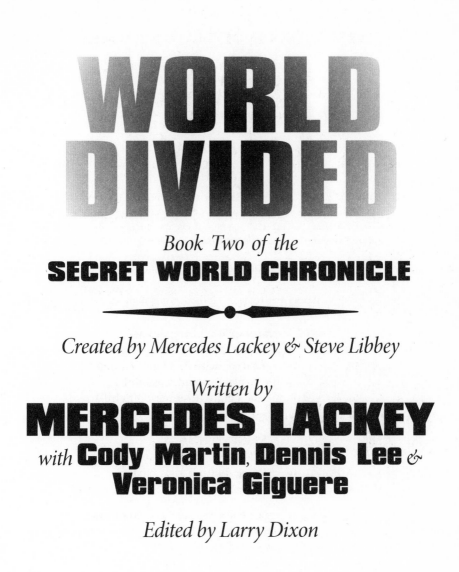

WORLD DIVIDED

Book Two of the
SECRET WORLD CHRONICLE

Created by Mercedes Lackey & Steve Libbey

Written by
MERCEDES LACKEY
with **Cody Martin, Dennis Lee** &
Veronica Giguere

Edited by Larry Dixon

WORLD DIVIDED: BOOK TWO OF THE SECRET WORLD CHRONICLE

This is a work of fiction. All the characters and events portrayed in this book are fictional, and any resemblance to real people or incidents is purely coincidental.

A Baen Books Original

Baen Publishing Enterprises
P.O. Box 1403
Riverdale, NY 10471
www.baen.com

ISBN: 978-1-4516-3801-1

Cover art by Larry Dixon

First printing, February 2012

Distributed by Simon & Schuster
1230 Avenue of the Americas
New York, NY 10020

Library of Congress Cataloging-in-Publication Data
tk

10   9   8   7   6   5   4   3   2   1

Pages by Joy Freeman (www.pagesbyjoy.com)
Printed in the United States of America

DEDICATION

To the awesome fans and friends of
the Secret World Chronicles podcasts.
We could not do this without you!

ACKNOWLEDGEMENTS

First and foremost:

We owe this story to the devs and designers of City of Heroes/ City of Villains/Going Rogue, the MMORPG by NCsoft and Paragon Studios where all these characters first were born. They evolved, grew, and changed from their original concepts, but much of that development took place in the world of Paragon City. If you would like to play in our favorite addiction, go to www.cityofheroes.com and give it a try.

You might have noticed that I (Mercedes) at least like to use song titles for my stories. This time I'd like to acknowledge the talented writers, singers and musicians and tell you which they are and why.

"Revelations" Iron Maiden. Seems to suit the confrontation of Seraphym and Verdigris.

"Running on Empty" Jackson Browne. Mercurye in captivity has a lot to think about.

"Nowhere Fast" The song I had in mind is the classic Jim Steinman tune from *Streets of Fire.*

"Every Breath You Take" Sting and the Police. This is perfect for the introduction of Vickie's Overwatch program.

"Watch Over Me" George Gershwin. It applies both to Vickie and to the Seraphym where John Murdock is concerned.

"Baby I'm an Anarchist!" Against Me! This is the quintessential John Murdock theme song.

"Cold-Hearted Snake" Paula Abdul. Really sums up Verdigris.

"Thunder Road" Judas Priest. Mostly because it's good, visceral fight music.

"She Blinded Me with Science" Thomas Dolby. I'm not sure why it fits, I'm only sure that it does.

"Respect the Wind" Eddie and Alex Van Halen, from the *Twister* original soundtrack. This music absolutely *is* the Seraphym for me.

"Bad Moon Rising" Creedence Clearwater Revival. As JM notes, the lyrics do sound as if they have been written for the Invasion.

"Dark Angel" VnV Nation. The lyrics definitely fit the Seraphym. I have to say that VnV Nation songs have come so close to encapsulating the mood of several of these stories that it is as if we had some sort of psychic link.

"No Illusions" 78 Saab. Such a cheerful melody for such borderline tragic lyrics. Definitely fits Mel.

"Sleeping with the Enemy" Rodger Hodgson. Oh Jack, this sure sums up everything in this story for him.

"Total Eclipse of the Heart" Bonnie Tyler. There are lines in this that fit just about everyone in the story.

"Precipice" VnV Nation. There is definitely no going back for Jack now.

"Thunder in Heaven" Ten. More good visceral fight music.

"Boulevard of Broken Dreams" Green Day. When everything seems lost.

"Pay It Forward" Thomas Newman, the original soundtrack of the same name. Very emotional.

"Suffer" VnV Nation. Again, it's kind of spooky how often VnV Nation manages to write songs that distill the essence of Secret World Chronicle stories. In this case…Vickie and Red.

"Illusion" VnV Nation. I actually had a dream with the entire sequence of this story playing like one of those wordless movie sequences to this song. That doesn't happen often and it is amazing when it does.

"Heroes and Thieves" Vanessa Carlton. A glimpse of hope.

"Roll the Bones" Rush. John at this point in his life has struck a balance, but believes in nothing but what he can experience for himself.

INTRODUCTION

Victoria Victrix paused for a moment, checked her watch, double-checked her watch against the time on her laptop. Hard to believe she still had almost an hour.

But there was a lot of story to get through before...

Better get back on it.

Her fingers flew over the keyboard.

Still with me, my unknown audience? By this time you've read how it all started for us, how the Invasion arrived all over the world concealed in delivery trucks that disgorged horrors right out of a Hollywood science fiction film. How we learned that the enemy was an old one—because he wore the swastika and was led by Nazi metahumans everyone had thought long dead. How we also learned that not all of our enemies were human.

How Echo, the organization that until now hadn't needed to worry about anything more organized than a few gangs of four or five metahuman criminals, suddenly found itself facing an army and losing. And how, eventually, the seeds of real organization against the Society of Ultima Thule came to Atlanta, where in Echo's ruined headquarters the repercussions were only just starting to shake out.

And among all those players converging on that southern city, there were a handful that would make a difference. A handful that could save the world. But first—first, we had to save ourselves.

And there were going to be some we were going to lose. Battles... and people. That's the nature of war.

For this was—is—a war. Make no mistake about it. Even though the enemy had evaporated into nowhere, anyone who had any brains knew that the Thulians would be back.

PROLOGUE

Dinner Date

MERCEDES LACKEY AND CODY MARTIN

The Invasion provided an unparalleled opportunity for anyone who wanted wealth or power to grab both. There were plenty who did. Politicians began to rise or fall based on their "solutions" or lack of them to the "Nazi Menace," or (more often than not) who or what they chose to point fingers at, agitate about, or scapegoat. It was a free ride for the criminal element. Even—well, especially—the media used the initial Invasion and the subsequent attacks we began to call "pop-ups" as fodder for their nightly barrage of fear-inducing infotainment. Shortsighted? Oh hell yes. But it brought in money, and the world over, "follow the money" will never steer you wrong when you are looking for human motive. It's human nature to figure that nothing bad will ever happen to you, because you, of course, are so much smarter, faster, better armed than the poor rubes in the Nightly News bodybags.

But probably the single most self-centered opportunist on the planet was about to take the gloves off and enter the arena. And what was the most dangerous about Dominic Verdigris III was this:

He actually had the brains to pull off just about anything he wanted to. He just had to be motivated enough.

When it all came down to it, Dominic Verdigris III, multibillionaire, supergenius and all that *and* a bag of chips, was a man who liked to enjoy the simpler things in life.

"I think the shark tank came out beautifully. And ahead of schedule, too!" He folded his arms across his chest, a self-satisfied grin creasing his lips as he glanced at his companion. "Don't you think, Khanjar?"

The stunningly beautiful Eurasian woman in the white silk jumpsuit could have been in just about any profession that required amazing good looks. World-class supermodel good looks, almost; save for her being slightly too-well muscled. In fact, she was Verdigris' personal bodyguard, preferred assassin and lover.

"Why a shark tank, Dom?" she asked, her cool tone betraying no emotion whatsoever. "Isn't that a little...over the top? Next thing, you'll want a white angora cat."

"Order one, have it shipped to my New York penthouse." He grinned, the sort of grin that meant he got the joke and didn't want the cat. "But, my dear, being over the top is the point. People, regular people, like to have everything laid out for them in easy to understand bite-sized chunks. They don't like to be ordered or forced to believe something is so, but they like to be led to that belief and have it reinforced according to the way they think the world should be. This all plays into the belief that I'm nothing more than a rich, lovable and eccentric scamp. I intend to keep it that way; everything is so much simpler." He looked back to the shark tank, watching the sleek predators gliding through the water for a moment before turning and walking towards his desk. It was the sort of desk featured in high-end architecture magazines, a long sweep of black plexiglass without even a speck of dust on it, facing the window and the "endless pool" outside. "This lovely villa, for example. I usually prefer something a little simpler, but such extravagant luxury fulfills its purpose. Eccentric billionaire equals brainless twit. But such a nice man."

Khanjar followed him, and took a seat on a butterscotch leather chaise lounge. "Speaking of 'nice man,' you wanted me to remind you about Save the Seals."

He waved his hand. "Oh, of course. Pick a nice round number, six digits, and donate it to them. And at least three other charities or funds that are obscure enough to not be passé, but still do well in opinion polls. I've got the schedule set for when each should be done, so that the PR from one cascades nicely into the next."

"Not Weasel Welfare, then?" Khanjar deadpanned.

"Wouldn't want any of my competitors to get a dime, so no." He laughed at his own joke. "Anything else that needs attending to?"

"There's the meeting and attendant press conference that you're doing with the families of some of your employees who were killed during the Invasion attacks. Scheduled next week, Friday, in California. Everything is already booked."

"Ah, right. I'll put in the paperwork to start a trust for that one office supervisor who died saving some people, include it in the ceremony." He frowned. "Why, whenever things go seriously tits-up, are there always Nazis involved?"

"Speaking of Nazis, what do you want me to do with that Blacksnake assassin we caught in the garden?"

"Him?" The villa's automatic traps had gotten the merc before he'd penetrated too far. "Scrub him of identity, kill him, and dump him once you find out where he came from. Don't bore me with the details unless it's interesting, and try not to have too much fun. If anyone is going to wear you out, it's going to be me."

Khanjar gave him a little bow, and left the room. Verdigris sighed happily; having someone he could be comfortable with and depend on to make sure things happened his way truly made everything easier and more enjoyable. Still, it was time to work. He settled down at his laptop, calling up several different encrypted emails and communication programs. This was all trivial stuff, no need to wake the desk up for it. Just a few finishing touches were needed for some issues; final orders and payoffs to ensure that a military junta that he was backing would succeed in toppling their country's corrupt government, more bribes to a slew of officials to ensure that the right people would look away when large shipments of drugs were crossing their routes, and that a reporter who had been causing problems for one of his shell companies would meet an unfortunate end. Typing rapid-fire, he was able to finish everything over the course of five minutes. Some of these plots were the result of careful years of planning and dealing, others mere footnotes for other larger schemes. *It's all in the details.*

A thought occurred to him as he finished. Tapping the touch-surface that activated his voice-recorded notes, he said, "Follow-up; need to order more research concerning potential and heretofore unknown OpFive metahuman or metahumans first encountered during the Invasion. Colloquially called 'angels' by mainstream media sources. End note."

The desk alerted him to the fact that it had more camera feeds on the "Mountain Incident," and he spared a moment to watch them. Tesla had bungled that one badly, and he found himself shaking his head over it once again. If there was one thing that Dom knew how to micromanage, it was the perception of his employees. He would never, ever, in a million years, have allowed some petty bureaucrats with an itching outbreak of Not In My Backyard dictate what he did or did not do with any of his employees, even one as problematic as the Mountain.

Hell, given the Mountain's case of profound depression, the disaster that had unfolded when the governor of Georgia essentially ordered him deported was something even a moron could have predicted. They were all just lucky it hadn't been worse, that the Mountain had killed so few and wrecked so little on his final rampage into the sea. He watched all the camera feeds of the behemoth's walk out into the ocean, correlating them with coordinates and ocean currents from NOAA buoys, adding it all to the mix. Everyone assumed the Mountain was dead—drowned, crushed by the depths—

Not bloody likely. So far as Dom had been able to judge, the Mountain didn't breathe and only used air to speak. And he was solid rock; how would the pressure at the bottom of the Marianas Trench bother him? Most likely, he was in a depressive coma down there, like some Japanese movie monster.

Dom aimed to retrieve him. Leaving him down there was a waste of an incredible resource, and given his treatment at the hands of Echo and the US government, it should be no problem whatsoever to recruit him once he was reawakened. Dom already had a staff of six shrinks standing by to turn him into Dom's most loyal employee ever—barring maybe Khanjar.

Khanjar strode back into the room just then, stopping in front of his desk.

"Perfect timing, my dear!"

"Dinner will be ready in half an hour," she announced. "Chef Ausanat also asked me to remind you to stop stealing in there to snatch food and ruin your appetite." Dominic held up his hands in mock innocence. "If you're finished, then the matter in the upper observation room is ready for you to attend to it. Before it starts bleeding on the carpet."

"Right. Let's not delay then, shall we? The carpet up there is worth more than he is." Standing up, Khanjar led him up a flight of metal stairs blended into the wall of the room. The glass door opened soundlessly as they approached, closing behind them. The observation room gave a commanding view of the bay below; from this vantage point, Verdigris could see his own personal yacht at port, as well as his sport fishing boat bobbing among the waves. He had loaned it to some of his lower-tier security operatives and engineers for the weekend; they deserved the break. With Verdigris, results counted, and he always made sure to reward those of his people who produced results. Several of the companies he owned openly appeared every year on those "best companies to work for" lists. He rewarded his shadow staff even more generously. The best way to ensure loyalty was to buy it and reward it. If you worked for Dominic Verdigris, and someone tried to bribe you, your best course of action was to report it. You would be rewarded by a bonus of at least twice the size of the bribe, and sometimes a promotion.

This was how Karamjit Bhandari had come to be in Verdigris' observation room. He had been a little too interested in Freshette Filters, LLC, after it had gotten the contract to supply Bombay with a series of new pure water treatment plants when their water infrastructure was destroyed in the Invasion.

Karamjit had never been very imposing before Verdigris' people had gotten hold of him. A typical Bombay specimen of the prosperous sort, he was a little soft around the middle, and just starting to lose his hair. His suit had been very expensive, and nicely tailored to hide that beginning spare tire. Just another CEO in the never-ending flood of same that poured out of business schools every year. He would have looked at home at any boardroom table across the globe.

But he was not at a boardroom table. He was handcuffed to a steel chair that was itself a work of art—and as a consequence, not very comfortable to sit on. He'd clearly been handled roughly in transport. That lovely suit was abraded and torn, as was his shirt, and his face was bruised and battered.

"Glad to see you made it, Mr. Bhandari. We don't really need to go into how you got here, or what brought you here. You know it, I know it, so on and so forth. It's a really old story; you got greedy. So, I'll cut to the chase." Verdigris held up a small PDA. "This controls several charges that have been placed in your home. Your family is currently asleep, as of about thirty seconds ago. It's a lovely gas, my own invention, so there will be no traces that police forensics will find. It'll be enough to keep them asleep until I want, and paralyzed while still experiencing everything when they do wake up." He pursed his lips. "It's not ideal yet, the paralysis is permanent, but I'll work that out later. I'd like you to direct your attention to this screen." He pointed at an LCD monitor positioned on a table in front of Karamjit. Pressing the touch screen, the LCD flared to life, showing a live image of a rather impressive three-story home. Activating a function on the PDA caused the house to burst into flame, with gouts of fire spewing out of almost every window. Karamjit started trying to shout and cry through his gag, bucking in his chair against the restraints. "That takes care of the Bhandari clan. You'll be fingered as the one responsible for the arson; a cleverly constructed trail of evidence that hints at your coming psychotic breakdown will make sure of that. It'll also show that you fled the country after raiding your bank accounts, heading for parts unknown and never to be heard from again." Dominic pocketed the PDA after switching off the LCD monitor, and began to pace in front of Karamjit.

"This could have been avoided quite easily, you know, but don't worry, your death is rather convenient for me. You are actually doing me a bit of a service, here. Criminals of all stripes have a habit of forgetting loyalties and debts fairly quickly." He paused in front of his victim, who was now sobbing uncontrollably through his gag. "This will be a reminder, not just for your associates, but for everyone: don't fuck with Dominic Verdigris." Khanjar stepped behind Karamjit, and in one smooth motion brought a small kuboton down on the back of his neck with a sickening pop. Karamjit, now limp, went into shock almost immediately, though he retained consciousness.

"You're paralyzed now. I think this concludes our business, Mr. Bhandari."

Khanjar released the helpless man from his bonds, and shoved him out of the chair. He rolled to the very edge of the observation platform, which did not boast anything like a railing. Verdigris did not care for "nanny architecture." If you were too stupid or helpless to avoid falling . . . too bad, welcome to Darwin's Waiting Room.

Dominic and Khanjar both walked towards the helpless man. The shark tank was directly below. Verdigris smiled; a model of efficiency as ever, Khanjar had applied just the right amount of force to Karamjit when she ejected him from the chair. He dug a toe—elegantly clad in a gorgeous Italian shoe—just under Karamjit's pudgy waist, and shoved. Sometimes it really mattered to add a personal touch when making business decisions.

The former CEO of a company that was shortly going to be as dead as his family plummeted into the shark tank. The sharks had been primed by a high-tech version of "chumming" that left the water crystal clear. Also Verdigris' invention. On the way to it, he'd come up with a brand new BBQ sauce flavor as well. The sharks reacted to the sudden intrusion with a ravenous feeding frenzy.

Verdigris observed for a few long moments before turning to his confidant and companion. "I'm starting to get hungry. Want to shower, and then we'll work up an appetite together?"

CHAPTER ONE

Revelations

MERCEDES LACKEY

Some people worshipped her. Most people feared her. Some people hated her.

Few of these people mattered.

She was a seraphim; *the* Seraphym, as the media were calling her now, some in jest, some in good earnest. It troubled them all that they could not take any sort of picture, no matter what sophisticated equipment they used. The images showed only a brightness, a wash of flame with a slim, vaguely human-shaped brighter space in the midst of it, and the flames spreading out like wings. There was no use in telling them that this was her native form. It would not make them worship or cease to worship, fear or love her any more nor less. This did not matter.

She had killed; one innocent, many guilty. The innocent life troubled her no less than the guilty—but she had removed him from pain at his own request, and that was, in this case, permitted. Her life revolved around what was permitted and what was not. Her life centered on somehow being able to steer the course of the present to a future in which there *was* a future. There were so many paths in which the instruments of the Fallen had won... and there were some in which there was no world of humans here at all, only charred rubble and the crawling things that could even survive Apocalypse. The Infinite did not wish that. Though the worlds that had been blessed with life that was aware, and alert, and sentient were myriad, the Infinite cherished each and every one. When a sparrow fell, the Infinite mourned: how much more so for a world?

So there it was. This world was in her charge, to steer by imperceptible degrees. Save a life here; let fall a word there. Nor did the instruments matter, only the end.

Thus she found herself, for the moment invisible, hovering in the study of the man called Verdigris.

He was a bad man, an evil man, evil in the way that only the most steeped in evil can be: he was utterly, utterly selfish and self-centered. A sociopath, one might call him, and yet how much of that was due to the atrophy of one little, little part of his brain? Properly stimulated, that part might grow, might learn, might grant him, one day, that thing called a conscience.

But today, this was not her concern. It might never be. Today she was going to use an evil man to steer the future.

She allowed herself to become visible, filling the room with her flaming wings.

Verdigris, she said into his mind, as he looked up, and she felt his surprise, and his surprise at his own surprise, for she was a new thing to him. She was doing what she rarely, rarely did. She was forcing the image *she* chose of herself into his mind, past his unbelief. He saw her as the frightened little magician had seen her; as the thing that turned the knees to water.

She would not tell him, *Fear not.* She wanted his fear. She needed his fear.

And he did fear her, but, typically, he refused to show it. That did not matter.

He leaned back in his chair, full of insouciance. "Well," he said. "This is new. The Vatican taking out a contract on me now?"

It would not matter if they did. Your own methods would foil their mortal attempts, and I am not their creature.

"You interest me."

I should. You have never seen my like. You may never again. You cannot control me, measure me, persuade me, nor ever understand me.

"You think?"

She did not answer him, or at least, not his challenge. *I come to tell you of the Thulians.*

He laughed. "I doubt very much you can tell me anything I don't already know. Unless it's where their base is or how I can negotiate with them?" He waggled his eyebrows.

There can be no negotiation with them—for you, she said gravely.

You are on a list; a handful of people they wish removed from their more perfect world.

He laughed again. "Bunk! There never was anyone I couldn't negotiate with sooner or la—"

She did not let him finish the sentence. She simply opened the most likely future to him, narrowed in focus down to what *his* most likely future, at this moment, would be.

Oh, the Thulians wished Verdigris removed from their more perfect world, indeed, but they never, ever *wasted* anything. Verdigris had a brain, an intellect, the likes of which was unmatched in this world for sheer inventiveness. And for every twenty inventions of his that were of no particular use to them—new flavors of foodstuffs, a seat cushion that could be compressed down to the size of a thimble and uncompressed to memory-foam softness, a way of creating neon signage that took a tenth of the power the same signs took now—there would be one that was something they could use.

So here was the future for Verdigris; the worst future he could possibly imagine.

He would be a brain in a box.

Removed from his body, that body he loved so much and loved to pamper, removed from all physical pleasures, provided with no sensory input but visual and auditory, he would be left with nothing to "play" with except his own tremendous intellect. And they would take the children of his intellect, discard most, and use the rest to further enslave what was already in bondage, taking their rule further out among the stars.

And he would live forever, or nearly so.

She felt his reaction as he did; he could not care for the billions dead, billions enslaved. But he could care—a little—for those he personally knew and to a lesser or greater extent, depended on as they depended on him. He was not altogether a sociopath; there were some connections there, atrophied as they might have been. He prided himself on being able to take care of "his own." As she slowly unfolded the Thulian progress to him, he watched as they smashed that pride in the dirt, wiped out his empire, and rendered him into an attachment to a computer system, the ultimate AI. And he could not even have the satisfaction of denying them the fruits of his neurons. They had the ability to wrest them away.

The future, for Verdigris, was imprisonment, impotence, and a futile immortality.

Then she shut the future to him. He sat in his chair, no longer insouciant, no longer carefree, and his fear of her and of what he had seen naked on his pale, sweating face. No one had ever seen this expression on his face before.

"That—"

Is a future.

He seized on the article. "*A* future? So there could be others?" Fear gave way to hope.

It is the most probable. For now.

"But I can change that!"

Any mortal can. If he is in the right place, at the right time, and does the right thing.

"You wouldn't have come here, shown me that, if you didn't think I could change it!" He would have seized her by the shoulders and shook her if he had dared. His hands clenched and unclenched on the arms of his chair. "Tell me what to do!" he demanded, in the tones of a man whose demands were *always* met.

That is not permitted.

That stopped him short, anger blooming in him. "That's bullshit! Why bother to show this if you won't tell me how to fix it?"

I answer to a higher power than you. It is not permitted.

He stared at her in outrage. She knew all the things he would have done if he could have. It mattered to her not at all. She knew that in that moment, he had joined the ranks of those who hated her. That, too, mattered not at all.

You know the ending of the journey. Find a way to make another path. Or do not, and find yourself there. I have shown you what is permitted. Go well, and wisely.

And with that, she took herself out of his world. She had done what she could. He was not the only, or even the best, of the choices for those who could make those changes, but he was now one of the most motivated. He would see that future in his nightmares from now on, and he would do everything in his considerable power to prevent it. That he would use any tool went without saying.

But so would she.

The future of this world depended on it.

CHAPTER TWO

Running on Empty

VERONICA GIGUERE AND MERCEDES LACKEY

So much we didn't know—including the flip side of the frantic warning from Mercurye, and that last image we had of him, battered and running from the captors that should have been our saviors.

The room resembled the inside of a gallon of milk. White walls, white carpet, white ceiling, even white microfiber furniture that seemed to absorb any spill or stain dropped onto the opulent cushions. The pants they had given him after a few days' containment were also white, a light silken fabric that made a soothing shushing sound when he walked from one side of the room to the other. Color, he realized, came in the form of food, entertainment, and the occasional visitor. Left alone in this pristine prison, Rick Poitier decided that he would give anything for a fistful of crayons or a few pots of fingerpaint. Anything to make his quarters in Metis less... perfect.

This was his second room in the forbidden city of innovation. When Mercurye had boarded the saucer to accompany the body of Eisenfaust, the ambassadors had mentioned that he would be quarantined for disease following his exposure during the Invasion. They never mentioned what sort of quarantine, and so he had spent a good portion of the trip trying to get details. The only ones who bothered to talk to him without the Stepford glaze in their eyes were the three young women on the bridge of the ship. Wearing identical gold and silver jumpsuits, these gray-eyed and violet-haired Metisians spoke with Rick at length without making him feel like a piece of dumb human ribeye, answering his questions as best as they could. When they couldn't answer due to some security protocol, they seemed genuinely sorry and apologized that they couldn't say more.

Once they had dropped him off, Mercurye had gone into a holding room in their medical center, where Metisians in skin-tight cleansuits swabbed him from ears to toes. The cleansuits covered them, faces and all, with a breathable yet sterile second skin that made them all resemble the creepy horror flick aliens who were rumored to sneak into bedrooms and perform probing experiments in all sorts of uncomfortable places. They scanned him with a host of chirping boxes, and when that was over, had him ingest some pureed concoction that they assured him was full of protein and nutrients to compensate for his journey and any ill effects that the Metisian environment might have on him.

He thought it tasted like cheap elementary school paste. No amount of Tabasco would have made it any better.

The discussions about the Invasion and Eisenfaust took days, it seemed. Not only did the faceless cleansuits record every answer, they seemed interested in the society reactions to the Thulians as well as the technological response. Any questions that Mercurye tried to ask were met with a shake of the head and a reminder to adhere to the standard interrogation protocol. When he would lose his patience, the cleansuits would stand as one and shuffle out of the room as soothing music was piped in through unseen speakers and the faint smell of vanilla and peppermint wafted through the air.

It was maddening. Infuriating. Insulting, considering all that he'd been through with the Invasion and with Echo. They denied his requests to speak with Tesla or to contact anyone, but they did allow him into his current room with a collection of every clichéd science fiction series ever created. And so, Rick spent his days alternating exercise with reruns that had kept him company during his teenage years in New Jersey.

Which meant that he watched the entire series of *Star Trek: The Next Generation*. Twice.

He had the volume turned up as he exhaled and kicked himself into an armstand against one of the walls. The lack of dirt made footprints impossible. As the precocious teenage heartthrob got in over his head once again, Merc mouthed the lines and began his post-breakfast routine. Fifty press-ups, slowly and deliberately, not even trying to go for speed. This was something he had started long before Echo. Between breakfast and school, he would turn on the television and try in vain to build up his ropey form into something that the cheerleaders would notice. He wanted to be that kid on the screen who stumbled over words with girls but who would inevitably save the day at the end with some key skill or lucky happenstance.

By the end of his second year of high school, Rick Poitier was just as stringy and acne-ridden as any other fifteen-year-old kid. He hadn't saved the school or become a standout in any of his classes, but he had gotten pretty good with the armstands. He watched the show to obsession and his mother even humored him with his own blue shirt as a birthday gift, but there were still no cheerleaders nor any rise in popularity. Instead, he took the bus home, walked a few blocks, and finished his homework like the good son he was supposed to be.

He passed one hundred, a light sweat on his skin that the Metisian environment tried to correct with a rush of cooler air. If he was lucky, one of the ship navigators would show up after he hit two hundred and hang around for a while to chat. They rarely gave him a lot of information about what was going on back home, but they did try, which was more than he could say about the rest of the population. According to one of the navigators, there were well over ten thousand Metisians, from the very young to the very old, and they all had a say in how the society functioned. It reminded him of a Law and Justice class he'd had to take in high school. Every rule was voted upon, all options explored alongside consequences, and each vote was equal. The teacher's vote didn't count more or less than a student's, and they voted on everything from exam dates to project requirements. The shared responsibility had its perks but the biggest drawback was the time involved. Every decision took minutes, sometimes hours.

In Metis, these same sorts of decisions took days, weeks, even months. The sheer fact that he remained in this room, upside down against the wall as he pressed into his two hundredth push-up, was the result of some grand vote among the populus. On days like today, Merc wished there was some Metisian equivalent of a starship captain who could overrule and make things just so with a wave of his hand.

The door chimed, beeped, then opened to reveal the three ship navigators. They grinned at Mercurye as he lowered himself to the floor and gave them an easygoing smile. "Good morning, ladies," he offered with a goofy yet practiced bow, same as he did every time they came to visit. "Are you the crew that's here to take me back home? There's just not enough dirt here."

Their smiles faded a bit. "We can't do that, Mr. Mercurye," one of them answered with a faint shake of her head. "The consensus remains that you should stay here until the Thulians progress to a later stage in their attacks on Earth and Echo."

He clenched his jaw, forgetting for the moment that these young ladies had no personal control over whether he could stay or go. As with many things in Metis, they were only messengers. "A later stage? So I get to stay here until it's a burning wasteland? That's really mature and hospitable. Will I get to go home with a party favor? Maybe a balloon or a picture of my jail cell?"

The first one winced as his voice rose. "It isn't like that, Mr. Mercurye. We voted for you to go home. We want you to go back and have you pursue your friendships and continue to assist the people of Echo. Unfortunately," she said, twisting her fingers nervously, "we were overruled."

"Overruled?" He snorted and padded across the white carpet to one of the chairs and flung himself onto the cushions. "By how many? All of them?"

"Fifty-two point three percent." The second spoke more softly, her expression sad. "We were so close this time, too."

He stared at them. "Fifty-two point three? But that means that—"

"That forty-seven point seven percent agree that you should return to Echo to assist in the fight against the Thulians," the third finished in a tone that was closer to Mercurye's than her co-navigators. "If you ask me, the simple majority is faulty. Two-thirds should be the prerequisite to hold someone against their will. It goes against the very model we attempt to emulate."

"Simple majority is sufficient for our purposes, especially in our fully democratic model, Trini," the first murmured. "Even if we do not agree with the majority."

"Simple majority is not sufficient in the case of personal liberties, especially in this instance where the subject has committed no crimes and is not considered a threat!" She jabbed a finger in Mercurye's direction. "He should not be detained! Even Mr. Tesla and Mr. Marconi argued as much!"

"Tesla?" He sat on the edge of the couch. "Alex Tesla is here? Can I speak with him? I thought—"

The one they called Trini threw her hands up in the air in a gesture that reminded Mercurye of Detective Ferrari. "No, not Alex Tesla. Nikola Tesla. The *real* Mr. Tesla, as far as anyone should be concerned. None of them will listen to either him or Mr. Marconi, in spite of their perfectly logical reasoning...." She began pacing around the room as the other two offered him apologetic smiles.

"She is rather emotional." The first of the navigators slid onto the couch next to him and took his hand in hers. "We all feel the same way, Mr. Mercurye. While it would be untrue to claim that you are not welcome here in Metis, you should not be held against your will and we should be providing you substantial aid against the Thulians during the first part of the conflict."

His stomach bottomed out at her words. "First part? You mean, there's more?" Mercurye pushed his other hand through his hair in disbelief. "You know that there's going to be more?"

She patted his hand as she spoke. "Well, of course. These things come in stages, as we have seen many times. We cannot intervene when doing so would keep humanity from learning in its progression, however painful that learning might be."

"Wait, wait." Mercurye stood and clasped his hands behind his head as he began to pace a slow circle around the room. It forced him to focus on his thoughts and organize the jumbled mess of emotion that the navigators' news had brought. "There are ways to stop this, there are ways for you—Metis, I mean—to help us so that we don't wind up a smear of humanity on what'll be left of the planet after the Nazis—"

"Thulians." The one called Trini spat the word with obvious distaste.

"Fine, Thulians. Whatever." He drew in a deep breath and exhaled, counting to ten as he did. "Point is, there are ways to stop this, but the majority of people here don't want to help. It'd be like...cheating, right?"

"Coddling is perhaps the closer approximation." The young woman on the couch tried to smile at him sympathetically, but it appeared to Rick as a weakly apologetic gesture and irritated him.

"It's not coddling. This isn't like some whiny little kid who can't stand up to a bully. This is the kid who's getting the snot pounded out of him every time he steps out of the classroom, and you're acting like you're committing a crime by not helping him! If you can help, why don't you?" His voice grew louder and more frustrated as his pacing increased. "Are you in some kind of competition with the rest of us? Are we just some sort of neat toy for—"

"In case you forgot, we voted to help." The soft-spoken one interrupted him, her tone full of patience. "We came here because we wanted to help, but we wanted to ensure that you were committed to your cause. The comforts of Metis can be tempting."

Her words took most of the anger from him. Rick turned to face the three of them, his wry smile showing signs of fatigue. "To be honest, I can't stand it. Your media collection's about the best thing going."

"Then we can help you, but we must move quickly." She pulled a slender bottle from her hip and unscrewed the lid, then gestured to Mercurye. "You'll need to remove your clothing in order to use the secondary skin coating. It provides a completely protective and flexible shell, much like the Echo uniform you wear. In order to be most effective, however..."

The other two women had already begun to shed their clothing without any regard for modesty, and Rick confirmed with a very red face that Metisian women were pretty much identical to lingerie models. He turned to face the wall and stripped off his own clothing, careful to not look too much to either side. Rick prepared himself to ask "what next?" when an icy tingle hit him between the shoulder blades and traveled down his back and down each of his legs. He let out a yelp in surprise, hands quickly moving down for modesty's sake before turning around. "That's cold, you know? Give a guy a warning!"

"You were without a shirt during your entry into Metis. I did not think that the cold bothered you."

"I'm a registered speedster, not a heating pad." The tingle across his skin wrapped around his body. Rick looked down as the white cleansuit layer quickly enveloped his skin. As if she knew what would happen, the one who had sprayed him grabbed both of his wrists. She was a lot stronger than he would have guessed as she held his hands away from his face. The sensation crawled up his neck and across his face, a film temporarily covering his eyes. He blinked, the film clearing without effort. There was a soft whistling sound as he breathed through his nose, the layer finally settling softly over his mouth. Rick parted his lips a few centimeters, relieved to feel the second skin move with him and allow air to filter through. Suffocation would not have been the way to go in Metis.

Two of the navigators wore the same off-white cleansuit layer. The third grinned at them, collecting the clothing and vials and depositing them on the couch. "Now, the three of you can leave. We've arranged a meeting for you, but you'll have to hurry."

"A meeting?" They pulled him to the door, not answering his question. He began to repeat the question, but one put a finger to his lips and shook her head. For now, the priority was to escape.

Hallways twisted and turned, white and gray marble in a blinding labyrinth. The two young ladies pulled him around corners and through doorways until Mercurye couldn't tell how far he had run or if he was even on the same level of the building. Was it even a building?

They pushed him ahead into what he assumed to be a wall as footsteps clattered somewhere behind them. He braced for the impact, drawing his hands up to provide some cushion. Rather than hitting the wall, Mercurye tumbled through something not unlike cotton and hit the floor with a grunt, skidding a few feet. The fibers of the cleansuit layer shredded over his face and arms with the impact, the threads hanging off of him in thin white strands. Neither of the women followed him; Rick flipped onto his back and held his breath in the pitch-black room, waiting to see if they might reappear.

Nothing.

In the vast darkness, a soft hum grew to just over a whisper and echoed, indicating the room was an immense size. Rick squinted as a faint blue glow pulsed above him. A second pinprick of blue light appeared, followed by two more to the left. Three appeared on the right, then a field of blue came into view such that it arched far beyond where a normal ceiling might have been. The humming grew in harmony, additional tones adding depth and richness as the blue glowing dots began to form a network in the darkness.

Rick stared, his jaw slack while something connected the ever-emerging dots to one another to craft an enormous wire-frame bust of a severe young man with perfectly coiffed hair and a necktie. He scrambled back as the "head" turned and seemed to focus on him. The face seemed to study him before nodding in approval and allowing the rest of the wire frame to continue. "Mr. Poitier," it thundered in a precise Eastern European accent that Mercurye felt should have been accompanied by a three-piece suit and a cup of strong tea. "A pleasure to see you away from your quarters. I have heard much of you from my nephew."

How did someone run from a glowing blue head of electrons that knew names and business associates? Mercurye tried to get the words out, but his mouth continued to open and close in shock.

He did not remain in shock for long, however. Maybe it was because this was too much like the apparition of the Great and Terrible Wizard of Oz ("Pay no attention to the man behind the curtain") or maybe it was because somewhere out there, his friends were still facing the Nazis—Thulians, whatevers—and not doing well at it.

"What the hell is going on around here?" he demanded. "Scratch that, what the hell is going on *out there* and why aren't you *doing* something about it?"

The Giant Head regarded him thoughtfully. A pipe would not have been out of place. "Permit me to answer your middle question first," said the Head. Rick was not going to call it "Nikola Tesla" until he had better verification than the word of three pilot/models in lavender wigs. "Your enemy is a group who refer to themselves as Thulians. They have a base of operations that corresponds to Metis. We have been aware of their presence for some time—and have been careful to conceal ourselves from them. This is not a royal 'we,' you understand; I refer to the Metisians as a group. Since you joined us, there have been two more small attacks in the Atlanta area, both thwarted by Echo or its allies. Neither I, nor I and Marconi, nor the strategists of Metis as a whole, have been able to deduce a pattern in their behavior. Other groups are acting opportunistically, some with attacks on citizens, some filling the void left by the decimation of Echo."

Rick felt his heart sinking again. Damn it all, he was needed back there, and here he was—

"To answer your first question, my colleague and I founded Metis shortly after my breakthroughs in broadcast power and electronic storage. We collected some of the finest minds of every country and continue to recruit, generation after generation. They are all democratic citizens of Metis, and together we have made incredible breakthroughs in every line of scientific investigation." There was no mistaking the pride in the Head's voice. "When my nephew founded Echo, we arranged to filter these discoveries into the world through him in a controlled manner. Controlled, because we were aware of Ultima Thule's existence after the end of the Second World War, and did not want to reveal our own existence, which would likely occur if these were released in too precipitous a manner."

Rick was beginning to get a very creepy feeling that he had seen or heard of something like this before. Then it came to him. The "Super-Science City" in the movie *The Shape of Things to Come*. These people—well, except for the Triplets—even had that same haughty, "you are not advanced enough for this, monkey-boy" attitude that the Wings Over the World people had....

"So—" he began belligerently, but the Head cut him off.

"Unfortunately... our safety here, and our intellectual powers, have induced both an arrogant sense of spiritual and mental superiority, and a state of moral cowardice." The expression on the Head's face didn't change, but the tone sounded deflated. "I blame myself for not offering enough guidance—or not insisting on more contact with the outside world. Some of those who have voted against you do so out of that misplaced superiority, and some out of fear that aiding you will reveal our whereabouts to the Thulians. Marconi and I will continue to attempt persuasion, but we need you to warn my nephew that for now he must soldier on alone."

Rick blinked. "What, me? Why me? And how?"

"Because at the moment, Marconi and I do not have any direct access to a communication device that will speak to Alex," the Head explained. "We can establish that contact, but it will take time. Meanwhile, Alex should not live in hope that—in the American idiom—the cavalry will come riding over the hill to rescue him. You can get to that device and warn him. You can also give us the—back door, I think it is called—so that if Alex attempts to contact us, we should be able to answer him, if only for brief moments."

Slowly Rick let out the breath he had not been aware he was holding. "All right. Say that I do that. Then what?"

"Then we commence the business of convincing five percent of the populace that it is better to die like a lion than live like a dog," the Head said grimly. "Have I your cooperation in this effort?"

Rick didn't even have to think about his answer. After all, this was something right out of one of his beloved *Next Gen* episodes. "*Heghlu'meH QaQ jajvam,*" he said.

The wire-frame lips of the Head lifted in something like a smile. "I had the feeling you would say that," replied Nikola Tesla. "Now, this is what you must do..."

But fifteen minutes later, having delivered his warning to Alex Tesla, nursing the bruises and aching bones his Metisian guards had given him as he resisted them...he wondered if he had, or would, ever be able to accomplish anything more than handing Alex an express ticket straight to despair.

CHAPTER THREE

Nowhere Fast

CODY MARTIN AND MERCEDES LACKEY

We didn't know any of that, of course. By "we," I mean Echo and CCCP. Merc was incommunicado, and the Seraphym didn't exactly talk much. Well ... not to most of us anyway.

One, though, she did speak to ... unlikely confidant that he was.

We had to save the world, but first we had to save ourselves ... but some of us had help from unexpected sources.

John was restless, again. He hated lying around and having people wait on him. Hospitals were the worst, and the CCCP HQ's medbay wasn't too much better than any of the hospitals he'd been in. He seemed to be taking longer to heal than usual too. Either he'd been hurt worse than he thought, or he'd been running on fumes for so long there wasn't enough left to heal with. He had been feeling dizzy the last few days, and inordinately sore. Granted, he was lucky to be alive and he was far sturdier than the average person, but his unease was palpable.

Nightmares didn't help either. But the real tragedy was that there wasn't any beer.

He was sitting on the ledge of the CCCP HQ's roof, staring towards the west and his neighborhood. There were a depressingly small number of lights on. The one thing to be thankful for was the lack of light pollution; he reckoned that it was rare to see the stars so clearly in Atlanta, or any major city.

You should see them from the depths of space, John Murdock.

"Stars are stars, Angel. I like lookin' at them from the ground."

He turned his head to glance over his shoulder. Her fires were muted tonight, only enough of a glow to see by. As always, it was her eyes that marked her as profoundly *other*, the smoldering golden glow without even a hint of pupil. She offered a bottle beaded with condensation. "Much obliged," he said, accepting the beer. "How long have you been watching me?"

Just now, or in general?

"Just now. The latter answer might scare me. An' let's talk for real. This mind stuff doesn't sit well with me." He took a long swig from the bottle, staring out over the cityscape.

She moved, lightly and gracefully, to perch like a bird on the ledge beside him. Not too near, not too far. "I arrived only a minute or so before I spoke."

"Busy night for ya, Angel?"

"Somewhat. Some rescue . . . some other things. Much sorting through possibilities." She moved her head restlessly, her smoldering hair stirred like little campfire flames. "So many threads, so many lives, and things changing all the time." Now she turned her head to look at him again. "Had you rather I looked more mortal?"

"How would that work?" John didn't turn his head to look at her, instead focusing on the stars above. He had never been able to stare at Sera, except for the first time he ever saw her.

"I can look as I please. This is not my true form, but no one mortal could bear that." She tossed her head, and between one moment and the next, she . . . changed. Changed to a red-haired woman, in a gown that looked like the representation of fire, rather than fire itself.

He risked a look at her. "Cute trick. I'd rather that you look like whatever you're comfortable with." He shifted where he sat, obviously uncomfortable with her effortless power. "Whaddya think of this bunch below us?"

Her eyes were the same. She blinked slowly. "They are . . . important. Very important. For so few, they have the potential to do so much, and they are not fettered by the self-doubt and constraint of those who could do as much, were they not bound by things that, in this confrontation, are meaningless."

"So, what you're saying is, that they'd be good sorts to stick around with?"

She blinked again. "I believe it is important that you do so. For your sake, and for theirs. You are the keys to each others' locks."

He looked at her sideways. "Never a straight answer with you, is there?" John shook his head, sipping at his beer again. "I figure I'll stick with them. My neighborhood is going to need all the help it can get, and a mutual support network will keep my ass out of the fire if things get hectic. Plus, their uniforms don't look that bad."

"A straight answer...I can give you some. First: there are more things I am not permitted to tell you than there are things that I may. And there is a reason for this. The Infinite...it does not, as Einstein said, 'play at dice with the universe.' It does not 'play' at all. All those beings that think...they are not toys, nor slaves, nor"—she winced a little, hardly more than a flicker—"things of entertainment."

John chuckled. "I seem to entertain ya a fair bit."

She tilted her head to the side, quizzically. "I am sorry if I gave you that impression." She stared at him a moment more. "The creatures that think are...possessed of Free Will. The Infinite rarely meddles in their lives. It took...a great violation, a great peril, for me to be permitted to be an instrument here. You are in a moment where... Free Will and all the right choices may not save you."

He looked at her soberly. "Even if we play our cards right, you think we can beat something like this?" His hand swept over the ruined metropolis. Over the destruction corridors, the scattered lights, and the smoldering remains of buildings in the distance.

Her lips parted a moment. A single tear, like a bead of crystal, moved slowly down one cheek. John's hand twitched to wipe it away, but he kept it at his side. "Insofar as I can do what I am permitted to do...I am trying, John Murdock. I am trying." The tear splashed to the tarpaper roof.

John nodded. "I think that that's more important than actually winning. The fact that we are fighting. It's all in the struggle." He sighed. "Besides, if it were easy, where would the fun be?"

She smiled wanly. "I had rather you all did not join my Siblings too soon. Life...is a vast blessing, when there is joy." She was silent a moment. "This, I am permitted to say. There is not one future. There are many, many. Threads and threads and threads, weaving, reweaving, being broken and knotted up again. More than you can possibly imagine. Something...happened. Something terrible grew and grew and began to change the endings of many, now most, of those threads."

"Y'know, if you were really trying to cheer me up...well, that sucked." He grinned, flashing his teeth.

Unexpectedly, she gave him a real, dazzling smile. "But that is why I am an instrument here, now, John. I am trying to find the way to the bright-ended threads. That is why it must be me, and not one of you—you can see only what you know, but I can see it all, and not go mad." She paused. "And I must weave my own way through Free Will, show a little here, do a little there, save a life, guide a very, very little...a touch here, a touch there. Do... do you understand?" She lost the smile, and a look of unbearable sadness came over her. "So many...do not. They cry for miracles. They do not understand that for a miracle to occur, something equally miraculous must be sacrificed. Those who would make that sacrifice are not always the ones that should, and seldom the ones who can."

He sighed. "I stopped praying years ago. Too many prayers, not enough to show for it. I think I understand what you're saying, but I—I'm not sure I'm ready to commit an' subscribe to your magazine, if you get my drift. I've been making my own way for most of my life; all the good that's ever happened to me has been because of *me*...for the most part." His eyes glazed over slightly, staring out across the empty space again. His eyes lost their spark, looking like they belonged to a corpse more than a breathing man.

Without him noticing, she had moved closer; she could be preternaturally graceful, and didn't move so much as glide next to him. The lightest touch of a finger on the back of his hand, the first time *she* had actually touched him, punctuated her next words. "All the good that happens does so because we reach out to each other, John. The more we connect, the more we achieve."

He started, almost recoiling from her. After a moment, his eyes took on their normal sheen, animated and ablaze with life again. He whispered, "And the bad?"

Her eyes blazed. "I make no apology for evil. It is the choice of those who seek it. Were I given a free hand..." The fires died in her eyes. "But I am not. That must be the choice of the good, to oppose the evil, to battle it, to succor those who have suffered from it. To reach out." There was a small, grim smile on her face. "But in the here and now, I have been given some small ability to fight it directly, and where I can, I do, and I will."

"And what happens if you overstep? If you take things into your own hands?" There was a hint of something else in his voice, but Seraphym couldn't place it. He was guarding something.

"For myself alone...I am bound by stricter laws than any mortal." Her grim smile turned wry. "With great power comes... great restrictions. I must be a surgeon with a...weapons-grade laser. But for mortals?" She looked away, and up, at the stars. Each word came slowly, as if it was being chosen with infinite care from a hundred thousand dictionaries. "Mortals are not granted infinite knowledge. They can only act on what they know. Mistakes are made. Terrible things are done—sometimes, nay, oftentimes, under the pressure of terrible things done *to* them. Much, much can be forgiven."

John shook his head, stifling a deep cough as he did so. "Not everything." Again, more that was being hidden. More that he was keeping from her specifically.

Again, she lightly touched his hand. "Look at me, John Murdock. Please." With what looked like monumental effort, John raised his eyes to meet her unearthly eyes. This time the fires that burned there were not of anger, nor sadness, nor the reflection of whatever place she had come from. There was within them, not a fire, but a glow. If he could have put a name to it, it would have been *compassion*. Not pity, which he would have rejected. It was something raw, unadulterated, and primal. "John, I pledge to you on my very existence. *Forgiveness is always possible.* There must also come acceptance of that forgiveness, and repentance, and sometimes reparation. Repayment. Atonement. But the forgiveness itself? It is there, as the air you breathe is there."

John stared in her eyes for several long moments, and opened his mouth to speak. There was pain in his eyes, and Sera knew that something important to John was about to be said. Before he could speak, however, the door access for the roof swung open, bathing the entire rooftop in a wide swath of amber light.

"Comrade Murdock. You are not to be moving from your bed." Jadwiga, the CCCP's doctor, also known by the callsign of Soviette, stood in the open doorway with her fists planted on her hips. "All over, I have been looking for you."

John looked to where Seraphym had been sitting. The only thing left was a golden-red feather, resting peacefully next to him. "I hear ya, Nurse Hearse. Gimme a second." He smiled to himself, and then finished his beer, setting the empty bottle on the ledge. "Back to the salt mines, huh?"

"You should not joke about salt mines," Soviette scolded. "Some of the comrades were sent there by Stalin." She shooed him down the stairs as if she was herding a chicken. And then looked back. "In bed with you. And...where are you getting beer?"

CHAPTER FOUR

Every Breath You Take

DENNIS LEE AND MERCEDES LACKEY

...and some of us were spurred to find new resources.

Victoria Victrix Nagy felt as if someone had hit her in the head with a brick; the revelation was so sudden, and yet, so logical.

It had struck her as she closed herself up in her office and began tickling the firewalls of the various networked Echo computers to see what she could get into. Their systems, of course, were severely compromised, as were most of the computer systems of the world. Great damage had been done in cyberspace by the Thulians. Inadvertent, but nonetheless, real. Security systems were offline or damaged, there hadn't been new security updates for most software in weeks, and Echo was actually in better shape than many.

But they were still compromised, which was why she had been able to hack into Tesla's datebook and personal scheduler as fast as she had, a few days ago.

Vickie's secret vice was hacking, and of course, because of her talents and training, she had a few more tools at her disposal than even the most sophisticated geek, be he white-hat or black. She was a techno-mage, which was a very rara avis indeed; she was one of only a handful that she knew of, and the only one who specialized in computers and computerized systems. A great many mages had a lot of trouble with technology, some to the point where things stopped working catastrophically around them.

Not Vickie. She could do things that were not technically hacking to get in, should she need to.

And it was clear that if she put her mind to it, she could get as deep into the Echo system as she wanted right now. Or rather, as deep in as she had patience for, given the limits of her own system. Why, at this very moment, without much trouble, she could pull up the feeds for every single security camera they had, and if she worked at it, she could empty their personnel files—it would take a lot of work, though, and more storage space than she actually had. She had thought to herself that it was a pity she couldn't do this to other people, instead of getting dragged out into the field—

And that was when it hit her. The revelation of how she could be of real use to Echo, and not end up so sick with agoraphobia and panic attacks that she couldn't eat for days. More than that. The way she could—or so she hoped—prove to Red Saviour that she was worth trusting.

She scooted out of the Echo system, leaving herself a back door, and went shopping.

She was under the desk with a flashlight in her mouth and her hands full of tools when she heard Bella's key in the lock. She knew it was Bell, because she knew the sounds of all three deadbolts on her door, and she had only left the one Bella had a key to in the locked position.

She dropped the flashlight and called out, "I'm in here!"

Bella's footsteps marked her path to the office, then the sounds stopped at the doorway.

"Holy mother-of-pearl—"

Vickie finished making the last of her connections and emerged from beneath the desk, hair messed, nose smudged. She put the tools back where they belonged in the correct drawer in desk number four, and surveyed her new kingdom.

What had been a Spartan spare office—she had three bedrooms and she used the biggest for her writing office—with just the desk, a chair, and her admittedly very good hacking/gaming PC, now looked like something out of a TV producer's idea of a CSI or CIA computer room. There were twelve identical flat-screen monitors, a server that would make a geek weep with desire, the kind of storage rack most big law offices would envy and four of the best multi-core computers not available on the market. They were not available, because the friend of a friend who had made them for her did not make these for money, only trading favor for favor. He was currently very happy with the favor he had gotten in return. He'd always wanted to see and verify with his own eyes real magic. Not metapowers. Real magic. Now he had. For most of his life he had lived with the haunting fear that the only thing that had made his hellish childhood bearable had been nothing more than a hallucination. Now he knew it had been real, he was not crazy, and suddenly there was a suppurating wound in his soul that could heal.

But that was another story.

"Romances must pay well," Bella said dryly.

Vickie shrugged. "Well enough. When you never leave the house, there's not a lot to spend money on." She sat down in the brand new zero-gravity chair. Since she was likely going to be in this thing for long stretches at a time, she had gotten the best. She put on the feather-light Echo-tech headset and microphone, took a deep breath, and hit the switch.

All twelve monitors came to life, and the room filled with the hum of computer equipment coming online and testing itself.

Quickly. Very quickly.

The plain blue screens began to switch to other things as her systems booted up, but right now, there was only one picture she wanted to see. Her fingers flew over the keyboard as she used her back door into the Echo systems. She got to the sysadmin screen, which asked for a password. Now she moved her right hand to the Ouija-board planchette, next to the keyboard, mentally detached her hand from her own control, triggered the spell, and picked out the word with her left hand as her right spelled it out. Techno-magecraft. The system "knew" which password it "wanted." The screen image "knew" which password worked, as a combination of letters and numbers which was the one most often tried. The one most often tried would be the right one, because the ones that failed, due to mistyping or other hacking attempts, would not be tried again, or at least not with the frequency that the correct one was. Her spell linked her to the screen image, to the system behind the screen image, and let her hand pick out the right sequence on the Ouija board. This was the Law of Contamination at work; it would be even faster if she had some personal object belonging to the sysadmin.

As it was, it was no more than a minute. And she was in.

As Bella watched in utter fascination, Vickie worked her way through directories and subsystems until she found the one she wanted—the feed to Alex Tesla's desktop. Once again, the planchette gave her the password, and she was in. This time it was faster; she had Alex's hair.

And she took his computer over.

A few keystrokes, and his camera was activated. A few more, and so was hers. He stared at her—or rather at his monitor, with startled eyes. In the monitor to the right of the central one, Vickie's solemn face appeared, a reflection of what he was seeing.

"Good afternoon, Mr. Tesla," she said, and smiled. Behind her, Bella stifled a chuckle as he jumped.

"Who—who the hell are you?" he asked hoarsely. "And what are you doing in my computer?"

"My name is Victoria Victrix Nagy, and I am one of your Echo Ops," she replied, keying up her own file and causing it to appear in a new window in the bottom left of his screen, "as you can see there. That's my file. You met me with Red Saviour and Belladonna Blue in your office a few days ago. I was the one with all the papers and the information."

Strange. Now that she was here, physically here in her safe place, the place where she was in control, she felt as assured, as cocky even, as her old long-ago self had been. Small wonder he hadn't recognized her. "As to what I am doing—I am giving you a little demonstration. Not just of how I can get into the Echo computers, but how I can get into a great many other places as well. Name a place. Any place."

"Uh—New Orleans. Cafe du Monde."

Her fingers flew. A new window opened, while one of the left-hand monitors came to life. In the new window, a grainy black and white feed of the Cafe du Monde appeared from an odd angle. "Traffic cam at the stoplight," she said, as the same feed appeared in her new monitor. Then the scene changed to directly across the street from the famous home of beignets. "Security cam in the ATM across the street." Last of all, a view from inside the cafe, partly blocked by a large young man frowning at something. "Camera in the laptop of Daniel Soleil, a stockbroker, currently on his lunch break and using the wifi hotspot. Silly man, doesn't even have a firewall. I'll show you what he's surfing if you like—"

"No, no!" Tesla exclaimed, and she slid out of Daniel's PC as easily as a fish swimming through a kelp bed. "That's fine." He took a deep and visible breath. "You're one of my people, which means you've passed a lot of rigorous security checks. I realize that especially at the moment the Echo systems aren't as secure as we'd like. Is that what you're trying to prove to me? Or is it something else you want? Did you want to be moved to the computer systems group? Why are you showing me this?"

"What I want..." She hesitated a moment. "Let's take the last question first. I am showing you this to prove to you that I can do what I say I can. And what I want—" She gazed solemnly into her own camera. "What I want is to be Echo's all-seeing eye for select teams, not the ones patrolling or handling calls, but the ones doing special ops or covert work. Your guardian angel. Your invisible guardian angel." She managed something that was not quite a laugh, but would pass for one. "I can be with your chosen field team, assisting them, feeding them information, warnings, accesses—"

He nodded. "Like something out of a spy movie."

"A lot like that," she replied. "Sometimes I will even be able to disable alarms and unlock doors remotely or run distractions. This isn't just computer hacking, Mr. Tesla. This is magic-based computer hacking. There isn't anyone in your organization who can do this. I want to be a full and valuable Op, but I also want to make you never ask me to leave my house again." She took a deep breath. "What I want, sir, is nothing more, and nothing less. Now, give me a team. Give me a test."

In the monitor, Bulwark tried on his headset. Djinni had already gone somewhere out of sight to remove the red wrappings that swathed his head, neck, and shoulders and put the headset on underneath. "This is rather melodramatic, isn't it?" he asked.

"I can cue the *Mission Impossible* theme if you want melodrama," Vickie replied. Bulwark was looking into the security cam of what was laughingly called the "briefing room" on the Echo campus—laughingly, because, like just about everything else there at the moment, the room was in a portable office building trucked to the site. "How comfortable is that?"

"Very," Bulwark replied, which was pretty much as Vickie expected. The Echo-tech headsets were practically invisible. They should be comfortable. They were what some of the higher level Ops had used in the pre-Invasion days on their crime-fighting sessions. "I've never needed to use one of these before."

"Is this thing on?" Djinni did not appear in the monitor, but Vickie hadn't expected him to.

"As soon as you put it on, yeah," she replied. "Here's the fast tour, full disclosure, Djinni. You're on an Echo-tech comm unit, one each. It's powered by you; uses your body heat. I can't actually see you unless you are in view of a camera I can tap. I can't see what you're looking at unless you also wear the minicamera that goes with the headset. Yes, it has something like a GPS so you can be tracked with it. That's so I know where you are so I can scout for you, by using security cams in whatever area you're in. Right now you're on an open feed, so you can hear and be heard by the whole team. You can elect to talk only to your team leader, and you and I can also talk privately."

She knew where he was going to go with that before he opened his mouth. "So, does that mean you wanna talk dirty to me, Victrix?"

She was in her safe place, and it wasn't the fear-paralyzed neurotic that answered him. "That'd be five cents a word, and my agent would get fifteen percent, Djinni. I don't think you can afford my rates."

Bulwark's mouth twitched and his eyebrows arched. While he took a moment to be amused, Vickie switched to private mode on the Djinni's pickup. "I know what's going through your head. It runs on your body heat and the kinetic energy generated by movement. Do the math. You can shut it off just by taking it off, or making it cold, or just doing your shifter thing and giving it no heat. But remember, if you shut it off, that means not only won't we know where you are, it means I can't help you. This isn't another control thing. I just want to be your eyes in the sky."

Before Bulwark could notice or Djinni respond, she switched back to open channel. "Most of Echo isn't going to need this system, only the people going covert." She wasn't entirely certain why she had told Djinni how he could disable his system. Maybe it was honesty. Maybe it was because she knew from his new Echo file how much he hated having a leash on him. If he saw it as a lifeline rather than a leash, if he was in control of it, maybe he'd be less inclined to dump it. "Which would be you, obviously."

Djinni still wasn't going to like this, but he would probably put up with it . . . she hoped.

Bulwark's mouth twitched again. "Maybe you *ought* to cue up the *Mission: Impossible* theme then."

"Oh, I don't know about that, Bull," Djinni drawled, in a tone of voice that practically promised trouble. "I think the first thing we should do is take in a little entertainment."

✦   ✦   ✦

Djinni and Bulwark settled into the cramped and primitive passenger seats of the Echo cargocraft; the sight of those skeletal contraptions in Bull's headcam made Vickie's back ache with sympathy. As they were strapping their gear down and themselves in, she gave in to a whim.

"Welcome to Echo Atlantic City Flight Two-Eleven," she said, in her best stewardess voice. "Please stow your carryons under the seat or whatever looks most like an overhead bin. There is no meal or beverage service, but feel free to scavenge for whatever crumbs or dropped items might have been left by the previous passengers. Your inflight entertainment will be me. In the event of an emergency, figure out where is a good place for an exit, because that's where you'll be putting one. In the event of a water landing, this thing floats about as well as a boat flies. If the cabin depressurizes, it will be important to know how long you can hold your breath, because it will take the pilot ninety-three seconds to drop to breathable altitude. If the passenger next to you is a child or acting like one, feel free to cold-cock him. At the conclusion of the flight, please stow your flight attendant in the upright and locked position. Thank you for flying Echo Airlines."

After a moment of surprise, Bulwark grunted what passed for a laugh and even Djinni unbent enough to make a sound that might have been a chuckle.

"I meant that about the inflight entertainment," she added. "You two got any preferences, musicwise?"

"Doubt you've got it," Djinni grunted. Victoria smiled to herself and gazed fondly at the multiterabyte storage stack that was music only. "Try me," she challenged him.

"Apoptygma Berzerk," he said. Smugly.

Stump the DJ, hmm? She cued up "Welcome to Earth" and sat back. In the window that showed Djinni's headcam, she could see Bulwark's face. He looked pained. She switched the feed to Djinni's personal freq, and cued up Miriam Stockley for Bulwark. His eyes registered surprise, then amusement. He closed them, and settled back in the dubious "comfort" of the seat.

"This might not suck," was all Djinni said. The rest of the flight passed in silence from both of them.

The target was in Atlantic City, and—as was to be expected, considering that this was a petty criminal—the target was not in a nice part of Atlantic City. Vickie ignored the buttonhole cams for the most part, as Djinni and Bulwark took their rented beater past the new casinos and the Triumph Tower and all the rest of the frenetic glitz, tracking them by the innumerable security cams, getting used to switching from cam view to cam view. She had an ace in the hole if she lost them: two more of the elaborately folded spell-packets plugged in via USB cables.

The "bit of Bulwark" had been easy; she asked for a couple of hairs, told him why, and he obligingly gave them to her.

Djinni, however, was not someone she wanted to approach for a "sample," and he was surprisingly careful. She had resorted, at last, to Jenson, Bulwark's superior. Jenson didn't like Djinni. Jenson would do everything he covertly could to put Djinni back behind bars. And Jenson didn't know her from Adam. So using her old FBI credentials, she'd gotten Jenson to get her something of Djinni's when he and Bulwark were out on a recruitment. Something personal. And what Jenson had brought her were books.

The Count of Monte Cristo, and *Franny and Zooey*. The former was marked with margin notes in a tiny, precise script; both were paperbacks so often read that the covers were soft. She photographed the notes and took tiny scrapings from the covers of both, then had Jenson return them to their proper places. She hadn't studied the notes, but the scrapings and one of the note pages were in Djinni's packet.

It wasn't only that she wanted an arcane way to track them, it was that she couldn't work actual magic for them at that far a distance without a magical connection to them.

The books themselves, the fact that they were something he read over and over, said a lot about the man. Add to that, the notes—she was not sure she wanted to know that much about him.

Well, right now, as they drove deeper into the seedier part of Atlantic City, it was moot. "Where exactly are we going?" Bulwark asked, as Djinni finally parked the car in front of a boarded-up storefront.

"I told ya, we're gonna take in a little entertainment." The glee in Djinni's voice made Vickie close her eyes and count to ten. He was going to try to do something to punish her for this. Never mind that what she was doing would be useful and might even be life-saving—

"You have bogeys at your eight o'clock," she said softly, as the security cam in the parking lot showed her movement behind them. She zoomed and clarified the image as much as she could. "Three, males, large, weapons. I see a pipe and a baseball ba—"

Djinni moved. Fast. He was beside the three before they could blink. "Hello boys," he said, genially. "Out for a stroll?"

The widest of the three cursed and started to swing; the tallest grabbed the pipe before it had moved more than a few inches. "Yeah, bro. A stroll. Fresh air, good for ya."

Djinni nodded. "So they tell me. Well, you boys keep on strolling."

Red turned his back to them and moved away, whistling. The thug with the bat made a gesture to follow, but the tallest held him back, shaking his head. Pipe boy cursed and turned away and the others followed. Djinni didn't look back and favored Bull with a chuckle as they continued across the lot.

"Preventative action?" Bulwark asked dryly, as Vickie's sophisticated sound analysis picked out most of what the would-be muggers were saying. The first continued to swear but the second silenced him. "—was a meta, you idjit. You wanta mix it up with a meta?"

"Something like that." Djinni was unwrapping his face. "There. Anything showing?"

In Bulwark's camera view, Djinni was wearing a face she hadn't seen before. It might have been pleasant, if it hadn't been marred by a couple of scars. He evidently wasn't going to bother with a hairpiece this time. She looked for the throat mike, the wire for the earpiece, and realized with a shock he'd grown skin over them both to conceal them. Oh, smart. "No, nothing," she replied. "Not even a lump."

"Good." Oh, she didn't like that grin. "All right, Jarhead. Let's go take in the nightlife."

The seedy-looking bar he was heading for was the only establishment showing any signs of life on this street. She already had a sinking feeling, and when the sign managed to flicker on long enough for her to read GENTLEMAN'S CLUB, she knew what he was planning to do to try to shock her.

She shook her head as they paid the cover charge and passed the bouncer, emerging into a barely lit room throbbing with pounding music. There was a runway-type stage with three poles; a very limber girl with patently artificial enhancements was twined inelegantly around one of them. Djinni sat down at a table near the stage, right in front of the middle pole, and ordered a beer. Bulwark did the same.

"I hope that girl didn't pay too much for those bazookas," she said dryly in their ears. "In ten years they're going to be hard as rocks and she can rent them out as paperweights."

Vickie was doing her job; seeing if the club security cams were running on wireless. They were; within moments, she had them all. "Eight wireless cams," she said. "Four in the main stage, one in each of two private rooms, one in the office and one in the dressing room. In the main stage area you have one in each corner. They have fish-eye lenses, so there's not a lot of blind spots. There's two people in the office, none in the private rooms and four more girls in the dressing room. Besides the bouncer at the door, there's another one down behind the DJ, and the bartender has a sawed-off at each end of the bar."

Djinni gave the slightest of nods to show he'd heard.

The girl with the artificial chest untangled herself from the pole. "Let's give it up for Brandy!" said the DJ, with staged enthusiasm, to a spattering of bored applause. "And let's hear it for Kara Kane!"

The replacement was met with some real response; it was easy to see why. If her boobs had been pumped, it had been by someone who knew what he was doing. She was long-legged and long-haired and looked like a head cheerleader that you just knew was as active under the bleachers as in front of them. She was also a much better dancer than Brandy, who was making the rounds of the tables until she found someone who would "buy her a drink."

The new girl was concentrating on her dancing, right up until she switched poles to the one that Djinni had parked in front of. As she finished her first swing around it, she got a good look at him. Her eyes widened. In recognition?

If so, Djinni gave no sign, other than tucking some bills in her g-string. And she didn't linger at "their" pole, but she didn't hurry the routine up, either.

But when her place had been taken by a woman who looked and danced as if she ate men alive on toast, Kara Kane managed to sidle her way to Djinni's table. She meandered through the crowd, giving her clients devastating and winsome looks full of promise. Seemingly on a whim, she stopped by Red and Bull.

"Hey, handsome," she purred breathlessly, planting one hip on the table and bending over so that her chest was just about eye level. "Buy a girl a drink?"

"Actually my friend and I were lookin' for a private dance, darlin'," Djinni drawled before Bulwark could say anything. "Think that can be arranged?"

"You just follow me," she replied.

What the hell? Vickie thought.

"Djinni—" growled Bulwark over the channel. "Just what do you think you're doing?"

"Come on, Jarhead," Djinni said genially, slapping Bulwark on the shoulder and propelling him forward into the private room. "Time for you to loosen up and have some fun."

Kara closed the door; in a remarkably short period of time, Djinni was in a chair, she was grinding her pelvis into his lap and her natural endowments were filling the screen in Djinni's button cam.

"Djinni, what the hell is going—" Vickie kept her voice as even as possible.

"Say hello to Miss Nagy, Kara," Djinni said in a throaty whisper. "Right now she's got the best seat in the house."

Vickie was aghast. "Jesus Cluny Frog!" she sputtered. "You just want to go out and announce to everyone that you're wired?"

Djinni chuckled. "Just Kara. Or, actually, Ms. Barbara Kronstein, to use something besides her stage name. This is our target, Victrix."

"Red? This is you, right?" The girl's tone of desperation was at complete odds with the way she was "dancing." "Red, I can't believe you just showed up; it's like you knew I needed help! Please, you've got to get me out of here—"

Bulwark interrupted. "Victrix. Audio?"

She'd already checked. These guys were cheap. "Nothing. No audio monitor in this room. But tell her to keep dancing, the camera is hot and the guys in the back are watching."

"Eyes in the sky, darlin', keep making the customer happy. Tell me what's going on, and give 'em a show. Bull, pull out that stack of bills. As long as there's money on the table, they'll leave us alone."

The girl pulled her long hair up on top of her head and shimmied. Vickie opted to watch the other cam feeds. "There's this creepy guy." Kara's voice was strained. "He bought into the club about six weeks ago, right after the Invasion when no one was coming in and Jimmy really needed the money. Now he's here all the time, and Red—" there was an edge of panic in her voice "—Red, I think he knows about me! He keeps dropping hints about my talent, and how he knows a better use for it, it's not the regular kind of come-on!"

"Blacksnake?" Bulwark asked, alarmed.

"This isn't their approach, they just come in and make a direct offer," Djinni replied, sounding remarkably detached for a man with a pair of mammaries a centimeter from his nose. "Besides, I know their recruiter."

"Who, then?"

Kara leaned back and did a belly-dancer-type undulation. "He kind of slipped once. He sounded German."

"—oh, hell no—" Vic muttered.

"What is it you actually do, miss?" Bulwark asked carefully.

"That's what I don't understand," she said plaintively, as she somehow did a fast reverse on Djinni's lap and the mammaries changed places with a shapely derriere. "It's nothing—weapony. I just turn sound into light."

"Oh, hell no," Vickie said again, aloud this time, aghast. "A pocket amplifier—"

"Or a convenient source of a lot of sound," Bulwark agreed, grimly. "And you have a living flashbang."

At just that moment, on one of the main stage cameras, Vickie caught sight of something that set all her internal alarms ringing. A man had just come in, and the bouncer was showing him deference. Quickly she froze a half-dozen frames as he turned, and ran them through her facial-recognition program. The answer set her nerves on fire.

"Oh, *bloody* hell, no! Bull, Djinni, get out of there now," she snarled, fingers flying over the keyboard to look for exits. "Your girl's mystery date is out in the main stage area and I am pretty sure it's Doppelgaenger, 'cause whoever he is, he's wearing Doc Bootstrap's face."

Bulwark was quicker at remembering what kind of an asset she was than Djinni. "Exits?"

"Checking." She called up the plans from the last Health and Safety inspection. And meanwhile she started futzing the feed on the cameras—all of them, to put suspicion off for a few more precious moments. She told the wireless signal to drift; on her monitors she could see the feed start to get static. "Out the front, the way you came. Both bathrooms have a window big enough to squeeze through if you break it, but take the women's if you have a choice; the girls have their own and it's likely to be empty. Fire exit directly left as you exit the room. Roof access—pop the panel in the center of the room you're in, it's a hard ceiling, crawl ten feet south and there's a hatch."

"Don't leave me!" Kara begged. She froze on Djinni's lap.

"Tell her to keep dancing. I'm screwing with their feed but it'll take a minute."

"Keep dancing, darlin', we're working on something."

In the office camera feed—which was, of course, also starting to snow out—she could see one of the men hitting his security monitor with the flat of his hand.

"You can't take the chance that Doppelgaenger will recognize you, Bull," Djinni was saying.

The monitor feeds went to pure static.

"If you're gonna go, go now!" she urged. "The cams are down, but if they're smart, they'll have it fixed in a second. The fire exit's a mechanical alarm, I can't shut it off."

"Split up?" suggested Bulwark. "You take the girl, I'll make the noise."

Djinni nodded. "Roof. You get the car if you can. See you back at the airport."

Bulwark headed for the bathrooms. Djinni pushed Kara off his lap and climbed onto the chair. The buttonhole cam got confused, then dark, then there was dim light as Djinni popped the roof hatch. Bulwark's cam was more straightforward; in through the door marked "Dames," he did something and an invisible force punched the window, frame and all, out of the wall. Then he was out and running down the dark alley, heading for the parking lot and the car.

Djinni wasn't wasting time with finesse or niceties. He sprinted to the edge of the roof, tossed the girl down into a dumpster, followed her, tossed her over the side to the ground and tumbled out himself. Djinni glanced down, noted Barbara's elaborate stiletto heels with more straps than a racing harness holding them to her feet. He grunted, threw her over his shoulder and sprinted down the alley.

The monitors in the club all came back to life. The men in

the office were just now realizing that the men and the girl were gone from the room. Doppelgaenger was shoving his way towards the back; he must have heard Bulwark punching out the window.

"You're going to get pursuit in a few seconds," she warned. Meanwhile she was calling up everything she could for both men. "Bulwark, your car's been 'jacked. City bus is approaching the lot, get on it. They'll never look for you there."

In Bulwark's cam, she could see the bus; no one would think twice about a man running to catch it. The driver must have had a modicum of heart; he stopped and waited. Bull got on, dropped change into the fare box until it beeped and threw himself into the nearest seat. The bus pulled out. Vickie switched her attention to Djinni.

"Next right," she said, just as the monitor showed Doppelgaenger in the private room. He looked up, his face contorted in a snarl. He leapt like a cat, presumably caught the edge of the open trap, and pulled himself out of sight. "Left. Doppelgaenger is on your tail." She tried to remember what the file said on Doppelgaenger. From what she'd seen, he was fast. Very fast. No way of telling if he had some enhanced-senses way of tracking Djinni but best to assume he could. Above all, he was ruthless, cold and brutally efficient and if he caught them... "Left again."

She had them on the map; with a sudden burst of inspiration, she called up the utilities map and layered it underneath. Yes! There—

"Left and left again."

"Where're you—"

"*Stop!*"

Vickie grabbed Djinni's packet to connect herself and him, gathered power—

—and the earth opened beneath his feet and swallowed Red and the girl whole.

Djinni had wrapped the girl in his coat; it didn't cover much, but it was better than just a g-string in the storm sewer that Vickie had dumped them into. He was muttering under his breath.

Vickie was exhausted. It took a lot of power to operate at that much of a distance. That power had to come from somewhere; in this case, since she'd had no time to prepare, it had come from her.

"Next right," she said. "Then go up the ladder. The manhole is in the alley behind the Triumph Tower. Bulwark is waiting right at it with a car."

She hadn't just dumped them the twenty feet down into the sewer; she'd made sure to give them a ramp. And it was a storm sewer, not a sewage outlet...

She'd closed the earth up after them, too. Fifteen feet of dirt should be enough to confuse even the keenest of meta-senses. And she'd been watching their trail in aboveground cams the whole way; there'd been no sign of Doppelgaenger. Bulwark had been able to get another car without a lot of trouble, and she'd given him directions to the nearest place she could bring Djinni and the girl out.

"We're here, Bull."

Bulwark pried up the manhole cover.

Djinni helped the girl start up the ladder, then stopped. "Private mode," he growled.

Too tired to question or argue, she switched.

"That was magic," he said, in a very flat tone of voice.

"Yes." She matched his tone.

The string of curses that followed left her wilting in her chair. "If you ever do something like that to me again..." He paused, then left the sentence unfinished.

"You coming, or sightseeing?" Bulwark called down the hole.

Without another word, Djinni climbed up.

He didn't say another word to Vickie after that. Not when Kara (or Barbara) thanked her, not when Bulwark said in a warm tone of congratulations, "Good work, Operative Victrix," not when she cued up more music for him for the return trip. He talked to the girl, he even talked to Bulwark, but he ignored Vic's presence as if she didn't exist. Just after touchdown, he got up and moved out of sight. When he came back out, he was wearing his wrappings, and he had the throat mike and earpiece in his hand. He dropped both in Bulwark's lap, detached the button cam from his coat, added that, and walked out.

"Terminating link now," said Vickie. She shut the rig down, took the spell packets and filed them in a box of others, and left the room, turning off the lights.

She was too tired to get any further than the living room. Bulwark would definitely green-light this. Djinni could sit and rotate; his opinion wouldn't count.

But now it hit her: those girls—

She sat down hard on the sofa and cried bitterly, her face in her gloved hands, crying until the gloves were soaked and her eyes were sore. Not one of those girls, could they see what she really looked like, would trade their lives for hers. The handful of people who had seen had been unable to control their revulsion. She would never again have the things that they took so much for granted that they didn't even think about it; people looking at them with pleasure, men wanting to touch them without a second thought, or indeed, any thought at all. Sun on their bare skin. Beautiful, unmarred skin. Feeling where they were touched...

It took a tremendous effort of will, once she had stopped weeping, to get up off the sofa, to go into the dark bathroom, strip off the gloves, bathe her face in cold water, and find another pair of gloves and pull them on again. But will was what a magician was all about; regardless of what she was, she had skills that were needed.

She went back into her Overwatch room and fired everything back up again, checking the time. Not a moment too soon; she switched to an entirely different set of comm frequencies.

"Reading me, Bella?" she asked, pleased that her voice was not too hoarse.

"Five by five," came the cheerful voice. "Video input coming online now."

A room in CCCP HQ appeared in the live-cam monitor. A room that was, in comparison to the one she sat in, what the radio room of the *Titanic* was to the comm room of the average supertanker. But it was what the CCCP had, and there was her counterpart, looking frail and wide-eyed, the tall, storklike Gamayun, just now putting on a headset of her own.

"*Vi menia slishite, tovarish?*" Vickie asked.

The woman nodded her head, a dark forelock falling into one eye. "*Slishu vas gromko e chetko, tovarish Victoria,*" Gamayun replied.

"I think we're ready to rock and roll." Bella moved and the camera viewpoint proceeded down a hall, around a corner, and into Red Saviour's office.

"*Shto?*" Saviour asked, the essence of impatience. "What silly toy you are having to show me now that Echo thinks we are needing?"

"Not a toy, and not Echo, Comrade Commissar," Bella replied. "A little something Comrade Victrix cooked up that I'm going to demonstrate for you. Ready, Vic?"

Vickie's gloved fingers flew over the keys of her computer. Once again, it was magic time.

Doppelgaenger had faith in the universe. It was a perfect machine. Things ran as they should. For everything, there was balance. Harmony. His brethren believed in contingencies and fail-safes. In strategy. They had their place in the way of things, yes. He saw the strength one could attain simply by planning ahead. But when all else failed he believed in the simple waxing and waning of order and chaos. When plans failed, when strategy couldn't hope to predict your opponent, the universe would provide. One simply needed to look hard enough.

Take the video feed, for example. His quarry had vanished. There was no trace. Aerial support had reported no changes in the spectrum above the establishment. No one, cloaked or otherwise, had taken to flight. Where there were three, became two, then none. The ignorant security of the club had lost the first man. No matter. It was the girl who had been important. But where her and her rescuer's footsteps went cold, so had their trail. Detailed readings of the location revealed nothing. As for the in-house surveillance logs, they had been replaced with hours of footage from the *Kill Bill* films.

At least those had been somewhat entertaining.

Still, all visual record of the infiltrators had been irrevocably lost.

And then, and here Doppelgaenger had to smile, the universe had stepped in. Was it chance that brought these men here last night? Had the girl gotten word out somehow? Had she sensed danger? If so, they were men on a mission. Echo men, there was little doubt. The heroes of Echo, doing their good deed. And they had been careful, oh yes. They had erased all evidence of their passing...

...save, of course, for the base, desperate actions of lesser men.

Doppelgaenger motioned, and the frightened man played the tape again. His name was Douglas. His last name didn't matter. A regular at the Silver Corral, Douglas' favorite pastime was sneaking in a small, portable camcorder and capturing, to be watched over and over again, his little slice of heaven. A small, sad little man, who had been tolerated because he did bring money to a club in desperate need of it. He had been caught once, and now paid hefty bribes to one of the club's bouncers. When Doppelgaenger had expressed his displeasure that the security footage was missing, the bouncer had been quick to remember Douglas and his hobby.

Doppelgaenger watched the scene play over again. The girl, those men...they had been men of Echo, he was sure of that now. He recognized one of them. He had, in fact, studied the face and mannerisms of this Bulwark several times. It had been enough. The huge man would barely waggle his brow, much less make any sustaining expression. And the other...?

"Kindred," Doppelgaenger whispered. He recognized the talent, having so much more of it himself. "You see it, small man? You see what this man does *not* do?"

Douglas stared at Djinni, and back at Doppelgaenger. He shook uncontrollably. Any word could mean his death. And probably a very painful one. He risked a glance sideways and flinched away. The remains of his wife were still twitching.

"Nn-nnnn-no—" Douglas stammered finally. "What do you mean?"

"His skin," Doppelgaenger purred. "It doesn't...it doesn't *breathe* right." He fixed Douglas with an encouraging smile. "Look closer; don't you see it now?"

Douglas stared back at Djinni's boyish grin, and looked helplessly back at his captor.

"*Look closer!*" Doppelgaenger roared, and smashed Douglas' head into the television, an old-fashioned cathode ray tube. The screen exploded. Douglas screamed, jagged glass shards slicing his weak flesh, his screams becoming gurgles. His body shook a few times from the current, then fell still, smoke bellowing from the debris.

Doppelgaenger rolled his eyes.

"*Wunderbar.* American electronics are *scheisse*. Someone find me a good German television set."

Behind him, a soldier saluted smartly, turned on his heels, and made as if to leave.

"Wait!" Doppelgaenger barked. "On second thought, we will return to base." He reached down and picked up the blood-spattered camcorder lovingly. His fingers moved with a surgeon's grace as he plucked out the cables.

His grin was beatific as he glided away.

"Finally, I get to *play.*"

CHAPTER FIVE

Keeping Up Appearances

VERONICA GIGUERE

It's really odd, looking back on all this, to see how people who would be vital to us were folks we never would have sought out, or who would even have passed anywhere on our radar. Like... one ex-Special Forces bartender in New Orleans.

THREE FOR ONE, or so the sign in the window proclaimed amidst a jumble of neon and gaudy metal plates that advertised the joys of both domestic and imported refreshment. Water stains rose three feet up the wall, the peeling wallpaper and discolored linoleum proof of rough times. The chairs were secondhand, the tables pitted and stained, but the bar along the west wall gleamed with a shine that said maybe, just maybe, things were starting to turn around. Old pictures in new frames hung on the walls, fresh signatures and messages from tourists and regulars were scribbled between the yellow water stains. Everything was in transition, from bad to better, in the bar on Bourbon Street. Everything, including the woman picking glass out of her hand.

She gritted her teeth and dug deeper with ragged fingernails, ignoring the mess she made. Someone had been careless enough to leave a broken glass behind the clean ones, and she had discovered the mistake seconds too late. Melisandre Gautier shot a dirty look towards the back office, knowing full well who was really responsible and who would avoid any blame. The bartender for the early shift was an airheaded little thing who couldn't tell rum from vodka, but the boss kept her on for morale.

Morale. It was a tasteful way to say something baser, but it did keep Elliot from chasing her. For Mel, that was reason enough to just dig out the glass, wrap her hand in a towel, and get back to work. The afternoon was warm and humid, the beer was thankfully ice-cold, and the combination made for good business. Good business meant good tips, and good tips meant another week of paying the rent.

For now, the bar was dead, save for a few good ol' boys knocking back longnecks as ESPN droned on. Yesterday at this time, she'd been treated to a visit by a pair of suits flashing Blacksnake IDs and waving a contract. The first "no" hadn't made an impact, nor had the sixth and seventh. Echo might have deserted her, but Mel's pride would not allow her to stoop so low as to become a weapon for hire. And so she told them that and more, reaching underneath the bar for the sawed-off shotgun that Elliot kept there for these sorts of emergencies...

And found a bottle opener. *That damn dancer...* A colorful stream of Cajun-laced invectives had filled the tiny space, and Mel brandished a double-barreled shotgun at the two operatives. They were surprised but not scared, and hadn't made any motion to leave. That was, not until the door had opened and a third person had strolled in.

Bulwark's presence had tipped the tide in Mel's favor, and he had stood by calmly as the Blacksnake boys backpedaled and left the bar. The stoic man had even gone so far as to give Mel the courtesy of a lookout and an all-clear, which was when she caught the semblance of a smile as the shotgun dissolved to nothing more than a flimsy bit of metal hot-glued to a magnet. Two others had followed him inside, a frightened woman with a pretty face and a man whose face was obscured by a swath of red fabric. She had answered questions, offered them drinks, and then sent them on their collective merry way with the best information she had.

Had it been anyone else, she wouldn't have said a damn thing. Echo had left her out in the cold years ago, but she didn't hold it against Bull...much. Orders had been orders, chain of command and all that, and she knew that he hadn't made the decision to put her out to pasture. So, she didn't hate him, and that was why she had pointed the three to the places that she had heard the Stone brothers frequented.

The glass was nearly out, blood running from wrist to elbow in a neat trickle from her attempts. Mel grimaced and reached for a clean rag, then contemplated the collection of liquors in front of her. "What says 'don't give a damn 'bout nothin' these days'..." She smirked, picked up the bottle of Jack Daniels, and wet the cloth. Gritting her teeth, Mel pressed the whiskey-soaked rag to her wounds and slowly began to clean herself up.

She wondered if Bull and his team would be back after their recon or if they would pack up and return to whatever HQ had sent them. For what it was worth, Mel told herself, she would be perfectly content to never see the Echo man again.

She'd been part of Echo, once upon a time. Mel Gautier—Reverie, according to the database—had been part of the Army's 2nd Ranger Battalion from the day she had turned nineteen. Enlisted out of high school, her commanding officers had nearly wet themselves when they had discovered just what she could do in the field. Illusion was her forté, concealment and mind games her companion as she accompanied seasoned troops on covert operations. By twenty-one, Mel had been deployed in operations throughout Somalia, Egypt, and Iraq. By twenty-seven, she was sent back to New Orleans with medical discharge papers and a promise of rehab and recovery that never came.

It had happened outside of Fallujah, during a raid on a rogue cell that was keeping trucks from getting supplies to the area's only makeshift hospital. When they'd left that morning, there were six of them. By that night, she was held in front of a video camera and made to recite from a script, the rest of her team held hostage to make her behave. It had taken the Echo boys and the Marines weeks to find her, even with one of their mindfraggers using his own specialized radar. Mel had hidden behind layers of her own imagination, projecting horror after horror on any who had dared to come near her, including the rescue ops who finally managed to knock her out. Sedated until they arrived in Germany, Mel was poked and prodded and questioned for days by Army and Echo psychologists alike. When the doctors had satisfied their curiosity, they had called in Bulwark to deliver the final verdict.

To say that Mel was bitter would have been akin to calling Mardi Gras a backyard barbeque. She had devoted more than a third of her life to both the Army and Echo, and both organizations had put her out to pasture rather than try to fix what had been broken. The Army's second-string psychiatrists had offered drugs to suppress her abilities and counter the unavoidable post-traumatic stress disorder that wracked her body and soul after her ordeal, but Echo had left her high and dry. With their staff of telempaths and neurofixers, the woman known as Reverie could have gone back to service in a year overseas, less than that stateside. Mel wouldn't have cared either way, she just wanted to be useful somewhere. For something. To someone.

The day that the Nazis had stormed through the French Quarter, she had been useful. For a few days, she had been worth something. To someone.

The day that the Nazis had landed, she had been working the noisy bar by herself while Elliot had stayed in the back, teaching the new girl how to "make drinks." Mel had ignored the lie—Elliot bought the liquor, but he couldn't mix it properly—and remained out front, gathering tips and popping longnecks as fast as she pulled them from the cooler. And then, all of a sudden, the Quarter exploded and she was out on the sidewalk, staring down the street as a line of metal giants cut a swath through strip joints and sandwich shops alike. When the sun had come up the next day, she had been back at the bar, cleaning up and rebuilding and hauling bags of ice to the distribution center in the middle of Jackson Square. Waiting for more help...for the same sort of help that had gone to New York, Las Vegas, Atlanta, Boston, St. Louis, and that had somehow conveniently missed her beloved New Orleans. The government forgot about their little corner of the world, ravaged just as badly by the inexplicable arrival and hasty retreat of the metal men, but less important than those cities that Echo had called home.

Although the government had forgotten the Big Easy, the businesses hadn't. The less-than-reputable organizations hadn't. The opportunists, the swindlers, the cheats and the liars, they all moved in on the broken city like sharks on a bloody shipwreck and had a hell of a feast, dividing the city amongst themselves and forcing the residents to choose sides. Without outside help, they built the city back up far more quickly than any government agency could have—dirty money had that ability, but it came at a price. New Orleans' resurrection courtesy of the underground had cost it that carefree spirit, that *bon temps* that used to roll through the Quarter night and day.

These days the krewes kept the city running and business thriving, with the powerful and resourceful at the top of the unique New Orleans ladder. Before that day in August, krewes kept the distinct flavor of the Big Easy in check, planning the festivities and letting the good times roll throughout the city from mid-January until the crescendo of Mardi Gras peaked. Since the Invasion, the krewes had become more than just a trendy organization for a few parties and an elaborate float. They were still part social club and part charity, but mostly enforcers for their own carefully guarded territories. Petty crime was a thing of the past, thanks to the strict control they maintained. Instead, the thriving criminal underground gained and lost ground through business deals and questionable rebuilding contracts.

Mel looked up to see the television flicker as gunfire rang out across the street. She paused, her hand reaching for the real handgun she kept next to the register as she waited for someone from the Krewe of Perseus to answer the challenge. This newer krewe had brought together hustlers, business owners, natives, and newcomers to exert control from Dauphin Street to the Mississippi River, between Canal Street and St. Peter's Cathedral. In that four-by-five square of city blocks, they controlled the lucrative entertainment district, the livelihood, the very pulse of the city. Others held the waterfront or the Garden District, but the Krewe of Perseus laid claim to this corner of New Orleans.

From the front of a nearby novelty shop, bolts of electricity snaked across the street to answer the gunshot challenge. There was an acrid smell of something burning, followed shortly by a car alarm and a fair amount of shouting. Mel let out a long breath and smirked as a stream of vindictive Creole reminded the shooter that there were worse things than bullets to worry about these days.

She turned away from the door. The three men stared at her, the NASCAR race on the television a staticky mess. One of them waggled an empty bottle at her, his smile a probable attempt at charm that just resulted in being snaggle-toothed and creepy. "'Ey, darlin', you know how t'fix this?"

"Sure thing. Won't even take me half a lap," she drawled. She hopped over the counter, hand still wrapped in the whiskey-soaked towel. With her uninjured hand, she reconnected the fraying wire to the cable box, then thumped the set for good measure. Sure enough, the image returned on the same lap as when it had gone to static. The men chuckled and snorted, and Mel set down another round of cheap domestic beer before turning back to the bar.

"*Well, well. As pretty as you are in my dreams, Revvie-baby.*" The voice pushed at the space between her eyes, the tone familiar yet nearly forgotten after so long away from the service. Mel froze, then turned to see a lanky man in denim and a worn but clean T-shirt hanging in the doorway. Her jaw dropped, and he repeated the words aloud in a rough Cajun drawl.

She threw her head back and laughed, her easy tone a mask for the familiar ache in her heart. "An' when did you get int' town, Kip? Coulda used ya in a fight yesterday." She moved around to the barstools to meet him with both arms around his neck. The faint smell of cheap cigarettes clung to his shirt and mingled with the sweat that came from an easy walk through the Quarter on a summer afternoon. His hands moved around her waist and he returned the embrace before lifting her up to sit on the polished bartop. Mel winked, then bent to press her lips to his in another more intimate greeting. The shared kiss was as much for show as for sentiment, and it had the boys in the back staring in envy at the everyman who'd just walked in.

He laughed and patted her hip, his thumb hooked in the worn beltloop of her jeans. "Got in last night, actually. Been doin' work here an' there, an' figured I'd stop in an' see how life's been treatin' my favorite Army girl."

Mel's smile faded, and she swung her legs around to slide back behind the bar. With Kip came a host of memories, mostly involving their combined days with Echo. She had met the man during her first tour in Somalia, and the two had become fast friends and more as the years had gone by. Any relationship was of the on-again, off-again sort, with no real animosity between them when they had drifted apart after assignments on opposite sides of the world.

He still looked like she remembered him; pale gray eyes and jet black hair complementing a wiry build, the caramel tone of his skin only bringing more attention to the lazy smile he still bestowed on her. She shook her head and bent to retrieve a bottle from the cooler. "I ain't Army no more, Kip. Ain't really Reverie no more, neither. I do have say over who gets a beer in this place, though. Y'want one?"

"Sure wouldn't say no." He settled on one of the barstools and leaned against the counter, nodding politely to the men in the corner. "The place looks good, even after all the hell that went through here. Guess you keepin' busy, Mel?"

She shrugged, the bottle cap lifted with a practiced flick of her wrist. "Busy enough. Work, sleep, gettin' by. Keepin' my head down an' my nose outta trouble, helpin' out where I can. Tizzy's shop got burned up good back when them things came and she lost Roscoe a few months ago, so I work Sundays for her at the shop so she can get to church."

It was the same story for everyone here, she mused. For Mel, it was just as much therapy for her as help for others. Serving cold drinks or spooning up fresh jambalaya, she could prove to herself that she was worth something to somebody. "Y'know," she began, "if you're around for a few days, they could use another set of hands to help fix the tile in the front..."

The man shook his head, taking a long pull on the bottle before answering. "Sorry t'hear about Roscoe, but I'm just passin' through. I did come by special to check on you, though. An' what's this about a fight yesterday? Anythin' t'do with them Stone boys an' what went down at their little club?"

Mel paused, her thumb running over the raised edges of the bottle cap. While she had sent Bulwark and his two associates in the direction of the Stone brothers, she hadn't heard anything about the results of that meeting. Instead, she pushed the conversation in another direction, not wanting to be reminded of the Echo group. "I dunno, Kip. Fights happen 'round here all the time. I do my best t'stay outta it all, earn my keep. What about you these days?"

"I got a decent gig out in Biloxi, actually. Not too far from Keesler, working security at one of the big casinos. Decent money, too," he added with a wink. "Better 'n tips here an' there. I mean, if y'wanted, I could put in a good word for ya there, get you workin' with a clientele that tips in Grants instead of Washingtons. That, or you could get a security detail there, too. With those pretty tricks of yours, th' cheaters an' swindlers wouldn't see you comin'."

The blonde woman sniffed, her arms folded across her chest as she thought of the people who were still recovering and rebuilding. Going to Biloxi would make her just as bad as the Echo brass, and that wasn't something that she wanted on her conscience. Besides, the stretch of casinos along Highway 90 were garish tourist traps even more than before, now that so much dirty money had been poured into them to build them back up. "Thanks, but I'll pass. Workin' here pays the rent, and I got people to look after."

"Like who?" He shook his head and gestured to the door and the dirty window that looked out onto Bourbon Street. "This place is falling apart left and right, Revvie-baby. It's not like they're looking out for you because you get 'em a beer at the end of the day." Kip shook his head and turned away, his gaze focusing on the NASCAR race. Regardless, his words pushed between her eyes, the touch a sweet caress against her mind such that she immediately relaxed. *You used t'be so good at what you did, Revvie. Best combination of raw talent and special skills I'd ever seen ... and Uncle Sam kicked you to the curb, with them Echo punks shutting the gate behind you ...*

She swayed slightly, her eyes closing as the familiar and soothing tones washed over her. All other noise disappeared behind Kip's mental "voice"—the television, the clink of bottles against the tables, the shuffle of feet on the linoleum. When Mel spoke, the words came slow, soft and dreamy to match the brush against her thoughts. "Yeah, they didn't give me nothin' for all I did. Just 'goodbye an' have a nice life' for all I did for 'em ..."

Could make 'em pay, Revvie. There're folks out there who appreciate what you can do for 'em. Ain't like Echo, where you gotta kowtow t'some bigshot who ain't gonna understand what you been through. He took a long pull on the bottle, a boot resting on another stool. Behind him, Mel hummed in contentment as a bittersweet smile lifted the corner of her mouth. His own posture relaxed to match hers, he smiled as the race went to a commercial. The fans kept a steady rhythm, the click-click as much hypnosis as the voice that surrounded her like the August heat. *How 'bout we pack up your things and drive down I-10? Stop off in D'Iberville at the old house, find a few memories left there, an' start over. You an' me, makin' some sweet dreams t'gether—*

A crash followed by the sound of chairs scraping against the floor jolted Mel from the trance, the touch abruptly pulled from her mind. In front of her, Bulwark flexed a meaty hand before setting the amber bottle upright on the bar. The three men at the table in the back had discarded all semblance of backwater ignorance, each reaching for his sidearm while Kip staggered to his feet. He licked the corner of his mouth, grimacing as he tasted blood. "Was wondering when you'd come back here, Bull. Didn't take you for the sentimental type," he said.

"Likewise. So, did you start working for Blacksnake after the Nazis landed, or did you get a head start after that dishonorable discharge? I didn't keep up with your stellar career after the court-martial." He folded both arms across his chest and nodded to Mel. "Heard that Damon got into town shortly after we left, and after your run-in with Blacksnake yesterday—"

Mel turned a hate-filled gaze on Kip, who smirked as the mercenaries moved behind him. Her face reddened as she realized what had happened. "You . . . oh, you didn't. No, wait . . . you did. You lyin', two-timin', selfish sack o' shit, you came here t'turn me over to 'em because the ones here yesterday couldn't." Her eyes narrowed and she wiped her mouth with the back of her wrapped hand, wishing that she could get the smoky taste of his kiss off her lips.

He spread his arms in a gesture of faux welcome. "What can I say? They knew your weakness, Revvie. When reason don't work, they give ol' Kajole a call, an' he answers. So an old flame comes walkin' back int' your life, an' you're lonely enough to believe whatever he tells you. I'm makin' you an offer. It's good money, an' Blacksnake'll put you to good use. People like you an' me, we're hot property these days."

"I ain't a traitor, Kip," she spat. "I'm tendin' bar, I got a right to refuse service t'anyone, an' I'm refusin' t'serve you. Get movin'."

"Look, the only way y'make money this good out here is down on your knees," Kip answered, his lip curled into a sneer. "An' I'm pretty sure that you don't wanna go back to that. You're what, ten, twelve years outta practice?"

Mel tensed up, then reached under the counter to come up this time with the actual sawed-off shotgun. The group behind Kip chuckled amongst themselves, and Kip took a step forward. She cocked the hammer, snarling. "Get outta here, Damon. You an' yer thugs. I ain't so low as a snake's belly t'decide t'go crawlin' in their lair."

Kip tut-tutted and shook his head. "Now, Revvie, you an' I both know that ain't a real gun—"

A blast shattered the table behind the four men, the sound prompting them to jump and draw their own weapons. Bulwark moved next to the bartender, his expression still unwavering in spite of the threat of more gunfire. "I'd bet that *is* a real gun, Damon. I'd also bet that if you attack an Echo operative in that fashion, as her commanding officer, I'd be forced to take action."

"She ain't Echo no more, Bull."

"She is if she wants to be."

The offer hung in the air as both men looked to the bartender with the whiskey-soaked rag about her hand, the can opener in the back pocket of her frayed blue jeans, and the expression that said she had had just about enough of the entire conversation. She looked from Kip to Bulwark and back, then smirked at the Blacksnake operatives.

"Like hell I'm not Echo." Mel took aim and shot again, this time silencing the television above the heads of the Blacksnake men. A rain of glass fell and the bartender smirked as the group scattered. "I'll decline that offer, Kajole. You an' yer boys can find somebody else who wants t'play traitor. I ain't biting."

"Think about it, Revvie. We got people who can get you fixed up proper. No more nightmares, no more shots, no more wondering if what you see is really there..." Kip's wheedling tone slipped into her thoughts once more, but Mel stiffened against the onslaught. A hand went to her face, fingernails digging into her forehead as she fought to get his voice out. *We got the medical records, the reports from Fallujah. Nearly turned your boys on each other. You think the walkin' wall there wants that sort of liability?*

"Cut it out, Kajole." Bulwark stepped between the two, his size allowing him to look down at the wiry mentalist. "Like I said and like she said, she's Echo. You're done here."

"Done? Boy, I'm just gettin' started."

Mel grimaced as she felt the twist behind her eyes, the pressure rising as her vision blurred and she cocked the hammer back. Her arm rose of its own accord, and Mel tried to drop the weapon even as she felt a pair of strong hands pull her down and around the bar. Bulwark pulled her into a headlock, one palm pressing her shoulder to his chest as he wrenched the shotgun from her hand. Stars blossomed in her field of vision just as shots rang out, and for a moment everything around her had an azure tint to it. Above her, Bulwark grunted as the shots from the Blacksnake men found their marks. Just as suddenly, there was a crash and the shooting stopped, and the grip around her neck and shoulders loosened.

The Echo man stood straight, helping the bartender to her feet. The bullets that had been intended for them had ricocheted off of Bulwark's personal force field, the kinetic energy mirrored upon contact. While he had to contend with a few bruises, the Blacksnake operatives were not as lucky. Two tended to shoulder wounds while Kip stood on one foot, his jeans bloodied from a shot just below his left knee.

Mel picked up the discarded shotgun and aimed at the meta's other knee. Behind her, Bulwark stood expressionless, arms folded across his massive chest. She cocked the hammer back and sneered. "Now, get outta my life, Kip Damon. An' get th' hell outta this bar."

She locked the front door once the mercenaries had left and filled a clean towel with ice from the cooler. She set it in front of Bulwark, along with two fingers of the best whiskey they had as a "thank you." Elliot had run out of the office to find Mel aiming at the four men, and a scowl from the bartender had sent him right back. She'd have to explain things later, once everything had calmed down and she'd cleaned up.

Mel filled a shotglass with bourbon and raised it in a toast to the Echo man. "Look, I appreciate you steppin' in, Bull. Not that I don't appreciate you comin' back an' playin' along when I needed it, but makin' the offer was a nice touch."

The seat squealed underneath the big man's weight as he sat at the bar. He pressed the ice against his shoulder, but didn't touch the glass. "I was serious, Gautier. You want in, you're in. We lost a lot of good people that day, and we're hurting for help."

She paused, the glass at her lips. With a fair amount of restraint, Mel set the glass down and knocked her fist against her thigh as she struggled to come up with a suitable response. "So, second string, then. Wasn't good enough the first time around, but now that there's this need, you'll just take anybody?"

"It's not like that, Gautier. I'm not talking about a charity case; I don't have time for that. I need answers, and I need good people to help find them." Bulwark fixed her with a look that none of her illusions could have ever equaled. "Are you willing to be worth something, Reverie, or are you only good for a barfight and Jack Daniels these days?"

"It's Maker's Mark."

A pause. "I don't drink bourbon."

"Yeah, you don't look the type." Mel turned away and braced herself against the back bar, a long breath escaping her lips. If she stayed, it wouldn't be long before Blacksnake came back with more people to retaliate rather than recruit. If she left, it would be a chance to prove herself again and maybe start fixing what was so very broken. "If I come with you, and join up," she said. "If I do that, do you think they could"—she made a vague motion with her unwrapped hand, fingers gesturing to her temple—"fix it?"

The barstool creaked as he shifted again. "We've got some good docs who might be able to tackle it. Some of the newer recruits have experience in that sort of rewiring, and they've got a gentler touch than the army docs. Multiple therapy sessions, so you don't lose what you've got. What happened to you isn't uncommon, Gautier," he said, his tone matter-of-fact. "It gets fixed every day."

"Then why didn't someone bother fixing it the first time!" She barked at his reflection in the glass, her hand coming down hard on the counter in frustration. "If I was so good, why did they push me away? Damn it, Bull, I *loved* what I did! I didn't want to leave, even after what happened! I wanted to be worth something again, and they kicked me out!"

"So be worth something now." He raised his head to meet her gaze through the mirror, neither sympathy nor pity in his expression. "Pack up, turn in your notice, and be at the Jax Brewery building in two hours. Leave the self-pity here, and don't be late. I've got a schedule to keep."

Her eyes narrowed at his reflection, and she finally dropped her chin to her chest as she took a deep breath. Hands relaxed before she turned around, and Mel sized up the man with a trained eye before speaking again. "Scotch."

"Pardon?"

"You're a Scotch man." Without waiting for an answer, she poured him a double of the top-shelf brand they stocked and set the glass next to his hand. She left the bottle on the counter before walking to the back and throwing a few words in the direction of the office. There was a shout of indignation, but Mel returned seconds later with a lazy smile on her pretty face.

"So," she drawled as she leaned against the bar. "How long 'til we leave for Atlanta, boss?"

CHAPTER SIX

Watch Over Me

MERCEDES LACKEY

One thing never left my awareness, ever. The creature that the media was calling "the Seraphym." She hung in my magical awareness like a second sun. I knew what she was. I just couldn't figure out what she was doing here. Sometimes I wondered if even she knew.

The Instrument of the Infinite, the Flaming Sword known as Seraphym, was walking almost invisibly over the dirt of a playground. "Almost," because some of the smallest children could see her. She was wearing her gentlest aspect because of that, and little faces, tan, white and brown, turned towards her, bright eyes gazed at her thoughtfully and then went back to the important business of reenacting the battle that had so recently raged here with small plastic figures, cans and broken bricks. There was no need for a rescue at this moment, the threads of the futures remained momentarily unchanged, and for as long as both those conditions held, she had chosen to walk this place. The power that could take down a Thulian ship with a single blow was sifting through the dirt at her feet, seeking glass and rusty metal, brick, cement, wood fragments, and stone. And when she found such things, she reduced them to powder. Step by step, she walked this playground, making the ground safe for the children. Once, she felt a tugging at her gown, and turned to find a small one holding up a ruined plastic figure, bright with the colors that had once adorned the meta known as Kid Zero.

She took it, and sought in her mind for that fleeting spirit, and found him, safe and full of wonder. With a sigh, half of regret, half of relief, she let the fires run over the plastic in her hands, reshaping it until it was restored to playability again. Then, on a whim, she changed its colors: black jacket and pants and boots, gold star on its chest, red cape. CCCP. Let them know who their new protectors were. She handed it back to the toddler, not noticing she had changed the hair too, to a certain chestnut brown.

John Murdock patrolled his 'hood as he had before, but slowly, cognizant that he was still not fully recovered. Sometimes she sensed trouble in the futures, dangerous things intersecting with that blankness that was him. She intercepted these things if he was not strong enough to handle them himself yet—and if he was, she still waited and watched, to be sure he would not come to harm. And when she had nothing urgent to tend to, Sera shadowed him, staying just out of sight. Watched him, paid attention to what he paid attention to. Tried to read his thoughts from his expression. And still, he was an enigma. The blank place in the futures would not resolve, and somehow she shrank from invading his mind to read what was there. But she had to unravel this if she was to find the way out of doom.

In the community garden, the seedlings drooped. Planted by inexpert hands, overwatered, in sour soil too heavy with clay and urban contamination for healthy growth, they were fighting a losing battle with root rot, and no one who tended them knew that.

Seraphym knew. She had seen John Murdock here, staring perplexed at the unthriving seedlings, knowing something was wrong, but not what, nor how to mend it. No one here was a gardener. And this garden meant more than mere food. It represented the hope of the community. Instinctively, John understood this.

She came here in the dead of night, stood in the middle of the plot in bare feet, and became more truly herself for a moment than anyone had ever seen her. A pillar of flame, she breathed in the contamination and burned it away, and breathed out healing. The sacrifice had already been made here, of time and torn hands and tears. She repaid that sacrifice with a tiny, tiny miracle. The seedlings raised their heads to the night air, strong and healthy again.

Then she walked the garden as she had the playground, speaking to the earth, softening it, and making it fit to nurture.

John spoke to a distraught mother, promising he would have a talk with her son. But Seraphym reached the boy first, manifesting in a burst of fire between him and the house where he would find... poison, for the body and the soul. Her eyes were angry, and her sword was in her hand. This boy was nothing in the futures; they would not change with him in them or out of them. So... that oddly gave her freedom.

She *forced* him to see her. The blood drained from his face, and his legs crumpled beneath him. His mouth worked, but no sound came out. She let him feel the force of her anger—not the full force, for that would kill him, but enough. And then she was gone. And when his legs would work again, he staggered home, and thrust the money into his mother's hands, and went out to mend the roof that she had been begging him to fix for six months.

In the informal day-care center, the old woman left in charge of the preschoolers drowsed in a scavenged recliner. And children whose eyes had seen terrible things, and who hid hearts wounded by terror, gathered around the glowing lady who had appeared when their caretaker fell asleep. She had summoned them with a glance of her strange eyes, collected them around her, let them cuddle close to her, and emanated compassion and purest unconditional love. She told them things without words, told them stories they would never afterwards quite remember, and slowly, their hearts healed.

CHAPTER SEVEN

Baby, I'm an Anarchist

CODY MARTIN AND MERCEDES LACKEY

People had begun to relax. It was stupid, of course, but when there was no more sign of the Thulians, people began to dare to think that maybe, just maybe, they had thrown their entire force into the blitzkrieg effort, lost, and had crawled back into a hole and all we had to do was figure out where they were and smoke them out of it.

Red Saviour, Bella and I never believed that, of course. Sometimes paranoia is useful. We had gotten the "shock and awe." Now we were in for the terror.

John Murdock hadn't seen much of the CCCP base except for the infirmary and a couple of offices. When Soviette had declared him "fit to fight," he had pretty much headed straight out the door without looking around. He'd had a lot of thinking to do.

He was sitting on his usual "thinking spot," the corner of a ledge on his squat's roof, Guinness in hand and the moon high above.

Finally, he'd settled on a decision. CCCP was still a hierarchical organization. It answered directly to a government, though it seemed the organization was a bit of a black sheep, from the research that he'd done. Anarchist as he was now—and looking at the Soviet abuses of power in the past—it weighed on his mind. The paramilitary aspect was...something that was comfortable for him; it was structure, and a welcome change after his past few years of wandering. Things were different, and he wouldn't be able to face this fact alone. His newly acquired "family" through the neighborhood certainly couldn't fight against it, even with his help.

65

The situation was still better than Echo and a damn sight better than Blacksnake and . . .

With a shudder, he turned his thoughts away from what that tattoo on his wrist represented.

He'd made up his mind. All that was left now was bucking up and making it official. Leaving the empty beer bottle on the ledge, he headed downstairs.

One cold shower—since he didn't have the time or inclination to set up a solar-powered one, at the moment—and a change into the cleanest and least abused clothing he had, and he was back on the CCCP's doorstep.

This time, he came in through the front door.

He didn't recognize the person at the front desk, but as he addressed the stony-faced man, he noted with relief that at least the fellow spoke English.

Though when he keyed a handheld walkie-talkie device in lieu of an intercom, he spoke Russian. All that John could make out was his own name.

The reply was faster than he expected. And evidently faster than the man expected too. "You may go up to the Commissar's office, Comrade Murdock," was all he said, leaving it up to John to find his own way.

This was very clearly a former warehouse and factory. Brick, two stories of offices in the front facing the street—Saviour had kept this area as offices, and the CCCP's makeshift sickbay, it appeared—and behind that, the vast expanse that had once had heavy machinery and storage piled to the ceiling. Now this section was being partitioned up into barracks, a larger infirmary, kitchen, garage, armory presumably. It was all very impressive, though clearly in its early stages; there was still a lot of building going on back there. Still, he'd kill to have even half of those resources for the neighborhood. The pounding of hammers echoed around him as he climbed worn wooden stairs to Red Saviour's office. Construction dust made him want to cough.

Finally, he reached her office; it took some navigating to find it. *Leave it to Russians to make a maze out of their HQ.* The Commissar remained seated as he tapped on the side of the door. "Come," she said, and nodded at the Spartan wooden chair in front of her desk. "I assume you have something other than a pleasant good morning to be telling me?"

John cleared his throat. "I've given the matter some thought." Red Saviour stood impassively, waiting for him to continue. "I figured that it'd be in my best interests and the interests of the neighborhood if I were t'join y'all. If you'll take me, that is."

Red Saviour regarded him enigmatically. And with remarkable calmness. "Comrade Parker argued your case for you with some vehemence," she replied. "She expected that you would be making this request." The Russian woman chuckled dryly. "You could not have a more enthusiastic advocate. If you had not been incapable of such things when you were in our care, I would have suspected you had become lovers."

John flushed, but didn't otherwise outwardly react. But Saviour was bulling right on. "However, since that is not the case, it must be your ... other merits. So"—she leaned over her desk—"you will be telling me about your scars. And how you got them. And do not attempt to deceive me. This is *my* territory and these are *my* people and it is my right and duty to see they are not put in harm that *I* do not put them in as their commander."

John began to sweat. During his years on the run, he had been especially careful about his past. It was his one weak point; the one thing that could get him, and anyone near him, killed—faster and more completely than a bullet. John moved to close the door to the office, looking to the Commissar for permission; she merely raised an eyebrow, which was enough for John. Closing the door, he turned to face Saviour, gripping the back of a shoddy chair positioned in front of her desk. "There's not much to tell. I was taken in as part of a research gig, run by the government. They made some changes to me; strength, reflexes, endurance, senses. Nothing outstanding, but enough. I ... took an 'early' release for myself when my powers first manifested. They didn't take too kindly to that, an' I've been avoidin' any unnecessary entanglements since." It wasn't the whole truth; the whole of it was damning, and would have taken much more out of John to tell. But it was, hopefully, enough; he hadn't lied, at the very least.

Finally, Saviour seemed to be content. Or as content as she was going to get. She made some notes. "Now ... we talk ideology."

This time she made him sweat in other ways. Never before had he been forced to articulate the philosophy he had come to—well, it was more than "embrace." It had become his life preserver in a way, and now he had to justify it and reconcile it with Leninist/Marxist Socialism. It was a long, a very long, hour. Mostly he expanded upon his personal beliefs concerning free will, self-determination, social and individual contracts, the nature of hierarchy and coercion, and so on. He didn't lie during this portion of his "examination" either; when asked questions pertaining to Statist Communism, he stated his unflattering opinions of all of the examples of the systems. She made notes the entire time.

When she was done, she pulled a file off the top of a stack of others, and pretended to leaf through it. Pretended, because he was sure that she knew it by heart. "Comrade Parker gives you a clean bill of health. Comrade Soviette does likewise. So. Now, we go beyond ideology. Is not enough to say one thing, even to believe it, but do another. Practical application, comrade." She put both hands on the desk and leaned over at him. "There is a bag of kittens on the railroad tracks and a train is approaching at 75 kilometers an hour. Nearby is a group of Young Pioneers about to succumb to the blandishments of a capitalist with an Xbox. What do you do?"

John stared at her, stunned. But before he could react—

Something crashed down through the ceiling, piercing and shattering the desk between them, scattering the files in a snowstorm of paper. Something huge, metallic . . . something he had seen before—

—the metallic tentacle of a Nazi war machine.

It withdrew as quickly as it had smashed down. John snapped into his fighting mindset without even thinking about it: calm, analytical, and mind going one thousand miles per second. Pure instinct, reflexes, and training; muscle memory, as opposed to calculating, conscious thought. He dashed to his right, crouching down into a half-stance and looking to the gaping hole in the ceiling. Red Saviour had gone to the opposite side, overturning her desk for cover; her fist was already glowing malevolently with charged energy. Within moments, the sunlight streaming into the room was blotted out by the huge and terrible form of the Nazi war machine. Both of them heard the telltale ultrasonic whine of the machine's signature energy cannon charging, preparing to fire and erase them from existence. Even with realization of their impending doom hitting them in microseconds, there was still no time to react; even their tremendous powers couldn't beat the speed of light, beams of coherent energy lashing out instantly.

They stared into the glowing mouth of the thing. And then there came an inarticulate bellow of rage from somewhere on the street outside. A huge rust-bucket of a sedan hurtled into the side of the war machine, impacting just below the muzzle of the cannon. The analytical part of John's mind recognized it as a '69 Chevy. The whole war machine *boomed* with the impact, ringing like a bell, and probably shaking up the pilots inside. The Chevy disintegrated in a cloud of scrap against the machine's armored hull, raining around John and the Commissar. A second vehicle followed the first; this time it was the remains of a delivery van. And that was followed by a chunk of concrete almost as big as the Chevy. With that kind of barrage going on, not even a computer could have kept the guns aimed.

That was the only opening that they needed. *"Davay, davay, davay!* To the roof, comrade!" The Commissar literally *flew* through the hole in the roof, kicking off of the desk. John got a running start, and then vaulted forward and as high as he could; he felt his strength ebbing, trickling away with each exertion. His injuries were still healing, and he was going to pay the price for that. Grasping, he barely caught the edge; still a Herculean leap for an average man, but well below what John was normally capable of. With a grunt, he pulled himself up above the lip of the hole and immediately began moving; a still target is a dead target, and he needed to go from the defensive to the offensive as soon as possible if he wanted to get out of this fight alive.

With the cannon inoperative, the controllers for the war machine activated the mechanical tentacles, snatching and stabbing towards John and Saviour. John immediately put on a burst of speed, running faster than any Olympic athlete could hope to. He vaulted over an air conditioning unit, catching a glimpse of it being speared by a tentacle. He pivoted, feinted, and then spun off in the other direction, a trio of tentacles jutting into the roof behind him. He slowed for a moment to focus, sending a blast of flame at the war machine; his fires weren't nearly as strong as he had hoped, merely reddening the hull instead of blasting through it with concentrated plasma. His Russian counterpart was flying out of reach of the beast's tentacles, sending concussive blasts directly at the cockpit's viewscreen and at any tentacles that threatened too closely.

Another abandoned car fractured against the side of the war machine, this one hitting so hard it actually clogged the muzzle of the energy cannon. From below came a whoop of triumph in a familiar female voice. "*Good* one, Chuggie! Keep it up!" John darted towards the corner of the roof; out of the corner of his eye John caught a glimpse of blue that quickly ducked under cover as the craggy creature called Chug dodged a tentacle, bellowed again, and picked up the remains of a set of cement stairs and flung it at another cannon muzzle. Was Bella managing to direct the creature? John didn't have time to contemplate it; another set of automated tentacles flew towards him, too fast; he barely managed to duck under them, one of the tentacles scoring flesh from his back.

Saviour's face was a mask of mingled fury and calculation, and—joy? She was *enjoying* this? Chug's assault had given her the space to think, and she turned blazing eyes towards John. "Fire kills these things!" she shouted. "Can you fly?"

"Hell no!" John rolled behind the roof access, two tentacles embedding themselves into it inches away from his head. "But I can jump pretty damn well!"

"*Nasrat!*" she spat. Before he could move, she had swooped down and seized him by the back of his jacket. The next thing he knew, he was twenty feet above the roof and accelerating towards the Nazi contraption, dangling from her hands. She didn't take her eyes off the thing, but shouted at him. "I am heading to the top!" she screamed over the cacophony of combat. "Being ready when I drop you!"

He didn't have much warning, just the sight of the top of the curve of the hull. She let go, and he dropped like a rock; John barely managed to roll into a crouch, still landing harder than he wanted to on the unforgiving hull. She dropped down beside him and began punching at what looked like a seam—a hatch maybe?—her fists glowing blue-white. Five punches and she was through, the remains of the hatch clattering inwards, swinging on what was left of a hinge. Below them, John could make out, through the smoke and sparking electrical systems, crewmen looking up, mouths agape with shock, and hear someone shouting in German over some sort of intercom.

"Fire, *tovarisch!*" Saviour screamed. "*Davay!*" She matched her words to a barrage of energy from her fists. John thrust his right hand into the opening she had created, relaxing his concentration ever so slightly. A plume of flame sprung forth, filling the interior of the war machine with brilliant fire. Unintelligible screaming followed, and then a jet of backdraft. Saviour grabbed his collar and kicked off as the machine began to tilt radically to one side. She only got a one-handed grip this time, and it canted her off-balance. They spiraled down to the roof and landed heavily. Not wasting a moment, both of them sprinted to the edge facing the street; the Nazi war machine had canted wildly, spinning down to the street below. Breathing a half sigh of relief, John watched it come to an almost-controlled landing. It didn't tear at the roof of the HQ or crash into any buildings. With a tremendous boom, it came to a rest, skidding along the asphalt before ending up against an abandoned warehouse.

In the half second after the war machine had stopped moving, both John and the Commissar had assessed the situation. To the right of the machine, Bella and Chug were fighting off six Nazi armored troopers; Chug had resorted to wading in to deal with them hand-to-hand, while Bella stood back with a terrible scowl of concentration on her face. Since the shots from the troopers' arm cannons were going wild, John could only assume she was interfering with them somehow. On the left, a group of five Nazis were standing in a circle, blasting away at the surrounding neighborhood.

"You! Take those five! I go right!" Saviour slapped something on her belt and sirens blared inside the CCCP HQ, though how anyone could have missed the sounds of the combat going on escaped John. It occurred to John that only a few minutes, two at most, had passed from the time the war machine had attacked till now. That might not have been enough time for people inside to react—and was there a plan in place if an attack came here? But the sirens would at least tell them that their leader was alive and outside and that was where they should be.

In a flash of red, black and gold, Saviour was already over the edge and flying towards Bella and Chug. Not even half a second behind her, John bounded over the lip of the roof, heading down to the group of Nazis on the left. In a flash of bizarre humor, he remembered a quote from the Blues Brothers. *Illinois Nazis. I hate those guys.*

The front door burst open—literally burst; it had been jammed shut by pieces of shattered car and concrete—and the mustached man who had been at the desk when John came in hurtled through the door and charged straight at John's targets. John touched down—again, harder than he had intended—on the now smoking hull of the war machine. One of the Nazi troopers noticed the CCCPer rushing at him, screaming unintelligible Russian curses; about the only thing that John could make out sounded like "Fascists!"

The man did a baseman's slide under the legs of the Nazi trooper, springing to half his height in a fighting stance in the middle of their circle. In an instant, he was striking them; mainly at their joints, with open-handed and closed-fist strikes that made John queasy just watching. The Nazis' armor rang with the impacts, but didn't give. They took notice of a threat in their midst, turning around to face it. In moments, the mustached CCCPer adjusted his tactics; he was now focusing on dodging and deflecting attacks directed at him. He swatted aside energy cannons an instant before they fired, ducking under swung mechanical arms with air whooshing along their passage.

It was amazing for John to witness; he didn't waste any time, though. This ballet of destruction could only last a few moments longer before the troopers got organized and destroyed their adversary. Just as the Russian redirected a discharging energy cannon into one of the adjacent Nazis, John fired off the strongest blast of flame he could manage. It splattered against the closest trooper's helmet, sending the armored hulk stumbling forward several steps. The Russian man immediately withdrew from the troopers' circle. Immediately, the air was filled with energy blasts, splitting concrete and walls all around John. The rank scent of burnt ozone filled his nostrils as he darted back behind a section of the downed war machine's hull.

Startling him, the CCCPer who had been fighting the troopers rolled behind the same cover, breathing hard. They both shared a look for the space of a second. "*Privyet*, Amerikanski. You are not bad fighter. For a *kulak*."

"You're not too bad for a Commie. Ready to give these bastards what-for?"

"*Davay!*" came the grim reply. John sprinted from cover, his enhanced legs pumping furiously against the street. He blasted gouts of flame at the group of troopers, but without tangible result; his fire wasn't as strong as he wanted it to be. Coruscating energy blasts rocked the ground around him, rippling through the air. John kept firing, covering each of the remaining Nazis in fire until they were glowing red-hot. From the corner of his eye, John noticed his Russian compatriot burst from cover, screaming curses again. The man launched himself towards the nearest trooper, hurtling into its right thigh. The Nazi lurched forward, hitting the street face first. In moments, the Russian was striking at the troopers in the rear; with their armor and defenses weakened by John's flames, the CCCPer was somehow able to cause much more damage to them. His fists deeply dented metal, even cutting through joints.

John fired off more blasts, focusing on the death's-head helmets of the Nazi troopers; they weren't able to coordinate an effective defense on two fronts and were firing their arm cannons wildly into the ground and air. The Russian pounded them relentlessly, twisting limbs at the right time and beating in vital parts. Soon, three of the armored behemoths were incapacitated; dead or on their way to death's door. John had run himself out; he couldn't move anymore and was using all of his energy to stay conscious. Slumped against a wall of what he vaguely recognized as a bookstore, he gathered his remaining reserves. Concentrating every single bit of willpower he had, he focused and then released everything; a concentrated stream of plasma burst from the palms of his hands before he went limp. The stream took off the head of a Nazi trooper poised to club the Russian man, toppling the fascist backwards. John slumped back, useless and utterly spent.

That was when salvation in the unlikely form of the CCCP doctor, Soviette, appeared, sprinting to John's side from the remains of the door. And scrambling over the top of the wrecked machine came the rockman, Chug, flanked by the Commissar and Belladonna Blue. John's vision was beginning to blur, going dark at the edges.

The Commissar let loose with a barrage of concussive energy blasts that looked to John as if her strength was fading, too. The blasts flew over the Russian man's head, impacting squarely with the remaining Nazi's armored chest. It was enough to drive the trooper back against the wall behind him. In a flash, Chug had ripped a plate free from the war machine that he was standing on, and heaved it with incredible strength at the dazzled trooper. The hull plate bisected the Nazi, cleaving his torso cleanly from his hips. With a shower of sparks and spurt of hydraulics, the invader was dead. It was over.

And *now,* with a howl of sirens, an Echo team appeared.

Enough strength washed into John to allow him to stand, propped up with the help of Soviette as the Echo team looked for something to fight and found nothing left. Red Saviour tossed her head a little, jumped down from the ruined hull of the war machine, and strode towards them.

"I am Commissar Red Saviour of CCCP, and we have the area secure, comrades," she said, not bothering to hide her smugness. "We will be wanting some of this technology for study, of course." She glanced around. "These are my team. Chug; our physician, Jadwiga, known as Soviette; Georgi Vlasov, known as Untermensch; and our newest comrade, John Murdock." Even as out of it as he was, John could only cringe at hearing his name pronounced in front of strangers. *So much for low-profile.*

Belladonna seemed to have disappeared. Then again, Belladonna was supposed to be Echo . . . it was probably less than politic for her to be here.

Hot on the heels of the Echo team had come a pair of reporters; Saviour consciously turned towards them. They had already caught her introductions on camera. "As you can see, the allies of the CCCP are on the job, protecting the workers of the city," the Russian said proudly. "And that is with but a handful of our comrades. When we are at full strength, we shall show you what we can really do."

The barracks weren't quite done yet; John staggered back to his squat, bearing—with Untermensch's help—several sets of the CCCP uniform. After working the numerous locks and getting inside, John flopped into his bed, breathing hard. It took him a few minutes to regain his composure; thankfully, his new Russian compatriot waited.

"That was being quite a first day, *tovarisch*," the man finally said, without cracking a smile. "But was a good interview. Even the Commissar said as much."

John climbed painfully to his feet, trudging towards the ancient refrigerator in the corner of the room. "Yeah, it was a decent scuffle. Suckers were lucky I wasn't at my best, though." He retrieved two bottles from the refrigerator, tossing one to the Russian as he stumbled back to the mattress. "So, what's your name again? I've got a mind for details, but I was way outta it by the time we'd finished with those goose-steppers."

"Georgi. My"—he made an expression of distaste, searching for the proper word—"callsign was not my choice. It is a long story for another time. I am older than I look." He grimaced. "I was the guest of such a very long time ago."

John took a long pull on his bottle of Guinness. "Well, pleased t'meetcha, Georgi. Name's John. John Murdock."

"*Budem zdorovy.*" The Russian tilted the bottle towards him before downing about half of it. "I suppose," he continued, his voice heavy with irony, "I should be grateful to them. I should not have been able to fight this lot if the first of them had not decided to use me to test some of their little theories." He held up his hand. "For all intents and purposes, these are invulnerable. There were some difficulties in getting the serum to work on the entire body. Their invulnerable soldiers were invariably dead within a day of injection. My healing powers were supposed to counter that." Another smirk. "Luckily, some of my comrades came to my rescue before the *fashista* could finish the procedure and learn from it. As such, I am a relic to that era." He stretched, cracking his neck. "There is a certain satisfaction in breaking their skulls again."

"Won't argue 'bout that, comrade." John finished his drink, setting the bottle down beside the mattress.

The Russian didn't seem much inclined for small talk, so after a little more conversation, he left. The room got uncomfortably warm after a while, so John managed to drag himself off the mattress and head to the roof hoping for a breeze. Unfortunately, the Russian had drunk his last beer.

He leaned wearily over the concrete parapet and looked down on his neighborhood. Even the small walk up here had caused him to breathe heavily; his wounds were giving him more trouble than they should have. *Maybe I'm growin' old.*

The breeze finally came from behind him, a breeze with a hint of cinnamon and vanilla to it. He knew what it was, even before he realized that it was coming from the wrong direction for it to be natural. "I thought you might appreciate these, John Murdock," the angel murmured quietly, as she stepped to the parapet beside him and held out a cold beer and a newspaper.

"And where were you this afternoon?" he asked.

"Tending something. Why? Did you need me?" She patted the paper, where the headline screamed *Echo Ops Trumped By Russkies.*

John chuckled raggedly. "Wouldn't say 'need,' Angel. But...it would've been nice. Still tryin' to heal up from gettin' skewered by a sword." He pondered for a moment. "The Commissar figured that the Nazis were part of a suicide squad; sleeper cell designed to stir up trouble, keep everyone on their toes after the Invasion. Pain in the ass, for a broken-down jerk like me."

She tilted her head to the side, regarding him for a moment. "That...the wound...I can help with. A little. If you would like. It is permitted." John shrugged, trying his best to hide the pain that the movement gave him.

"Is that a yes, a no, or a 'just go away'?"

"Forgot that y'can't read my mind that easy, Angel. Have at it."

"Then give me your hand, if you would." She held out hers. John paused for a moment. He tentatively removed the fingerless glove from his right hand, the tattoo of a snake eating its tail was visible again, and he hoped that the way it unsettled him wasn't visible to her. She looked at it a moment, and blinked once.

"That explains a good deal," she said, then took his hand in both of hers, covering the tattoo with her right. For a moment, she went so still she seemed to be frozen in space as well as time. And then a sudden rush of strength engulfed him, as if fire ran into all his veins and nerves; his senses flared, and he felt *completely* awake and aware to all the world in a way he had never been before. She released his hand.

"Y'know, if y'could bottle that, you'd make a fortune, Angel."

She looked at him for a moment, and there was something in her face that disconcerted him...and also tore down something guarded in him. "There are few who could bear it, John Murdock," she said. And then she looked away for a moment. "Sometimes... even I cannot bear it."

And with that, she spread her wings and lifted into the sky, vanishing in a flash of feathers and flame; flying with a speed that should have been impossible. The feeling quickly dissipated from John; he was still invigorated, but now more puzzled than ever. *Just another night in Atlanta, Johnny. Just another night.*

CHAPTER EIGHT

Cold-Hearted Snake

MERCEDES LACKEY AND CODY MARTIN

With so many resources tied up, it was a free-for-all among the criminally inclined. And no one did—or could—take advantage of that like Verdigris. No one else had his resources, his organization or his intellect. And no one else was quite so willing to feed off the misery of others.

From this high up, the destruction corridors through Mumbai—or Bombay, according to the old maps—were very clearly visible. The Thulians hadn't wasted too much effort on Mumbai, just two ships and attendant troopers, and they had gone straight for the one thing in the entire city that would cause the most damage if lost. Half the population was used to doing without electricity, without food, without adequate shelter—there were some families that lived on plots of sidewalk no bigger than a queen-sized bed—but nobody could do without water. The Bhandup water treatment plant was in ruins because of the Nazis, and people were dying. People were always dying in Mumbai, but until the aftermath of the Invasion it had not been at a rate so fast the corpse wagons couldn't keep up.

Of course, Dominic Verdigris had helped things along there, just a little. It wasn't all that hard to dump a few slow-release biotoxins in a water supply amid all the chaos. And there was nothing quite like having such an enormous population start dropping like flies to put the pressure on.

Such a nice, well-rounded plan. Further degrade the water. Sell treatment plants via a shell corporation—treatment plants that would, of course, entirely fail to take out the biotoxins. Wait for the ensuing outrage. Dissolve the shell, nuke the fragments, plant the blame on certain government officials, then come in with one of his overt corporations and sell them the same plants with the appropriate add-on at "compassionate" prices and suddenly not only do you make a double profit, you have the entire population of one of the world's most populous cities fawning at your feet. When he was done here, he would have a secure base of operations and a loyal workforce willing to do just about anything for him.

Provided, of course, Khanjar could deal with that little problem that had come up.

What was he thinking? Of course she could.

Verdigris' gaze drifted from the jet's window, sweeping over his bodyguard's delectable physique. Khanjar—her real name was probably lost to her, he mused—was perfect for what Dominic paid her to do. A metahuman assassin who could turn her skin as hard as diamonds, she was supremely skilled in several different forms of unarmed and armed combat, ranging from blades to firearms to heavy weapons, not to mention whatever goodies that he had managed to invent that week. He had first found Khanjar early in his rise to power; she was an independent contractor who had become popular with several international drug cartels. She was extremely mercenary, always going to the highest bidder, but professional, never leaving a job uncompleted. Given who Dominic Verdigris was, he never had to worry about anyone paying her more than he could. After a trial period where she proved her worth in some rather interesting ways, he hired Khanjar permanently as his bodyguard and chief of security.

Their "romance" started very soon after she was hired full time, and Verdigris was fully aware that it was a tactical move on her part. She was moving in closer to him in order to fulfill her own needs, and that suited him perfectly fine. Since those early days, they'd come to reach a mutual respect beyond the monetary one, especially when Dom relied on her exclusively for many matters. It also tickled him to test and see how far his assistant viewed the power dynamic between them as being in her favor. No matter how clever she thought she was, he could always outthink her, and be at least three steps ahead.

"If you stare any harder, and if I were any other sort of woman, you might make me blush. Almost."

"Sorry, m'dear. The view out the window was boring me. Still reviewing the security briefing?" He nodded slightly at the stack of folders and clipboards on the table by her seat.

"Yes. Rather routine. The main convoy will go with you; we've got one of our local teams acting as your personal security while I take care of the errand that you assigned me. Once I'm done, you should already be back at the airport and we can go home." As soon as Dominic had made it known to her that they would be traveling to Bombay, Khanjar had started the process of making sure that all of the necessary precautions had been taken for his visit. Security details on the ground, reviewing route plans, potential ambush sites, escape plans, surveillance and counter-surveillance, local demographics—the list went on and on for all of the factors in successfully keeping someone as important as Dominic Verdigris protected. She liked to imagine that even the President didn't have nearly as good a security detail as her employer, not even counting Dom's personal inventions that he kept on himself at all times. Then again, the President didn't have a personal assassin. At least, not that she knew of.

He grinned but otherwise kept his body language enigmatic and controlled. "Excellent, as always. Care for a drink? If my internal clock is right, we'll be landing shortly. I need something of the whiskey persuasion if I'm going to be dealing with politicians and the teeming masses."

She shook her head. He should know better. "None for me. Rain check for the end of the day, however."

He smiled, standing to pour himself a drink from the cabin's stocked bar.

Hopefully not too long of a day, she thought. She hated India.

There were a few paparazzi when the jet touched down on the tarmac, all being kept a reasonable distance away by the already-in-place security detail that Khanjar had set up in advance. Stepping out of the plane ahead of Dominic, she scanned the area quickly, taking in everything, then gave the go-ahead subvocally through her implanted microphone.

Verdigris stepped out of the exit hatch, giving his best movie-star smile. There would have been a larger reception, except that Khanjar had deliberately filed not one, but seventeen flight plans, all showing the arrival at different times. Only their host knew the real arrival time, and only after Khajar had phoned him in the air.

Their host was waiting by a running limousine, his arms spread in welcome. "Mr. Verdigris! It's an honor and a pleasure to have you here in our city. I only wish it were under better circumstances." Raghav Singh was thoroughly contemptible, and seemed to represent everything wrong with developing nations' politicians. India, for all of its poverty, was a powerhouse in the making on the world stage. And it was in the hands of men such as Mr. Singh, which was probably why next to none of its citizens would ever prosper beyond where they already were in life.

"Pleasure is all mine, Singh. Shall we?" Verdigris motioned for the limo, not waiting for a response before sitting in it with Khanjar trailing immediately behind him. Once Verdigris and Singh were seated inside and secured, she spoke into her radio to signal for the convoy to move out. Police cars and unmarked SUVs stayed ahead and to the rear of the limousine, rolling towards the slums of Mumbai; the poorest, as in most disasters and wars, had been hit hardest by the loss of the water processing plant.

Khanjar waited a few beats, listening to the radio chatter as she watched the convoy speed away. Satisfied, she made a circle in the air with her finger. Three more SUVs pulled up in front of her, each filled with hand-picked security operatives. She quickly strode forward, entering the passenger side of the middle SUV. "Let's go. I want to be back at the airport for a final inspection of the ground before Dominic is back from his speech. Step on it."

"Gods, this man is stupid," Khanjar fumed. Verdigris had given very specific instructions to their host, Mr. Singh, that the patsy was to be kept in a secure location that couldn't be tied to anyone involved. Apparently, Singh had interpreted that to mean his personal mansion. *I'll need to remember to question Mr. Singh on that particular point.* Forcefully, *if Dom will allow me.* Khanjar had an uneasy churning sensation developing in her stomach about this task, but forced the feeling from her thoughts. *No plan ever goes according to plan; you need to adapt to the conditions that develop, and quickly, or you die.* That simplified things for her.

Khanjar was unsurprised to see them approaching a ten-foot-tall wall, which probably had some form of interdicting materials at the top, invisible from down below; likely some shrouded razor wire, maybe even electrified fencing. At length, an equally solid gate appeared in the wall, which swung open at their approach. *Stupid, stupid, stupid. What if someone else had carjacked these vehicles?* This was becoming entirely too sloppy; she would never allow anything she did as part of her job to be this half-assed. It was all "for show" security; it looked scary, but wasn't very threatening for a determined aggressor.

The guards that waved the vehicles in were all dressed in smart khaki uniforms, and armed with submachine guns. The inner courtyard was paved, dotted with impressive planters full of exotic flora, with two rows of banana trees lining the driveway.

The building itself was a modern interpretation of a Victorian-era provincial state house, the sort that the British overlords had built to rule the Raj from. *Typical. He probably doesn't even know what he's copying.* Four stories tall with a colonnaded portico, it was a security nightmare. All those huge cement pots would make perfect cover, at least for a little while.

The McMansion itself might just as well have been made of straw, or swiss cheese. Big windows—and she would bet that not one was bullet-resistant. The sides of the house had lovely gardens; the place was too new for big trees, so the landscaper had made up for that with tall hedges. More concealment.

She already knew what the back would look like. Two open marble terraces, going down to a sloping lawn, with a nice big artificial pond or lake at the bottom and more landscaped gardens around. Possibly a swimming pool and some guesthouses tucked out of sight. Again, built on the British Stately Home model. But the Victorian Kings of the World hadn't needed to worry about squads of kidnappers or assassins armed to the teeth with twenty-first century weapons. More places for attackers to hide, and potential hostages. Brilliant. Just brilliant.

It was probably too much to hope for that the package was being held in one of the guest cottages, or better still, a window-less cement workshop or storage area. At least a small building would be defensible by her team.

The majordomo for the household greeted them as they exited their vehicles, arms spread wide and a magnanimous smile creasing his face. "Welcome, welcome. Mr. Singh told us to be expecting you, friends." He spoke with a slight accent, but in otherwise perfect English.

"Dismiss your help to their quarters, and have done with the pleasantries. When you've finished with that, please take me to the 'guest.' We are here to do a job, efficiently; we are not guests to be entertained. Understood?" Her stern glare must have impressed him. The man bowed, turning quickly, and then jogged over to talk with the servants. Khanjar turned to the security team. "I want team one to patrol the grounds in a roving sentry; keep in touch on the standard frequency. Team two, by the gate and the back entrance if this place has one. Team three, with me. Two of you on the main door, and one posted outside of the 'guest.' Go to it." The men and women nodded and went off to perform their assigned duties. The majordomo had returned, sweeping his hand towards the entrance. Khanjar followed him, three security operatives trailing her.

The interior was elegant, in a sort of obnoxious way. After traveling the world, dealing with the rich and powerful on a daily basis, and having Dominic Verdigris as her employer, Khanjar had developed an eye for tasteful decoration. This looked as if the decorator had been told "make it look like I am a billionaire" and had then been overridden to add more gold and mirrors wherever possible. Actually... it looked rather like a movie set out of the 1930s. Impossible ostentation. Narrow arched windows dotted the receiving room, with several hallways branching off to the rest of the house. She filed the details away as they descended a staircase to the cellar. Dry goods and high-end sports cars filled an underground garage, which they bypassed. Their destination was apparently the home's wine vault; the door looked impressive, but like everything else in this house, it was an expensive facade. Khanjar could already see at least three ways to breach the door without damaging the contents and with only minimal damage to the surrounding structure. "Madam, the one you wish to see is in that room."

"Take the guards upstairs, and have them join the rest in patrolling the perimeter. My team will take it from here."

"Madam, Mr. Singh was explicit in his instructions that—"

"Don't argue; just do it. The people involved in this can buy and sell your cheap life a thousand times over. Don't be a problem; just be a part of the solution."

"Y-yes, madam." The majordomo bowed deeply, retreating from the room without delay for politeness.

The two remaining security operatives with Khanjar flanked the door, with the one closest to the hinge opening it for her. Without pause, she walked inside.

The patsy was there, with his wrists and ankles tied to a rolling chair. The door hissed shut behind Khanjar, making the bound hostage visibly jump in his seat. "Do you know why you're here?" She spoke softly but firmly, keeping her expression completely neutral.

"You won't get away with this!" the man replied, with shaky bravado. "Singh won't keep me quiet by having a lot of goons work me over! You would be wise to let me go."

"You're here," she continued, ignoring him, "because you've become a problem for Mr. Singh that my employer doesn't trust can be handled by his own talents. You're a whistleblower who was intending to expose Mr. Singh's dealings concerning the faulty water treatment units that have claimed scores of your fellow countrymen. Normally, this wouldn't concern us at all; all the better that corrupt and evil men like Mr. Singh be made examples of. But, since Mr. Singh is working for my employer, it has become our concern." Khanjar grabbed a wine cask and effortlessly placed it in front of the man. "First, are you injured?"

"Only my faith in my fellow man," the man replied, taking her words as a sign that he was probably going to get off easily, perhaps with some sort of dire warning. Which he would ignore, of course; his kind always did.

"You appear to be honest and intelligent. I will be honest with you. I am here to silence you permanently."

He stared at her as if he could not understand what she was saying. Then something about her expression convinced him that she was quite serious. Before he could say anything else, she continued.

"Now, we wish to make this as tidy as possible. You can die alone, apparently by your own hand, confessing a trifling peccadillo that my employer has arranged for you. Or you can resist, you will still die alone, apparently by your own hand, and your wife, wild with grief, will smother your son and kill herself." She put pen and paper on the wine cask in front of him. "We would like your suicide note in your own hand. We have one prepared by a computer, and it is a good match for your handwriting, but my employer prefers reality when at all possible. I will dictate to you."

The man looked on the verge of tears. "And my—my family? They will be spared if I comply? They won't come to any harm?" Khanjar could tell that he was broken at that point, and she nodded.

She cut the man's hands free. He looked at the pen and paper, and gingerly picked up the pen as if it was dangerous. He looked up to her, resignation on his face—but then his eyes went wide. Khanjar snapped her head to the right, looking over her shoulder just in time for the world to explode into a hail of stars. She went flying, crashing into the wall and sending several bottles smashing to the floor.

Khanjar's thoughts slowly started to become less muddied. She'd been kicked, and hard; it was a good hit, and if she had been a normal person, she might have been sent into unconsciousness with a concussion. As her vision cleared, she could make out a figure clad in black kneeling next to the hostage; the intruder was covered in tactical gear and had his face obscured by a balaclava. "Sir, I'm here to get you out of here. But we need to move quickly. When I disappear, I need you to scream. Okay?" The hostage nodded shakily, still in shock from the sudden turn of events. Giving a thumbs-up, the intruder stepped back through a shadow and completely disappeared. Khanjar had to shake her head once, but she knew what she had seen. *A metahuman!*

The hostage then screamed as loudly as he could, crying for help. This went on for a few seconds before the door opened. Both of the security operatives stepped inside with their PDWs drawn, pointing at the hostage. *"Where did she go?"* one of them barked.

A disembodied foot lashed from a shadowed corner, right where the ceiling met the wall. The heel connected with the temple of the guard who had been talking, sending him sideways into the other man. As the second guard stumbled to regain his balance, the intruder's upper torso snaked out of a shadow to his left, grabbing the guard's jacket; his head was violently jerked into the wall with a wet crack. With both of Khanjar's people down, the intruder materialized out of a shadow near the door. "It's time to go. We're behind schedule, sir, so we need to move in a hurry. I can't travel with you, so we need to go on foot."

The man said nothing. He simply ran out into the corridor. The meta followed, grabbing his arm and hustling him along.

Khanjar tried again to clear her head, this time with a little more success. Without a second thought, she drew and readied her pistol. In the dim light, her skin also took on a glinting sheen. *I need to stop the package, at any cost.* She had never failed Verdigris before, and she didn't intend to make this the first time. She broke into a run, activating her radio with her left hand as she did so. "Package has been taken, making for the first floor. Repeat, package has escaped. One intruder, probably more, stop them—" As she reached the exit for the cellar, she heard the gunfire. Checking her corners, she slowly exited the stairs; doorways were a natural choke point in a building, making them easy ambush spots. The guards inside as well as the operative she had left at the front door were all gone.

"Someone, report!" Nothing but static. Someone was probably jamming her team's comms. If that was the case, then Dominic didn't know what was happening, and could be in danger. A renewed sense of urgency added to Khanjar's actions. Crouching, she moved towards the door, cracking it open. Immediately, it was cut into splinters by gunfire. She peeked around the corner for a fraction of a second, taking in the scene. All of the resident guards were dead, scattered around the driveway and inner courtyard. She could see two of her own people down, and cursed silently. The rest of her security team were pinned down in two positions—at the gate, and behind a low wall at the end of the driveway. Their attackers were dressed exactly the same as the intruder who had disabled her: black uniforms and tactical gear. They worked well together, and were going to soon outflank her men. There was a slight pause in the gunfire as the attackers had some of their people reloading; Khanjar shot three of the closest ones, and then sprinted to her men on the driveway.

"Report!"

One of her men, his right arm bleeding from a gunshot and hastily bandaged, whirled on her with his pistol before recognizing her. "Shortly after you entered the house, the on-site security personnel began attacking each other. A small element surprised the rest with coordinated fire, and created a lot of casualties. While the rest were dealing with them, these new players came in. Killed all of the guards, and then started in on us. We've been holding out, but we're running low on ammo and they've got superior positions. Where's the package?"

"He's out; a meta ambushed us in the cellar. We need to neutralize the package, at all costs." Her mind was already running through ways to spin this. Best was that Singh was protecting the man, and the intruders killed him. So tragic, someone important must have wanted him dead before he revealed whatever it was he was going to spill...

But that was for later, after he was safely neutralized.

She'd let Dominic worry about it. Right now, she had to focus on what she did best: killing. She leaned around their cover, shooting two more of the attackers. They were wearing armor; she noted this and adjusted her aim, finishing the two off with a controlled pair to each of their craniums. Satisfied, she began to scan the courtyard. *Couldn't have gotten far; the attackers are holding the courtyard, so the package didn't get out through the back. There!* The target crouched behind a large planter. She couldn't get a clear shot at either the meta or the target... but the man's leg was partially exposed. Taking careful aim, she fired off a single round from her pistol. It tore messily through the man's calf, causing him to scream loud enough to be heard over the cacophony. He wouldn't be running anywhere now. The metahuman spotted Khanjar, and then blinked out of existence.

Knowing what was coming next, she threw herself backwards, doing her best to stay concealed from the other attackers. The metahuman sprang from the shadow cast by the wall she had been hiding behind, where it was deepest in the afternoon sun. He kicked the pistol from her hand, flowing gracefully as he moved. Before she could react, her legs were swept out from under her; she rolled with it as best as she could, but she was still vulnerable. The meta shot one of her men before he was tackled by the injured one; he fell backwards willingly, falling through a shadow. The security operative hit the ground hard, gasping for breath, holding nothing. Khanjar scrambled for her pistol. The air around her was suddenly filled with bullets; the meta had come out of the darkness in the house. Rounds pinged off of her skin; it still hurt, but none of them penetrated. Her team wasn't as lucky, all of them dying from the precise shots. She aimed to return fire, but the meta had already disappeared again.

Khanjar knew where he'd be going; as expected, the meta appeared next to the target. She'd accomplished this much; he couldn't walk, much less run, unassisted. The attackers were pulling back in an orderly retreat, still firing on her position. She was able to see the gate; four of her people remained, fighting as best they could with the cover that was left after the furious gun battle. She controlled her shock as a lithe female figure leaped over the wall and landed soundlessly among the last security operatives.

The two who turned to face the newcomer immediately froze; the woman's eyes were unobscured by goggles, unlike the rest of the attacking force, and were fixated on the two men. She swept her arm behind her; discharging a short assault rifle point-blank into the backs of the other two men. The two men that had been transfixed in the woman's gaze were now on the ground, writhing uncontrollably and bleeding from their eyes and ears. *This is it. They're going to get away unless I can stop them. They've killed everyone else.*

The meta who could jump between shadows appeared from a corner near the gate. He spoke briefly into a shoulder-mounted comm unit. The door opened, revealing two up-armored Hummers, all-black. But Khanjar spotted the telltale, the one thing they had forgotten: a small grill-mounted insignia.

Blacksnake. Dom is going to have a cat.

The male Blacksnake meta looked back to the package, gesturing. Khanjar had a quick flash of inspiration. She felt for the belt of one of her downed ops, pulling off a flashbang grenade. Flashbangs produced an intense flash of light and an extremely high-decibel bang without any fragmentation, making them ideal for hostage rescue situations. Khanjar wanted to use this one for a very different purpose. Taking a chance, she stood up to get a better throwing stance. Gauging the distance, she pulled the pin and did her best fastball throw for where the hostage was lying. Her timing was perfect; the meta was mid-blink when the flashbang went off mere inches from his intended destination. Every shadow in the surrounding area was blasted away for a fraction of a second by the blinding light the grenade produced. It was enough; when she could see again, Khanjar smiled, grimly, when she saw that only the upper half of the Blacksnake soldier was there.

The remaining Blacksnake meta took in the situation instantly; she fired a barrage of rounds at Khanjar, forcing her back behind cover. When the gunfire ended, she saw the meta dragging the target into one of the waiting Hummers. Time seemed to slow down for Khanjar as her adrenaline spiked. She vaulted over the wall, all of her muscles taut. She saw an HK91 on the ground, its owner dead. In one deft motion, she scooped it up and slid into a kneeling

position. The target was being hauled into the vehicle, and the door
was just starting to close. She indexed the trigger, lined up the sites
and, exhaling, pulled the trigger. A splatter of blood blossomed on
the target's back, right in the eight-inch box that indicated most
of his vital organs. Time flooded back to regular speed; the door
slammed shut as the Hummers sped off, leaving Khanjar alone in
a silent courtyard populated only by the dead.

Verdigris listened in silence as Khanjar concluded her report,
then turned to regard the semiconscious body of their "host"
propped in the limousine next to Khanjar. "I must admit I was
a bit puzzled why you drugged his drink," he said.

"After the 'complications' we suffered during the errand, I felt
it prudent not to allow any further factors to potentially cause
problems for you, Dominic." She glared harshly at the unconscious
form of Mr. Singh. "The sorts of problems that cost the lives
of seven of your employees. Almost eight." She glanced back to
Dom's eyes, briefly.

"Spin, spin. Well, we have the computer-sampled handwriting,
so I'll change the letter. Make it a whistle-blowing document that
names Singh, but not us. Despite our patsy's altruism, he wasn't
a terribly inspiring man." Verdigris paused for a moment. "Kill
Singh, plant him somewhere with a Blacksnake bullet in him. I'd
like to find out who hired Blacksnake for the extraction, so I'll
get my intel on it. For the families of the security personnel lost,
make sure that they all receive the standard benefits along with
the cashed stock options that were saved up for each of them.
One of our standard letters should suffice; if not, have one of
the paralegals draft something and forward it to me for review
before it goes out."

Khanjar made the error of allowing her jaw to drop for a single
moment before clamping it shut again. "Of course," she said, steel-
ing herself. "I'll personally make sure it's handled."

"Also, we're going to start the process of buying out all of the
assets of Blacksnake, until Blacksnake itself is just a shell. I like
their work; they gave us a little bit of a run for our money, as it
were. They've got some spunk. Besides, buying out rivals is always
so much simpler than destroying them, especially when they still
have some usefulness." He actually *twinkled* at her. "Don't you
agree, m'dear?"

She gulped hard, trying her best to keep her emotions suppressed. "I'll see to it as soon as we're back at the island, Dom." It wasn't often that Khanjar wondered why she worked for Dominic Verdigris. The money, the protection, the luxury—they were all the obvious draws. He was wealthy and intelligent beyond anyone else that she could possibly come under the employ of. But it was times like these when she wondered if she would survive her employment long enough to enjoy the fortune she was amassing while working for him.

The Ides of March

MERCEDES LACKEY

The document left by autistic precognitive Matthew March had been a nightmare to transcribe. The poor man's handwriting and spelling had been erratic at best—he was the next thing to illiterate, given his condition, and all of his visions up until the final ones had been transcribed by Echo psions.

But now, here it was, in legible form in Alex Tesla's email, and it was . . . devastating. Fata Morgana, the head of Echo in Chicago, had dubbed it "The Ides of March," and it more than lived up to the name.

It wasn't so much a document as a long, long list. Names and places, and initially it had made no sense. Not until more time had passed, and Fata had a leap of intuition and began correlating those names and places with dates.

Then it became clear. The places were all places of Thulian attacks. Or "Kriegers," as the media had dubbed them now, for "Blitzkrieg." Why "Nazi" wasn't good enough for them . . . but then they weren't Nazis, exactly. . . .

Alex pulled his attention back to the annotated, utterly devastating document. This was an accurate list of Thulian targets and deaths—almost every death, not just of important people or metahumans. That was what had confused the issue and had seemingly made no sense; some people were still listed as missing, for instance, and why would Matthew have bothered to count civilians in his death tolls?

Well, because he was Matthew.

What had also made no sense was that some deaths that had

occurred well after an attack had been listed with that attack, like the Mountain, for instance. But, as Morgana had said, if you used autistic cause-and-effect reasoning, things like the Mountain's suicide were actually attributable to the Invasion; if he hadn't come out of his self-imposed exile to help, he would certainly still be alive and inside Stone Mountain at this very minute.

And the list went on, and on, and on. No dates, only targets and deaths. No way to plan, no way to warn. There were just too many of them. It only said what the media idiots were saying, that everywhere was a target.

And then, at the end, the final words. *Fire and death, fire and death. Nothing left. No one. The end.*

Alex Tesla could only stare at those words as despair crushed him into the earth.

CHAPTER NINE

Thunder Road

MERCEDES LACKEY AND CODY MARTIN

Meanwhile . . . I was proving myself to Saviour. Now she was going to give me a trial by fire. Only I wasn't the one with my feet in the fire.

John had been called into the Commissar's office earlier than usual. On most days, it took Natalya until after lunch (did she eat?—he wasn't convinced that she even slept) to call him in to review whatever policy transgressions he'd committed during his patrol earlier in the week. All usually minor, and all certainly written off. But it was important that he still be called to task to answer and maintain the standard that the Commissar had set. She often wrote it off, sans the souvenir busts of Lee and his generals taking flight, as a product of his American individualism clashing with the "*bolshoi* efficiency" of her Russian command structure.

He'd become used to it, finally, after butting heads with the Commissar subtly. Resigned to his fate of being lectured sternly on regulations and standards for a spell, John knocked on the office door.

"In!" Saviour bellowed. "*Davay, davay,* Comrade Murdock, you are holding up boat!"

How the hell did she know it was him? John opened the door, strode in, and saluted after coming to attention. "Comrade Murdock, reportin' as ordered, Commissar." She didn't deign to rise from her chair, but she did look up from her computer monitor, casually saluting him.

"Nagy sorceress is being on bottle cap," she said with satisfaction. She took a box from a pile on her desk and shoved it across to him after checking the name. "Daughter of Rasputin is computer wizard. Comm is tracking all comrades in HQ. Very efficient. She is to be your overwatch, whenever not on patrol. *Da?* You are to be receiving assignments once acclimation has been accomplished." She put her hand up to her ear and adjusted something there, then stood up. "Sorceress has Blue *devushka* convinced, and we gave this system trial, myself, Ubermensch, and Blue Girl. Most satisfactory. Now all comrades will be on overwatch for special assignments." As John snapped to attention, she reached over the desk and ripped out a slender tuft of his hair. "You are giving sample for magics voluntarily, *Da?*"

"Jesus, shit! Um, I mean, yes. I do, Commissar." John had enough discipline not to reach up and rub his scalp while at attention.

"Good. You are dismissed. Be taking package and becoming briefed on system." She sat back down, put the hair in a labeled plastic bag, and tossed it in another box. There were about a dozen more in there like it.

It wasn't a large package, but then, if this was spyware electronics, it wouldn't be. He headed to the locker room, opting to change out of his issue coveralls for his patrol uniform so that he could get to work. He set the box on the bench in front of his locker, and began to strip out of the jumpsuit.

His comm buzzed. He keyed it, pulling up his fatigue pants. "This is Murdock, go."

"Nice ass. Open the box, comrade Amerikanski."

John hesitated for a moment, looking around. "Who is this?" He bent to flip open the cardboard top of the box, revealing several manilla envelopes. "The box is open. Who is this, and how are you on this frequency?"

"Put on the earpiece, please. Nice pecs, too."

Too weird. John opened and shook out the contents of the first envelope. A small, clear earpiece like the Secret Service and spies use, minus the cord that hooks behind the ear. He wiggled the earpiece into position. "Now what? And you still haven't answered my questions."

"Welcome to CCCP Overwatch, Comrade Murdock. I'm Vickie." The voice came from the *earpiece*, and *not* his comm unit, which went LOS. No service.

"Victrix. The sorceress, right?"

"One and the same. You have in your ear a nice little item of Echo tech, which Echo does not know you have, and which, for the moment, we will not let Echo know you have. Runs on kinetic and heat energy from your body and a much more secure signal than your comm."

"All right, I follow so far." He shrugged on the rest of his uniform, strapping the bullet-resistant vest last. Attaching the comm unit to his belt and snugging up his boots, he was completely ready now. "So, this is the part where you lead me through what all of this junk that the Commissar gave me does, right?"

"Actually the stuff is pretty much plug and play. I'm not 'Q'—you're smarter than James Bond—and what I need to demonstrate is what I can do for you so you aren't tempted to ditch the stuff on the first job. So, call it a hands-on demonstration."

He nodded, patting his sidearm in its holster. "Walk me through it as we go; I'm on patrol." He strolled out of the locker room and towards the garage. There, he signed out one of the Urals minus a sidecar. Bear and Georgi were busy arguing in Russian, buried elbow deep in the engine of one of the CCCP's vans. The Ural came to life underneath him, and he eased it out of the garage and out into the shining sun.

"For starters, until I get your sample, I know where you are by a complicated triangulation system off the earpiece. *Much* more secure than GPS, which I do not like for that reason. Tracers work both ways, and only I and the programmer know about the system I'm using."

"Okay. So you have my position locked in at all times, so long as I keep the earpiece. What's this about the sample? Is that why the Commissar damn near took a chunk of my scalp out?" He couldn't help but notice the personality difference between this Vickie and the terrified, silent, white-faced thing in Saviour's office. He liked this one better. This one had moxie. He had to wonder just what it was that turned her into the rabbit when she was out with people. Whatever it was, it had to have been bad.

"When I get that, I can loc you by magic. *No one* can follow that protocol but me. No one can see where you are unless I send them the feed."

"Not even other witches and warlocks?" *Or goblins or faeries? Does the Commissar really buy this magic crap?*

"Warlock means 'oathbreaker,' by the way. And no. It's secure and heavily shielded, plus encrypted. Now since I know where you are, I can hack into security cams, traffic cams, even some ATM cams in your area, and tell you...that 150 feet from you right now and closing, someone is going to blow through the intersection without stopping in a POS green Honda Accord. So you might wanta slow down a touch, or speed up." John, willing to indulge her for the sake of an experiment, sped up. Just as he got to the intersection, a green blur accelerated at him at close range on the right. Reflexively, he gave the Ural more gas and the car narrowly missed his rear wheel.

"Dumb jackasses!" he shouted over his shoulder. "Kids play in this neighborhood!" A collision while riding the motorcycle, even with his armor and helmet, would've ruined his day. Maybe ended it, permanently.

"Something's hinky...he didn't even try to brake."

"Let's get back to it. What's the rest of this stuff y'gave me?"

"Cams. mostly. Buttonhole, helmet and one on a stick that I'm dubious about, but which Echo seems to like to use to poke around corners and in through holes. I suppose it could be useful in a rescue sitch. The rest is various dingus..." She paused momentarily. "Heads-up."

John's comm came to life. "This is Gamayun, HQ Control. Patrol Unit Troika, do you copy?"

He activated the comm, keeping a hand on the accelerator. "This is Unit Three—uh, Troika, heading south on Whistler and Fifth. Whatcha need, Control?"

"Metahuman break-in last seen moving south on Whistler in vehicle."

"Control, vehicle wouldn't happen to have been a green Honda Accord, would it?"

Gamayun paused, and John knew the CCCP metahuman was using her own powers to check. "*Da.* Affirmative."

"This is Unit Troika, in pursuit of suspects. Feed me more information as you can, Control." John keyed off his comm, hitting the handbrake and slidding the bike to a stop. He gunned the engine, revving after the Honda. "That goes for you, too, Vic. Consider this your trial by fire."

"Use the new feed, Gamayun. Give it to me in Russian, I'll translate. Murdock, Target is still on Whistler. Whistler intersects with a feeder road to the interstate in about half a mile and it's a good bet he'll take it. You can take a short cut. Next left, 100 feet, right right." John cut onto the path that Vickie described, dodging what little debris there was left.

"What's the opposition like?"

There was some Russian. "Gamayun says we have six perps crammed in that can, all loaded with semiautos. One is a meta, described at the scene as having put everyone to sleep."

"Damn it. All right, anything further? Running out of time before I come up on 'em."

"You're ahead of them. Next left puts you on the feeder in front of them. I'll see what I can do about the meta."

"Time till I intercept?"

"Thirty seconds on my mark." A pause. "Mark." She began counting down. John slowed the Ural a few miles per hour. He wanted to come out just behind them; too soon, and they might decide to just make a grease spot out of him with their car.

"This section coming up, what's the population like?"

"Industrial. Shift change in one hour, more or less." More Russian. "Gamayun says there are some trucks . . . ah . . . three on the feeder road. Not many cams, so I can't see much. But you have high chain-link and razor-wire fences on both sides of the street most of the way to the interstate."

"Copy. Gonna have to stop them before they get to the interstate. En route." John saw the intersection. His timing, with Vickie's assistance, was good; he got there less than a second after the green car went speeding past. His tires skidded as he performed a suicide slide through the turn, speeding after them. One of the thugs must've been paying attention; John saw a lot of activity in the car, what looked like waving and moving around excitedly. Two thugs leaned out of the windows, one on each side. Each of them was holding a gun. "Shit!" John swerved to his left just as gunfire stitched the pavement and the air where he had just been.

"Cut right, side street parallels the feeder road—it's really an industrial alley." John forced the Ural to turn; a few of the rounds from the thugs found him, though. The Ural took the brunt of the assault, but John felt a sharp impact in his upper chest.

"Okay, that's three metas in there. No way anyone can fire from a moving car with that kind of accuracy without being meta. You okay?"

He coughed hard; it hurt like hell, but he was too amped up on adrenaline to care too much at the moment. "Fine. Patch me through to Control."

"She already hears you. Shared freq."

"Roger. Control, this is Unit Troika. Got multiple suspects using deadly force in suspect vehicle. One confirmed metahuman, two potentials. Advise on ROE." The engine for the Ural was beginning to smoke; he knew that one of the rounds had pierced the gas tank, but luckily not low enough to be an immediate concern.

He heard Vickie giving a rapid fire translation into Russian. He heard Gamayun talking, then her voice, stronger, in halting English. "Lethal force authorized, Commissar's orders."

"Sec," Vickie said. He heard mumbling. "Lethal force authorized from APD and Echo. Clear to roll, Murdock. One of the sleepers back at the scene isn't going to be waking up."

"Roger." John coaxed as much speed as he could from the damaged Ural. Something clanked *hard*, and an intense squealing, screeching noise came from the engine. "Cut the shared freq with Control, Vickie."

"On private."

"I'm out in front of the suspects, right?"

"Roger. About 200 yards ahead. Any of these side streets brings you back to the feeder."

John hit the brakes, sliding to a stop before rocketing back onto the main feeder again. He could see the car; they'd slowed down, thinking that John had been persuaded not to follow them anymore. "Don't tell the Commissar, but we're gonna have to put in another form for a new Ural." John accelerated the protesting Ural, aiming straight for the green car.

"Yah, I don't think that sound is anything good anyway." A pause. "Shit. You're playing chicken."

Ignoring the protests from both Vickie and the Ural, John continued straight ahead. The driver had recognized that it was John by this time, and sped up to the ratty car's top speed. Seconds from impact, John released the handlebars and kicked off of the bike, sailing to the right. He curled up, protecting his head and sides with his arms as he crashed bodily into the chainlink fence. It acted as a sort of heavy-duty net, absorbing enough of his momentum before the poles snapped that the impact only bruised him. Of course, if he'd been a regular human, it would have killed him anyway.

The green car and the Ural, however, didn't fare so well. The driver didn't see what was happening until it was too late, with no time to swerve out of the way. The Ural slammed into the Honda and what didn't end up halfway into the radiator rolled over the hood and into the windshield, and what was still left after that somersaulted over the top.

The Honda driver tried to correct, taking it into a short spin. Now top-heavy from its motorcycle addition, the car flipped, rolling—

—until it came to a sudden halt, slamming into an upthrust of dirt and asphalt that hadn't been there before.

To John, whose head was just beginning to clear, the pillar of earth looked strikingly like a middle finger. He dusted himself off, swayed for a moment, and then stalked towards the stopped car. John wrenched a car door open single-handedly, almost tearing it off of the frame. All of the men in the car were battered and bloody, and in no shape to put up a fight.

"I think this is the part where you're all under arrest. And you owe me a new bike." John hauled each of them out of the car amidst groans and cries, secured them with zip ties, and sorted their weapons into a pile. "Cut me back to Control again, Vic."

"Roger. By the way, I can't usually do that on this kind of remote. But you're about six blocks from my place on a road I know. I'll be able to do some more of that sort of thing once I have your sample and if you are in ground contact. You're live, go for report."

He nodded, surveying the destruction. "Control, this is Unit Troika. I need a bus for the injured and a pickup. All suspects apprehended. And, uh, the Commissar needs to buy a new bike. Murdock, out." John switched off his comm before Natalya—who was no doubt listening in—could offer *her* input. "Vic?"

"Roger, you're private and Saviour's having a cow."

"Consider yourself hired."

She laughed. "Like you had a choice? It's me, or no field trips."

John chuckled, wiping a trickle of blood that had come from a cut on his scalp. "Time to look forward to more paperwork, excoriation, and the Commissar asking for my head." Just another day on the beat.

CHAPTER TEN

She Blinded Me with Science

DENNIS LEE AND MERCEDES LACKEY

Overwatch was a success with everyone except Red Djinni. Tesla loved it—well, when you could pry him out of his depressive sinkhole long enough for him to express approval for anything. I guess I should be grateful in retrospect about that depression, at least in this case, since Overwatch was still very much a closed secret used only by Bulwark and his Misfits. That was going to prove vital later. I knew why, too, and I leaked it to Red Saviour; I'd gotten the contents of the Ides of March. I wasn't impressed, to tell the truth. Not because the Ides were inaccurate—because so far, they were quite accurate. But because as any magician or precog will tell you, looking into the future is like being one of the blind men with the elephant. You can only see the part of it that you already know something about. There was nothing in the Ides about CCCP—only Echo. Nothing about the Seraphym. Nothing about the mysterious Nazi-free zone in Alaska.

And as any precog or magician will tell you, the future is not immutable. March had seen a future. Maybe the most probable. But it was not inevitable.

Right at this point, though, Red Djinni was making my life too miserable for me to worry about Alex Tesla's problems.

Every once in a while the intrepid detectives of Echo hit a wall. It didn't happen very often. They had access to an incredible wealth of information, to the very best in forensic support, and not in the least, to their own considerable deductive talents. During the chaotic period after the Invasion, they found themselves on the receiving end of a flood of more-than-urgent directives, and had to accomplish them with a staff cut in half by virtue of casualties.

Top priority was: "Where in hell did these Nazis come from?"

Not far below that was: "What the hell was their armor made of?"

The Echo research labs were slag and rubble. The Echo database was only now recovering from the Nazi worm. Sources were silent or dead or had defected.

It was time to look elsewhere for answers—and help.

Two detectives were tasked with pooling whatever information they could on the Nazis of yore. No level of detail was to be overlooked. "There is no such thing as useless information," they were told. All data was to be collected, filed and assimilated. Such a task might have proved daunting to most. The sheer volume of information would have taken even the most learned of scholars, the quickest of speed-readers, years to absorb.

Instead, the Pennyworth Twins had merely shrugged and assured Alex Tesla they would have the job done in three months.

No one really knew how they did it. They were metas, to be sure, but no one had ever seen them do much more than sit quietly together, sip their tea, and stare out into space. Or at computer monitors. Whatever it was that made them into something frighteningly close to a human supercomputer wasn't obvious even to the Echo psychics. Not that the psychics hadn't tried. Once. The overwhelming rush of information had driven the talent in question into an instant state of catatonia that didn't lift for weeks.

When asked later what she could remember of the incident, she likened the event to being at ground zero of a 30-megaton information bomb—then she jabbed telekinetically on the controls to her morphine drip.

Today, surrounded by distinguished members of Echo's senior staff, the Twins stood at attention. They were ready to give their answer.

Everyone waited expectantly as the Twins' unfocused gaze came to rest on Alex Tesla.

"We are ready to answer your queries," they said together.

Tesla, who had been waiting impatiently for this moment for months, did not hesitate.

"Where did the invaders come from?"

The Twins closed their eyes and seemed to tense up. Their eyelids fluttered.

"No clue," they said after a moment.

The room echoed with audible groans and angry muttering.

"Great," Tesla said, his palms pressed hard against his face. "What *can* you boys tell us?"

Speaking alternately, they began an infodump of everything Nazi related, from the most obscure occult societies to the philosophical foundations of the SS. It had a mesmerizing effect. Eyes began to glaze over.

"Enough!" Tesla shouted. "That's ... quite enough, thank you."

Yankee Pride nudged Ramona. "I didn't know Hitler sucked his thumb."

"Or that he believed in self-administered enemas to treat genital warts," Ramona answered absently.

"Everyone shut it!" Tesla ordered through clenched teeth. He put both his hands on the table to keep them from shaking. "All right then, the armor. Can you tell us what that blasted armor of theirs is made of?"

"On that, there are numerous possibilities. It could be from Atlantis, the result of Doctor John Dee's alchemical experiments, some completely new alloy from aliens, originating from mined asteroids, derived from demonic conjurations..."

"Well," Tesla sighed, giving up. "That was a productive three months spent, boys."

"... or the completion of initial documented experiments on a novel alloy by Doctor Judah S. Goldman, military munitions inventor and chief scientist of the Third Reich."

"Goldman?" The muttering started again; Goldman was the infamous Nazi scientist who had vanished before the Fall of Berlin, and he was almost certainly dead by now. The only real "survival," if you could call it that, was the legend of the Goldman Catacombs, a storehouse of impossible riches where allegedly most of the missing loot of the Third Reich had been stashed. Of course, no one knew where the Catacombs were, and by this time (and after two Geraldo specials) no one really believed in their existence.

"We assumed there would be skepticism," one of the twins said, without any inflection. "We enlisted a previously unused source. As a result, we have a probable location of the Goldman

Catacombs—Nevada, reasonably near Las Vegas. We also have what appear to be early blueprints."

There was stunned silence. Finally, someone in the back asked, "Who was this source? If it was Geraldo—"

"As it turns out, Mr. Rivera missed the mark the second time by only five miles. The source in question is a new recruit to Echo. Her name is Victoria Victrix."

Tesla started a little. The woman had already shocked and impressed him with her Overwatch program, but that could have been a fluke. On the other hand...she'd brought in a handful of magicians already, and seemed to have far more than her share of—

—damn it, he didn't like magic. He didn't believe in it. It had to be some sort of previously unknown psionic ability. Right?

Whatever. She was able to get jobs done. When he didn't put her in the field—even when he did—

And she clearly had access to information that was off the standard databases.

He spoke up before he had a chance to second-guess himself. "All right. It's the only lead, pursue it."

Yankee Pride shook his head. "Sir, assuming that this isn't some wild goose we're chasing, the Catacombs are supposed to be impossible to get into. And if you do get in, it's one death trap after another. We'd need at least a dozen metas and a couple of trap squads just to try, and we don't have them."

"No," Ramona disagreed. "If half the stories about the place are true, we'll need a smaller group anyway. This is strictly recon, and large numbers in there would just complicate things. And they should be volunteers. People who know the odds of them coming out are not good. The only ethical way to handle this is with volunteers and who have we got that we could spare? No one. Right?"

Yankee Pride gave Ramona an appraising look, then turned to gaze at the man seated behind him. Jenson met his look, and sighed.

"You want to *ask* him to volunteer?" Jenson said.

"That's right," Pride said. "No orders, just asking."

"And what makes you think he will?"

"He will," Pride replied firmly. "You know he will."

He tapped gently on his comm unit. "Alison, would you please have Operative Bulwark come up to Control?"

✧   ✧   ✧

Bella was angry.

No, that was a magnitude below what she was feeling. She was furious.

Knowing that Vickie subsisted on tea, coffee and whatever freezer-burned microwave meals she could chip out of the frost, she'd picked up something at the soul food restaurant. She'd come in full of relative cheer to find the sorceress in a compacted ball of tears and misery.

Vickie had tried to cover it up, but Bella had the cause out of her. And now Bella was going to take it out of the *cause*'s hide.

The fact that she'd just gotten a directive assigning her to the cause's team only put the froth on the cappuccino.

Bella reported to the ready room (yet another temporary portable building on the Echo campus), looked right past the team leader and everyone else and focused on her target.

Red Djinni.

It looked as if he had just arrived there himself, since he was still standing. Good. That would make this easier.

"Bella Parker?" asked the team leader, Bulwark. Somewhere in the back of her mind a little fangirl let out a squee, because he was a lot handsomer in real life than he was in his file photo, but she ignored it and let the anger take over. She nodded and headed for the Djinni. Being both a tomboy and a paramedic had taught her not to telegraph her punches. She just walked up to him and let him have it with her best uppercut to the chin. No sissy slaps for her—

"Ow! Sweet mother o'—!"

Her hand went numb. What was his chin made of—concrete?

At least he went down. Like most metahumans, she was a lot stronger than she looked.

She stood over him, shaking her hand, and glaring. "*That* is what you get for making a cripple cry, you rat bastard," she snarled. She shook her tingling hand some more. "Frick."

"Christ," Red groaned. He came slowly to his feet, massaging his jaw. "If I knew Acrobat had a mommy with a strong arm, I wouldn't have...and to be fair, he's not a cripple. He just needs a bit of backbone."

"Not Acrobat, you moron. Vickie. My neighbor. My patient, you frickin' sadist." At this point she was about ready to clock him again, sore hand or not. "She can hardly move without pain and you have to go and make fun of her on the Le Parkour course and tell Tesla that...." She couldn't go on. She'd kill him. Twice.

"That *what?* That I don't need her over my damn shoulder twenty-four/seven? Grow up..."

"Ms. Parker," Bull supplied helpfully.

"...Ms. Parker!" Red shouted. "Maybe you should let your precious patient fight her own battles instead of sending in her pet Smurf!"

"Very clever, asshat. She didn't send me in the first place, and in the second...." She couldn't finish. Instead, she popped him again. Left hook, this time. Red fell to one knee, cursing.

"Ow," Bella grimaced. "Worth it."

Bull nodded in appreciation, and glanced down at his handheld tablet. "They neglected to mention your prowess with fisticuffs, Ms. Parker." He scribbled a few notes down.

"I was a paramedic with LVFD, which allegedly is why they assigned me to you for this operation. I've had to cold-cock many a drunk in my time." She shook both hands now, but since the feeling was returning to the right, she offered it to Bulwark. "If you decide you'd rather not have me as your DCO, I'll understand." She glared at Djinni. "And I'll be using Overwatch, thanks. It's been working a treat with CCCP."

"Which is why you've been assigned to us. You are also a Nevada native, and your files indicate that you know the area particularly well. You have a colorful record here, Ms. Parker," Bull mused, still scanning his tablet. "Goodness... disobeying direct orders, abandoning duties to take offensive measures..."

"Not to mention working directly with another organization, and"—she grimaced—"a little matter of 'elimination with extreme prejudice' of a thug that tried to kill me and my hippie friends."

"Yes, I read the report on that too. A bit one-sided, perhaps, as much of your statement was edited." Bulwark drew himself to his full height and crossed his arms. "Did you have any other option?" he asked, his voice dreadfully quiet.

"I'm a distance empath, a touch-telepath, and he was holding me," she said steadily. "I got memory flashes of what he'd done in the past—I think they eventually tied him in with six murder-rapes and another dozen or so rape-with-violence—"

"Did you have any other option?" Bull interrupted.

She could have told him why. How she was pinned. How she

had seconds to stop him. How at that moment, given her fluctuating abilities, she was sometimes limited to "extreme mental
force" and "petting kittens" with nothing in between. Okay, at
that moment, she had been honed straight in on killing him.
He was a rabid dog, and you didn't coddle rabid dogs in ken-
nels, you shot them. Maybe she could have done something
else. Maybe.

Instead, she simply answered, "No."

Bull nodded. She was telling the truth. "Very well. Your record
and abilities suggest you can be of use. You will find that this
particular outfit has something of a reputation of..."

"...of coloring outside the lines?" Red suggested helpfully, as
he climbed into the nearest chair.

"...of exhibiting independent thought," Bull finished. "But I
would warn you, Ms. Parker, that I do not tolerate recklessness.
We have a mission, then we execute it. I will not endanger our
tasks or our operatives with counterproductive conflict in the
field."

"Suits me, sir," she replied. "I have no argument with the
DCO's primary objective, just the...hmm...the restrictions. I
packed heat as a paramedic, sir. Where we went in, you had
to. My FD station wasn't exactly...by the book. My captain's
motto was 'Lead, follow, or get run over.' The idea that healers
don't hit is stupid."

"Uh...if you don't object, sir, I'd rather Ms. Parker didn't touch
me." Harmony looked awkward and nervous. "Telepathy...I don't
want a telepath in my head."

"I can heal you without touching you, just not as well." Bella
shrugged. "You aren't the only one squeamish about psions."

Bulwark nodded. "I think we might have an understanding
then, Ms. Parker. We are scheduled for a briefing. It seems our
intel has unearthed something and they are requesting volunteers.
Please join us."

"I'll get my kit." She saluted—sketchily, but it was a salute, while
her internal fangirl made heart-shaped eyes at the hunk—and
headed back to the car.

Bull turned to Red. "Don't you get tired of being beaten up
by girls?"

Red stood up, all pretense of injury gone.

"Actually, it kind of turns me on."

✧   ✧   ✧

Vickie had hated, hated being caught by Bella in one of her moments of weakness. But it had been a bad day to start and had gone downhill from the moment she'd opened her eyes.

Weather systems going through had a tendency to make all her scars tighten, which meant she'd awakened in pain. But she had pledged to herself that she would run the Le Parkour course every day and she knew that if she gave herself a break once, it would be easy to find excuse after excuse until she was back to never leaving the apartment. So she went out. No one was ever on the course in the predawn.

Except, as she reached the halfway point, someone was. And that someone was the Djinni, who had gone over the course three times in the same time it took her to finish—in no small part because everything hurt, and what didn't hurt, didn't work. His snide little comments as he passed were like ninja stars between her shoulder blades, shattering what was left of her self-respect.

Then she'd gotten home (speeding the whole way, and thanking the powers for the special Echo tag that made her immune to cops), cleaned up, plugged herself in, checking Tesla's office first as she always did, only to be in time to hear Djinni telling Tesla just what he thought of "nanny cam" and particularly its operator. And that was it. Five minutes later, Bella came in with a sack of soul food for lunch to find her a wet mess.

When Bella had gone, Vickie cleaned herself up (again) and tucked the lunch into the fridge for when her stomach wasn't doing the fandango, reflecting as she did so, that having the blue medic move in next door was one of the best things that had ever happened to her.

Back to the Overwatch room and she saw the "urgent" flag blinking on the main monitor as she opened the door. Less than sixty seconds later she was the silent observer of the briefing for Bulwark's team.

Bulwark's team. Craptastic. More Djinni.

That lunch was probably going to go uneaten now.

Funny. Djinni wasn't smart-assing. Well, after that monologue for Alex Tesla, it wasn't likely he was going to be wearing the wire. Bull already had one run-through, so that left Scope, Acrobat and Harmony to bring up to speed.

Ah, there was Bull's mic and ear lighting up. "Overwatch," she said, feeling a lot better to have him coming up first. "Reading me, Bulwark?"

And there was his camera feed, showing the three newbies to Vickie fumbling with their gear.

"Affirmative, Overwatch, you are five by five," came the crisp reply. And then, in a stern tone, "No, Acrobat, that goes in your ear."

Bella lit up. "Testing," came over the private channel. "I am reminded irresistibly of *F-Troop*."

"The sound you hear is my head hitting the desk," Vickie replied. She switched over to the briefing room intercom and gave simple instructions on what went where. One by one, the lights by their names lit up, and she tested the links.

"...don't know what I'm... *oh!* I can hear something! Hello! Uh... Operative Acrobat, um, five by five, whatever that means."

"Hello, Acrobat," Vickie grinned. "Just let it mold to your ear, son. It should only take a moment."

Scope and Harmony followed suit, and then...

"Red Five, standing by."

"Djinni?" Vickie asked. "You using telepathy now instead of the wire?" Actually she was aghast; didn't know whether to be apprehensive or relieved.

"Don't get cute, Victrix. I've been overruled. Just start the damn show."

"Right. Nobody hum the *Mission: Impossible* theme, please, I've heard that twenty times already. Rolling briefing tape." She cued the mission tape, which would, yes, self-destruct—or rather, erase—when they were done with it.

They were, as far as Vickie could tell, about forty feet underground, which was fine for her communications and bloody well supreme for her magic. They had earth all around them.

The Goldman Catacombs were the stuff of legend. No one seriously believed it existed. The few that did, the few that dared to actually go *inside* were never heard from again. Like the myth of the Minotaur Labyrinth, it was said to contain great treasures. One simply needed to make one's way along the twisting maze of insanity, defeat the great guardian at the end, and claim the goods. Of course, each section was rumored to be lined with more death traps than a bad B-movie. That was what made the Catacombs so unbelievable. What could be *that* valuable, even in aggregate, that anyone would go to so much trouble, when a secure vault with a small army of guards armed to the teeth—like Echo had—would do the same job at a lot less cost and astronomically less hassle? Part of the legend was the eccentricity and ingenuity of the man himself. Doc Goldman had been one of the finest minds of the Third Reich, so much that his boss was willing to overlook his heritage. Considering that the Third Reich would have happily gassed Einstein himself, that was saying something.

For the tenth time, Bulwark asked Red the question.

"And none of this is familiar to you?"

"Why would it be?" Red deadpanned. "Goldman Catacombs. Wow. The myth of this place. It's a thrill to be here, Bull. Quick, someone take my picture."

"If he's never been here before, I'm the mything link," Bella punned on the private channel.

Vickie wasn't entirely sure. None of Djinni's vitals indicated he was lying. Then again... would they? Given the colorful stories about his past, his file was surprisingly scant of anything solid. It was obvious that he was, at the very least, schooled in subterfuge.

"Well, my map says right again," she replied, peering at the low-res digital file of a poorly scanned map. "There's a squiggly bit, it might be a notation or cockroach crap, about ten yards down that might mean... something."

"Crack outfit we're running here, huh?"

"That's enough, Djinni," Bulwark said. "There's something to what he says, though. Overwatch, this might be a good time to inquire about the source of your intel."

"I have here before me a digital copy of a set of schematics allegedly plotted by one of the bricklayers that lined the Catacombs. It was the best I could find, which is a damn sight better than anything Echo has." Already she felt weary. "They're old. And the copy isn't good. But they were in FBI classified files, so evidently the FBI thinks they're valid."

Acrobat stopped. "Thinks? *Thinks?* Overwatch, this is the *Catacombs!* We need better than *thinks!*" Acrobat's heart rate accelerated, and he started to breathe fast and shallow.

"Bulwark, he's going to hyperventilate and pass out in a second," she warned over his channel.

Bull motioned Acrobat to silence. "Bruno, calm down..."

Acrobat started to shake. "You don't understand! No one's survived this place! *No one!* Oh God...except..." He turned to Red. "Not cool, dude! Not cool! You've been here before, right? You're just messing with us, right? I mean...who just walks into a death trap, I ask you?"

"Acrobat, take a deep breath," Bulwark said. He laid a hand gently on Acrobat's shoulder. "We all knew the risks coming down here. I know what you've heard of this place, but do you really think I would let you, any of you, come down here if I didn't think you could handle it? You may be trainees in the eyes of our superiors, but you have all proven yourselves to me. I know you can do this. We're here. We're committed to this." He paused. "Straighten up, soldier. Let's get to work."

Bruno stiffened up.

"Oh, come on, Bruno," Red said, giving Acrobat a noogie. "It'll be fun."

"Gerroff!" Acrobat said, from underneath Red's arm.

Vickie interrupted them by clearing her throat. "Well, since I didn't ask before, I suppose I had better now. Have I your formal approval to work whatever magic I have to in order to keep your asses reasonably intact?"

"No," Red answered. "You've got uncertain plans and are working relatively blind here. We do this right." He looked at Bulwark. "We do this my way."

Bella glared at him. "Vickie, you have *my* personal permission, since laughing boy here doesn't seem to have any more clues about this joint than you do."

Bulwark regarded them both, and finally spoke. "We're not going into this divided. What did I tell you about counterproductive conflict in the field, Operative Blue? Overwatch, feed us what intel you can. Djinni, scout her findings. Disable what you can. I'll head in first if anything seems uncertain."

"Yessir," Bella replied. And added on Vickie's channel, "And if the shit hits the fan, I hope you can think of something to pull me out with." She spoke up where they could all hear her. "And why are you heading in first, sir?"

"Because I'm the least likely to get hurt," Bull answered, turning on his force field.

Whether this was part of Bulwark, or created by some dingus he'd come up with, was irrelevant. What it *was,* however—a transparent sphere, visible mostly because of light refraction off it—sprang up around him.

"A force field?" she breathed. "Holy Klingons, Captain Kirk! Bull can stop bullets?"

"Yeah," Scope whispered. "And more. Kinetic mirror. Whatever hits it, bounces back."

Bella shook her head. "Wowsers. How much can he take?"

"He hasn't tested that yet, but once a building fell on him." Scope's eyes grew reverent. "Have you even seen a building... bounce up?"

"He *survived* that?"

"It almost killed him, actually. But he didn't have much choice. It was during the Invasion, and there were too many lives at risk. Einhorn healed him up afterwards, but for a while it was pretty scary. Lots of internal bleeding. We almost lost him."

Bella gave her a speculative look; stuff was leaking out of this girl as if her empathic barriers were cheesecloth. There, mixed in with the hero worship, was pain and regret and a deep longing. *Oh boy. Mama always told me that it wasn't a good idea to get into romance at work....* Of course, Mama had herself, and here was Bella as the result of it, but hey, don't do as I do, right? And, she had to admit, Bull was smokin' hawt *and* a Boy Scout, which was a combo that was irresistible to Bella and, it seemed, to other women as well.

Vickie coughed in Bella's ear. "Much as I hate to break up this fangirl moment..." The common channel cut in. "As I said, there is a squiggle about ten yards ahead that might mean there's something there."

"Define 'something there,' could you?" Djinni drawled. "You're supposed to be a writer."

Bella could hear Vickie counting under her breath. "There is something on the map that is not one of the usual symbols like 'electrical junction box' or anything else I can recognize. I would logically assume it means 'trap here,' all things considered, but I can't tell and I've been overridden by Field Command from trying to tell what it is by magic. Happy now?"

"Could use a bit more alliteration."

The response was two muttered words in a language Bella didn't know, but which sounded Slavic. Then, "Terpsichorian tragedy transpires on tripping traps." A pause. "Twit."

"Can you give us anything more, Overwatch?" Bull asked. "I can stop objects, but anything energy-based is going to cut right through."

"I wish I could. Without doing a magic scan, I've got nothing but the map."

"We do it the old-fashioned way then. Scope, give me a scan. Harmony, I'll need a boost. Acrobat, I've got point, you're on rear guard. Djinni, if you have anything to add, this is the time."

Scope stepped forward, drew a sensor unit from her belt and did a sweep. "Nothing out of the ordinary here. Looks clean."

"Of course it looks clean," Bull said with exaggerated patience. "Give me energy readings."

"Negative, sir. In fact, readings are lower here than the last bit of hallway."

"Shielding," Bull grunted. "Walls are probably lined with it. At least we know something's here."

Harmony took a nervous step forward. Bull's field shimmered at her presence, and accepted her in. She laid a hand on Bull's back, and the field flashed in intensity. It seemed to hiccup, then expanded with a jerk, crunching into the floor, walls and ceiling. They yielded, leaving curved dents that groaned from the pressure.

Acrobat let out a surprised yelp as they all tensed up, preparing for whatever hell was about to be unleashed.

Nothing happened.

"Easy, easy...." Bulwark murmured. "Remember our last session. Picture what you want to happen."

Harmony squeaked in apology and closed her eyes. Slowly, the field receded until it just covered the width of the hall. After a moment, the field's glow intensified.

"That's good right there," Bull said. "Good girl. Djinni, give me something."

"Like what?" Red snapped back.

"You've been here before. Forget about implicating yourself, our lives are at stake here."

"Recording off," Vickie said crisply. "I'll fake something later to fill in the gap. Jeezus, step up, would you?"

"This is the problem with having a reputation," Red muttered. "Everyone thinks you have all the answers. Christ, are you serious? Overwatch really *doesn't* have complete prints on this place? Did we come down into a death trap with a sketchy floor plan and the trust that I've done this before? I've surpassed traps, sure, but even I know not to go in without a really good idea of what to expect. What were you thinking, Bull?"

"That you have already been here, and that you wouldn't let us die just to protect your own sorry ass."

"Goddamn you..."

Acrobat flinched and backed away in fright. "Oh, this is bad, so bad..." If Harmony had been cheesecloth, Acrobat was a bucket with no bottom; his fear and even some of the thoughts that accompanied it slammed into Bella like a fire hose.

Red and the boss are fighting, right on top of some trap. We are so dead.

Shaking, he connected with the wall. Yelping as if he'd been stung, the surprise drove him forward. Tripping, he and Bella heard a click as his knee triggered something in the floor.

She didn't even have a chance to react as the roof came down on them. No—not down on them, *behind* them. Reacting instinctively they all drove forward; Bulwark's shields were all ramped up facing forward, there was next to nothing in the back.

"Reposition to the rear," Bull ordered, and Harmony dropped her hand. They let the others run past and continued behind them after the force field flared up again.

"Wait, that's...*stop!*" Red yelled, driving his arms to the side as he skidded to a halt. They collided into him, bowling him over as they fell to the ground. Ahead, with an audible whirling and clanking of gears, the floors retracted into the walls, revealing a deep pit. Red hopped up to assess the situation. They had stopped in time. Well, almost all of them.

Scope had been looking back in concern for Bulwark. She hadn't noticed Red's warning until it was too late. Tripping over Bella, she sailed into the pit.

Acrobat, racing towards them from the rear, reacted immediately. He dodged over Red, somersaulting with ease, and let fly a thin sturdy trip line from his gauntlet. The end, affixed to an odd, supple putty, made hard contact with the ceiling. He dove, catching Scope in midfall. The line drew tight and they bounced, jerked into a soft pendulum motion. It all happened in so little time that Bella could only watch with her mouth open.

And a voice, soft and relieved, from within the pit... "Nice catch, Bruno."

"Thanks," Acrobat replied. He was still shaking.

"Fortify," Bulwark growled as he came skidding to a stop behind Bella. She looked back, and witnessed an awesome sight. Arms wide, Bull had braced himself for impact. In a desperate move, Harmony had simply wrapped herself around him. The force field was brilliant in its defiance. Immovable. The falling ceiling caught up to them, and with a tremendous crash bounced back, heavy pistons buckling under themselves as the revealed stonework of heavy ceiling tiles cracked and shattered to rubble. The shock wave echoed back, rippling like an earthquake through the walls and floor of the tunnel, demolishing everything in its wake.

When it was over, there was still the sound of bits of stone cracking off and falling down into the rubble. And an odd whirring noise. They turned to the pit, noting the glint of what appeared to be some very nasty spikes at the bottom. The whirring sound was Acrobat retracting his line, as he and Scope zoomed up into view.

Bella swallowed hard, and coughed out a lot of dust. "Um. Nothing like the classics, I guess," she said, trying hard for something like humor.

Bulwark let out a soft breath and turned. "Report."

"Pit trap, sir," Scope answered. "The falling ceiling drove us to it. I . . . I messed up, fell in." Her jaw tightened in anger. "Lucky for me, Acrobat kept his head."

Bull gave Acrobat a curt nod. "Nice moves, son."

"Just like the training room," Acrobat gulped. "Just like—"

"This shouldn't be here," Red muttered. They turned to see him glaring at the pit, as if offended by its presence.

"So that's what a squiggle bisecting a circle with a V-shape underneath it means." That was Vickie, her voice sounding strained even over the radio link. "How nice. If there were more of those on this map, I might be more useful. Oh, and the next time I call up his ghost for a little séance, I'll be sure to tell Goldman you disapprove of his design, Djinni."

They took a moment to regroup. Bella was checking over Scope and Acrobat, making sure the fall hadn't left any injuries masked by the surge of adrenaline. Harmony had begun to sob uncontrollably, and Bulwark had taken her aside and was speaking quietly with her. She was shaking but she nodded along with Bull's reassuring words. Bella made as if to touch her, and she shied back violently. Then, immediately, shook her head. "S-s-sorry," she said. "It's not you. It's—telepaths."

Bella nodded with a wry expression. "Don't worry about it. It's pretty common even in Echo. Not too many people like the idea of someone rummaging around in their mental dirty laundry."

Red was crouching off to the side, watching them.

"What did you mean by 'this shouldn't be here'?" Vickie asked him. The dead air behind her voice told him it was on private channel. He grimaced.

"Nothing," he muttered. "Who the hell builds a pit trap after a collapsing ceiling? Goddamn overkill."

"Uh-huh. Seems to me if that trap was disabled in the first place, you wouldn't have even known the pit was there. Something someone who's been here before wouldn't have expected, if that someone had someone else who was disabling traps ahead of them. Yes? No? Rice cakes?"

He told her what to do with her rice cakes.

"Wouldn't fit," she snapped back. "And don't you think it's time you started being a little more proactive? Like it or not, you're stuck down there with everyone else, and what happens to them is gonna happen to you."

He didn't answer. It was all going to hell. He had never expected to be here again. It was always the game, the prep work, the thrill of running the gauntlet. Each job a wild ride, Red and his crew always beat the odds. But then, they always knew they would. They had checked everything, planned down to the second how things would go. They had trained for each test. And they had gone in knowing the risks, the *calculated* risks. What was it this time? Why had he let them come down here? This wasn't what he did. Just in the door, and they had almost died. There was no planning, no calculated risks, no calculation at all.

A part of him loved it. Dungeon delving, relying on wits and luck and gambling it all with nothing but the thrill of imminent danger. It was the ultimate escape that he craved yet never let himself experience. Ever. All those years he had been holding back. It was the one line he couldn't cross. It was the line that ultimately got people like himself killed. Of course, everyone crossed it eventually. Whether from a moment of weakness or finding that one last, great challenge, every pro crossed it. And died. Or retired after one too many close calls; he heard that it *did* happen on occasion. Had it come to this? Was everything gone, anything that mattered in the least to him? Was nothing left except that one last, uncertain moment?

Perhaps.

He watched them. In turn, the team watched back. The hall had gone silent as their eyes came to rest on him. They were demanding answers now. His flip attitude, his confidence and his damned reputation had brought them to this. Bulwark had called his bluff. Only now, Red realized he didn't know everything about this place. They might have a brief map, and his denied-but-real experience here, but there were blind spots now. He didn't know what was going to happen anymore. Acrobat had been right. These were the Catacombs. Uncertainty here meant death. Their deaths. This wasn't his old team; they were amateurs in uniform. He almost laughed. They were his *new* team.

And if he didn't smarten up, he was going to get them killed.

And *again,* her voice. That nagging voice, telling him what was right, and that rebellious jerk inside of him just *had* to lash back at it. He hated her for that. What was it with Victorias that they just couldn't let things alone, they had to keep digging until they uncovered...

...the truth.

"You know if I could be down there I would. We both know I'm a liability in the field. This is all I have, all I can do. But I'm trying, you rat bastard. If you would let me, I'd be dumping every magical hoo-ha I have down there right now. As it is, I poured every red cent I had of my own cash into this rig. If I didn't have the paycheck from Echo, the lights literally wouldn't be on right now. And I know it's not enough, but at least it's something, and right now, we're in a fight we're gonna lose unless everyone brings everything he's got. I brought mine. You gonna bring yours?" The voice sounded very tight. Not with anger, with something else.

"I always do," he snarled. "You should know that more than anyone."

"Say what?" The bewilderment alerted him to the fact that he'd been snarling at the living and a ghost, both.

"Nothing, wrong number," he muttered, standing up. He nodded towards Bulwark. "Harmony all pepped up now? We should get going."

Bull nodded and they gathered together.

"Overwatch?" Red said finally.

"Djinni?"

"Magic is a go."

Bulwark looked at him oddly, then said, "Confirmed, Overwatch."

"Roger that." No sound of triumph or "I told you so." Maybe relief, but that was it.

Somehow that didn't make him feel any better.

Vickie didn't feel as if she had won anything ... just relief, relief that she could finally do her whole job. Maybe a little gratitude that Djinni had bent his rules. Mind, she still didn't know *why* he had a pinecone up his butt about magic but ... well, he did, and he'd made a compromise.

As a consequence, she sent in her "feelers" with extreme care, more so than she did with Murdock and the CCCP. There was "wrongness" ahead of them, in the tunnel that both her map and her scrying said to take. If there was a pattern to the tunnels and traps, this was it. So far, there had never been anything that was line of sight for more than forty feet, and so far, all the traps had included corners or bends.

"Team, disclosure here. I have a piece of what we are looking for and I'm using that as a kind of compass—it's a scrap of paper with some of Goldman's original calculations on it. The compass says take the next left. But the magic sensors say there is something bad waiting for you there. You guys ought to stop at the turning and see if you can get anything...."

"We're already getting something," Bella replied. "Smells like dead things."

"Oh God!" Harmony shrieked. *"Looks like dead things!"*

"Somebody point your cam in there, please?" There was some shuffling and she lit up the darkened tunnel with magic. Carefully. Gradually. So the horror was revealed slowly.

The camera views flared to life, and she scanned her screens to get a clear view. She noticed Scope's view was the steadiest. Acrobat's shook uncontrollably, and Harmony's wasn't even pointed in the right direction. It looked actually like she was going to ...

She did. Vickie managed to switch views to the tunnel before she lost her own lunch. Strange how a mass of bodies didn't affect her nearly as badly as someone hurling.

"That's an impressive sight."

"What you got, Overwatch?" Bulwark asked.

"Incomplete." She let out more magical feelers. The walls were brick, stone, and earth. The things in them were not. She picked up a planchette with a pencil stuck in it and let her hand trace what she sensed. Slowly her drawing formed on one of the monitors. "I'm doing something, call it scanning. The designs look like the walls house..."

What the hell were those things? They looked like...hoses?

"House what?" Acrobat shouted.

"Easy, son," Bulwark said. "We're not going to move until we get confirmation. Djinni? Anything?"

Red knelt down to examine the corpses. "Doesn't seem to be any visible flesh wounds, Bull. No apparent damage. It's like they just...fell and died."

"It's something complicated," Vickie was talking more to keep them in the loop than anything. "What I'm doing is kind of like a scanning electron microscope. I'm getting the picture bit by—"

Harmony stood up just in time for her camera to point back down the way they had come. Just in time for a hint of movement but not enough time for Vickie to warn them before a wall dropped down behind them, sealing them in.

Damn it! She took a chance and "glued" Acrobat's feet to the floor before he could jump and trigger something else. Then, frantically, she scribbled more design, more design—

Water pipes?

No, the feeds to the side, she recognized the housing.

"Guns!" Vickie yelled, her hands clenching in panic, then she lurched for the keyboard and sent her warm, flat Coke and her cat flying. Could she crunch the guns in the walls? Jam the feeds?

They jumped as the darkness broke. Panels of lights lining the hall blared to life, each punctuated by the staccato of adjoining turrets that sprang from the walls. A low humming rose as they powered up.

Vickie went for the guns, willing the earth around them to close in on them, jam the mechanisms, crush them. Sweat poured down the back of her neck. Her arms burned, the muscles screaming with exertion, as if she was doing this with her own two hands. Which she was...

It wasn't enough. The guns were too heavy, too *tough*. She wasn't making a dent in them without bringing the walls down too, and the humming continued to rise to a deafening pitch. They continued to ramp up, the barrels were spinning, they were going to fire!

"Get in close and behind me," Bulwark said calmly. "Harmony, boost me."

They leapt to him as Harmony reached out with both hands. His field flared into existence, barely shielding them all as he braced himself for the bullet storm.

And...nothing happened. The barrels stopped spinning. The humming subsided.

"What?"

They relaxed, confused.

"Weapons malfunction?"

"Then what killed these people?"

"Did you do that, Overwatch?"

"No idea what—"

"They don't even look like they've been shot—"

"Shut up!" Red barked. Everyone froze, and in the sudden silence they heard the buzzing.

"Bull!" Red shouted. "Shield down!"

"Are you insane?"

"Just do it!"

Red detached himself from the group and sprouted his claws. Bella watched in shock as pointed flesh tore through the tips of Red's gloves. Bulwark nodded to Harmony, who removed her hands from his shoulders, freeing him to relax his power. As the shield fell away, Red lunged forward and dove into the floor, which was paneled with embossed metal. Grunting, he ripped open the paneling and tore into a mesh of wires and circuit boards. The grid screeched blue fire and hissed in protest as the tunnel was plunged back into darkness.

"Can I help?" Vickie asked urgently, for Djinni's ears only.

"You hear that buzzing anymore?" he asked.

"No."

"Then I'm done."

"Lights up," she said on the common channel, and again, slowly caused the rock of the ceiling to glow.

Red turned to the others and stifled an involuntary laugh. The trainees were huddled around Bulwark, locked in transparent confusion and wide-eyed fright. Bella's eyes were squeezed tightly shut. And Bulwark...well, he was Bulwark. Nothing ever seemed to faze him.

"What did I miss?" Vickie asked. Humbly.

"Another diversionary trap," Red answered. "When the guns didn't go, I felt the humming ramping up in the floor, like pins and needles on my soles. They were coming from"—he pointed to the mess of wires and broken circuitry in the floor—"here."

"What were they for?"

"Here," Scope answered. She beckoned them to the walls. "Holes in the walls, they weren't there before. Must've opened up when the guns came out. Djinni's right; the guns were a diversion."

Bella knelt close to examine them. "You've got good eyes, Scope. I can barely see them."

"That's what I do," Scope replied. "Up there too, you can see little stopcock valves in the ceiling now. Really little ones, like miniature fire sprinklers."

"And here," Red called out, his head submerged in the now exposed floor panel. "Got conduits running the length of the floor down here. Electrical trap." He rose, shed his claws and ran an exposed finger along the holes in the wall. "Sarin gas." And on the ceiling. "Acid, concentrated sulfuric."

"Those are the most stable over time," Bella said flatly.

"The shield should have been enough to handle the acid," Bulwark said. "Maybe the gas, but the electrical would have cut us down."

"Magic wouldn't have worked fast enough to see all that," Vickie admitted. "Not before it triggered." She sighed, then muttered, "I need something more...tech." She muted the mic so they couldn't hear her, pounded her fist into the table and swore at herself. It wasn't enough, damn it. Not even her best was enough.

But it was all she had, and they were on the clock.

Punish yourself later. Help now.

"Come on," Djinni said, beckoning them on. "I think I see our objective."

He led them forward, his step a bit more confident. He stopped at a widened portion of the hall and ran his fingers over one section. He grimaced as his hand passed over a section. Rearing back, he grew his claws out again and plunged his hand into the wall. There was a crunch, followed by a brief pop and some smoke. He withdrew from the fried circuitry, and slid a panel aside. A secret door, and beyond, darkness.

"Remind me to call you next time I'm locked out of my car," said Bella.

"Not sure your insurance would pay for the collateral damage," Vickie murmured.

"I usually go for finesse," Djinni said. "Right now, I'm just not in the mood. Give us some light here, Overwatch."

Vickie obliged and lit up the hidden room. It looked a little like a storage room at the Smithsonian. Lots of crates. Lots of shiny things on shelves. Lots of really big shiny things, too big for shelves or crates. She recognized a lot of artifacts, or at least the styles, but there was a lot of art and some techie stuff too. And—were those wall panels of carved amber?

"Fan out," Bulwark ordered. "We're looking for documents, but keep your eyes open for dark metals or sample casings."

They worked the room over, bringing back anything that looked promising. Bulwark grunted as he broke envelope seals and ran a pocket scanner over the documents.

"Reading e-copies and resending," Vickie reported.

"Copy that," Bulwark said. "We got anything yet?"

"Those docs in your hands now all resonate with my sample, so you're on the right track. It'll take a better math-head than me to know which is the right stuff."

"Scope," Bulwark said, raising his voice. "Overwatch reports a hit from your sector of the vault. Bring me everything you got."

"Yessir!" Scope shouted back as the others joined her.

Meanwhile, Vickie was ever so carefully increasing her "field." She wasn't sure what she was looking for, only that she was getting a hint that there was something else down here. Something off the map, and big.

While they sorted through their finds, she got something. "Uh . . . sir? I've been doing some scouting of a sort. This isn't the only vault. There's something . . . nasty down there. Four hundred ninety-three point four meters south."

"Define 'nasty,' Overwatch."

"I'm pinging an extremely large storage area with a lot of tech in it. A lot of the same metal as in the armor."

"So perhaps they're samples in another area of the Catacombs," Bulwark said. "How much of it?"

"Ballpark?"

"Sure."

"About what hit Atlanta."

Bella whistled. "That's no 'sample.' We heading in, bossman?"

Bulwark nodded, slipping his scanner back into his belt. "We're done in this room, might as well check it out."

"Have you gone right around the bend?" Red objected. "Didn't you hear what she said? There's enough of that crap in there to build a small army."

"And?"

"Have you considered the possibility it *is* a small army? We got the primary objective, we should book."

"We had three directives: to see if infiltrating the Catacombs was possible, to obtain Goldman's research notes, and to get a sample of the material in question. We are in striking distance of all three. We should move on."

"Within the realms of *reconnaissance*, Bull! There's no telling what's in there!"

"Then we investigate. Really, Djinni, this labyrinth was sealed in the sixties. Do you really expect there to be the fully armed troops and weaponry we faced during the Invasion?"

Red looked like he was ready with an angry retort, but instead turned his back on Bulwark and marched away.

"What's up his grill?" Scope asked.

Bulwark watched Djinni storm off, his face pensive. The trainees relaxed. They knew that look. Bull was sizing the situation up, and would have an answer soon. They waited patiently. Bella looked from one to the other, wondering what the hell was going on. But Vickie already had an idea, and she was right.

"We're walking into the unknown," Bull said finally. "This is as far as the Djinni's gone."

"Backing up all intel and locations now, Team Leader," Vickie said very formally. "Sending backups to Echo database...now."

What she hadn't said was obvious to anyone who knew her: if the team was lost, the data was still safe.

As they continued, Vickie switched to Bulwark's private channel. "Sir, I'm not sure this is a good idea, from the perspective of me, outside, safe. Relatively."

"Understood, Overwatch. You realize this puts us in a very bad situation. We'll have to look to you more than ever."

"Yessir." She cut back over to Djinni's private freq. "Djinni...

there's probably a pattern here. I think you may be better at spotting it than me; I've never gone treasure-hunting and I don't know jack about modern traps other than trying to scan for crap in the walls, and we saw how well that worked. Ideas? Hints? Buy a vowel?"

"I have no frickin' clue," Red muttered. "You're asking me to think like a man who, despite his high profile, managed to escape capture after the war and still managed to build a monstrosity like this in the heart of America without being discovered."

"Well, he had to have assumed there were going to be metas on both sides of the law coming down here. And normals."

Red stopped. "Right, so he would have realized he had any number of possible abilities to overcome. Time to think this through." He turned to the others. "Okay, so if you needed to keep your goodies safe in a maze from *anyone* in a world filled with metas, what would you need to do? Who would you need to overcome?"

"Hounds," Bella piped up. "Metas who can find the path."

"Right," Djinni nodded. "So assuming there are those who can circumvent the maze, like we have with Overwatch, you would need to line the most direct route with hazards that, in combination, would take down anyone."

"I'm running a quick search on abilities that we know metas had by the time Goldman died." Vickie's hand flew over her keyboard, calling up multiple screens that flashed streaming hits before her. "Invulnerability—well, call it 'really hard to kill'—that's top on the list. Followed by flyers, so your traps would not have to count on people stepping on things to trigger them. TK/TP, samey same."

"What about those powerful enough to simply kick in the door and storm their way to the target?" Bulwark asked. "Surely Goldman would have prepped for them."

"Autodestruct." Vickie's answer was prompt and confident. "Ubermensch the first could probably have gotten away with that, so it looks like Goldman took that into account—one of the reasons it's so hard to read this place. Every time you turn around my magic is going 'Don't touch that!' You know, Goldman must have been willing to let people get to his goodies *if* they were able to meet his challenges. There's a cold, psychotic logic to this. From the scraps of blueprints we have, to a brief feel of the ley lines of this place, it all points to what appears to be a massive power source deeper in the complex. Best guess, the whole place is set to blow if anything comes in not willing to play by the rules of the labyrinth."

"Can you estimate the power level?" Bulwark said.

"On the scale of Hiroshima."

"You're joking."

"Do you *hear* a rim shot? This guy was playing for keeps and quite prepared to take out the neighborhood for spite."

Red looked them over. Even their breathing had grown cautious. They were afraid to move, perhaps even to think. They were so close now to their objective. Five hundred yards. Still, a lot could happen in five hundred yards...

"Okay," he said, urging them to keep thinking. "Goldman's tried to crush us, then gas, melt and electrocute us. What's left?"

"Vacuum?" Vickie suggested. "Flood? Hordes of ROUSes?"

Red shook his head, it didn't sound right. "No, seems he's already covered his bases with the brute squads."

"You *are* the brute squad," Bella muttered. No one laughed.

"Beam us into space? Could he have had that tech?" Vickie answered her own question. "No, or he'd have built this out there. Djinni, do you think we should just feel our way along? I'm concerned there might also be timers on some of this shite. Timers would fit the parameters of a 'keep moving' rule."

Red shared a look with Bulwark.

"Your call, Bull," he said finally.

"Slowly," Bulwark said. "Everyone around me, tight as you can, I can only extend protection so far without running into the walls. Harmony, I need you to ramp up Scope. We're going to need her eyes. Overwatch, can you keep the light source ahead of us, at least a hundred feet?"

"Can do," Vickie replied. The light crept slowly forward, a few inches at a time, and they began to advance. "So what other powers did Goldman know about? Motion sensors to get flyers and TKers? How would he stop a TPer, other than limit line of sight?"

"The labyrinth itself would have taken care of that," Djinni said. "Nothing's line of sight here for more than forty feet."

Scope had finally started sweating. Her eyes were everywhere. Her gaze flickered from side to side, floor to ceiling and back so fast the telemetry could barely keep track of it.

"Okay, what about flyers and TKers? You know, the floaty kind."

"If the first ceiling didn't cave them in, they would have been strangled, oozed and fried by the second. No, we're definitely missing something."

Of them all, Bull was a rock...and, if he wasn't futzing her reads, Djinni was surprisingly cool. Of course given how much he could control his body, no telling what was going on in his head. Harmony was tighter than a banjo string at this point; Vickie suspected that only the constant physical contact with Bull kept her focused.

"What could a sonic power do to get through that you guys can't? Something a sonic might trigger. Uh, someone with sonar, so they wouldn't need light at all?"

"We're miles beneath the surface," Djinni said. "Anything physical or mechanical in nature is going to get picked up here. There's almost no background to compensate for, Overwatch. Be it sound, light, he could have filtered out earth tremors...what's left?"

"Boy bands? Drive you crazy with perfect hair?" Vickie was running out of ideas. "A pheromone weapon to make you all strip naked and have an orgy?"

What was left? Of course.

"The one thing that the Thulians are missing is they don't seem to recognize that magic works," Vickie said, thinking aloud herself. "But...wait...that wasn't true of the early pre-Na—"

Too late.

Ahead of them, Vickie's light source came to a sudden stop and flashed as it completed the mystic circuit. Too late she saw the Nordic sigils flare as they were fed with her power, and something else. A collapsed hole of energy, contained and tethered to a small point in space by a thin ley line. As her magic probe brushed the point of contact, the tether sparked and collapsed, igniting the arcane trap. A massive cell of raw energy erupted, was grounded, and channeled itself into the nearest mystical matrix—Vickie's light spell. It was a lot like having the sun go off in your face. Blinding light followed by pain so intense it wasn't even pain anymore, but a primal force.

Bella had been looking back the other way in case there was something sneaking up on them. She caught the flash as reflection down the tunnel and instinctively closed and covered her eyes. "*Stop!*" she shrieked. "Nobody move!"

She opened her eyes again.

It was dark. Cave dark. Scope was sobbing. "Who's hurt?" Bella snapped, turning and groping for them.

"My eyes! They're burning! I can't *see!*" Scope cried, sounding as if everything she owned in the world had been taken from her. Which, of course, since her power was in her eyes...

"Honey, none of us can see." Bella found Scope's elbow, followed the arm up to the woman's face, and clapped a hand over Scope's eyes, ruthlessly opening herself up to everything. This psychic healing thing... you had to let go of everything you knew and let what felt like pure instinct tell you what was going on—at least, you did when it wasn't something obvious like a gaping wound. Which was hard for a control freak like Bella. Getting easier though, with the angel's help....

"You'll be okay. Not right now, but the optic nerve's intact..." She let the cells tell her what was going on. "Retinal damage, it'll heal. Corneas are fine. Lens too. Lens is where your power is. Scope, you'll have it all back in a couple days, faster if I or Sovie or another Healer can concentrate on you." She gave Scope a quick burst just so she could start seeing something (at least, once they had a light again), to let her know that Bella wasn't blowing smoke to make her feel better. She felt for her flashlight and turned it on.

The others were blinking and rubbing their eyes, but they seemed to be recovering.

"I knew it," Red spat, turning on his own flashlight. "I *knew* it. Magic, of course, it's *always* magic..." He paused to run the light over the length of the hall. "Overwatch? We're in the dark here. Anything stirring around us?"

He was met with silence.

"Victrix? Report."

More silence, and a very faint hiss in their earpieces.

"Terrific."

"Well, shit," Bella said sourly. "Keep going or bail? We've got the notes. Is it worth going on without Overwatch on the basis of what we think might be out there?"

She rested one hand on Scope's shoulder and gave the woman another dose of healing. It was working, actually. She felt it making the undamaged cells replicate, the ones that were not too damaged... were they regenerating? Hard to tell.... "Scope, you're currently the weakest link. Can you go on?"

Scope shot her a dirty look and stood up. With a flourish she drew out her pistols and came to attention next to Bull. She was still squinting.

"Just tell me which blurry thing to shoot."

Bulwark motioned them forward. "Let's go."

Acrobat hesitated. "Sir, we've lost tactical, Scope's vision is in question and Djinni's got no clue what's ahead. Are you sure that's wise?"

Bull shone his flashlight down the hall. "Son, what we have are some notes on what may very well be the key to handling everything the Kriegs can dish out—but it might not. Around that corner is a cache of the stuff in question, or better yet, prototypes. We get our hands on those, and the boys back in the lab might be able to piece together enough data to crack open a Krieg death trooper and take him down in seconds. That sound worth it to you?"

"Yessir."

"Then what say we head down there and finish this?"

Slowly sight came back; consciousness had come first, and it had taken all of her discipline to stay where she was when she came to and couldn't see.

Vickie had trained herself a long time ago to be aware of where she was as soon as she was awake; the zero-gravity chair kept her upright and in one place even unconscious. And fortunately for her, sight started coming back pretty quickly.

The first thing that jump-started was the realization that she'd *almost* had the right answer when the answer blew up in her face. These Thulians didn't know magic, but Goldman had; he'd been around when Himmler was messing about with his SS-elite magic society. So he'd trapped the place against magicians.

The only thing that had saved them all was that she hadn't been physically present, and all she was using was a simple, low-level light spell. The trap had been designed to take whatever magic touched it, amp it up exponentially, and blow it back in the caster's face. If she had been there, it would have charred her inside and out, and the gods only knew what it would have done to the rest of the team. But the caster wasn't there. Just her computer—

Computers! She didn't hear the noises of her Overwatch suite! No fans, no pings, no...nothing. That jolted her into full consciousness, and she flailed in her chair. And that awoke more pain than she'd been in since she'd been in burn rehab. Her skin seemed to have tightened all over where there were scars, hardening up, and hurting.

For a moment that put her into pure panic mode. Then a particularly gut-wrenching spasm brought tears of pain into her eyes, and that cleared them. She blinked and saw all her computer screens dark, and got the mental flash of her team down in the Catacombs just as blind as she was.

There were no more traps. Before Vickie had gotten knocked offline, she'd downloaded the latest iteration of their sketchy map to Bull's PDA, with "where you've been" and most importantly, "where you're going" marked on it. It had been updating regularly all along, so he could only assume that she had that function automated.

That meant that, since they were almost line of sight to what Overwatch thought was their goal...it was within reach.

"Halt," he said quietly.

His team, huddled nervously about him, came to an immediate stop. Bull shone his light ahead of them.

"We turn right, and we're there," he whispered. "End of the line."

"Overwatch able to give you any details before she fizzled out?" Red asked.

"Just some rough dimensions," Bull said.

"And?"

"It's...big. Roughly the size of the Echo main hangar."

"You mean that hangar bay with the supersonics?"

"No, the *entire* hangar."

"Jeebus," Bella muttered. "What's he got down here? The Neue Graf Spee? Hitler's Escape Rocket? Walt Disney?"

"If we're lucky, Operative Blue, perhaps some hard evidence that his experiments worked."

Bull motioned them close and nodded to Harmony. Again, she laid a tentative hand on his back and the force field intensified around them. He jerked his head at the bend in the path, and they inched forward.

They came to a portal. Big, massive, and circular, much like an old-fashioned bank vault door. The door was reinforced, and as importantly, the frame was just as heavy. No blowing this thing off its hinges.

Red handed Bella his flashlight and motioned her to hold the beam steady. They watched as he knelt next to the door, in front of an ancient access panel. After a moment, his claws flashed out again.

"More hack-and-slash disabling?" Bella asked.

"Not this time," Red muttered as he slipped his claws beneath the panel casing. With a grunt, he pried the cover off and examined the mess of wires and circuitry beneath. "If this place is as big as Bull says it is, we might need to do more than open the door. We might need light."

He fell silent as he gracefully snipped some nondescript wires apart. He shed his claws again and his nimble, unencumbered hands reached in and brushed a few wires together. There was a crackle as sparks flared and a low hum crescendoed all around them. Darkness fled as fluorescent bulbs lining the path flickered to life. A few continued to flicker.

"Are you insane?" Acrobat demanded. "You just turned on... what if you set off another trap?"

Bella decided to try something. The kid was ramping up again. She more or less shoved *calm* at him, all the while keeping her voice soft and soothing. "Anything down here doesn't need light to get us. But we need light to see it coming."

Red nodded, still focused on the panel. "And if this chamber is as big as Bull says it is, no way our flashlights will be enough. Ah, here we are..."

He reached in and withdrew a large circuit board still tethered to the panel by ropes of wires. The circuits were printed in gold. The transistors on it were vintage 1960s—about as big as grains of corn rather than the head of a pin.

"Wow... that is brilliant work." Bella's eyes were like dinner plates. "Vic'd kill to see this. Have you got any idea how much that would be worth to a museu—"

"No idea," Djinni said, and proceeded to smash the board against the wall. There was a mighty crash as the glass-walled transistors shattered. The silence that followed was interrupted by a steely hiss as the portal slid open.

Bulwark sighed. "Was that really necessary?"

"Sorry, Bull," Red chuckled. "I'm a sucker for the dramatic."

They turned as Harmony uttered a small squeak. She was standing in front of the vault door that had swung silently inward. "Then you're going to *love* this."

Before them ... was something that could not possibly be described as a "room." It had walls, a floor and an arched ceiling, and it was underground, but this was no mere room. Red squinted, and thought he might, just possibly, be able to make out the wall at the opposite end. But he wasn't entirely sure, the light was too dim.

This place was easily big enough to hold a small family farm with some space left over for, say, a racetrack.

"What the hell is in here?"

The lights in the room began to fade up—standard fluorescents slowly warming up and flickering on in sequence.

There was an army below them.

Row after row after row of powered armor, beneath a huge vaulted ceiling, looked uncannily like the rows of clay warriors in the tomb of Emperor Qin Shihuang in Xian China. Stiff and at attention, each suit of armor gleamed in the new light. Despite being still and lifeless, each held the promise of unthinkable violence. And there were *hundreds* of them, packed into neat little rows, four abreast, trailing off into the distance. The only interruption lay in the center of the chamber—a massive structure with a square base and a smooth domed roof.

Red turned and punched Bulwark in the arm. "Told you."

"This ..." Harmony paused, unsure of how to continue. "This makes the kind of sense that ... doesn't."

"How ..." Acrobat's voice broke, he gulped, and tried again. "How do you get all this crap *down* here? And this room! We must be hundreds of feet underground! They *built* this?"

Scope swore. "Would someone please tell me what the hell I'm supposed to be seeing?"

"An army, Scope," Bull said. "We're looking at an army of metal. Based on what we fought, though, these look a bit archaic. Not primitive by any means, but first generation. I'm sorry, Acrobat. I have no idea how this is possible."

It was Bella's turn to swear. "Bomb tests."

They all turned to blink at her. "What?" asked Acrobat.

"Bomb tests. A-bombs, H-bombs. I live here, remember? My grandparents worked for Oppie. In the forties, fifties, even the early sixties, Las Vegas was a handful of mob-owned casinos on Fremont Street and a few divorce ranches. The only thing that was important out here then was the military and the test site.

And if it was military, no one ever asked questions. You could move *anything* out here as long as you stuck your crew in Army Surplus uniforms and painted the trucks olive-drab. Everyone would assume you were doing something with the bomb tests and no one would say a word." She shook her head. "Brilliant. He installed all this right under the noses of the military." Then her face soured. "He could even have done blasting timed with the bomb tests and no one would notice. Seismographs weren't that accurate back then, and the bomb test times were posted in the papers so people could gather and watch in Vegas. Mom has postcards. Mushroom cloud with Vegas Vic."

"Great," Djinni muttered. "Fabulous. Make sure to add that in your report. So, mystery solved. We'll be going now, yeah?"

"Not yet," Bulwark said. "We should investigate, see if we can take a sample with us."

"And just *how* are we supposed to do that, Bull?" Red scoffed. "Those things weigh a ton. What, you think you can grab a helmet and be off?"

"You could crawl in one and pilot it out," Bella suggested.

"Right," Djinni said, rubbing his temples. "I'm sure there are simple Gameboy pads and instruction manuals in each. And you're assuming they aren't automated death machines. Christ, they might wake up the minute we get in there."

"The suits all had organic pilots," Bella told him. "That's in the Invasion debrief."

"Enough," Bulwark said. "We go in. Stay tight. Anything looks wrong, we still have our path of retreat. Djinni, you've got point."

Red gave Bull a hard look, then swung himself onto a nearby ladder. He began to scale down, his eyes never leaving Bulwark. They followed him cautiously, making their way to ground level. Bella winced as her feet made jarring sounds on the metal rungs, with each clang echoing off into the giant room. She softened her descent, flexing her knees to ease her feet onto the rungs. She noticed the others following her lead. Except for Djinni, who slid silently away from them and down to the bottom.

"How the hell does he do that?" she muttered to herself.

Once on the floor, the space was even more intimidating. The lighting wasn't bright enough to illuminate the whole place, just enough to make spooky pools of shadow everywhere. But there was one thing Bella noticed. These suits weren't like the ones she'd seen in Groom Lake. They looked...clunkier. Just as big as their modern counterparts, perhaps, but noticeably less articulated. She supposed if you managed to get one on its back, it was out of the fight. No arm cannons either. Each held their hands close to the chest, gripping...

"Are those...are those swords?"

Bulwark nodded. "And battle axes and clubs."

"First gen?" Bella said aloud. "If they are...a sample from one of them might tell the techs a lot."

Djinni crept up to one, like a stalking cat, his curiosity overcoming his apprehension. Gingerly, he took hold of a sword, his hands running up to the hilt. He pulled. The sword didn't budge.

"Somebody didn't eat his Yankee Doodles this morning."

Red didn't answer; instead, he somersaulted up and sat on the armor's immense shoulders. Reaching down, he strained to pry the cold metal fingers from the sword hilt. Nothing. They were locked tight.

"Well," Bulwark said, "so much for that idea. Let's move along. There might be something else salvageable further on."

"Maybe a spare parts bin," offered Scope.

"Or a scratch-'n'-dent section," Acrobat chuckled. "Fifty percent off, only used to invade on Sundays."

Laughing, they moved deeper into the room, their initial panic at seeing the extent of the place quickly lost when nothing moved or offered a threat. Red hopped down from his perch and watched them go. He didn't join in on the laughter.

Neither did Bella. The rest might not be spooked—but she still was. There was a vast maze out there to prove Goldman was a psychotic nutball bastard. This was still part of his creation.

And despite what they had gone through to get this far, she still couldn't shake the feeling that it had still been far too easy.

The image of her team blind down there jolted her. Hard. Right into thinking mode again. The pain didn't matter; she'd gone through worse. What did matter was her team. She'd let them down already; she couldn't leave them.

Right. From cold boot and see what comes up. Vickie powered everything down and, one piece at a time, powered them back up again. She nearly wept to see the tests run and most of them come back live. A couple hard drives lost, that was not a problem, she had backups of her backups—but no BSODs, oh gods be thanked. Grabbing her kit she plunged into the belly of the beast, taking care of the purely mechanical and electrical first.

Then the Overwatch system. Known quantity first: JM. Murdock wasn't expecting her to ping him, but he was getting into the habit of always wearing his wires on patrol, and—

—yes. Yes, he was, and he was live. She got his camera and mic-feeds and the mechanical locator on the map. So the mechanical part of Overwatch was working.

Now the magical... She pulled Bulwark's packet from the USB interface and plugged JM's in.

Nothing. And it wasn't the packet. Back she went to the spare parts shelf and hauled out a new interface, blessing her own paranoia. Plug and plug, cast the spell, and there he was on the map without benefit of the mechanical locator.

She pulled JM's packet and plugged in Bull's.

Nothing. She tried not to scream.

Their progress was slow at first, until they realized they were inspecting the same thing, over and over again. With each new row, each new battalion, they found the same armor, wielding the same weapons, each as immovable as the last. They sped up, moving to a cautious march, their eyes everywhere, until they came to the giant domed structure.

It towered over them. The dome appeared to be a flawless ceiling of metal, glinting softly in the dim light, atop a tall, square, metallic slab.

Red squinted to make out the details. Unlike the domed roof, the square walls of the base seemed rougher. He inched closer and finally ran his hands along it. He realized his mistake. The walls were smooth as well, but inlaid with intricate carvings. He shone his flashlight over them, and was surprised to see a brilliant relief of an enormous wolf, beautifully portrayed midbattle with human soldiers half its size. He could almost hear its snarls, feel its rage...

He nodded to Bulwark, and made his way around the monument. Another relief, this time of a bird. An eagle, he would say, wings spread, claws extended, captured in that flash of time just before snatching its prey and hurtling up into the sky. A rabbit, perhaps? Red looked closer, his eyes widening. No, a horse.

Giant animal predators. What kind of whackjob carved these, I wonder?

Continuing, he found two more similar carvings, again depicting the savage wolf and the triumphant eagle. But no doors, no panels, nothing suggesting that this structure was anything more than a monument to the crazed inner workings of the mind of the Third Reich's most infamous inventor.

"Well?" Bulwark asked as Djinni joined the rest of the group.

"It's official," Djinni replied. "Goldman was a nutjob."

"Take a look here, Djinni," Bull said, shining his flashlight on a new row of armor. "We're finally seeing something different."

Red gave the armor an appraising look. "No more medieval weaponry, and thicker arms too. No, not arms..."

"Arm-mounted Gatling guns," Bulwark said. "And no, they won't come off. We just tried. Acrobat, I hope you're getting all this."

Acrobat nodded, guiding his sensors over every inch of the armor. Strobe lighting pulsed from the handheld accompanied by soft clicking sounds as the miniscule camera snapped a steady stream of pictures.

"Odd," Bull said. "It's like we're walking through more than just an armory. They're lined up in some sort of historical order. More like a museum."

Red jerked a thumb back towards the dome. "That would explain that monstrosity."

"Sir!" From ahead, they heard Harmony's surprised squeal. "You should probably take a look at this!"

They rushed ahead, and came to an impossible sight.

"No..."

"The hell...?"

"That's...not possible..."

"Hello!" Scope cried out. *"Still blind here!"*

Bella shook off her shock long enough to grab Scope's shoulder and give her another dose. Which wasn't going to help her see much now...

"Um...it's...modern armor suits. Like *we* fought."

"Like we fought?" Scope repeated.

"Yes," Bella answered.

"In here?"

"Yes."

"In this really, really old vault?"

"Yes."

"Modern armor, in this really, really old vault, like we fought *three months ago?*"

"And lots of it."

"Okay," Scope nodded. "I'm with Red. Let's get out of here. Before the bears come back for their porridge."

"Seconded," Bella said promptly.

"Agreed," Bulwark said. "This goes beyond any measure of uncertainty. If these are here, someone's been here recently. We're gone. Now."

"Wait," Red interrupted. "Don't panic. Panicking tends to get you dead a lot faster than thinking something through."

"That's easy for you to say!" Acrobat blurted.

"Uh...guys, I can't see but I still got my ears." Scope said, pointing a thumb behind her. "What just happened back there?"

They all turned. The light at the entrance was dimming. And the door was closing. Not quickly, but fast enough they'd never get there before it shut and sealed.

"How 'bout now? Panic good now?"

"Yeah," Red muttered. "Panic good now."

With a steely hiss, the door shut. Behind them, from the labyrinth, a warning bell began to peal. The room, once dimly lit by a few panels high in the ceiling, exploded with light.

Vickie froze a moment with despair. *Please please please don't let them be...* but her hands were already moving by themselves, grabbing six fresh spell-packets from the storage bin, and plugging them into the interface. And...

Yes! All six lovely, lively little dots on a blank screen, one she quickly overlaid with the last saved version of the map they were making as they made their way through the Catacombs. They were in a big space—the big space they'd been heading for when she got knocked out.

Now in a fever, she brought up the mechanicals. *Please let the headsets and mics—*

Nothing on the headsets, only static on the mics. Vickie hammered her fist down on her desk.

"Gather up," Bulwark ordered. "I want eyes everywhere."

They clustered together, their backs to Scope, and waited. They had each drawn their firearms and they let their eyes adjust to the sudden light. The ceiling had become one giant light source, so strong they could feel its rays beating down on them. It was as hot as movie lights. And through the heat, the klaxon blare of the alarm grew louder. And still they gathered, with hairpin triggers, watching through the glare, listening through the din, for an enemy.

"There!" Bella screamed.

As one, they turned and fired. Hurtling through the air towards them, something all metal wings and razor talons. A giant bird, steely death, and with a start Djinni recognized it. Its eyes were huge, out of all proportion to its head, even by raptor standards, giving it the look of a cartoon designed by a homicidal maniac.

"The hell? That's—"

"Krieg Hunter!" Bella yelled. "It's got an energy cannon!"

"It's real?" Djinni yelled back. "It was a goddamn hieroglyphic five minutes ago!"

The eagle hit the power suit above them as they all reflexively dove to the side. It bounced off, and headed back up for another dive. "That real enough?" Bella screeched.

Djinni shot a look towards the massive structure that loomed over them. Sure enough, a large bird-shaped hole was now where the bas-relief eagle had been.

"Real enough," he growled. "Bull, you can't shield us from that!"

"Affirmative," Bulwark said. "We need cover."

They dove as the Hunter descended on them, this time firing long steady blasts that reflected off the armor around them. They scattered again, diving behind power suits. Bella let out a yelp as she tackled Scope to the ground, the blasts just missing Scope's head. The smell of scorched hair and metal filled the air.

"We can't just keep dodging this!" Acrobat yelled. "Escape or fight?"

"Escape to *where?*" Djinni yelled back, dodging another blast. "Keep moving! Who's got Scope?"

"Here!" Bella barked, gripping Scope's arm and desperately leading her through a row of armor. "Harm's with us, too!"

Bulwark rose from cover and aimed his gun at the Hunter. He fired off three steady shots and cursed as they ricocheted off the robotic bird's massive hull.

"At least there's only one—" Acrobat began. Whatever he was

going to say was drowned in the massive crash of an entire row of suits going over. And through the hole in the ranks leapt—

"The wolves..." Djinni muttered. "Well, this just got festive."

Tactical mess.

Bulwark prided himself on being able to assess any situation. He glanced around him, mapping the scattered positions of his team. Bella and Harmony were on the run, guiding Scope as best they could from the deadly energy blasts of the Hunters. That's right, *Hunters,* plural. There were four of them. Djinni had started off in hot pursuit, but had flagged the attention of one of the wolves. Cursing, Red screamed something about the wolf's mother and led him away from the women. That left Acrobat, a damn weak reed to lean on—

Not mess. Disaster. Tactical disaster. Escape route cut off, no obvious plan of attack...

The guns were useless on Krieg armor, unless it was heated white-hot first. He wasn't carrying armor-piercing loads, which *might* have had some effect on the joints, provided he was a good enough shot, which he wasn't. He ran through their options at lightning speed. They didn't have any. He came to the conclusion that Djinni had been right. This had been ill-advised. The Djinni was right. He hated when that happened.

There were two raptors, circling and descending like missiles on Bella, Harmony and Scope. And two wolves, one off chasing the elusive Djinni. Which left...

The hair on his neck rose in instinctive reaction to a sound his caveman ancestors knew only too well.

It's growling at me. A robot wolf is growling at me.

Bulwark never laughed. He shook his head, suppressing an insane thought that this would the perfect time to start. The growl reverberated with an electronic tinnyness, like some demonic Speak-and-Spell.

Like all the Krieger constructs, the wolf was art deco, and very stylized; sleek, streamlined curves broken by angular joints. The ears were clearly functioning as antennae, but were far too solidly built to break off, and had been constructed as if the creature had laid them back in anger. The huge lenses of its eyes were protected by overhanging brows of metal that gave a look of rage. There were no nostrils, not even hints of them. But there certainly were teeth. Huge scythes of metal, ending in needle points. Functional; they didn't need to tear, only to pierce, and they could probably pierce anything.

It crouched. He heard a whine that was just barely on the edge of his hearing range. It ramped up, the tone going higher. The head swung from side to side a little; the thing was making sure of its target, which was, of course, him. Probably assessing him for weapons.

Bulwark watched him with a clinical level of detachment. Leaning forward, he spread his arms wide and braced himself. His shield flared into existence, defiantly lighting up the area around him, but paled by comparison to before, before...

Perhaps he had been relying too much on Harmony of late.

The wolf charged. Bulwark leaned into it. The wolf crashed into the shield at full force. There was a slight give, then it flexed out. The wolf flew back and fell into a line of armor suits, knocking them over like bowling pins, and landed unceremoniously on its back. Growling, it rolled and came back up on its feet, legs spread wide and back arched up defensively. It continued to growl, and Bull heard the whining again.

Without Harmony to bolster his defenses, he'd felt that. Not badly; just as if he'd been gut-punched. Still, take enough punches to the gut, and eventually your insides will begin to bleed.

Assessment: Stand-off. Advantage: Robot. I will eventually tire. He will not.

Bella had found a spot where some of the knocked-over suits had formed a kind of teepee. The young women squirmed into the space in the middle. The Hunters couldn't reach them in there—but they couldn't stick as much as a finger out without losing it. She took a moment to examine Scope, placing a hand calmly over the girl's eyes. No improvement, and through the damage, deeper and saturating everything in her, she was bombarded with Scope's rage. This was a woman with a desperate need to prove herself. It was her constant, the drive that shaped almost everything she was. She could always do *better*. She had made a mistake earlier, and had been saved by Acrobat. Ever since, Bella could feel an uncontrollable frustration within the girl, almost deafening at times. It wouldn't happen again, she would make sure of it. And here they were, in a situation where if she'd had her eyes, she could *fix* it. If.

Bella sighed. There was nothing to say to her. Scope was in

her own personal hell right now. All that Bella could do was keep trying to give her the most important thing back. Her eyes. Where was a jolt of angel juice when you needed it?

Three thousand miles away, that's where.

So what was left? They were trapped. She could tend to their wounds, but there wasn't much else she had offensively. The Hunters were machines, not humans, which meant her telepathy was worth squat against them. Hell.

That left Harmony. Shielded as she was, Bella could still read her body language. The girl was in her own bad place. Her eyes darted nervously to catch whatever glimpse she could of the diving Hunters. Her lips quivered, shaping a silent and nervous prayer, her hands clasped in fear.

All right. "Harmony, can you give me the same power-up you do for Bulwark? I might be able to do more for Scope."

Harmony shied away, refusing to even look at Bella. She crumpled up against some fallen armor. She was shivering.

Perfect.

Bruno had always heard that there was a perfect moment, when suddenly, you knew exactly what you were doing, what you needed to do, and how you were going to do it. A moment when everything went right and you were in the groove and everything else just fell away.

He'd never expected to feel a moment like that. Ever. He'd always been the not-quite, the never-was. Like all of Bull's squad. "Bulwark's Misfits." He'd heard enough of the insults, the jabs, the sneers, had been overwhelmed with them. Enough that he had taken the words to heart. Half-baked and halfway there and never quite good enough for a "real" team.

Which was why the sudden certainty, the feeling of That Moment, was all the more astonishing. He could see it, feel it, taste it. He knew what to do. He knew he could do it. All he had to do was take the steps through time, and to trust. Trust in his teammates, and in their leader, because while no one placed any faith in Bulwark's Misfits, no one discounted *Bulwark*. The training kicked in, the endless hours spent optimizing their strengths, compensating for weaknesses, weeks and months spent exploring their potential as a team. All it took was an idea, and they could see it through.

Acrobat skidded to a halt, and watched the wolf bounce again off Bull's shield. The big man fell to a knee and coughed blood, and after a moment, rose again. He wasn't beaten yet.

Acrobat grinned. Bull wasn't beaten yet.

Bella turned away from Harmony, who was a wreck. A liability, a civilian who needed protection, for all intents and purposes. Taking a deep breath, she laid her hands on Scope's shoulders.

All right then, let's work with what we've got. Do what she could for Scope with the limits of her own strength. She dug deep, and poured it out.

"Scope, the weakness of those birds is the mouth. They have to open up to fire the energy cannon. That's your best target."

She ignored the tunneling of her vision, and the fact that it was starting to gray out to give Scope everything she had. After all, if Scope couldn't pull this off, it wouldn't matter. They'd be toast. And the Goldman Catacombs would win again. Bella knew her limits, and she was approaching them fast. Vision went first, fading, so she just closed her eyes. She was already crammed into a nook in the armor and that was holding her up, so when her knees started to wobble, she stayed where she was. Just had to hold on, a little longer. A little longer...

"Hope that was enough," Bella croaked, as her legs gave out and she crashed to the ground. Still awake, but not by much. With numb, weak fingers she fumbled at her belt for a glucose pouch.

Dive.

Red flew forward, tumbling away with smooth execution. It was barely enough. A desperate slash of claws found a tentative grip on his shoulder and drew blood. Red vaulted left and made a break for it through a row of power suits. It bought him a moment as the wolf crashed into a line of suits, toppling them over. At least that was something. But he couldn't keep this up, and as far as he could see, he couldn't hurt this thing.

Run. RUN, IDIOT!

He needed a breather, a second to stop and think. Better yet, to watch. Everything had a weakness, damn it. The trick was to stay alive long enough to see it. Behind him, he heard the screech of powerful claws digging against indestructible steel as the wolf righted itself, and then a hard repetitive clanging as once again, the monstrosity propelled itself in hot pursuit of its quarry.

That would be me.

The wolf was closing the distance again. Red risked a look back, and immediately wished that he hadn't. He had seconds, *seconds*, before it tore into him...

Dodge...left. No! Feint left, DODGE RIGHT!

He flew up, caught the pommel of a power suit's sword and let his momentum swing him up and around. The wolf shot past him, letting out a surprised yelp as it fumbled to a desperate stop, its limbs flailing and rump skidding on the ground. Red stifled a gasp as he felt his shoulder give and managed a clumsy flip to land on his feet. Maybe he shouldn't have showboated out there on the practice course today in front of Victrix. Hubris. It always comes back to bite you in the ass.

It's bigger, stronger and faster, but it can't maneuver worth shit.

He watched the wolf lose control, skid, tumble over and roll to a stop.

Now hide, fool.

Red gritted his teeth, popped his shoulder back into place, and raced for cover in the dense forest of armor, shifting his weight to muffle his footsteps.

Behind him, the wolf came to his feet, and growled, the sound rumbling among the metal pillars of the armor suits. His quarry had vanished. He trotted back and found drops of blood. The baleful glare of his eyes intensified as they followed the trail, leading away through the rows of armor. He started off towards Red, knocking over power suits impatiently, arrogance and purpose in every step.

Personal Damage Assessment: Minimal. Minute points of exposure in shell.

Quarry Status: Badly injured. Losing blood.

Conclusion: Quarry termination imminent.

Scope drew her guns and peered out through the cracks and breaks in their cover. She could make out the Hunters now, to some extent. They had begun to synchronize their attacks, swooping from opposite sides and concentrating their fire.

Bella could hear it, but her own vision hadn't come back yet. One glucose pouch was empty and she sucked on a second desperately.

"You got a shot?" she asked.

"I don't know," Scope admitted. It killed her to say it, but she couldn't be less than honest.

"Take what you can get," Bella advised. "If I can get my legs under me again, I can maybe give you more eye. But damn it, Scope, watch the strain. Your eyes are dying now, all I can do is regenerate new tissue. It's delicate. If I do much more, if we push things too far, it might rupture the optic nerves. Permanently."

"Don't worry about me," Scope muttered. "Look to yourself. We might have to run soon, and you're no good to us if you can't even stand up." She turned to her right. "That goes for you too, Harm. Pull it together."

"And *what*?" Harmony demanded. "What do you want me to do?"

"Whatever you can," Scope answered. "Or we die, here and now."

She took a breath and dove for the opening. The Hunters were turning, and descending, and firing...

She trained both pistols on one and emptied her clips into it. She missed.

Vickie dove under the desk again, flashlight in her mouth. Then she swore, dropped the flashlight and fired off a spell for light—the same one that had caused all that trouble the first time. Now she could see.

Paranoia was damned useful. She'd built every bit of this rig with an eye to losing components and having to switch in a hurry. More expensive and tedious to do, but in a sitch like this one—

Ha. There and there and there. Two of the components were just her own version of surge protectors. Just because there was no evidence the Thulians used magic, no reason not to protect things she might use for other applications. She pulled the blackened, shattered crystals in their clear boxes, scrambled out from under the desk, and grabbed two more and a patch cable made of silver braided with horsehair and pure linen thread. She plugged those back in, and watched as the circuit came to life, magically. The third was easy; a real surge protector had tripped. She reset it. Back in business?

She could only hope. She killed the light spell and scrambled back into her seat. The trace pixels were still there. Taking a deep breath, she ran a full reset, with a prayer that this time the whole system would come back live.

✧   ✧   ✧

Bulwark was holding steady...for now. It was a classic standoff. The wolf couldn't reach him directly, but he couldn't do anything to the wolf, and the wolf was wearing him down. The laws of physics were harsh, and the force fields didn't cancel out blows, they only reflected the energy.

Some of it got transferred to him. Inside his bubble, he was taking a pounding. He couldn't keep this up forever.

His nose was starting to bleed. He wiped it off on the back of his sleeve. He felt as if he had gone six rounds in the ring with someone in a higher weight class than he was—someone with a grudge.

As the wolf rammed into his force fields again, raging at him from a mere four feet away, he caught sight of something moving above and behind his opponent.

Not the other—

No, it was Acrobat.

Careful not to *look* at the lad and give the wolf a second, unprotected target, he gave Acrobat an unobtrusive hand signal.

Acrobat grinned, pointed to the wolf, pointed to the armor and held up two fingers.

Oho...clever boy. Bulwark gave the slightest of nods, and braced himself for impact.

The wolf backed away and set up another charge. It launched itself at Bulwark, head down, changing its tactics to ramming. Maybe whatever AI was operating it had noticed that slashing and biting wasn't getting through, but bludgeoning was hurting him.

It barely noticed as Acrobat launched himself from the shadows and laid a mocking slap across its face.

"Tag, shithead! You're it!"

Hooting with laughter, Acrobat somersaulted away.

The wolf stopped its charge and watched the boy run off. He turned to look at Bulwark, then to Acrobat, and back again.

I really want to know what it's thinking, Bulwark thought. *Probably assessing the new threat. A much simpler one than me. If it was me...*

The wolf turned and charged after the boy.

...I'd go for the target without the force field.

Bulwark watched the wolf run off. He gathered himself, let his bubble fade away and sprinted towards the rows of older armor.

✧   ✧   ✧

Scope felt the hands on her back, grabbing fistfuls of her hair and shirt, yanking her unceremoniously back under the shelter of the fallen armor and flat on her ass. She snapped to her feet, her eyes furious and ready to give Harmony the worst beatdown of her life, when she saw the scorched earth at her feet. Harmony had pulled her out of the blast fire.

Saved again, and by Harm this time. How much do I suck?

"Are you *insane?*" Harmony screamed. "Death machines on the dive and you step out from cover?"

"This cover won't last forever, you dumb twit!" Scope shouted. "We need to take them out now!"

The Hunters answered with a heavy burst of fire. Their makeshift fortifications shuddered and groaned under the strain. One suit of armor twisted on its pivot and threatened to roll away, but fell back in a mad screech of grinding metal.

"They're starting to direct their fire," Scope muttered. "They're peeling away the layers."

"Oh God," Harmony whimpered, sinking back down and covering her face with her hands. "We're dead. We're *dead.*"

Geez, this thing is FAST.

Acrobat dodged another swipe, bouncing back and over the wolf's deadly descent. The wolf was quick and Acrobat was extremely mindful of how it used its entire body to generate speed. Still, it was chasing a target that could turn on a dime, could leap in impossible directions and safely land with barely a toehold. It was like trying to catch a bouncing ball.

But an unprotected bouncing ball. This was a target that was not sheltered behind an invisible force field. All the wolf had to do was catch it.

God only knew what was making the calculations in there. What Acrobat knew was that he had to make the equation come out in favor of him being the tasty one. Which meant . . .

Slow down. He had to slow down. Crazy as that sounded, this would all be for nothing if the wolf switched targets again.

Keep in close, within reach. Stay tasty. Stay tasty.

He felt a shiver as he leapt between outstretched claws in midswing, and shock as he felt the tag, one sharp claw grazing his ribs. He cried out as he watched a spray of blood droplets spatter away, following the track of the claw.

He landed awkwardly, one leg buckling as his hands rushed to survey the damage. Painful, but a graze.

Move!

He vaulted backwards, barely avoiding another mad swipe, pushed off the ground with his hands and rolled away. He leapt up again, and was on the run, his breathing now labored and sharp with fear.

Okay...maybe stay just a bit out of reach.

He risked a quick look over his shoulder. The wolf was gaining. Of course it was. And where was Bulwark? Surely he had bought the man enough time...

He cursed as he dove to the left away from another pounce. He righted himself and ran on.

...enough time to get set up.

And then, in the distance, he saw it. Rising high with a gorgeous arc, ablaze with a brilliant warmth of amber and screaming its beautiful head off...Bull's flare. It sputtered at the apex, up near the very top of the domed ceiling, then cooled and burned away.

Acrobat turned and raced to Bull's position. He grinned again, his hand pressed to his wound. He couldn't remember the last time he had had so much fun.

...oh...God...

The glucose wasn't working nearly fast enough.

But that wasn't nearly as crucial as what this strain was doing to Scope's eyes. Too much, too soon, and the damage could be permanent—and then what would Scope do? Her metapower *was* her eyes.

But it was Scope's decision. Not Bella's. No matter how strongly Bella felt that this was a catastrophically bad idea, it was still Scope's decision. If she had learned anything from the Seraphym, it was that you didn't argue with informed Free Will.

Bella sucked down another glucose shot, then decided to make a bad Free Will decision of her own. She grabbed an Echo stimulant patch (prominently labeled as "Emergency Use Only") and slapped it on the side of her neck. She'd never used one before.

As the drug hit her system, she privately vowed she was never, ever going to use one again. It felt like being hit with a semi-load of Cafeebucks double espressos made with caffeine water. Her heart sounded like a Buddy Rich solo.

Well, if you can't get angel juice in an emergency...

She clamped her hand on Scope's neck and poured everything she had into the healing, seeing the neural nets and the scorched areas of the retina that needed fixing with hyperclarity, and cursing that her power couldn't make things work faster.

She was so focused that she had no idea she was about to run short. Until about a microsecond before she passed out cold.

...uh oh... She felt her knees just starting to buckle. Then lights out.

"What did you do?" Harmony screamed. "What just happened?"

Scope grunted an answer, as she caught Bella and eased her to the floor.

"She's done," she muttered. "Took everything out of her."

Scope turned and glared at Harmony.

"Your turn," she said.

"Me? What do you want *me* to do?"

"Get her up," Scope said. "C'mon, juice her. I'll bet she can turn some of that healing stuff on herself with a boost."

"Oh...I don't know about that...I don't think it works like that. She's out! I might have, before—"

"Well, then *why didn't you?*" Scope demanded, furiously.

Harmony put her back against the machine, shrinking away from Scope's rage. "What do you want from me? I'm not like you! I'm not...*I'm not cut out for this!* I got scared, all right? I panicked! I'm still panicking! I'm all sorts of panic right now! Call me Panic Girl! Call me—"

Scope leaned forward and slapped Harmony. Hard.

"Ow! What the hell are you...?"

"Stop it, Harm. Take a breath. Remember how you were at the beginning? Remember why Bull gave you your callsign?"

"Be-because I was...I was kinda...excitable."

"You were batshit psycho, yeah. But we helped you, didn't we?"

"Yes," Harmony said in a whisper.

"You learned to bring it down, to ease it out, to breathe. Harm, *breathe.*"

Harmony took a breath.

"Now exhale."

Harmony exhaled.

"Again."

Harmony took a few long breaths and then let out a long, wavering sigh. Her lips began to tremble. She looked up at Scope with terrified eyes.

"I don't know what to do," she said softly.

"Help me," Scope replied, with a firm conviction that she wasn't sure she actually felt. "Juice me up. We need to take these bastards down and get back to Bull."

Harmony raised her hand and tentatively laid it upon Scope's shoulder. She gripped hard, then stopped, her eyes going wide.

"But what if Bella was right?" she asked, her voice shaking. "What if this messes you up for good?"

Scope didn't answer. It was possible. Her eyes were on fire. She could feel the light hitting her retinas like daggers. Bella wasn't kidding—her eyes were dying. She gritted her teeth, and made her choice.

"Do it."

If there was one thing Bulwark was *really* good at, it was waiting. Hundreds of stakeouts, countless patrols, shifts on guard duty and an overly stalwart sense of responsibility lent itself well to patience. But this time, even he had to admit he was feeling a bit...itchy.

He knelt motionless between the still rows of the old armor, his head back, his eyes steady on the highest point of a dislodged power suit, upturned by the battle, its sword angled up and locked in place. He glanced up once, as his flare died away. In the distance, he heard the Hunters descend again and again on the ladies. He heard their shots ring out, he heard the groan of metal shifting on metal, but nothing else. The shots continued. The women, at least one of them, must still be up.

The noise from Djinni's quarter had subsided. Red had somehow defeated his foe, or had been taken down himself. Either way, Bull kept a sharp ear trained in that direction. It wouldn't do to be taken by surprise from behind, especially now, with so much at stake.

That was, perhaps, why he felt a twinge of apprehension. He wouldn't be much help to anyone without taking out his current foe. And to do that, he had to rely on Acrobat.

Bruno was your typical Misfit. Here was someone with enormous potential, but with so many self-imposed limitations that active fieldwork was, at the time of his enlistment, completely out of the question. Still, a meta was a meta. Better to segregate them, keep tabs on them, keep them on the roster and out of trouble. They could hardly turn him away. The solution? As usual, the Misfit was sent to Bulwark.

Let Bull make 'em or break 'em.

Why Bull?

It'll keep him busy and out of our hair.

The few higher-ups that actually valued Bulwark as a capable officer, as a remarkably successful trainer, always wondered why he took such contemptuous and unremarkable assignments with little argument. When asked, he told them, but they never understood.

Bulwark didn't believe in Misfits. He believed that when you gave someone a challenge, they could rise to it. He believed that in their hearts, they wanted to.

"Rise up. They can break your bones, but only you can break your spirit."

He said it often; to his recruits and even, in the quiet hours of the morning, to himself. Why walk when you could run? Why run when you could fly? How will you ever know, until you test yourself?

As Acrobat flew into view, somersaulting over the toppled armor and down past Bulwark, Bull saw the crazed smile of sheer confidence flash across Bruno's face. Acrobat, the one-time loser and presumed lifelong member of the Misfits, had just graduated at the top of his class.

And behind him, in deadly pursuit, the monstrous wolf followed.

It leapt over the armor at full speed, determined not to let this silly, bouncing man escape. Bulwark watched it descend and rose quickly to his feet, his arms again wide, and willed his force field to flare up. Fast.

Time seemed to slow down, and Bull kept his breathing steady as he locked eyes with the roaring beast. He bounced lightly on the balls of his feet, his shield bobbing merrily with him, until just before contact.

Most of the time, Bulwark was a quiet man. Even so, his rumbling voice carried a strong undercurrent of force, as if anything above a whisper would tear down the walls around him. It was rare to hear him bark an order, rarer still to hear him shout, and to hear him scream? That was unheard of. But when he did, it was like the snap of a thunderous whip, a massive blow to the head, the crash of lightning landing at your feet. It was his *authority*, and it was a force of nature.

Acrobat had landed softly behind Bulwark, had grinned as he saw the shield light up around him, and turning...

...he fell back, in shock and awe, as he witnessed his mentor's fury.

Bulwark bore down, leaned into the impact, and screamed his rage and determination. The shield, flashing in strength and a burst of pure light, almost holy in its intensity, met the descending wolf. The wolf was not expecting this. Not that there was anything it could have done to stop itself, short of growing wings.

It hit the edge of the field, and exploded backwards, impaling itself with a deafening crack upon the tip of the fallen power suit's sword. It thrashed wildly, trying to free itself, emitting sparks and a horrible stench of burning insulation and plastics.

Acrobat stared as the wolf shuddered once, convulsively, then froze in its final contorted position. He blinked, and a wild, uncontrollable laugh erupted from his mouth. He leapt to his feet, his arms pumping high into the air as he hooted and hollered in triumph.

He turned to Bulwark, fully prepared to deliver a victory hug to the giant man.

"Bull! That was *amazing!* You were amazing! You were..."

He stopped. Bulwark was doubled over, his right arm bent at an angle that was horribly wrong. Bull grunted something unintelligible, and slowly dropped to the floor.

"*Bull!*" Acrobat yelled, scrambling to his commander's side. "Bull, what...?"

"Get to the others," Bulwark muttered, painfully turning onto his back. "They're going to need you."

"Not a chance, old man. *Semper fi.* We don't leave anyone behind, remember?"

"Don't be an idiot, boy. Arm's broken, and that feeling in my gut's telling me there's probably a lot of internal damage. I think my ligaments might have snapped too. Come back for me, get to the girls."

"Shut up," Acrobat replied, bending down and pulling Bull's good arm over his neck. "I've seen enough slasher movies, I know what happens if I leave you behind. Krieger zombies will show up and eat you or something. Get up. Giving up's for ordinary people. We aren't, and we don't got that luxury. Right?"

"Be realistic," Bull coughed harshly. "I can't help in this state, all I can do is give you another target you have to protect."

"Rise up," Acrobat said with a grin. "They can break your bones, but only you can break your spirit."

"Oh sure, throw *that* in my face now..."

Bulwark grunted as he sat up and, with Acrobat's help, struggled awkwardly to his feet. In the distance, they saw the Hunters raining deadly blasts down on some target they couldn't see for the intervening metal monsters.

"Let's go," Bulwark said. "Hop to."

"Yes, sir," Acrobat replied.

The wolf was confused. It had lost sight of the red man. Well, most of him. The telltale trail of blood had stopped between the rows of armor, ending in a heap of fabric. A hastily discarded combat suit and a long, red scarf. Millions of calculations passed through its systems. Probabilities. Maps of the storage facility. Game theory.

Scenario #1: Manifestation of metahuman ability—teleportation. Processing...

Conclusion: Improbable. Spontaneous manifestation of teleportation always results in inaccurate initial jumps. If already extant, quarry's appreciated limitations in speed and agility, while superhuman, would have necessitated earlier use of said ability in evasive efforts.

Scenario #2: Manifestation of changeling ability—mass and size manipulation.

Processing...

Conclusion: Improbable. Current metahuman registry lists three metahumans with mass/density/size-altering abilities. None can exceed size limits greater than a factor of two without severe compromise to internal organs, a factor of three without fatality.

Scenario #3: Guile.

Processing...

Conclusion: Probable. Quarry exhibits cunning and ingenuity, as well as agility. Shedding of garments may indicate a stratagem to confuse one's predator.

Transmitting data.

Course of action: Wait. Monitor. Quarry is now uncovered and vulnerable, targeting systems adjusted accordingly.

And from his ambush point, Red "watched" the wolf. Stripped, every cell of his skin fed him a constant stream of information from his surroundings. His fingertips, extended into hard, curved hooks, gripped the back of a power suit. He hung there, motion-less, surveying the minute movements of the wolf, just feet away on the other side of the armor. His skin had cooled to the exact temperature of the armor. Infrared sensors were not going to help the wolf now.

Red felt the crackle of electricity coursing through the mechani-cal predator, the echoes of tiny gears as its head swayed to and fro, the cooling of his blood on the robot's claws...

It wasn't enough. He had bought himself a moment to breathe, to think, but it wasn't enough. Even at rest, he sensed the power in the beast, the raw torque in its limbs and the snap of its jaw. All he had was somewhat mutable flesh, bone, and a meat-space brain. He needed something more. He needed a closer look.

More. Listen. Look. Center in on the damn thing...

It wasn't easy, focusing on a nonliving creature around the cold barrier of a steel statue. Slowly, Red felt for the echoes, the signals, and defined the wolf. It appeared a bit beaten up and battered. A few dents and scratches here and there. Of course, it *had* crashed into a few power suits during the chase, and at full gallop. What happens when indestructible things collide? Something's gotta give. And something had.

There.

It wasn't the largest opening, but as far as he could sense, it was the biggest he was going to get. On the back, at the nape of the neck, the wolf was...well, he was *bleeding.* Bleeding energy. A chink in the armor, enough to expose something within, something vulnerable enough to shed flashes of heat and electricity. Was it enough? Was there enough of a breach to gain the advantage?

In answer, a spark fizzled through the exposed crack and popped with a guilty burst.

Contact.

Red relaxed his body, took a breath, vaulted high over the power suit and crashed down onto the wolf's back. His legs gripped the curved sides of the torso and locked on as he leaned forward and threw his arms around the wolf's neck. He was anchored.

The wolf went wild. Its head reared back, jaws snapping in a futile attempt to ensnare its unwanted rider, but to no avail. The armored neck simply did not have the flexibility to allow such a maneuver. In desperation it began a series of jumps and hops, but Red held fast. It paused for the briefest of moments, growling, and threw itself on its back and began to roll about. Red grunted as the sudden impact almost knocked the wind out of him. He gritted his teeth, and willed the armor to come, to grow. It was sporadic, and very ugly, but he was soon covered in layers upon layers of skin, alternating between dense and chitinous to pliable and spongy. It took the brunt of the attacks, and the wolf roared in frustration. But it didn't stop moving. Red held on, his eyes locked on the tear in the wolf's neck.

Finally, the wolf gave up and came to a dead stop. It was pondering its options.

That's enough. Go time.

He released his arms from the wolf's body and reared back. His hands, held aloft to strike, spread wide as the claws erupted from his fingertips. He drove them downward, angling them sharply to drive into the wound and up the wolf's neck and into its brain. Red gasped as he felt his claws snap apart upon entry. He had overestimated the opening. Secondary armor and the jagged tear in the hull had blocked the killing stroke.

And now, the wolf was off again, leaping, spinning, frantically trying to buck him off. Red screamed as the bones of his fingers, now anchored in the wolf's neck, crunched and shattered. His breathing grew quick and shallow as he forced himself to endure, to keep pressure with his legs as his trapped hands held him fast to the wolf's back. Fighting off the vertigo, grunting through the pain, he let his broken fingers feel for cracks, for holes, for any-thing, any way through to the vulnerable brain. Nerve endings screamed for relief as he flexed the muscles of his arms, pulling at torn and broken ligaments in his fingers, in futile attempts to worm their way deeper through a mess of wire and torn metal and components he didn't even have a name for. He stared in disbelief as the middle finger on his right hand flexed and bent in a shape no finger should, and popped out to dangle free, like some grotesque horror movie prop. He was in danger of losing his grip. But he had to try, he had to find an opening...

And there, in spite of the pain, he heard himself erupt with a booming laugh as he felt the tip of a pinky finger inch its way through the armor and into the mesh of wires lining the wolf's spine. He dug in hard, thrust up the wolf's back and willed the pinky claw to heal, to grow and shoot up the inner tunnel of the neck.

He felt a moment of victory. Just a moment. The razor tip of the claw found its mark and shot through the jumble of nerves tethering the CPU to the body. There was a terrific flash, a sudden squeal and hiss of release as the wolf's brain lost function, lost its connection, and the enormous electrical potential housed in the head discharged through its body, through Red, and the combatants fell to the ground together, lifeless.

Scope took a stance as the Hunters went to the top of their arcs. They *had* to keep flying like real birds, it seemed; something of a design flaw, since it meant they had a limited time for a kill-sweep on a dive before having to climb again. This would have been a piece of cake if she'd had good eyes. It would have been ridiculously easy, in fact, since the Hunters had to present the target to her before *they* could open fire. She had her guns trained in opposite directions, ready to make the shots.

The Hunters opened their mouths.

It felt as if someone was throwing sand into her eyes. All she could see through the fog and the pain were the open mouths. She couldn't see the relatively tiny muzzle of the energy gun.

Damn it! She dove for cover just before they opened up in her.

Scope screamed. "No good, vision's better, but not enough for that shot."

"Well, what *can* you hit?" Harmony shrieked.

She couldn't *see*, damn it! How could she hit something if she couldn't see it?

...and how could *they?*

Their eyes were big, huge in proportion to their heads. Probably had several kinds of sensors packed in there. If she took those out...

By now she could tell where the Hunters were in their attack pattern by the timing and the noise. They were climbing again.

She threw herself out of cover, ignoring the harsh stabbing pain in her retinas, her guns blazing away at the glowing red eyes just as they turned into their dives.

As it always did when she was doing this sort of a shot, time slowed for her. Three bullets—one eye out on the right-side Hunter. Two more—the corresponding eye on the left-side Hunter. Their heads jerked around, bringing their other eyes around to face her. One more bullet each, and the heads were dark, the Hunters were blinded. She rolled back into cover as the birds tried to pull up, the wings making screaming metallic sounds under the strain. But it was too late, far too late. Gravity is an unforgiving mistress. The birds slammed into each other in midair, then fell in a tangle of mangled metal, thrashing as they did so.

Sounds came in on one channel. Not good sounds, and all in the distance. No telemetry or feeds on anyone.

Vickie didn't even have time to think of an easy way to signal she was back online. Not with several kinds of nasty bearing down on her team, from the sound of it, and her boards showing only one signal in, and no signal out.

And then, just as suddenly, before she could say or do anything, it seemed to be over. There was no sound at all.

Red's litle dot wasn't moving.

She started to type in commands, and—

Wait. Wait. She had signal out on *him*. And suddenly, camera too. A stunning view of a tangle of metal that he seemed to be hugging.

Of course she had him live. Of all of them, it would have to be *him*. Maybe it was the fact that he had grown skin over his mic, earpiece and camera that had protected them. She screamed into the mic. "Red! *Red!* Wake up, you miserable rat-bastard S.O.B.! Wake *up,* you're the only one I can talk to! If you're dead I swear to Hades I will resurrect you so I can kill you all over again! Wake *up!*" She unloaded all the invective she knew in the eight languages she was fluent in. The Russian was particularly choice. Russians really knew how to cuss. If only he could appreciate it.

And then... *"Pri tom, shto rot tseluyu tvoyu mat?"*

She froze. Her heart leapt. "You're *alive!* Oh, thank the gods, Red! You're the only one I have feed on, that surge blew out half my system. Are you all right?"

"I've been better," came the pained reply. "I feel like I've been stripped naked, had my finger bones broken and been electrocuted for good measure. Oh wait, I have..."

She briefly cursed in Hungarian. "I don't heal; damn it, Red, I'm sorry. There's some stimulant patches in a belt... Wait, you're naked?"

"Focus, Overwatch. How are the others?"

"Moving. That's all I can tell. I haven't gotten sound or camera feed or telltales back on them yet, and I'm afraid if I reboot again I'll lose you too. I have the feeling that if you hadn't skinned over your camera button I wouldn't have that either."

Red reached over, picked up his discarded scarf, and pulled himself up. "It's quiet," he said. "Fighting must have stopped. Are they *all* moving?"

"Acrobat and Bull are together, moving slowly. Harmony, Scope and Bella are together and moving faster. They're about two hundred yards left of you." She paused as his camera feed and dot showed him waddling off. "Your o*ther* left."

"Cut me some slack," he muttered. "I got a little fried. Only reason I'm still alive is about fifty pounds of extra skin insulation. My brain's still waking up."

She blinked. The writer in the back of her mind wanted to ask him several dozen questions about how that all worked. She clamped her teeth shut on those questions. "If you keep going in a straight line you'll meet them about the same time as they meet each other. You might think about finding pants, or you'll make Harm's head explode."

"No worries; I'm hardly my usual svelte self at the moment. It'd take a lot of exploration to even *find* Big Red right now."

"Right. I'll just call you 'Ken.'" A strange whining sound seemed to be coming from the area just past the others. "What's that sound?"

Red stopped, and realized he had been squinting. The fight had apparently singed most of the skin on his face. He was, so it seemed, without most of his eyelids. He followed the sound and looked up. He gasped as the harsh light of the room hit his eyes.

The camera view flared with bright light. He must have planted the button cam right in the middle of his forehead when he skinned it over. "What happened? What's going on?" she asked, in renewed panic.

"Sorry," he apologized. "Light caught me off-guard. I think..."

He stopped, as a heavy rumbling noise grew in the distance.

"Aw hell..." he sighed. "That can't be good."

"You took the words right out of my mouth."

Red broke into a run, and nearly tripped over himself. His impromptu armor of skin and tissue hung awkwardly, interrupting his stride and playing havoc with his sense of balance. He swore as he was forced to stop and will the excess flesh away.

"What's wrong?" Vickie asked, "Are you okay? Did you break something?"

"Just give me a moment," Red snarled. "There's a little too much of me right now, and..."

He doubled over, surrounded by steaming piles of his own discarded skin, and retched.

"Those were puking sounds!" Vickie said. "You're puking! What is it? Poison? Nerve gas?"

Red steadied his breath, and wiped at his mouth. "No, I just... I've just never gotten used to the smell of myself after...doing that."

The camera caught a few frames of the discarded skin and her mouth dropped open. It was one thing to know about his ability in the abstract, quite another to get such a graphic demonstration. "Uh...yeah," was all she could manage. "I can't think of anything to help," she finally said, humbly.

"Just another moment," he repeated, wrapping the scarf around his head. "I'm raw at the moment, too tired for anything fancy, the skin'll heal on its own."

"If you know where you left your stuff, there's glucose pills in the Echo belt pouch, and a stimulant patch."

"Forget 'em, the others might need—"

And right on cue, there came the sound of gunfire, terrible crashing sounds, and the screams of his teammates.

Red ran a hand quickly over his scarf. It was secure. He broke into a run and flew over anything in his way, over fallen pieces of armor and debris from the battle. He leapt over the fallen Hunters, a smoky and entwined mess of metal, noting the destroyed orbs that served as their eyes. He filed that away for future reference. Everything had a weakness. Everything.

"I want to be you," Vic whispered mournfully, engrossed in the incredible first-person view of a Le Parkour master's headlong rush across impossible obstacles, and painfully aware *she* would never move like that again. She wasn't even aware she had said it aloud. "Oh, I wish I was you."

"You'd be the first," Red muttered. "You'd be the..."

He skidded to a halt, and screamed.

"Oh...oh...*fuck!*"

Vickie gasped as she took in what he was seeing. It was so beyond not good that there weren't any words for how bad it was. Her mind went around in circles, frantically looking through her arsenal for an answer. The last time she'd been faced with one of these things it had been up close and personal, yes, but an angel and an entire team of Atlanta SWAT had come to her rescue. The Seraphym was nowhere around, and SWAT was a long way away. And her team, oh God, her team looked so *broken*. They huddled together around Bulwark, under a dim and fluctuating force field, and towering over them, magnificent in the harsh light of the vault, was a Death Sphere.

The Sphere hovered and hummed in place, its arms thrashing wildly. Two of them ended in broken stumps, crackling wildly with exposed energy.

The cameras, Vickie thought wildly. *Scope shot out the cameras! Oh, good girl!*

But it hadn't been enough. The Sphere was "feeling" about, bringing its tentacles down in mighty blows. Armor flew through the air, until finally a tentacle bounced off Bulwark's shield. The Sphere paused, then brought all its remaining arms down, *down*, and struck to destroy the huddled group of metas.

Bulwark stood, defiant, but even from Red's distant vantage point, Vickie could tell he was hurt. Harmony, wrapped frantically around him, screamed and recoiled from every blow, her cries mingled with pain and terror. Bella was tending to Scope, who lay motionless, blood flowing freely from her eyes. Acrobat bounced in agitation, seemingly trapped beneath the very shield that was saving his life.

How the hell did they ever get a Death Sphere down here in the first place? Vickie wondered. *Where did they hide it?*

"The dome," Red growled. "It came from the dome...the Hunters and wolves were just the advance sentries. This is the vault's real guardian. Overwatch! We need..."

"What?" Vickie screamed.

"I have no frickin' clue!!" Red screamed back.

"It's in the air, I can't reach it with magic! I don't have..."

"Magic again?" Red snarled. "Remember the last time you used your magic?"

"Well, what would you suggest?" Vickie shouted, now as angry as she was terrified. "I can't short out its systems, I don't know what they are! I can't hack it, I don't have a port or a wireless link to it! Echo's got no backup for you down there! Magic is all I've got—"

Then the answer came to her in a burst of icy clarity. It was time. Time to call in that favor; one she had earned so long ago she had almost forgotten it, a favor from another time, another place . . . another Vickie. A favor, strangely enough, born of simple friendship. Back then, she'd never thought she'd ever have reason to use it.

"Red," she said, her voice surprisingly calm and steady. "Please hold very still. I need your skin contact on the ground."

"For what?"

"You need to be my channel. I'm calling an Earth elemental."

"You need me to what and huh?"

"I need you to hold that position, and be *very* still! I'm going to . . ."

Red bolted upright. "Are you *completely out of your mind?* Do you know how unstable an elemental summoning is? Once you lose control, you can't get it back!"

And just how the hell does he know THAT?

"Can you take on that thing alone?" she demanded harshly.

He didn't answer. In the distance, they watched as a half-dozen tentacles crashed down on the failing shield. Harmony fell away from Bulwark as he dropped to one knee. She collapsed on the floor, and didn't move.

"We don't have time for this," Vickie said, and for a brief moment she felt that old Vickie come alive. The soldier. The *commander.* "Now shut the hell up and plant your hand on the floor!"

Red uttered a few choice oaths, and slammed his palms down on the ground.

"*Hold still.*" Most spells were complicated. This one . . . wasn't. As simple as the friendship that bound her and the elemental she affectionately called "Herbert."

She took a deep, deep breath, reached inside for the memory. Pulled energy from the Earth Her Mother, channeled that same energy *through* the Earth Her Mother to the Djinni, and called one of Her Children. "*Herbert, honey, Bad Things have happened. I need help, I need you, please.*" Never forget the "please." It was the difference between her and . . . well, other people, who would try to coerce the elemental kind.

Mom would murder me if I even thought about coercing an elemental. There was always, always that little voice in the back of her head commenting on everything. But she wasn't listening right now. Because now—

She saw the camera view shuddering as the ground shook, as if with an earthquake. Well, there was an earthquake going on, a very local one. Red's head, and view, snapped to the right as an avalanche of small stones—relatively small, compared to what was emerging—cascaded down the rock face of the vault, bouncing off the topped armor there. With agonizing slowness, something roughly the shape of a man separated itself from the wall, leaving behind the Herbert-shaped hole that was almost the height of the interior of the vault. The head turned blindly in Red's direction, and the creature made a sound like the earth groaning an unintelligible question.

"Pull off your earpiece! Point it at him!"

For once, Red didn't argue. The camera showed his hand shoving something in the direction of the elemental.

"There!" Vickie screamed through the earphone, amplifying it with magic. "Herb, there! They hurt Mother to make monsters! They hurt Vickie! They hurt my friends!" One thing that she *could* do with her magic against that sphere—she could light it up like a Christmas decoration for Herb. And she did.

The elemental turned its shapeless head towards the Death Sphere, and made another sound. If you could describe the sound of a volcano as "angry," this was that sound.

"Get it, Herb! Get it!" Vickie screamed.

It strode across the expanse of floor, each step crunching into armor and flattening it. Vickie had not seen the Mountain at work, but she had the feeling it had looked a lot like this. With another roar, Herb wrapped his stony arms around the Sphere, and the fight was on.

"Hold on! Pull off its arms! Hurt it!"

The Sphere didn't need cameras now; the target was grappling with it. The energy cannons on that side whined as they charged up, and blasts of actinic light pounded the elemental's torso and legs. Huge chunks blasted free, pulverized into powder that filled the air, along with the smoke of overheated rock.

In moments, Herb was half himself.

The elemental was made of sterner stuff than the Kriegs could ever have anticipated, though; as the cannon powered down to recharge, he reached into the floor at his feet and pulled up huge slabs of the marble flooring and the ground underneath it to replenish himself. In moments, he was back to his original bulk.

He tried to rip a tentacle out, and couldn't, tried again and made a whining, frustrated sound.

"Herb!" Vickie shouted, realizing the Krieg metal was too strong. "Herb, get a pointy thing! Hit it with the pointy thing!"

The head shape swiveled ponderously; Vickie lit up one of the giant "swords" from the armor lying near Red—one with an arm still attached. Herb didn't go after the sword, however. He reached down, picked up an entire suit of armor near his feet and, using the whole suit like the hilt of a tool, began to hack away at the tentacle.

"Good boy! That's right! Good boy! Keep hitting!"

The tentacle separated with a shriek of hot metal. Herb tossed it aside and grabbed another. Whatever was in charge of the Sphere registered the fact that it was in trouble; the Sphere tried to escape. Herb wasn't having any.

"Hold onto it!" Vickie screamed. "Hit it! Hit it!"

With dogged determination, Herb held onto two tentacles in one hand, as the rest frantically retracted into the body of the ship. He shifted his attentions to the Sphere itself, hacking at it with the armor and sword with all the enthusiasm of Sweeney Todd making meat pies.

Not even a Death Sphere could hold up under a battering like that. The Sphere dented, dented more, then started to split. Sparks showered out of it, and it spun on the tethered ends of its tentacles. Herb kept hacking.

Vickie expected the thing to explode. It didn't. It just emitted a metallic scream and dropped to the floor. Herb stood there for a moment, as if waiting for it to come back to life.

When it didn't—he flung the battered and unrecognizable armor aside, and clapped his hands gleefully, pebbles showering down from each smack. The pebbles bounced off Bulwark's weakening shield.

"Herb!" Vickie called. "Careful! You'll hurt—"

Herb's head swiveled again, and he caught sight of the team, still huddling together, still protected by Bull's force field. More enemies! He wouldn't let his friend down. Herbert was strong! Herbert never failed Vickie! Caught in the rush of battle, he roared and picked up another suit of armor. Brandishing it, he headed for the half dome of the shield.

"No!" Red screamed, his voice lost in the cacophony of Herb's charge. The elemental reared back, and brought his weapon down. The sword caught the shield on a strange angle, and Herbert uttered a confused rumbling yelp as it bounced awkwardly off to the side. And beneath him, Red watched as Bulwark staggered to his feet, one arm outstretched in defiance, his other arm hanging uselessly at his side. And Red was struck with a moment of horror, as Bull's legs shook and buckled beneath him.

Bull crumpled, and fell.

"*This!*" Red roared, again in a dead sprint towards the stone behemoth. "*This is what magic gets you!*"

Herb glanced up, watched Red tumble towards him, and then looked down again. The shield was tough. He knew he was tougher. He could beat it.

"*No!*" Red screamed as he flew over more armor. "*Goddamn...*"

Herb raised his weapon again.

"*...stinking...*"

Herb's face shifted, grimaced, as he leaned back for the killing blow.

"*...MAGIC!*"

Red hurled the earpiece at the elemental in a futile gesture—maybe hoping to attract its attention. But this was exactly what Vickie wanted. She shoved her own magic energy into it, powering it with magic instead of Red's body heat and kinetic energy.

"*HERB!*" she shrieked, using magic to multiply the sound of her voice a hundredfold, and letting her fear and hysteria come through. "*NO! FRIENDS! DO NOT TOUCH!*"

The earpiece fell to the ground, rolling end over end, and came to a stop at Herb's feet.

It was the sound of a friend that stopped him. His friend. His only friend. Through the ages, countless attempts had been made to harness the raw power of elementals. They had been chained, both literally and figuratively, bent and broken and forced to do the will of their masters. But never for long. The consensus after far too many documented cases of mages destroyed by their futile efforts, driven by their lust for power, was that elemental control was simply impossible for any appreciable length of time. It never occurred to any of them to befriend one. At least, not until Vickie gave it a try.

The behemoth paused, tilting its head towards the tiny device on the floor.

"No hurt. Friends to Vickie. Friends to Herb. Friends to Mother." Her voice broke for a moment on a strangled sob of relief that he was listening. She spoke soothingly, one old friend to another; Earth elementals were slow to anger and slow to cool. When enraged, they reverted to the temper and understanding of a four-year-old. "Calm down, baby. It's okay now, you saved Vickie's friends. They'll want to be your friends now, too."

The creature made an inquiring sound. Herbert had always been one of the easier Earth elementals to work with. He was definitely quicker on the uptake than most. As she watched him, she could tell when the anger petered out and his intelligence started to come back.

"My friends came here to find out what the Bad People were doing, and the Bad People sent metal monsters to hurt them. They're hurt bad. I couldn't help them. That's why I called you, sweetie. You did a great job."

She cleared her throat. "Bulwark? Drop the shield? Say hi to Herb? He's interpreting the shield as offensive."

"No!" Red shouted. But the shield came down; Bella looked up fearlessly—or maybe at this point she was just so far beyond fear it didn't matter.

"Hi, Herb, I'd come shake whatever you call a hand, but I have badly hurt people here. Thanks for saving us," she said, and went back to tending Scope, Harmony, and Bulwark, dividing her attentions among all three of them.

Herb knelt clumsily down beside them, and made an interrogative rumble. And then, one that sounded hurt and sad.

Vickie heaved a sigh of relief. She knew Herb, he *was* sad. He was a lot like Chug; he hated it when anything living was hurt.

"Give me the sitch," Djinni said, landing next to Bella.

"Harm's out cold," Bella replied as she checked Bulwark's broken arm. "She's got some bad bruises. She was probably taking some of the beating while amping Bull. Scope's got severe eye trauma and Bull's trying to pretend he's invulnerable, but he's not quite pulp." She gave Red a quick glance. Rolling her eyes, she pulled off her jacket and threw it at him. "Put that away. You're scaring the children."

Red grunted his thanks and tied the jacket around his waist. "And how you doin', Bruno?"

Acrobat stood in shock, no longer bouncing in agitation. Red's question took a moment to register, but when it did he looked down at his decimated team, then up at the grinning stone elemental. He shot Red a crazed look.

"I'm freaking out, man! What do you think *I'm doing?"*

Herb rumbled. Somehow it sounded...comforting? Or at least like an attempt to comfort.

Acrobat stared up at Herb, numb, and shook his head.

"Not helping, dude, but thanks."

"Herb is trying to tell you he understands." Vickie's voice came distorted out of the earpiece lying on the floor next to Bella. "Someday I'll tell you some stories."

Herb made another noise.

"He wants to know how you think you're getting out?"

"Good question," Djinni said. "Back the way we came? We could pick up Harm, Scope and..." He paused to speculate the weight of Bulwark's massive frame. "Yeah, good question."

"Path behind you should be clear," Vickie suggested. "I could lead an Echo rescue team to you."

"We don't have time for that," Bella interrupted. "Harm might be okay, she *might* be, but Bull and Scope need more than I can do for them. I'm talking full-on ICUs and med staff, and they need them now!"

"Damn it," Red muttered. "There's no way out of this place fast enough. No safe way, in any case..."

The relative silence was shattered by the bellow of five or six old-fashioned klaxons. A glaring light at the top of the room was replaced with flashes of red.

"Oh, come on!" Red screamed, coming to his feet, his hands clenched in fury.

The earpiece spluttered with curses.

"What?" Acrobat yelled. *"What is that?"*

"Goldman was a sore loser!" Vickie screeched, sounding as angry as she was fearful. *"I'm reading a huge spike in the power grid right under you! The place is set to blow!"*

Bella screamed something unintelligible and infuriated. "No, NO, *NO! Damn it, NO!"*

Acrobat began to bounce again.

Red simply let himself sink to the ground.

"Safe" in her chair, Vickie hugged herself, tears of exhaustion and frustration burning her eyes. She had...nothing. Exactly nothing. She'd have to have time to study the place to stop the explosion, she'd have to know the schematics, have to...

She shook as her sensors felt a surge in the energy core. They had seconds...*seconds*...

She had nothing. They were all going to die, and she'd hear it happen and wouldn't be able to do a damn thing about it.

Over the pickup mic still on Red, she heard Herb rumble; he was puzzled. The noise caused Red to turn his head.

Herb was confused. He knew something was wrong, but he wasn't equipped to tell what it was.

Herb... *Oh gods... I can't... I've got to.*

"Herb? Honey? I... Would you..." She choked. "Honey, this is going to be hard for you, dangerous. You might... you might not... you might go to sleep forever. But the cave you're in is going to blow up in about a minute—"

Herb interrupted her with an angry rumble. The others were utterly frozen, listening to them both, and only understanding her side of the conversation.

"That's right, hon. Like the bomb tests here. My friends—"

Herb rumbled again, cutting her off. Her heart practically stopped as Herb opened up his own "chest" with both hands, creating a hollow big enough for them all.

With a floor-shaking thud, Herb dropped one of his shovellike hands down beside Bella and Bull, and rumbled authoritatively.

"He's going to take you out of there! Get Bull and Scope into his hand!" she shouted. *"Hurry!* You've got a minute at the most!"

"You heard the woman, *move!"* Red shouted. Together they lifted their fallen into Herb's outstretched palm, and climbed aboard. Red paused only to retrieve his earpiece, and hopped in last.

The rock closed in around them. It was hot in there, and dark. And Acrobat started making choking sounds. "How are we going to breathe?" he gasped in a panic. "How are we—"

"Herb will make air for you," Vickie sobbed out of the speaker of the earpiece, as their tiny "cave" lurched from side to side. "If it was just him, he could swim through the rock, but he has to keep you guys in a bubble of air, he has to *make* the air, and he has to keep you from getting hurt at the same time, and..." She became incoherent for a moment. "It's hurting him. It's killing him. He said he had to do it. He had to... because he's my friend. And you're my friends. And... that's what a friend would do."

And for the rest of the journey to the surface, there was only the sharp muffled sound of a sudden detonation, and then silence.

✧　　✧　　✧

They only knew they had arrived when their "cave" stopped moving. And a moment later, it cracked open.

Red was out first; they were in the desert, miles from anywhere, which only made sense. He turned back to the creature that had carried him—in a sense, in its heart—

It had crawled out onto the flat hardpan. And it—he—looked curiously lifeless.

A moment later, pieces began to fall off, crumbling into sand. As Red watched, numb, while the rest of the team pushed their way out, carrying the unconscious, the entire elemental turned into another dune.

"Overwatch?" he said tentatively. There was no answer. Although he thought he could hear what sounded like muffled, heartbroken weeping. Red closed his eyes, and shut off his comm unit.

"Thanks, Herb," he whispered. "Helluva job."

He exhaled, and heard the sirens in the distance. When he opened his eyes, he saw Bella jumping up and down, waving frantically. A dust storm was approaching. No, not a storm. The dust was lit by swirling lights of emergency vehicles. And above, Echo Swifts, speeding towards them on silent wings.

They were safe.

The fact that the Catacombs had been breached was all over the command station in moments. Doppelgaenger was not sure why everyone was so excited about it. It was amazing—and a testament to Goldman's twisted genius—that they had been rediscovered so few times, and penetrated only twice, both times by criminals.

It had only been a matter of time before Echo—

Criminals. Echo. Could it be?

He was the ranking officer at this abandoned missile silo for the moment; that gave him access to virtually anything here that he wanted, and he used it ruthlessly. And the initial feeds from the Wolf Pack told him that his hunch was right. The last time the Catacombs had been robbed, it had been a team that might have included the Red Djinni. And now—here was the Red Djinni again.

As he collected all of the raw downloads from the Pack, the Cast, and the Sphere, he was smiling tightly. One of the Pack had fought the Djinni directly. Soon, he would know more, much more, about his counterpart.

The tech in the computer room gave him copies of all of it; it was a pity the Sphere had been destroyed before it was able to upload. He would very much like to know how such a small group had been able to defeat a Sphere. He carried off all the data on a standard thumb-drive, and reflected how ironic it was that Ultima Thule, for all its superior technology, could find no better way of giving its people copies of vital information than to use a bit of degenerate human tech that one could buy off a shelf in a store.

When he got to his quarters, he locked the door so as not to be disturbed. *Ah yes,* he thought, as the first images of the Djinni appeared on his screen. *There you are. Now, let's see what you are made of....*

Vickie stared dully at the cold cup of coffee. Beside it were flat cans of soda. She hadn't managed to choke down more than a sip of any of them.

At least the team was all right, even Scope. Especially Scope... she was going to get her eyes back. Bulwark was on the mend. Djinni no longer looked like he'd been parboiled and disjointed.

No thanks to her. No, it was all thanks to Herb....

She scrubbed the back of her glove across her eyes, and finally forced herself to pick up the cups, the cans, that had accumulated around her while she sat and cried and beat herself up. She hauled them all to the sink and began dumping them out, one by one.

There was a tap on the window above the sink.

"Grey," she said, hoarsely, "I am not in the mood. Let yourself in."

The tapping persisted. Vickie felt the tears come, she fought the trembling in her lips, and brought a hand up to wipe at her eyes.

"Stupid cat..." She gulped, as she reached up to open the window.

The tiny rockman, barely three inches high, beamed at her, and began jumping up and down, clapping his hands in glee. He had found his friend! He began to dance.

With a shock of recognition Vickie opened her window, folded her arms on the sill and rested her head on them. The rockman paused to lean up and embrace the tip of her nose, then returned to his dance of joy. He began to chirp in shrill whistles and clicks.

Vickie smiled.

"Of course, Herb," she said, gathering him up in her hand and bringing him inside. "Of course you can come live with me."

CHAPTER ELEVEN

Bad Moon Rising

MERCEDES LACKEY AND CODY MARTIN

It would take Herb thousands of years to grow to the size he had been, but he didn't seem to care. Maybe he didn't; living with me, he certainly had a more interesting life. He and Grey had a kind of "Odd Couple" relationship. Eventually I "told" Red about Herb's survival—by sending Herb out to him when he was on a stakeout—but that's another story.

We still hadn't heard from Mercurye—and if Tesla had, he hadn't left a record of it anywhere that I could get to. Meanwhile . . . and we had no idea how they were doing this . . . the Thulians were continuing to make their presence felt. Small groups, fast strikes, equally rapid disappearance, and no idea how they were doing it. The Seraphym thwarted some of these appearances, but the bulk of them—well—

That was us.

"Chonny!"

Upyr's pale face seemed to hover in the shadows of the doorway. Most of the lights were off in the CCCP HQ, not just to satisfy Saviour's penurious nature, but to cut the generation of heat. The only rooms in HQ that were air conditioned at this point were the computer room and Sovie's sickbay.

"Commissar is being want to see you. Matter of Ural."

John lifted his sweaty head off of the couch arm in the break room. "She read the report, didn't she?"

He had to assume Upyr shrugged; he couldn't see her shoulders.

169

"*Nechevo*. Is still being want to see you on matter. *Davay.*" John had become used to jogging everywhere when he was still in the Army; now wasn't any different for him. Tying the sleeves of his coverall around his waist, he started off at an easy lope to the Commissar's cramped office.

Red Saviour was clearly waiting for him. She had a stack of papers in front of her that she wasn't looking at, and an evil little smile on her face. "*Privyet,* Comrade Murdock," she purred. "I am having assignment for you ... to make up for destruction of CCCP transportation."

"Uh, roger, Commissar. Y'read the report, didn'tcha?"

She said nothing for a moment, just fixed him with a glare that was altogether too much like being fixed with twin laser beams. "About assignment. Daughter of Rasputin is finding difficult to find replacement parts for CCCP equipment. Also van comes with, solving transportation deficit. Is sturdy invention, 'Crags List.' Very useful. You will be obtaining both. In ..." She consulted a piece of paper that was two sheets into the pile. "Adair, outside of Atlanta. Is Borzhoi Bus going there in one hour. Here is ticket." She handed him a bus ticket with a running dog on it. "Better to hurry, or will be missing transportation."

Right. In stinking hot Georgia. He hoped the bus would have AC. "Any further instructions, Commissar? If'n not, I'd like to grab a quick shower."

"You are knowing where depot is?" That smile was back. "Is long walk, comrade."

She really wanted him to suffer. "I can move fast when I need to, Commissar. Y'don't need to worry 'bout me."

"Am not worried about you, Comrade Murdock." The smile was even broader. "It will be even longer walk if you are to miss bus." She paused, a long, significant, and very pregnant pause. She took the time to rake him with that wolf look of hers. "You are dismissed." John offered a quick salute and immediately dashed out of the office.

His seatmate had no front teeth, and constantly sucked air through the gap. "So, that's when I stabbed 'im and took his mints!" The man slapped his knee and started cackling loudly, drawing a few stares from the other passengers. Not that the other passengers were a sterling set either. They all looked like they could be his neighbors in Meth Heaven. "So, what's a slick feller like you doing around these parts?"

These guys were psychic. They always knew when you didn't want to talk to them. "Just through on business, ol' timer."

"You some kinda travelin' salesman?" The old man was not going to leave him alone. John decided that desperate measures were in order.

"You could say that." John flashed a fake smile. "I primarily deal in metals. Lead, for instance." The bulge of a pistol under John's jacket drew the attention of his seatmate, who immediately snapped his eyes straight ahead.

"All right, mister. I, uh, I's need to use the bathroom."

"Good plan, Stan." The old man got up and hurriedly found another seat as far away from John as possible. The rest of his trip was completely uneventful, for which John was very thankful. Also thankful that the bus had working air conditioning.

Adair, Georgia, was out in the swampland between Atlanta and Savannah. If it had been hot in Atlanta, it was worse out here. John got off at an open-air drop-off on Main Street, which appeared to be the *only* street, and consulted his directions. Adair was an island in the swamp, bisected by the causeway. It appeared from where he stood that half of the local population traveled by airboat, and the other by cars, trucks and vans no younger than twenty years old.

Finally he spotted what he was looking for: a swinging store sign that said T. TAYLOR: TV RADIO & TOOL REPAIR that was so faded as to be almost illegible. The humidity was so heavy he felt like he was swimming up the street towards it. The sun was setting, but there was no relief in sight from the heat that he could detect.

The sign on the door said CLOSED but there was someone moving around inside and the door was open when he pushed on it.

"Hello? Y'all open?" John scanned the store; dusty shelves piled high with disassembled parts and components for all sorts of electronics, some of which he could identify but most of which were alien to him.

"If'n yer"—the ancient, withered old man behind the counter tilted his bifocals and consulted a scrap of paper—"Chonny Murdock, then yep. If'n ya got money fer some-a this here stuff, then yep. If'n ya want somethin' fixed, then nope."

John nodded. "I'm Murdock. It's John, by the way, an' I got the cash. Mind if I check out the stuff first?"

The old man cackled. "It's all in the van, the van's in the back. He'p yerself." John circled around to the back of the shop, and was stopped short by the sight of the van. White, with lettering so faded it looked like ghost-writing, dented and rusty, it probably was old enough to vote and drink. *Is this heap of crap even gonna run? Or drop its guts out from under me?* It looked just as old as the shopkeeper, and even more banged up. The contents weren't any better; boxes of ancient electronics, dusty, probably functional, but certainly not pretty. If the Commissar thought it was worth wasting money on, it wasn't his place to argue.

Then again, considering the age and state of repair of most of the CCCP equipment... maybe this was the only way to get spare parts.

After a few abortive attempts at starting the van, the tired machine decided that it could be goaded into performing its job. No doubt that John and Georgi could get it fixed up once it was back at the CCCP garage... but the trip back was another problem entirely. By now it was dark, the little dried-up town was barely lit up with a few lights in windows, most of which were rivaled by the lightning bugs out in the swamp. And it was still hot. And humid. And, of course, the AC on the van was "two-forty"—two windows down and forty miles an hour. Which was all the van would do, flat out.

Ironically, the radio was the most functional part of the beast. At least as a radio repairman the old fart knew his job.

Of course, it was an AM radio, which meant—

Religious. Sports. Politics. Religious. Politics. Religious. Some kind of weird rant that was political, sports, alien abductions *and* religious...

Finally he found some sort of honky-tonk station that faded in and out, but at least it was music. It finally strengthened when the DJ announced that he was going for a break and was going to play a Creedence Clearwater Revival set. That suited John.

Or at least, it suited John right up to the point when the set cycled to "Bad Moon Rising." The tune was upbeat, but the lyrics? The lyrics sounded like they'd been written as a vision of the Invasion. It had gotten to the chorus, when John felt all of the hairs on the back of his neck stand up; something felt off. Over the years, his instincts had become fairly well honed; doing the work that he did with the Army, you had your training, your buddies beside you, and your gut. Nothing else. You had to trust all of them.

Instinctively, John scanned the swamp on either side of the road. It was nearing twilight, with the sun already sunk behind the trees, so details were harder to make out. The fact that he was trying to pay attention to the road—and the headlights on the van were in no better shape than the rest of it—didn't help matters. Slowly, he became aware of an odd hum; some sort of vibration that permeated the air. *That's familiar as all hell for some—*

When the Death Sphere screamed over the road, bathing everything in the sickly orange light from its alien propulsion; John had to slam down the brakes to avoid getting thrown off the causeway by the backwash—or whatever you'd call it. Near as anyone could tell the Death Spheres used antigrav and whatever was under them got shoved, hard. The trees that were under its path had smashed-off limbs, and some had been completely blown down.

"Time for the understatement of the century: that can't be good." John gassed the van, which was gracious enough not to die on the spot. A few dozen yards ahead on the road was a turnoff in the direction that the Thulians were heading; it was marked with a sign denoting a power plant ten miles away. *There's nothing else out here for miles; that has to be where they're going.* He skidded the van around the turn, gunning its engine for all that it was worth. John fished out his issued cell phone from a pocket, hitting the speed dial for CCCP HQ.

"*Privyet tovarisch.* Is to be hoping you are not walking to Atlanta, Comrade Murdock," said Gamayun's voice. "Commissar will be wroth."

"Comrade, I've got a real emergency out here. We've got Nazis headin' for a power plant along the highway about thirty miles from where I picked up the van. It's gonna beat me there; this piece of crap is too slow, and they're goin' too fast. I need help fightin' these guys." John paused a moment, listening for some sort of response. There was a rapid-fire burst of Russian in two voices, both female; Gamayun must be alerting—someone. Then—"Co—"

The phone cut out. "Goddamn it!" *Rotten cell phone reception might actually be the death of me.* He tried to raise HQ on the phone again, but no joy. He threw the useless device into the passenger seat in disgust and exasperation. "I've got bigger problems right now." Like how he was going to fight off an entire unit of Nazi troopers in power armor, along with air support from a Death Sphere. He'd never had to take that much on by himself. When the CCCP HQ got hit, he'd had Saviour, Georgi, Sovie, Chug and Bella.

Let's hope that Gamayun is getting everyone on their feet; even if they moved like demons out of hell, they'd still only get here in thirty minutes at best. More than enough time for me to have either saved the day or been turned into fine paste. Maybe both.

How many Nazis fit in a Sphere anyway? He didn't have a chance to see if there were any attached to the outside, either; that's how they picked up ground troops that got taken out. The number might be crucial. One too many would be fatal.

Never mind. He'd have to deal with all of them, no matter what. Pushing thoughts of getting atomized or burnt alive out of his mind, he focused on keeping the battered van on the road.

Before John knew it, he was around the last bend in the road.

"Oh shit!" There, across the road was a very nervous looking squad of soldiers, all pointing their weapons at him.

He screeched the van to a halt, being very careful to keep his hands on the top of the wheel. All of the soldiers were shouting commands at him. It wasn't hard to figure out he was supposed to turn the van off and get out with his hands up, and he complied quickly. He got his bearings fast; the plant was a good-sized one, with a large grassy clearing on one side and the other three sides bordered by forested swamp. There was a sign proclaiming that this plant had been converted to burn waste wood, and there was a series of huge mounds of the stuff along one side. The road dead-ended at a parking lot with a security fence and a tiny guard-shack, with the squad between him and it. The parking lot in front of him only had a few cars in it: one Humvee with a mounted gun on the coaxial turret, and then regular civilian vehicles. What caught his attention was the smoldering wreckage in one corner only a hundred yards away. Clearly some piece of military equipment; it was completely destroyed, preventing John from properly identifying it.

"Keep your friggin' hands above your head! Get down on your

knees, now!" The soldier was wearing a staff sergeant's stripes; he looked like the "average middle-aged white guy," with a face that could have belonged to a mailman or an office worker.

John followed the sergeant's instructions, moving slowly and deliberately; these guys had just been attacked, and John didn't want to get shot by a scared Specialist. "My name is John Murdock, and I'm a metahuman. I'm with the CCCP. I'm here to help, guys." He nodded at the still-smoking wreckage. "I saw the Sphere from the road."

"Sarn't Lawson!" One of the other soldiers moved forward from the staggered line, still keeping his rifle trained on John while he talked to the staff sergeant. "I've heard of these guys; commie metas that work with Echo in Atlanta. They're legit." The sergeant took in the information, and spent a few long moments looking John over before he relented.

"All right, stand down, squad." They all lowered their weapons; John noticed that no one engaged safeties, however. The sergeant walked forward to John, extending his hand as John moved to meet him. "Glad to see you. Name is Staff Sergeant Lawson, with the National Guard."

"I tried to get through to HQ but—all I have with me is a cell. Reception broke off 'fore I got a response." Now he wished he had Vickie on Overwatch. Even if she couldn't make the CCCP transport move any faster, at least she could keep him updated. "What's your status here, Sarge?"

"After the Invasion, we all got activated; they've got us tasked to protect key points in case there was another push. We had just got done with helping to do some clearing and reconstruction in Atlanta before we were sent here. We've been here a week with nothing happening, until that damned silver ball came floating over." He pointed at the burning wreckage. "That used to be our air defense—an *old* MIM-72 Chaparral that they dug up from God knows where. Maybe a museum." He shrugged. "Anyways, it tracked and fired on the Sphere as soon as it was over the trees; Army had outfitted the usual Sidewinder missiles with new warheads that they said were gonna burn the Nazis up. It did hit, and it set 'em afire, but it didn't kill the Sphere. The Charlie got zapped, along with two of my men." The sergeant shuffled his feet and had a look on his face that John had seen too often, especially when he looked in a mirror. *Never an easy way to deal with troops dying under your command. Something that I'm more acquainted with than most. I've gotta keep focus, and keep Lawson focused.*

"Is that it—Lawson, right? What happened to the Nazis after that?"

"We used up all the Stinger missiles we had on it; took a chunk out of them, but didn't finish it off. It limped away about due west, right over that clearing. We got off a call to McPherson Base, but they're on the other side of the goddamned state from us. Help is on the way, but it's gonna be a while before they get here."

One of the men had the squad radio with him, and he was listening with increasing alarm. "Sarge!" he interrupted, "We ain't the on'y ones! Them Nazis is poppin' up all over!"

Ah hell, another Invasion? We barely made it through the last one . . .

He could hear humming again. That kind of tooth-rattling humming that he could only associate with the Nazi antigrav drives. It was hard to locate, but he thought it was coming from just the other side of the grassed-over area. "Lawson, help isn't gonna get here fast enough, and they're comin' back. We need to take up defensive positions an' get ready for a fight. What other weapons do y'all have?"

Lawson held up his rifle. "You're looking at them. There's a .50 on the Humvee, but that won't do much against their armor unless we're shooting at the joints."

John nodded. "Deploy your men, and then grab cover. I'm gonna try to give us an edge."

"You heard it, girls! Mount up! Gilley, Jackson, Fieldhouse, get behind those barriers on the right! Move with a purpose! Rest of you, form with me on the left. Keep your spacing, and watch your sectors!" All eight men started running; the sergeant was shouting orders and positioning his soldiers. It was a small squad; two fire teams, with one of them short two soldiers. *Do we have enough? Would it matter if we had a dozen more soldiers?* John keyed up his enhancements, readying them and clearing his mind. He set off on a fast trot, getting to Lawson's position in a few strides.

"I'll be on the right, in the tree line. Try to keep from blowing my ass off; I'm rather attached to it, hooah?" *Friendly fire isn't, and Mr. Murphy isn't ever kind.*

"Hooah, roger that! Let's kill these bastards and call it Miller

Time." John nodded and began to run. His enhancements came up to full, and he was across the parking lot in less than three seconds; weaving through the trees at the edge of the swamp, he found a concealed spot behind a small mound of earth and dropped to the ground behind it. This was going to suck; he didn't have comms with the National Guard troops, and was the only metahuman. Lately, he'd gotten back in the comfortable position of knowing there was someone at his back. He was feeling better since his run-in with Blacksnake, but still wasn't quite up to par; it felt like he was always fatigued. *Count yourself lucky; you should have been dead from that stab wound, and any other person would have been.* He still wasn't sure how Sovie had kept him going. Then again, he'd never had a metahuman healer fix him before he stumbled up to CCCP's door.

The sound was what pulled him out of his reverie to focus on the fight. The trees in front of the field were breaking and splintering as something forced its way through them; the cracking and squealing sound of the wood being split quickly grew deafening in the still night air. Almost as if they had magically teleported, the Nazis were suddenly into the clearing. They seemed to pause at the edge of the open space for a moment. There were a dozen of them, in two staggered rows. It looked like they had learned from their mistakes; no more random stomping through the opposition without any sort of formation. The Thulians just stood and watched, probably analyzing what was in front of them, then started their advance again, and firing started on both sides: the National Guard soldiers with their rifles and the Nazis with their energy cannons.

The oncoming troopers were clearly confident that they were in minimal danger; while they were in formation, they hadn't bothered to move in leaps and bounds or utilize any other sort of tactics other than stomping towards their targets and firing methodically. John waited, keeping as still as he possibly could; the Nazis had some pretty good sensors and other vision enhancement gear in their helmets, and he didn't want to give himself away. Sweat was running down his back and sides.

This was the worst part. Waiting was always the worst part.

It didn't take long for the Thulians to all completely enter the clearing, moving well away from the trees and swamp.

Now.

John raised his right arm over the tiny berm he was behind and concentrated, relaxing his inner guard. Fire sprang up around his hand, then exploded outward to fill the entire back half of the field. The firing from the Nazis momentarily stopped as they were completely engulfed; the Guard held back a little, since they couldn't see definite targets through the inferno. John cut the fire off; his skin had pinpricks of pain from the flashover, and he was sweating even worse than before.

The entire field had spot fires where there was still anything left to burn, and smoke obscured everything. Thankfully, the Nazi power suits were glowing, they were so hot; immediately, one of them went down as the squad of soldiers concentrated their shots on its joints and weak spots. John popped up in a half crouch, focused, and blasted the nearest trooper with a stream of super-heated plasma. The Nazi was dead after a few seconds, a ragged and melted hole through its chest.

Time to move.

Tracers—and giant columns of fire—worked both ways. John ran, his enhancements still keyed; Thulian energy beams exploded trees all around him, sending deadly wooden shrapnel flying through the air. He was able to make a baseman's slide under one beam, skidding to a halt behind a hefty barrier that two soldiers had taken position at.

"Jesus Christ! Think you could've given us a little warning about the fire?" the nearest soldier shouted over the gunfire as he reloaded his rifle.

"I'll be sure to stand up and wave my arms next time, letcha know when the ambush is goin' off, kid." John punched him in the shoulder. "Keep firin'!" He didn't listen for a reply; he was already scanning for where his next bit of cover was going to be. There wasn't much; a few overgrown mounds of dirt left over from whenever this place had been built, some concrete highway barriers, and nothing else on this side. The soldiers had disabled another Nazi suit; with its elbow and knee joints shot out it couldn't lift itself up. If the trooper inside didn't bleed to death, he might live long enough to be interrogated. *Keep moving, keep moving; if I stay here too long, they'll nail these soldiers just to get to me.* John angled his upper body around the side of the barrier—it exposed less of him as opposed to going over the top—and blasted the Thulians with fire twice. With their suits softened up by heat, they were starting to take a lot of damage. One headless and one maimed; John hardly ever missed. Before the enemy could orient on him again, John was up and running for a barrier on the far side of the parking lot.

More dodging; the troopers were *really* unhappy with him, this unhappiness was reflected in the volume of energy beams coming his way. Well, when they were shooting at him, they weren't shooting at the unenhanced and poorly armored soldiers. Then again, when they were shooting at him, they were *all* concentrating on one target: his favorite hide, the one that happened to be covering his body at the moment.

Suddenly, out of nowhere, a mud-and-water geyser erupted in the middle of the field. It subsided, leaving behind a seething mass of mud with grass floating on top, roughly the diameter of a home swimming pool. A moment later, another erupted, this time in the middle of the troopers, leaving another mudhole. Then a third, a fourth, a fifth, all placed randomly, as if God was poking holes in the ground blindly from below. Startled, some of the troopers stumbled into the holes, and ended up sunk to their waists in the gooey, sucking mud. John didn't waste any time, and neither did the soldiers; while the troopers were mired, three more went down from grenades, plasma, and automatic fire. Some of the rest were splattered with the gouts of mud, their visors plastered with the thick ooze, effectively blinding them.

What the hell is doing that?

It wasn't one of the soldiers, at least he didn't think so. Well, whoever was lending a hand, he wasn't going to turn it down.

A strange thing happened; each of the Nazis sprouted what looked like a glowing orange umbrella in front of their left arm cannon. They expanded to cover half of the area in front of a trooper, leaving the right arm cannon exposed with part of the suit.

Shit. Energy shields? What other sci-fi crap are these guys gonna pull out next?

The shields absorbed any bullets that struck them. But the Kriegers seemed to be moving slower, as if operating the shields was draining them. *One less cannon for each of 'em, and they move slower. We can use this.* John was up and dashing again, this time for Lawson. The cannons couldn't keep up with him now, but he could still get whacked by a lucky shot; for his trouble, he snapped a plasma wave at the thighs of an entrenched trooper.

With both legs cut in half, it toppled forward onto its face, still firing. *Shields aren't too good when they get overwhelmed. Even at half of my best, I could still probably blast one.* A second later, John was at Lawson's position.

"Fancy seein' you around these parts, Sarge. How're you lookin'?"

"Not great. My RTO is dead, along with another specialist, and my SAW gunner is out for the count. We can't take much more of this." His words were punctuated by an energy beam impacting their shared cover, sending up a heap of vaporized dirt and rock. "Got a plan?" John looked over to see the mangled bodies of Lawson's soldiers. *Hell. Can't think about it right now. Got to save everyone we can, everyone who's left. Think, damn it!*

"Yeah, but it ain't much of one. I'm gonna take the Humvee, start usin' the .50. Try an' flank around their shields, if you can; they only face forward, it seems. I'm gonna burn these guys again, soften 'em up. You'll have to move fast after I do, though. Tell me when you're ready!" The Humvee had its front end hidden behind the corner of the plant; he'd still have a decent field of fire from the turret, though. John felt the tap on his shoulder; Lawson gave him the thumbs-up. His men were in position and ready to run when the order came. "Rock an' roll." John stood up to his full height, exposing half of himself. Relaxing, he sent another monstrous plume of fire rocketing towards the Kriegers; they continued to shoot wildly, but were at least temporarily blinded. "Now!" Lawson and his bloodied squad ran hard and fast for the swamp on the right side of the field. John tried to keep the fire going, but some of the cannon blasts were getting uncomfortably close.

John extinguished his fires and ran again, this time for the Humvee; he still had a few precious seconds before the troopers could focus on him.

I ought to sign up for a marathon or something after this; I think I've logged more miles running than most people have on their cars.

He hit the side of the Humvee with his shoulder, denting one of the armored doors. Flinging it open, he scrambled inside and into the turret mount; there was a lot of blood spread all over the interior. *Goddamn it. I should have gotten here faster. Taken out the Sphere, blasted it from the road, something—*

A cannon blast scoured the ground twenty yards behind the Humvee. He could beat himself up later, if there was a later. Racking the charging handle on the .50, John aimed down the barrel at the nearest Nazi; it was only now starting to ponderously turn towards him. Squeezing the controls, John felt the satisfying vibration as the machine gun rocked in his grip. The big, heavy, *fast* bullets impacted solidly with the Thulian's shield, making it shimmer constantly. John adjusted his fire; the rounds slipped off the left side of the shield and into the Nazi's right arm cannon. Still superheated from the fire, the cannon shattered into shrapnel after only a few rounds, leaving a stump that was leaking either blood or hydraulic fluid. Maybe both. The Krieger dropped his shield to fire with his remaining cannon; John tore him to pieces with sustained fire, blasting away chunks of armor and flesh with each round. *New target.*

The next Krieger was smarter; as soon as it looked like John was targeting him, the trooper angled his shield to face the mounted gun. This also had the effect of turning the trooper's arm cannon in a safe direction; namely, one that wasn't facing John. *That'll work!* John began raking the remaining Kriegers with the machine gun; whenever he began to fire at one, it would avert its arm cannon. Even slowed by their shields and the mud, they were still plodding forward; they'd be able to spread out and flank him, especially once they were up onto the parking lot.

Just as the first of the troopers was about to reach the asphalt, John barely made out the familiar chatter of assault rifles. That first Krieger did an awkward stutter step before falling over; dozens of holes were stitched through its back. "Lawson! 'Bout goddamned time!"

The troopers were done; when they turned their shields to face John, they also turned their backs to face Lawson and his squad. They weren't protected by their armor or their shields any more, between the M2 machine gun and the soldiers' rifles. The remaining Kriegers were cut down one by one; the last two switched off their shields. They were able to use both arm cannons for only a few blasts before they were cut down. John saw one connect with Lawson's position. Before he could react, one ripped through the corner of the building that the Humvee's front end was hiding behind. The Humvee's hood and engine both caved in exactly as if something big going ninety miles an hour had hit the front, and the Humvee bucked backwards. Suddenly the entire world was spinning for John. After an eternity, he woke up on his back, and could feel blood trickling along the edge of his scalp. *Must've been knocked out. How long have I been down? Where are the others?*

The sound of running boots started to drown out the high-pitched ringing that John had been hearing since he woke up. He tried to roll onto his side, and found that he couldn't. Something was pinning him to the ground.

"Holy crap, are you all right?" One of the soldiers? John heard something metallic scraping against the ground, and he felt the thing holding him to the ground come free.

"What happened? Is everyone all right?" Things were still blurry around the edges for John. *Probably a concussion. Like I really needed another one.* He was having trouble thinking, and the world seemed slower than it should be.

"Naw, man. Lawson ... he bought it with those last two." A pause. John was able to turn his head up far enough to see a nametape, "Fieldhouse," but nothing else. "Listen man, we'll get ya some help, just relax." Then there was the familiar hair-on-end feeling from before. What did that mean again? John's vision finally came into focus.

"Sphere ... Death Sphere is comin' back!" John struggled to stand up, and more details became clear. He stared at his hands and noticed that he still had the control mechanism for the machine gun; at his feet was the M2 itself, all easily fifty feet away from the Humvee wreckage. *How in the hell did I rip this beast loose? No time, no time, notimenotime.* "Fieldhouse, get whoever is left in position; we're gonna have company!" He stumbled to the earth berm where the others had taken cover, scooping up a discarded rifle from one of the downed soldiers. There were only six of them left, including John. The unease he was feeling was only growing. "It ought to be here by now. If we can feel it this much—"

John turned around in time to watch the damaged Death Sphere glide over the parking lot behind them, three troopers disengaging and landing with a crunch.

"Man, we're dead. We're so dead."

"Fire, soldier!" John raised his rifle along with the others. *This is it. They've got us, dead bang. To hell with it; we'll make them pay for it—*

Then, a new sound—no, sounds. In the distance and approaching. There was something coming. The Thulians stopped their advance, evidently hearing it as well.

It took him a moment, but suddenly the sound clicked for him; jet packs...and another set of engines, not as shrill, though nothing like the snarl of a fighter jet. What the—CCCP didn't have—

It wasn't CCCP.

First down, and coming in so fast it looked like a crash, was an aircraft about the size of a stunt jet. Except that at the last minute the engines suddenly rotated, and what had been a near crash turned into a vertical landing; something with V/STOL capability, like a Harrier jump jet. The rear canopy flipped up, and one of the biggest men John had ever seen in his life popped out of the thing like a giant out of a clown car. The plane was still setting down as he flung himself out of it, landing hard on a wrecked car and rolling. As he rolled, John could hardly believe his eyes as the car—and then the asphalt—rolled up around the man, forming a crude armor.

Right behind the little jet landed another pair of big men, both wearing Echo jet packs. One was black, the other looked like some sort of Pacific Islander. The black man was wearing nothing but boots, a pair of nanoweave trousers and a nanoweave vest with a helmet. "Matai!" he bellowed, pointing at the three Kriegers. "Light 'em up for your brother!"

The second man raised up what looked like a sleek paintball gun and began tagging the visors of the three troopers; fluorescing, self-illuminating paint splattered their viewports, obscuring any view they might have had. *Wonder if those damned helmets come with windshield wipers.*

By this point another Echo Op popped out of the front of the jet and vanished upwards before John got a good look at him, as a second jet landed and two more Echo Ops emerged from it. The first Op was head-to-toe in what looked like jousting armor—as armored up as the Kriegers were. The second was followed by a flood of dogs that looked as if they should have been the armored one's pets, since they, too, had helmets, armored neck braces, and shoulder armor.

The leader of the Echo group shed his jet pack and charged the troopers on the ground, colliding with them at the same time as the junk-covered giant. The troopers began blasting them, with pieces being torn and continually renewing themselves on the scrap-heap meta; the leader just shrugged off the beams that hit him.

John heard the sound of nails clicking against the ground; a blur of teeth, armor and fur streaked off from where the dogs had been sitting by their keeper. They circled around behind the Kriegers, whose attention was still diverted.

What the hell kind of good are dogs going to do against trooper armor?

Coming from behind, the pack launched themselves at the knee joints of the armored troopers, hitting them right at the bend of the knee with the sort of shoulder bump that two fighting wolves would use, and one by one the troopers fell over. The melee was too busy for John to fire into; he might hit the two Echo personnel or the dogs if he tried. But he could see why the dogs were in armor now; if they tried to smack into the Kriegers without it they'd probably break their necks or concuss themselves.

There was still that Death Sphere; if things started looking sour for the Thulians, they'd just give everyone a thermite bath, hose the field down with their energy cannons, or beat whatever they could reach to death with the tentacles. John turned to face Fieldhouse. "Get your guys and get clear of this! Unless you have any LAWs or surface-to-air stuff, you guys are just targets. Move!" The National Guard soldiers didn't need any more encouragement. John spotted the Echo operative that looked like an ancient knight, and sprinted to his side. "Got a name, buddy?"

A clean, synthesized voice replied, quietly, "Echo OpTwo: Silent Knight."

"Right, that figures." John gestured towards the Death Sphere. "We've gotta take that sucker out, or we're all dead. Can you help with that?"

"Yes." Silent Knight gave an approximation of a nod. "But you'll want to stand behind me when we do."

The man with the dogs didn't do anything, but suddenly the dogs all came streaming back to take a position behind him, as he fell in behind Silent Knight. He looked at John. "Leader of the Pack. Knight here projects coherent sound beams. Like lasers, only sound. SASERs." He leaned down and did something to the dogs' helmets, then tapped Knight's shoulder. "Okay, Knight, the pups are safed." He leaned a little to one side and spoke into where his lapel would have been if he'd had one. From working with Overwatch, John recognized he must have a button or throat-pickup mic on him. "Okay, Corbie. Hit it. Knight's in position."

A black blur dove down out of the equally black, smoke-filled sky, briefly hovered next to the damaged section on the side of the Sphere, then arrowed up before it could react. John actually didn't think the Sphere's operators realized it had been there, whatever it was; he wouldn't have seen it if it wasn't for his enhanced vision. There was a brief flash, followed by a gout of smoke and flame that emanated from the panels above the damage; they sheared away, falling uselessly to the ground, with the metal around the hole still burning. Silent Knight braced his feet.

Suddenly it seemed as if all the sound had been muffled.

John looked around, confused; the troopers were still wrestling with the two Echo people, and it should have created a ruckus. He felt someone yank the back of his collar, suddenly, pulling him behind Knight's shoulder.

"Now!" The black meta shouted, disengaging and clapping his hands over his ears. The Islander with the paintball gun shot up into the sky on his jet pack, and the asphalt-covered one rolled up into a ball. Knight suddenly thrust his hands forward, and there was thunder; all of the sound that had disappeared was back and amplified, projected in front of the meta. John saw the air ripple ever so slightly along a narrow band, impacting directly where the bomb had gone off on the Death Sphere.

There was shouting from behind them. John turned to look in time to be thrown to the ground; a Krieger flew over his head, glancing off of Knight's shoulder before clanking against the side of the Death Sphere.

The Sphere was collecting its troopers.

The junk-heap meta and the Echo leader tried to dogpile the last Nazi on the ground, but the inexorable force emitted from the Sphere drew it up the same as the others, sending both of the metas rolling on the ground. Pieces blown off from the other Kriegers earlier in the fight shot up to join the two live Nazis on the sides of the Sphere.

"Hey!" Leader of the Pack elbowed John's shoulder. "You've got fire powers; use 'em!" The Sphere was turning to make an escape; it rotated perfectly, the damaged opening in its armor facing directly at John.

A quick breath, the familiar twinge, and then a lance of fire. *Burn, you bastards. Burn!* John had been suppressing his hatred for the Thulians up until now, trying to keep things impersonal and objective. Now, he let it all flow into his fires, his entire energy invested in controlling them.

"Bull's-eye!" The Islander shouted. For a moment, John wasn't sure that the blast had been effective. The Sphere continued upward quickly; it looked like it was going to escape after all.

Just what I need right now would be for my powers to give out again, to fail right when everyone needs them most.

Then it slowly began to cant sideways. It barely skimmed through the lower layers of the clouds before it plummeted straight down, out of control. When it slammed into the ground, the impact was loud and hard enough to shake everyone off of their feet. Seconds later, something detonated deep within the Sphere, sending a huge fireball into the evening sky.

The National Guard soldiers were the first on their feet, shouting and hollering from the other end of the parking lot. They came running and limping over, clearly glad to have lived through the battle. John picked himself up off of the ground, still dizzy from when the Humvee had exploded. "Not a bad little bang." He turned to face the Echo Ops. "Name's John Murdock, with the CCCP. Pleased t'meetcha, comrades. I figure me an' the troops owe y'all one. Hell, a case." He extended his hand to shake the tall team leader's hand, wiping away the blood from his scalp wound with his free hand.

"We got a call from OpTwo Victoria Victrix that you were out here solo," the big black man said. *So it was Vic with all of the ground stuff. She's got her voodoo to tell her where on a map I was, even though she couldn't see anything without me being wired. That must'a been the best she could do blind. I guess Gamayun got through to her. I owe 'em both, big time; could turn into a nasty habit.* "Sorry about the small team. I'm Flak, team lead—the Kriegers are popping up all over tonight, looks like they're hitting mostly power stations and important electricity junctions. Happy to say we're holding 'em off at the moment."

John nodded. If the Thulians took out some key infrastructure, they could cripple the entire country; everything was codependent nowadays. Knock out a few critical junctures, and the entire power grid would go down. Power fails, so does shipping; shipping fails, so do most of the cities that depend on regular supplies. And so on from there; the trigger effect, in short. "Who else is on your team, here? Didn't have too much time for proper introductions. What with the explosions an' all."

A black shape dropped down out of the sky; for a moment he got a strange feeling of familiarity as the huge wings fanned the air. And…a sense of disappointment because it wasn't Sera.

It was a man in a mottled gray-and-black night camo suit and black camo paint, with black wings. "Cheers, mate," he said in a pronounced British accent. "Corbie. I'm liking these night gigs, makes a lad less of a target."

"That was you with the explosive charge? Pretty handy." John looked at his wings. "A whole bunch more stealth than the jet packs, I imagine."

"Flak's idea. Brilliant, eh?"

"Not bad at all. Who's the walking trash heap? I've never seen anythin' like that."

"My brother Motu. I'm Matai." The Islander, his broad face wreathed in a smile, came forward to shake his hand. Matai was huge. Motu was twice as tall and proportionately broad. "We're from Samoa, mon. I'm no meta, I'm just a big, growin' boy. Our mama, she feeds us good." The other Islander had shed his "skin" as he approached, and now was just clothed in his Echo nanoweave. "Come say hello to Johnny Murdock, of the commies, brother!"

"Comin', brother." Motu also shook hands with John as he reached the group. "Glad to see we didn't have to scoop you into a bag for Victrix." John's hand was completely engulfed in Motu's, but the big meta's gentle grip wouldn't have ruffled the feathers of a baby chick.

"Makes two of us."

Flak interjected. "You've already met Leader of the Pack and his mutts. Got them especially outfitted for fighting these Kriegers. Leader got the notion for armoring them when some of 'em kept knocking even the biggest of us over for fun when they were romping around. Knees lock forward, not back, even on those suits." The dogs lined up beside their—owner? handler? pack leader?—and sat down in a neat row. John could hear panting inside the helmets. It sounded like doggy laughter. "Then there's Silent Knight, here. Last thing a lot of Kriegers have ever heard, if you get my drift."

"I am very pleased to meet you, John Murdock," said the synthesized voice. "I hope you will forgive my abruptness. The situation was critical."

"Not a problem, comrade. You guys pulled all of our asses outta the fire, so to speak." John remembered suddenly why he was out in the lovely swamps of Georgia in the first place. "Speakin' of fire, if I don't get that sorry lookin' van an' its contents back to HQ, the Commissar is gonna use my hide as a rug in her office." He looked to Flak. "Can you radio in, make sure that these soldiers have help comin' for 'em? Their radio telephone operator and squad leader got taken out, an' if things are really goin' hairy all over, the message might not have gotten out."

"Of course. We have to move out again, but we'll make sure they get the help they need." One of the soldiers came trotting over—one of the ones that John never heard a name for.

"Uh, sir? You're Flak, right? If it's all right, could I get your autograph?"

CHAPTER TWELVE

Respect the Wind

MERCEDES LACKEY AND CODY MARTIN

I've probably mentioned before that the Invasion provided a vast smorgasbord of delights for the bottom feeders. In many cases, they enjoyed it unopposed. But not in Atlanta.

And especially not in the territory protected by CCCP.

The CCCP had changed substantially in the last few weeks. For one thing, Hensel had worked wonders, turning the old building into a real working headquarters. For another, there were more people here now than just Untermensch, Chug, People's Blade, Soviette and the Commissar.

A planeload of CCCP members had arrived to media fanfare; mostly just news jackals looking to capitalize on the controversy that surrounded Atlanta's newest "Reds." They were a mixed lot of the very old and the young, for the most part, led by a star-tlingly handsome and charismatic man about the same age as Red Saviour, who announced to the female reporter who was all but swooning over him that she could call him "Molotok."

John had learned that these were older Soviet metas from World War II and the Cold War era, and shiny new young socialists that Saviour said, enigmatically, were "unconventional" and thus did not fit into the Supernaut defense cadre. He wasn't sure what that meant. The Supernauts seemed to be mostly armored metas under the supervision of Worker's Champion (who Saviour called "Uncle Borets" or something like that) and Saviour's own father. There seemed to be a lot of shouting in this relationship . . . and John

189

got the distinct impression that the CCCPers who had arrived on this shore had been more unacceptable than unconventional, those whose powers were waning and had retired, and those whose powers were erratic and not yet under control. He had to wonder how many metas the Russians had lost. He'd heard numbers bandied about of the Echo Ops lost that ranged from a half to three-fourths. Certainly the numbers were bad if Echo was reduced to taking petty criminals now. Maybe not so petty. He'd heard things about Red Djinni, for instance, during his days on the run. . . .

If that was true, and if the Russians had lost a proportionate amount, he couldn't imagine how any of them would be unacceptable.

Except . . . maybe . . . in their loyalty to Red Saviour. Or maybe their unwillingness to compromise their socialist ideals to Batov's new way of doing business.

Maybe a bit of both.

Things were finally starting to shape up, though. With the increase in manpower came an increase in the amount of work that the CCCP could do. This included expanding the group's patrol routes to include the surrounding neighborhoods, like John's. The CCCP's attached soup kitchen was working around the clock, serving hearty meals to anyone who came by. A free, albeit limited, medical clinic that asked no questions about where injuries came from was operated by Soviette and whatever off-duty CCCPers she could wrangle. He could have used both in his underground days. Maybe if he'd had them, he'd already be one of the comrades . . . hard to say.

Jonas' community garden had been not quite ruthlessly taken over by the twins—a pair of sonic metas—and the strange, gothy Upyr, who had all come off a farm commune and had forgotten more about vegetable gardening than the entire neighborhood had ever known. Upyr was even a botanist, which seemed odd for someone who looked like a vampire. Chalk-white hair, skin so pale that it looked almost painted on like a China doll, proper little square-framed "socialist" glasses clearly handed out by the state—the kind that hadn't been in fashion since John Lennon died. "BCGs" is what they would've been called in Basic; birth control glasses. Upyr never wore anything but shadow-gray and black, always wore gloves, and was so self-contained, except when she was working with plants, that you would scarcely know she was there. The only bit of color about her was the scarlet CCCP star with the anachronistic gold hammer and sickle in the center that she wore over her left breast.

And Perun, an engineer before his metapowers over electricity had manifested in the Siege of Stalingrad, had personally rigged some kind of electrical feed to every building in Jonas' neighborhood, while his friend and fellow "old man" (who was a woman, though you'd hardly know it by looking at her), Rusalka, had seen to it that there was a clean source of fresh water coming into every household from across the destruction corridor.

The CCCP was truly making an impact on the surrounding area; the headlines in the newspaper and on the television had ceased to be totally hostile and were slowly becoming a shade of neutral. During the flurry of activity, John had barely any time to acquaint himself with any of his new comrades, save for a few. One, in particular, stuck out in John's estimation like a raw turnip in the middle of a posh buffet; "the" Soviet Bear. Of course, none of the media had ever spoken to Soviet Bear. Which was...just as well.

John had first run into Bear while working on the CCCP's rundown, thirdhand, and utterly ancient Soviet generators. They were supposed to be WWII surplus. He believed it. He'd run into Bear because Bear was supposed to be the only person who understood the damned things. That wasn't strictly true, but Perun was still rigging the neighborhood electrics, and for John at least that had priority. The man looked like a steampunk enthusiast's wet dream; except for his head, shoulders, and arms, he was almost completely mechanical. His "body," if that term even fit anymore, was made out of blued titanium, painted over with flaking Soviet military-gray paint. Hydraulics and tubes sprouted all over his joints and torso. The "centerpiece" was off-center in his chest; a glowing crimson, gyroscope-looking "heart." The grayed-out hair, "Ivan" mustache, and officer's cap completed the look. The old Russian also wore an eye patch over his right eye; no doubt a souvenir from some past fight. Though given the Bear's reputed age, which fight was up for debate.

John was trying to remove a panel in order to access the inner workings of the generator when he heard Bear. "No, no, *tovarisch*. Must use 'sock it to me' wrench for maintenance panel." John turned to see Bear, leaning against the doorway with a very, very large clear jug in his hand. Even from several feet away, John could smell the rotgut vodka that filled it. "Had to repair these when I ran camp in Ukraine." Bear shifted uncomfortably, coughing into a handkerchief he had in his free hand. John noticed that it had a few spots of blood on it, despite the Russian being careful to hide the handkerchief. "Where are manners? Name is Vladimir Pavlovich Polokhov, the 'Soviet Bear.' *Sovietski Medved.* You may call me Pavel; Americans have many troubles pronouncing Russian names. I assume you are our newest American comrade, *da?*"

"That's right." He extended his hand. "John Murdock; pleased t'meetcha." Pavel shook his hand weakly; John felt the gnarled joints enveloped almost completely in his own hand. "Now, y'said somethin' about me usin' the wrong wrench for this job? A . . ." John let it hang in the air for Bear to finish.

"*Da,* 'sock it to me' wrench. Is how you say it, *nyet?*"

John thought for a few moments before it clicked. "Ah, y'mean a socket wrench. Thanks for the tip, Pavel. If'n ya wanna stick around, I could use the help gettin' this up an' running. It's been mostly guesswork for me so far."

For the next few hours, John talked with Pavel while they disassembled and repaired the antique generator. John mostly listened; Bear went on about his exploits during the Great Patriotic War, his experiences with Lenin and Stalin, and a plethora of dirty and lewd jokes. The man was a compendium of bad puns. It was a good thing Bear was not patrolling the neighborhoods alone. Though it was unlikely that any of the folks hereabouts would know what a *kulak* was, or be insulted by being referred to as a Ukrainian.

Today the pack consisted of John, Upyr, Bear, and Untermensch. John wasn't entirely clear on what Upyr could actually do, but the Commissar seemed confident of her ability in a fight, so he was willing to go along with it. The four of them were riding in a pair of the CCCP's issue Ural patrol motorcycles, sidecar attached; they were cheaper on the ever-so-scarce gas (which had gone rare in-city ever since the attacks), and would take more punishment than WWIII could throw at them. John and Untermensch were driving the bikes, with Bear and Upyr riding in the sidecars, respectively. Bear was continually griping about how it was "below him" to be riding in the sidecar; he cradled an ancient and well-used PPSh-41 in his arms, cooing to it in Russian occasionally.

This wasn't John's first motorcycle patrol with the CCCP, so he was fairly relaxed. He made sure to stay alert, however; falling into a routine was the easiest way to have something bad happen.

And, of course, as soon as he was done processing that thought, the routine was broken. Jadwiga's voice blurted over the comms. "Patrol Hotel-1, this is Control. Receiving report from Gamayun. Stand by." Untermensch, who was leading the squad, signaled for everyone to come to a stop and "ruck up." Gamayun was one of the newer Russians to come to Atlanta. Named after a mythological prophetic bird in Russian folklore, she was one of the CCCP's trump cards. She was a true-blue remote viewer; anywhere in a ten-mile radius, she could be damn near omniscient. Not in predicting things, but in seeing what was going on there. She used an inverted shotglass over a map to narrow her focus. She was limited to one sort of "filter" at a time, though; right now she was being used as an early warning system, immediately alerting the CCCP about any wrongdoing or incoming threats in their area of responsibility. John remembered Saviour's reaction when she came in off the plane. She had looked at the frail little blonde and grunted, "Is only favor Worker's Champion is doing me." That passed for high approval, apparently.

It was less than a minute before Soviette was on the comms again. "Immediate action: we have a large group of Rebs, northwest of your patrol's position, heading South along the main thoroughfare. Traveling on motorcycles. Intel says they are very hostile, and are currently using deadly force."

A new voice on the comms. John recognized it immediately as the Commissar's smoke-hoarsened alto. "I am advising you that current law is no deadly force may be used by metas on non-metas unless life is in danger." Then her tone took on a darkly wicked tenor. "So use own discretion about life being in danger."

Untermensch drew a circle in the air with his index finger, signaling John to start his motorcycle back up. "We ride!" The two Urals roared to life, dust wafting into the air behind their mufflers. Bear laughed heartily, chambering a round into his antique submachine gun. Upyr smiled thinly, reached into the sidecar and came up with a Russian police-issue KS-23 shotgun. At John's glance she shrugged. "Rubber bullets, comrade!" she shouted. "I am not crazy old man like Bear." John shook his head—he didn't believe in "less than lethal" munitions, figuring if you were forced to shoot someone, you sure as hell better kill them—then gunned the throttle, rocketing along the road behind Untermensch. It was a good thing these Urals were as sturdy as advertised; Unter was riding over piles of debris and ruined pavement with reckless abandon, bouncing Bear violently in the sidecar. Signaling with his right hand, he made a sharp turn down an alley. John followed, staggering his bike off from Unter's path and allowing the distance to grow slightly between them; no sense in both bikes being taken out with one shot. Or grenade. *I really hope they aren't packin' grenades.* The Rebs were known for being rip-snortin' crazy; drugs, prostitution, and guns were some of the more tame ventures that they were hooked into before the Invasion. Now, it seemed, they aimed to build themselves a little Mad Max-style kingdom.

In a flash of daylight, the patrol was out of the alley and into the street, screeching their bikes to a halt. Less than a mile to their left were the Rebs; had to be at least twenty of them. Shotguns, rifles, pistols, and firebombs; every one of them was armed, and blasting everything they could see. Luckily, they were entering the neighborhood from the direction of one of the unpopulated destruction corridors. But it wouldn't be long until they reached areas where folks were actually living; at this time of day, the streets would have plenty of people on them, going about their lives.

The CCCPers dismounted from their motorcycles, forming a line facing the oncoming Rebs. Unter was the first to speak. "We find cover, then hold them here until backup can arrive. We need way to keep them from bypassing us." He surveyed the area for a few very tense seconds, then focused on an abandoned build-ing to their right. "That one. Pavel, Murdock; take it down!" The building had been previously gutted in the Nazis' invasion; the side facing them was open to the street. Without wasting a moment, all four of the CCCPers positioned themselves between it and the Rebs. Bear moved forward, adjusting the gauntlets on his arms. John noticed that the old Russian's mechanical heart, still suspended and spinning in his chest, sped up moments before the Bear fired. In a staggering blast of light, two coherent beams of energy lashed out from Bear's fists, striking key load-bearing columns left in the building. It began to topple uneasily behind them; John pulled up his scarf over his mouth, and then relaxed his concentration. A heavy wave of flame jetted from his own gloved hands, engulfing the ruins just as they hit the street. Dust and smoke filled the air; it would take a bit to dissipate, and might provide them a limited amount of concealment.

The Rebs were closing in. John moved left along with Bear, taking cover behind a water tower that had fallen from a roof and landed on its side. Untermensch and Upyr were positioned ahead and to the right of John's location, the two of them on opposite ends of a sedan that had been partially melted. The Rebs were less than one hundred yards away; the roar of their choppers and the staccato clatter of gunfire filled the air, punctuated by their cursing and whooping. John thought for a moment, then spoke into his headset. "Boss, how much did the Commissar get these bikes for?"

Unter looked back to John, an expression of puzzlement on his face. "We are on strict budget. She is getting them surplus—"

"Good to know." While Unter was talking, John had taken a small roll of "100-mile-an-hour" tape from one of his belt pouches. Engaging the brakes on his Ural, he revved the throttle up before taping it down. Just as the Rebs were within fifty yards, he released the brakes, sending the motorcycle screeching down the center of the Rebs' column. Their bikes scattered out of the way of the oncoming Ural, with one of the Rebs eating pavement, hard. Eyeballing the distance so that it was just at the rear of the Rebs' formation, John ducked out from behind cover, blasting plasma at the gas tank. In a brilliant fireball, the Ural exploded, sending the sidecar tumbling like a child's toy. The Rebs were now blocked off from both ends; debris and CCCPers in front, and a fiery wreckage behind them.

The Rebs, screaming, hollering and shouting curses, immediately returned fire. Rounds impacted all over the place as the bikers tried to provide half-hearted covering fire while they dismounted their motorcycles. One crazy pair continued to ride towards Unter's position; the Reb riding pillion was wielding two Molotov cocktails in his hands. Upyr and Bear both peered around cover with their weapons, firing almost simultaneously; "rubber" slugs and 7.62x25mm rounds lanced towards the bikers, striking both of them and tumbling the firebug off the vehicle. Both of the Rebs and their bike skidded to a halt, dead. The passenger was on fire; between Bear's bullets and the impact with the ground, his own Molotovs had shattered and doused him with burning fluid.

The remaining Rebs finally found cover; some behind their bikes, others among the debris. Now it was time for the real firefight. John, Bear and Upyr took shots at targets they could hit, blasting away concrete, brick, and motorcycles to reach their targets. Several bikes caught on fire, with another one exploding spectacularly while a pair of Rebs were still behind it. This was a ranged fight; Unter didn't look very happy.

"Nasrat! Fashisti svinya..." There was more growling in Russian, and finally Unter's temper reached the breaking point. *"Tovarischii!* Keep them pinned! I need a workout!" Without another word, Unter broke from cover and sprinted across the street to an alley, disappearing down it before the Rebs could train their weapons on him. John and Bear both immediately began to lay down a withering amount of fire; dozens of blasts of flame augmented by concussive energy bursts and submachine-gun rounds. Upyr manually chambered a round into her shotgun, peered around her cover, and then popped up over the top to fire a burst directly into the center of the Rebs' side. The impact point exploded into a small cloud of white, powdery gas; John recognized it as a specialty "Lilac" round for the KS-23, tear gas mixed with CS agent. The Rebs closest to the burst immediately began to cough and tear up; mucus streaming from their noses and mouths as the chemicals irritated their membranes.

John speared a single Reb who was trying to advance to cover with a lance of fire; the man went down without a sound, crashing to the ground as if he was a marionette whose strings had been cut. The Rebs were starting to get desperate; the fight had lasted for less than a minute, but in that minute they had lost over half of their numbers. Before John could fire at his next target he saw a dark blur drop down from a rooftop, right over the position of the largest grouping of Rebs. John almost felt it as the big Russian touched down in their midst, crying *"Ura, ura, ura!"* The Rebs, astounded, had no time to react before he set upon them. Hands flashing in terrible, brutal strikes, Georgi almost literally cut through them; broken bones and splashing blood resulted wherever he struck. Across the street, a smaller group of Rebs noticed what was going on, and turned, preparing to fire into the melee. John quickly tapped Bear's shoulder, directing his attention on the alleyway's mouth. Nodding, Bear put down his submachine gun, opting to use his energy blasts instead. Another cacophonous roar, his gauntlets discharged. The energy bolt impacted the building directly behind the Rebs, sending tons of brick and steel crashing onto their screaming forms.

And as quickly as it had started, it was over. All of the Rebs were dead, riddled with bullets, burnt or beaten to death. Untermensch strode down the street towards his comrades, a proud smirk on his face. "Threat neutralized, comrades. Let us clean them up, and report back to HQ—"

A barely visible blur rushed through the flames behind Unter, clipping his left side and sending him spinning pirouette-style. Before any of the CCCPers could register what the blur was, it had appeared at Upyr's side. It was one of the Rebs; shirtless, wearing a sleeveless leather vest, stained blue jeans, and a beard that would've put Father Time to shame. "You stinkin' commies just wrote a check your asses can't cash. Drop your guns, or the chick gets a permanent smile." Unter had recovered, and was circling to the biker's left, trying to get behind him. "Not so fast, sucker. Name's Bad Bowie; I talk fast, and I think even faster. You get right with your pals, or she bleeds. I ain't goin' to ask you again, chump." To emphasize his point, he drew his knife—unsurprisingly, a Bowie almost large enough to match a machete—against Upyr's neck. A line of blood stood out against her too-pale skin. "Last chance; drop the guns, or I drop her."

"Not going to happen, *svinya*." Unter walked over to stand next to John and Bear. "Here is your last warning. Put down your knife and come quietly, or we carry you to base. Choice is yours, Amerikanski." He stood nonchalantly; Bear had recovered his PPSh, and now had it trained on the Reb.

Strangely, Upyr was smiling, a little Mona Lisa-like smile, an "I've got four aces" sort of smile. Bad Bowie obviously couldn't see it. Nor did he seem to notice that instead of wringing her hands in fear she was calmly and methodically taking off her gloves.

In fact, he had no idea anything at all was happening, until she said quietly, "I think you do not want to hurt a little pale girl, Amerikanski—" and laid both of her white hands on his wrist. "I am not telling you my name, I think. It is Upyr. Do you know what that means?" She didn't wait for a reply. "Is meaning 'Vampire.'"

John blinked and shook his head hard. The moment she touched the man, it was as if all the light around them was being sucked towards them. He'd been in an eclipse once; it was like that. Not at all like sunset or twilight, for the source of light was still high in the sky—rather as if all the light in the area was swiftly being siphoned away.

Bad Bowie went white, as white as Upyr. His eyes rolled up in his head, his knees shook, and Upyr slipped deftly away from him and ran towards John and Bear.

The moment she let go of him the peculiar light effect stopped; as she reached John's side, the man shook himself like a dog, and recovered, snarling. "That's it, you damned Reds. I'm gonna make a pair of boots outta each of your hides."

Unter leaned to his right, speaking softly. "Take him alive, comrades. He may prove useful for...intelligence."

Upyr looked—oddly pink. Her eyes sparkled dangerously. She looked high, or drunk. Quickly she clasped one bare hand on John's wrist, the other on Bear's shoulder. John felt a surge of vitality... which "tasted" like the Reb. It was the only way John could describe it. It was nothing like the surge of wellness and aliveness he had gotten from the Seraphym. This was *stolen,* not gifted. The source was tainted with evil and in comparison, the source was a bucket of polluted water beside the free and primal ocean.

Upyr lost her flush, and that dangerous beauty. She moved behind John, but did not put her gloves back on again.

Bear was the first to move, breaking the stare-down. "I can't believe I'm missing Matlock for *this?*" The Reb charged the group; they broke ranks, with John and Unter on one side opposite of Upyr and Bear. Bowie went for Upyr first, slashing the air with his knife; Upyr sidestepped him, brushing her hand along his bare arm, and Bear rushed forward, plunging both of his energy-shrouded hands at the Reb. Bowie, not as fast but still way too fast, dodged one of Bear's fists, with the second glancing his shoulder. The Reb spun around, his vest ripped away where Bear hit him; he made a backhanded slash, scoring Bear's titanium ribs with the huge knife. Upyr moved in again, her fingertips brushing Bad Bowie's knife hand. He slowed fractionally as she slipped away.

John, keeping the pressure up, darted in; he was the one closest to matching speed with the Reb. Controlling his breathing, his enhancements kicked in; he was next to the Reb, dropping down and slamming an elbow into his stomach as he completed the spin Bear had sent him into. The blow knocked all of the wind out of Bowie, but he was still in the fight; an open-palmed, lightning-fast strike to John's shoulder pushed him away. Distance was exactly what he didn't want in this fight; it would give the Reb room to work with his blade. John closed in again, planting a foot hard on the Reb's instep. Down the knife came in response. John hadn't pulled himself in close enough in time; the knife was going to get planted square in his chest.

Another flurry of movement. *I'm not dead?* The knife was inches away from John's chest...held in place, stabbed through Unter's right forearm. The Russian man smiled, then chopped at Bowie's throat; the Reb staggered backwards, choking. Time had slowed down for John; he saw the knife slide out of Georgi's forearm, and saw the wound there begin to heal almost immediately, the bleeding slowing to a very tiny trickle. The CCCPers didn't waste any time; Bear keyed his gauntlets, firing at the asphalt directly behind the dazed Reb. The ground erupted behind him, sending him stumbling straight back towards John and Unter. John ignited both of his fists, "getting off the X" by taking an immediate step to his right. Unter shifted his stance, allowing Bowie to pass between John and himself. Both of them hit the Reb at the same time; John igniting the man's clothing, and Unter planting a firm kick to his midsection.

Bowie flew backwards, landing hard on the ground. He was completely disoriented, half-heartedly rolling on the ground to extinguish the fires covering his body.

Upyr glided towards him as if she were speed-skating. She stopped his roll with one foot planted on his chest, and didn't so much bend down as make a motion like a striking snake with both hands outstretched. She clamped one on each ear; once again that "light falling inward" effect started, and the flames snuffed out as if he'd had a canister of fire retardant emptied on him. His eyes rolled completely up in his head this time, he went white as chalk, and passed out entirely.

Upyr stood up, whirled with unnatural speed, and this time clamped both her hands on Georgi's wrists. Her hands were shaking, like someone who'd had an overdose of speed.

She kept her hands on Unter for longer than she had on John and Bear. When she let go, she wiped both of them on her black trousers with a look of disdain, and quickly put on her gloves again.

John turned the defeated Reb over, fastening flexicuffs to his meaty hands. Hefting the large Bowie knife, Bear secured it to his belt. Untermensch surveyed the area, then keyed his headset. "CCCP Control: area is being secure. One prisoner, metahuman, calling self 'Bad Bowie.' Hostiles used lethal force; replied with conventional weapons with extreme prejudice. Hostiles neutralized. Request fire suppression team and city 'wagon' for dead." He paused a moment. "Also be telling Commissar will be needing requisition forms for new Ural." He clicked the comm off before anyone could reply. "*Horosho* work, *tovarischii*. Now, let us police up bodies and get to HQ. Long day of forms ahead of us, *da?*"

"And excoriation by Commissar for Ural," Upyr murmured.

John shrugged. "What? It got the job done...and besides, we can say the Rebs did it." John eyed several of the still intact motorcycles that the Rebs had rode in on; there were a few very choice Harleys.

Upyr tilted her head to the side. "*Da*. And building full of bullets fell on them, *nyet?* Also mysterious exploding chemicals. And must have been incendiary grenades in saddlebags."

Bear nodded sagely. "*Da*, Rebs are sneaky, *nyet?*" He paused for a moment, realization dawning on his face. "You are to be using Amerikanski sarcasm, Upyr?"

Her deadpan was perfect, except for the little Mona Lisa smile. "I am not knowing what you mean, Vladimir. Am making observation I shall surely repeat to Amerikanski authorities."

Pavel—Bear's preferred name—guffawed in response. "Just as well, comrade. You must not have sophisticated sense of humor, like I." As the group began to walk back towards the carnage, he piped up again. "Did this old Bear happen to tell you one about man in bar with frog?"

John hadn't had much of a chance to clean up after the fight with the Rebs; his patrol had policed up the bodies, gathered the weapons, and inventoried the still-functioning vehicles before the coroner and a couple of squad cars had arrived. Unter spoke with the police officers, flashing his credentials and giving a quick summary of the events while John, Bear, and Upyr helped the coroners. When it was all said and done, the group still had to wait for another CCCPer to come with a van to transport their Reb prisoner; John and Pavel, being bikeless, rode in the back with Bowie.

Upon arriving back at HQ, John and Bear were very quick to get Bad Bowie settled into the CCCP's only holding cell; the sooner they could occupy themselves with paperwork, the better chance they had of avoiding Saviour "excoriating" them about the Ural. While filling out an after-action report—the second copy, that is—Upyr, clean and sleek and as mild looking as any kitten, tapped on the wooden desk. "Chonny, you are to being report to holding cell, please." She glided back out of the room just as quickly, not bothering to elaborate.

Bear looked up as John stood to leave. "Being sure to ask Georgi where my '#1 Stud' shirt is, comrade Murdock. I have suspicions that he has purloined it for antirevolutionary reasons!"

"Yeah, I guess there aren't a lotta those floatin' around the base."

"*Nyet!* Made it myself with iron-on transfers. Iron burn on back is distinctive!" Chuckling, John left the room and made his way through the base towards the holding cell. The barracks and most of the major facilities within the base were nearing completion; the living quarters were in passable enough condition so that the contingent of CCCPers had a place to sleep and shower. There was no air conditioning yet—but there wasn't any in his squat, either.

Knocking at the door of the holding cell and waiting a heartbeat before entering, John was certain that this was going to be his talking to for allowing the Ural to be destroyed. As soon as he opened the door, however, he immediately knew that things were going to be much . . . less interesting. Bad Bowie, the Reb prisoner taken after the firefight, was sitting in a chair. Both of his wrists were fastened to the chair legs with built-in leather straps; the same for his ankles. Across a battered metal table sat Unter, pen and pad of paper in hand. The Commissar was in the room, cracking her knuckles; sparks of energy ignited each time she did. It was then that John noticed that Bowie was sporting some new bruises and cuts. *Oh, hell.* This wasn't a session for John to get smoked by Saviour; this was an interrogation. And it didn't look to be of any legal sort.

Natalya was the first to speak. "Ah, Comrade Murdock. Good of you to join us. Our guest has decided to waive his right to an attorney. However, he is also refusing to talk. Since you and

Georgi were leads for the patrol, it is protocol that you are both being present during 'questionings.'"

"Commissar?" John stood in the doorway, a growing sense of unease building up in the pit of his stomach.

"What is it? This *svinya* won't wait all day. We need to persuade him to talk before we turn him over to Amerikanski police authorities for processing."

John paused for a long moment. "Commissar, I need t'speak with ya privately. Immediately."

Red Saviour looked at him coldly, but there was fury in her eyes. She motioned to him to follow her into an adjacent office, empty save for one flickering fluorescent light. "*Shto?* You have objections, *Comrade* Murdock? I am Commissar here. *I* am making decisions. You are carrying them out. Is *nyet* democracy."

"Ain't arguin' about chain of command or nothin', Commissar. But this is *wrong*. Not only that, it's illegal. We can't just beat the hell outta him until he spills the beans. It's unconstitutional." John made sure to keep his tone even; he was still a little shocked by the sudden change of mood, but he was starting to get angry, too. This was exactly the sort of thing he was trying to get away from, some of the worst excesses and abuses that hierarchical power structures engage in. "We just can't do this."

"And what has capitalistic constitution to do with us?" Saviour's teeth bared in what was not a smile. "I am needing information to save lives of workers. This is only one man. Good of many comes above coddling one. And I am not beating him. Am using sophisticated technique with electricity and water that leaves few marks."

John shook his head, speaking through gritted teeth. "The Constitution's got everythin' to do with us, Commissar. This ain't Moscow; we gotta hold to the rule of law. There are some things that can get bent and even broken, but not when it comes to human rights, damn it!"

"He is criminal! He has no rights!" Her glare turned icy. "Already you revolt, soft capitalist that you are, spoiled by TVs and MacBurgers! *I* am Commissar here! You obey, or you leave!"

John stared back at her, his eyes meeting hers with the same sort of dead intensity. Finally, he looked to the door. "Fine, *Commissar.* I'll lend my expertise, with your permission."

The Commissar showed the barest hint of surprise on her

face, before quickly masking it with her usual air of command presence. "So. You see wisdom. There is hope for you." With a curt nod, she opened the office door, leading John back to the holding cell. Natalya turned her attention to the sullen Reb; he met her gaze before snarling in disgust. There was still fight in him, and it was apparent that the Commissar was going to fix that. "Comrade Murdock will be assisting us in extracting what we need to know from you, *svinya*. Location of Reb hideouts, whereabouts of your leader, Rebel Yell, and so on. Think hard on this information while we prepare." She moved to the corner to the right of the door; a small crate covered with a beaten-up cotton tarp caught John's eye. Ripping off the tarp with a flourish, Natalya began to remove items from it and place them on the table. Pliers, a crank field telephone, a jug of rubbing alcohol. Bowie eyed each item as the Commissar set them down.

"You can't fake me out, bitch. I got rights, and you can't—"

"Can't, comrade? I seem to remember reading report; you died in fight with CCCP patrol. Shame, being burnt and blown to racist pieces. Don't remember corpses having rights." Natalya picked up the pliers in one hand, moving towards the Reb. She backhanded him hard; with her strength, it was more than enough to daze him. The Commissar began to angle the pliers towards the Reb's mouth before being interrupted by John.

"Commissar?" Saviour stopped right before the pliers were going to clamp around one of the Reb's teeth; Untermensch looked up from his writing pad. "That's messy. If he starts swallowing blood, he'll just vomit everywhere after a while, too." John paced around the edge of the table, occasionally glancing at Bowie; the biker's attention alternated between the dangerously close pliers and John. "I've got a couple of suggestions, if'n ya don't mind."

"Please, comrade." Natalya waved him on.

"Well, easiest is waterboarding. Y'tie him up on a board, with his feet elevated. Stuff a rag in his mouth or cover his head in a plastic bag with a small hole over the mouth. Pour water down on his head; it's supposed t'be simulated drowning. Pretty harsh stuff, but it doesn't leave any marks. Supposed to knock over even CIA agents, averagin' around fourteen seconds before the person cracks." Saviour nodded, considering it. "Then there's 'the Vietnam.' With that field telephone, a couple of trashbags, and a cinderblock, we could hook him up but good. Electrocution sucks; hell, even do away with the crank phone and get one of our people with the right powers in here. Practice, and whatnot."

The Reb was starting to shake, sweat flecking off of his brow with each convulsion. John pressed on. "If y'wanna get messy, though, we can just lay some plastic down and get an icepick. Precise, but he'll bleed out pretty quick. Knives an' shivs are better than guns for scaring folks; not everyone knows what it's like to be shot, but *everyone* knows how it feels to get cut. We can even get that knife he was totin', his namesake, for extra kicks—"

"All right, you damn Reds, all right!" Bowie exploded, on the verge of breaking down into uncontrollable sobs. "I'll spill, damn it! Just don't touch me! I'll talk!" Georgi began to write, apparently impassive to the goings-on.

Saviour's lips stretched in a wolfish smile. "So, you see reason. Begin talking."

John didn't waste any more time. He unfolded his arms, walking out of the room and shutting the door behind him. And found himself grabbed by the shoulder, whipped around and forced into the wall by one very angry blue woman. "What in the *hell* is going on here?" Belladonna hissed at him. "And how *dare* you be part of it?"

"Bella—"

"Don't 'Bella' me! What gives a torturer the right to use my name as if we were friends?"

John sighed impatiently. "But, Bella—"

He felt a mental *smack* inside his head as if she was slapping him.

"Bella!" John snarled, walking two steps towards her, forcing her to step back to avoid being run into. "Wouldja get offa your righteous rage an' listen to me? Or d'ya wanna beat *me* up? The first would save a lotta time, though the second would probably leave ya feelin' better."

"You're either an idiot or a thug, *Mister* Murdock," she snarled. But she backed off just a hair, and took her hands off him. "I know Red Saviour is a thug. I thought better of you. And you two have got to be *idiots* when you know I can pry anything you need out of that creep's skull without resorting to—"

John interrupted her, clamping a hand on her shoulder and another over her mouth. "Bella, *listen*. Y'hear any screamin'? Y'hear any dull thuds? How about smell? Burnt hair or barbequed skin?" He waited until she stopped wriggling in his hands, then lifted them up. "Well?"

"—No—"

"No. Y'don't. 'Cause I didn't torture him. More importantly, I didn't *let* the Commissar have at him, either. But he's in there, singin' like a canary." He took a step back, placing his fists on his hips. "An' the Commissar is happy without gettin' blood all over the place. Y'want me to explain, now?"

She glowered, and nodded curtly. "I'm listening."

"Good. I really wasn't lookin' forward to bonkin' ya on the head. It'd ruin my 'cool image,' or whatever the hell the kids say." He shook his head. "We ain't gonna torture him, though Nat was pretty set on that when I walked in. Torture just don't work, kiddo, though Nat might like to think, because it's visceral and she can effect it, that it does. Torture an' interrogations under physical duress don't produce good intel; just 'bout anyone worth their salt in the security agencies knows that." John took a moment to let that sink in, taking another step back to lean against the wall opposite Bella, hooking his thumbs into his pants pockets. "When y'put somebody in pain, it's their natural response to make it stop, ASAFP. They'll admit to anythin', and feed ya any story ya want. People will admit to killin' Hitler and Jesus Christ, just to stop the hurt."

"I know that."

John shrugged. "Despite that, there'll always be diehards that wanna try to mess people up anyways, just t'see if it'll get some extra info out. I couldn't stop Nat from torturin' that guy, not without it comin' down to a true-blue fight. I could've quit on the spot, but then she'd have gone ahead and cut him anyways. What I did, though, is redirect 'er. Y'see, the threat of pain is much more effective in gettin' someone to crack than actual pain. I went into plenty of detail on how we could tune that Reb up, and did so where he could hear it an' hear how much I didn't care if it hurt him. And it was all BS. Y'dig what I'm gettin' at?"

She looked as if she was going to protest angrily, and then deflated. "It's still psychological torture. All I would have had to do would be to touch him."

"Psychological torture? Ain't no different than threatenin' the guy, guilt-trippin' him, playing 'good cop/bad cop,' or any other trick to get 'im to talk. An' you weren't here. If'n you had gone in right when you got here, you would've walked in on a toothless or near toothless punk with Nat bashin' him in the face for not bein' able to talk past bleedin.'" He sighed, standing up and stretching. "What I did worked; it kept Red Saviour from messin' up that Reb, an' not too many laws were broken in the process."

She looked away from him, and seemed to shrink in on herself. "I hate this. I hate this. It's turning us into them."

John turned back to face her. "Y'gonna quit? Cowboy up." He squared himself in front of Bella, craning his head down to bring it to her level. "You're Nat's friend. I'm 'er subordinate. Y'see the difference in what each of us can do in that framework?" John started to move to walk away again. "Don't let 'er see you like that, though; put on your game face, kiddo."

Slowly she straightened. "You're right. She might be a rock; I have to be the water that wears her down into another shape."

John tossed a carefree hand over his shoulder. "Then be the friend y'are to her, an' do it." He started unzipping his dirty Kevlar vest. "Me, I'm gettin' a shower before I have to heat up the boiler again."

"You do that." A pause. "Thanks."

"Don't mention it, comrade." And with that, John disappeared around the corner at the end of the hallway.

John had just finished his shower in the communal head that the rank and file of the CCCP shared. Even with more comrades having arrived to fill bunks, there were still so few of them that John could manage to shower alone most of the time. Cleaned up and dressed in a pair of surplus fatigues and a black shirt, he settled down in the makeshift rec area; a few milk crates, a strange assortment of very abused chairs and a couch, and a TV shoved into a corner of the barracks, with a smattering of Russian culture magazines and newspapers laying around. Maybe the biggest difference between the barracks and his squat was that the barracks were so clean the floors squeaked when you walked on them. Then again, "excoriation duty" was a lot like punishment detail in the service. You messed up and you found yourself cleaning with a toothbrush; attention to detail was everything, and it felt comfortable to John. There were exceptions; the CCCP was Russian, and where it shined with efficiency in some areas, others served to illustrate how painfully cobbled together the group was.

Not wanting to ponder on his exchange with Natalya, then Bella afterwards, John flipped on the TV.

"...and in other news, it seems that Atlanta's Red Enclave managed to clean up a pocket of trouble today." The news announcer was one of the same ones he'd seen blathering about the initial arrival of the CCCP in the form of Saviour, her father and Worker's Champion. "A motorcycle gang calling themselves the 'Rebs' attempted to attack one of the neighborhoods cut off by a destruction corridor. A so-called 'CCCP Patrol' put an end to that with no civilian casualties and no property damage. Pretty remarkable, considering that last report about Blacksnake, huh, Steve?"

The other plastic anchor laughed. "Well, Stella, boys and their toys, and Blacksnake has the best toys around! Can't blame them for wanting to use them!"

John muted the channel with a smile. Things were changing. They'd likely get a lot worse before they got better. With the Rebs and other gangs stepping up their activities, everyone was waiting for the other shoe to drop. But, for just this moment, things seemed a little bit brighter at the end of the tunnel.

Red Saviour was shouting and breaking things again. Fortunately she never broke anything that was actually useful, but that might have been because the rest of the comrades knew her moods and cleared away anything that might be wanted later, leaving things within her reach, at times like this, like the hideous Atlanta souvenirs that people *would* insist on giving them. "I am devastated, comrade, but Saviour was in a rage, and..."

John had just entered the base to clock in for his patrol shift. He could hear her shouting in the rec room all the way from the front door.

There was a lot of Russian, but there was some English, too. "...Tesla is a credulous old *babushka*! Some babbling from crazy man not able to leave bed for twenty years and *poof!* He is quaking in boots and hiding under sofa!"

As John neared he could hear that there were at least two other people with Saviour.

"On one hand, Commissar, some of those things March wrote about have happened..." Bella said cautiously.

"On other," grunted Unter, "is like Nostradamus. Is vague enough to fit anything."

John was right at the rec room door and there was no way to get into the locker and barracks room without going through it. He hesitated, trying to remember the layout of the HQ so he could find something to occupy himself with until the Commissar was finished with her "meeting."

"You are not to be revealing this to comrades until I say so, maybe never." Saviour threw an ugly pottery "War of Northern Oppression" statuette against the wall and it shattered five inches from John's head. "Are enough old *babushkas* among comrades to believe in *nekulturny*—what is good word?

"BS," said Bella. Firmly.

"*Da*, BS. Prophecies! All world on fire, everybody dead, game over, comrade! Bah!" She threw another statue; this one of General Lee looking saintly. John remembered that one in particular; someone had drawn a felt-tip Hitleresque moustache on it. Still a little stunned by what he had just heard, he began to walk woodenly down the hallway. Apparently, he wasn't quiet enough.

"*Who is lurking?*" Untermensch's bark froze him in place. "Show yourself!"

Damn it.

John stepped into the room. "Not lurkin', just on my way to sign in on the duty roster, comrade."

Three pairs of eyes skewered him. "How much—" began Saviour, when Bella interrupted her.

"Everything important, Commissar." She grimaced. "Sorry I didn't pick him up before he did."

Saviour's glare was enough to tell him that the character mug of a Rebel soldier was about to impact on or near his forehead.

"With all due respect, Commissar, there's a difference 'tween listenin' in and not being able to help hearin'."

Unter lost a little of his glare as he smothered a grin. Bella shrugged. "He's got you there, Commissar. I'm surprised they didn't hear you over at the Piggly Wiggly."

Saviour turned her glare on Bella, who reacted not at all. "You might as well tell him the rest."

John slung his jacket over a chair, leaning on the back of it. "So...the rest of what? Heard something 'bout someone named March, and then a whole lot of not-too-happy-soundin' things."

"Comrade sorceress is uncovering idiocy that explains why Tesla is shaking like little girl in front of bear," Saviour said sourly. "Bah. *You* tell, blue girl."

"Apparently immediately after the end of the Invasion, an

autistic Echo precognitive rated between OpThree and OpFour got a head full of horrific visions, scribbled everything he saw down and set himself on fire," Bella said crisply. "Some of what he wrote down seems to have been accurate—and more to the point, could not have been 'predicted' by any means other than genuine precognition. The man's name was Matthew March, so in a burst of creativity they've called this stuff 'The Ides of March.'"

John took in the flurry of information, nodding once. "All right, I'll buy it. Now, what exactly did he predict? That's the million-dollar question, ain't it?"

"That the Nazis are going to win. You die, he dies, everyone dies, and those who don't die wish they had."

He chuckled, scratching his head. "You're joshin' me, right? This can't be serious."

"It's serious. Tesla won't believe in magic or angels but he'll believe in precognition, and he believes this."

John took a few moments to gauge Bella before speaking again. "Y'all really believe this, don't you?" He looked to the ground, thinking. "Well, all right then. If it's credible...then what're we gonna do about it? 'Cause I'm not really the sort to take much lying down, and I don't think y'all are, either." He glanced to each of the three in turn.

Bella scratched her head. "Well...Vickie believes it. She's more of an expert in this sort of thing than I am." She held up a finger to forestall his reply. "She also says that in her experience, prophets can only see things they can relate to and understand. She pointed out that there's no mention of CCCP, for instance, and given that the Nazis tried to put a war machine tentacle through Saviour's skull, I think you guys are not a small consideration to them. That means that maybe March didn't see everything. Or maybe he only saw what would happen if CCCP didn't factor in as a player here." She shrugged again. "Don't know, don't care. If I go down, by God, I am going down fighting no matter what."

John spoke again. "Still, that doesn't answer my question. I've pretty well figured on fightin'; the question I asked was what sort an' how."

The three exchanged glances. "Am having thought," Saviour said slowly. A sharp glance at Unter. *"Da, da,* is so *rare* for me, you may stop laughing behind hand. Sorceress has prophecy. Sorceress is *bolshoi* computer greek."

"Geek," said Bella.

"Geek, greek, whatever. She is good at getting things. So... let her be putting two and two together and giving us the nose-up—"

"Heads-up."

A haughty glare. "My English is being perfect! *Heads-up* when she is seeing maybe matches. So, is best plan I can be making with no intelligence to guide."

"So, our only source of intel to base a course of action off of is this gal, Vickie?" He looked to Bella. "Anything else we can get outta Echo, since they've got a bigger logistics base to work with?"

Saviour snorted. "Sorceress is getting into Tesla's own files without him knowing."

"All right, so we've got info comin' fairly much straight from Echo, but not exactly on the most friendly terms. Once we have somethin' more to go on... what do *we* do? The CCCP isn't at full strength by any means, and from what I understand our backin' from Russia is grudging at best. Am I right?"

"One sniper in the right spot at the right time, comrade." That was Untermensch, a sardonic smile on his face. "That can be all it takes to be changing history."

"Or prophecy," added Bella.

"All right, point taken. We figure out more on what to do when we have somethin' to go on." He sighed, gathering up his jacket. "What can a lowly comrade such as myself do t'help in the meantime, aside from patrollin' and fixing up this joint?"

"What else have soldiers like us ever done?" asked Unter, shrugging.

The futures were moving again. Seraphym sat in utter stillness in the shelter of a giant air duct, screened from below by the parapet around this roof that was also a garden.

It was a strangely soothing place to be, this bit of growth atop the CCCP headquarters. Planted by the twins and Upyr, but designed by Fei Li, the Seraphym had discovered it a week or so ago and had taken to giving it some of the same attentions she was giving the neighborhood gardens—though this one needed such things far less. Mostly she just encouraged the plants here to grow, so that they were as lush now as plantings that were several weeks older.

She needed a soothing environment at this moment. CCCP

had learned of the prophecies of Matthew March, and that was changing the shape of what might be; there was still that maddening blank spot where John Murdock was, but...there were new things, new lines, springing into existence and she had to close her eyes to concentrate on them.

If only she could see into that gap. If only she could get some inkling of what it was that John Murdock represented so that she could make some kind of a guess as to how to cross that gap to the one set of futures she needed to reach...

She was concentrating so hard that for a moment she even lost track of where and when she was. And before she realized it, John himself was next to her, a glass of water instead of a bottle of alcohol in his hand. "Evenin', Angel."

She did not startle or "jump" as a human would, but her eyes opened wide and she stared at him blankly for a moment. "Good evening," she replied, feeling off-balance. "It is a...pleasant evening."

John nodded, sipping from his glass. "Yeah. Skies are clearin' up from all the smoke and crap that got thrown into 'em." He leaned forward against the edge of the roof, looking down into the street. There were a few stragglers waiting in line at the CCCP's soup kitchen, as well as some children playing in the street. "Folks are startin' to relax again. Ignorance is bliss, I guess."

What to say? Anything might reveal too much.

John saved Sera the trouble of attempting to think of something enigmatic enough. "Got some news; suppose y'already know some of it. Stuff 'bout a fella named March. The folks downstairs seem to give it credence, and they're a sharp enough bunch. Still, I'm not really given to believing in all of that precognitive mystical stuff." He turned to look her in the eyes. "Which, given present company, might make me an idiot."

Before she could even think—which in her case, was less than an instant—*It is permitted* breathed into her mind. Her eyes widened.

"There is not...one future," she said, uncharacteristically hesitant. "There are...many. More than the stars in the galaxy. But...not all are equally likely. And some are born and others die, depending on what is done in the now."

He nodded. "Still, the experts seem to think this one is legit. Lotta 'gloom and doom,' involving—"

"The enemy, your enemy, the invaders of the broken cross...

they conquer all. Those that resist are destroyed, those that do not are enslaved. And the world ends in fire and death."

John raised an eyebrow. "Y'know all 'bout this 'prophecy' already, don't you?" He set his water glass down on the ledge to stand up straight and study her face.

"Yes. I have seen it. I . . . see the futures. This one ends in what Matthew March could not see because he could not imagine it." She gave him a penetrating look, and . . . felt even more unsettled. By *him*, and not just the absence of him in the futures. Perhaps that is why she told him more than she intended to. "The enemy takes its force from this world to spread outward and onward. And since this world is but a . . . a launching pad . . . it suffers the fate of such an object. When they are gone, there is nothing you would recognize that is left." She Listened. There was no rebuke. So this, too, was permitted.

"Huh. Commissar, Bella, and some gal named Vickie all seem to think that's 'cause they weren't countin' on the CCCP being . . . well, us. They've gone to some mighty efforts to take us out, and we're still kickin.'"

Something about him made her want to tell him things. She trusted that the Infinite would tell her when to stop at this point. "Mortals are limited in what they may see. Their minds . . ." She shook her head. "Those who have seen only a fraction of what we may, the Siblings, have gone mad. And they are limited by what they know. If they do not know of a thing, generally they cannot see the future that it contains." She took a slow breath. "Matthew March could not see you."

Nor can I . . . She wondered if he would remember that.

John shook his head. "Still sounds fuzzy through and through, if'n ya ask me. Whatever the case may be concerning the 'futures,' our bunch is aimin' to do what they were gonna do anyways: fight. Figure out how to hit back at the Nazis, get proactive instead of reactive. Rebuildin' is well and all, and damned necessary. But reacting to a threat isn't nearly as productive as eliminating it at the source. And those fascists sure as hell had to have come from somewhere." John's gaze drifted back to the street. "Speakin' of rebuilding, I meant to tell you thanks. Y'know, for helpin' out around the neighborhood. Subtle, but I figured I knew what to look for after a while."

That startled a smile from her, and she felt heat in her cheeks.

"You are...welcome." She felt impelled to explain. "There is so very much I am not permitted to do, or to say...it is a joy to find things, even small ones, that I can." She took a deep breath. "I am not permitted to change the futures. Only mortals may do that."

"Well, every bit counts. Lot of the folks in the neighborhood are lookin' to change their own future; 'bout the only good thing that came from the Invasion was folks banding together, for the most part."

"When they band together for the support of one another and not to prey upon one another. But yours are good people. They have chosen well." She blinked, once. "You say nothing about... what I just told you. That I am not permitted to change the futures, though I see them." John's lopsided grin broke out over his face, and he began to laugh. "Why do you laugh?"

"Sera, look at it like this. I'm not even sure if'n I believe in what you are. Y'think anyone would really listen to a dude spoutin' off about angels and the futures, prophecy and so on?" He shook his head again, still humoring her with his smile. "I imagine they've still got plenty of padded rooms that they wouldn't mind throwin' me in for that sorta thing. And money isn't very good in crazed street preachin', nowadays."

She blinked again. "Religions have been started on less," she reminded him. "But I had in mind...the more personal. There are those who do believe I am what I am who are offended that I do not respond to what they want. When someone is told that a Sibling can See the futures, they generally want to know only their own."

"Y'haven't much to fear from me, Sera. After all, I wouldn't wanna scare off my 'guardian angel.'"

That flustered her. And that was a very new feeling. "Why... why do you call me that?" Had he noticed? Noticed that she had been protecting him?

"I assume that you're not exactly everywhere at once. An' since there can't be a shortage of things for ya to do, it'd seem ya spend more than my fair share of time talkin' with me." He coughed hard a few times, taking another drink of his water and clearing his throat.

"You...interest me. I talk with others. But you interest me."

He chuckled again. "Fain my heart; I thought I was just a

dumb country boy that liked guns a little too much." He turned to face the roof access. "You're not bad company yerself, Angel. Even better, I can understand your English; some of the new folks we've got from Moscow don't know a lick, or got such thick accents I've gotta try not to laugh."

For the first time, *ever,* she laughed. It surprised her so much that she did it again. It was an intriguing and delightful sensation.

John cocked his head to the side before walking to the roof access. "Well, there's somethin' new. I'll catch y'later, Sera. Back to the salt mines for now. Though callin' it the *gulag* might be more appropriate." He disappeared down the passage of light coming through the doorframe, waving over his shoulder with his free hand as he left.

She gazed after him, examining this most remarkable interlude. The things he had evoked from her...not only the futures were changing. *She* was changing.

And there was a change in him as well. A lightening of the darkest parts of his spirit. The sense that there might be some hope, some optimism in him now. He was still a cynic but... not as bitter. This was what she had hoped for. Whatever lay on the other side of that blank ahead could not come from a John Murdock who was bitter and in despair.

With that thought, she was reminded of her duty. She closed her eyes, settled herself in stillness, and began sifting through a billion, billion futures.

INTERLUDE

Dark Angel

MERCEDES LACKEY

"Why me?" Bella blurted, finally. "I mean, you should have picked someone like Einhorn. Hell, that's exactly who you should have picked. She's a *believer,* goes to church Wednesday nights and twice on Sunday, obeys all the rules—"

Which is precisely why I did not choose her. The voice in her head remained calm, but had taken on a shade of amusement. *Belief is nothing. Mortals believe in many things that are wrong. Actions are what count. What one does is infinitely more important than what one believes.*

"Yes, but—" Bella shook her head. "Every time I turn around I'm breaking another rule—I thought you—I thought it was all about obeying the rules for you."

This time there was a definite undertone of laughter to the voice. *As I said, mortals believe in many things that are wrong. That is but one of them. The Infinite does not condemn those who rebel. The Infinite encourages rebellion. Rebellion gives birth to creativity. It was not through rebellion that the Fallen fell.*

Now the voice took on the color of deep sadness. Of mourning.

No, it was through something else entirely. Hate and scorn for the mortal creations. The certainty that they were superior to anything mortal. Pride, and the certainty that, at best, mortals were so vastly inferior to the immortal. In this case, pride, truly, goeth before the Fall. Her voice remained compassionate, but took on a touch of steel. *Now, I need you. Your world needs you. It will take more effort than you have ever put into anything before—but you will become—*

215

She paused.

—*something of an Instrument, yourself.*

Bella nodded.

CHAPTER THIRTEEN

No Illusions

MERCEDES LACKEY AND VERONICA GIGUERE

"Okay. So, you're Mel." Bella gave the arm of the chair she was in a swat. It was some sort of fancy rig from Doc Bootstrap's old office. It wanted to adjust to make her all comfy. She didn't want it to. "I'm Bell. Or Bella. Hi." She waved at the couch, also from Bootstrap's office. "Have a perch."

The blonde she was signaling to gave a noncommital nod and crossed the room, sitting stiffly on the edge of the cushion. The Echo uniform they had issued her was a bit loose, and she pushed the sleeves up to her elbows before crossing her arms over her chest. "So," she started quietly. "You a shrink, or do you just do the triage and pass me to the next person?"

"I'm not a shrink, but I'm also not triage." Bella rubbed her temples a little. "Doc Bootstrap, who used to own this furniture, is DOA in the Invasion. At the mo, Echo doesn't *have* anyone who did what he did. Shrinks, yes, but shrink-with-empathy... no. And no one can do, it seems, what I can." She grimaced a little. "They seem to think... and my mentor thinks... I can do a bit of empathic rewiring. If you're willing, I can try to fix you. Like, permanently. But I have to warn you, I've never worked on anyone as seriously messed up as you are."

Mel stared at her for a moment, trying to figure out if the blunt honesty and matter-of-fact statements were a cover for something else. "Seriously messed up. Yeah, you must not be a doctor like the rest of them. They'd always try to sugarcoat it." There was another pause, and the corner of Mel's mouth lifted in a very faint smile. "What's the worst that you've tackled before me?"

"Couple of people with hysterical claustrophobia after being buried in the remains of the Echo tower. I have a friend I am not even going to touch without a helluva lot more practice."

The smile turned into a smirk. "So you know your limits. I can respect that. You talked to Bull or just read what the Army docs wrote? 'Cause there's 'messed up' and there's all-inclusive FUBAR." Mel sniffed and shifted in her seat. "And if Echo's recruiting from the second, then things must be pretty bad."

Bella shifted in the chair. "Well . . . that's where the whole rewiring part comes in. There's FUBAR, which is what my friend Vic is, and then there's you. Which is . . ." She drummed her fingers on the chair arm, trying to select the right words. "Look, what happened to you got treated with drugs early on. So it's not the massive scar mass that Vic has. She's like a kitten got into a whole basket of yarn and turned it into a nightmare. You . . . I think . . . and my mentor thinks . . . I can untangle and heal. Am I making sense?"

"Sorta. At least you're being honest, which is more than I can say for anyone else I met before." She let out a long breath and pushed her hair away from her face. "People tried something besides drugs at the beginning. The issue wasn't that it couldn't work with time, it was more . . ." Mel paused, pressed her lips together, and looked Bella eye-to-eye. "What did you do before they hauled you here? You're too young to have been doing this since before everything went to hell."

"Paramedic, Las Vegas FD. Augmented class, empathic healing powers, Echo OpOne, on permanent assignment from Echo Rescue. Now . . ." She twisted a piece of hair around her finger. "They class me as an OpTwo-point-five, and I keep getting stronger, keep being able to do more stuff. It's kind of scary."

Mel nodded slowly, arms uncrossing as she leaned forward. "First person to try and help me was probably twice as old as you, a sweet and tough-as-nails nurse who'd been in all sorts of messy situations. It wasn't the ability, it was . . ." Her voice lowered, and there was a sense of shame in the words. ". . . What she saw. They'd start, I'd flip, and then they'd have to deal with the projections. It just got easier to drug me and let me go, for the sanity of whoever drew the short straw."

"Yeah, read all that. And . . . well, this is gonna be a lot different. It's either gonna work, or not. My mentor thinks it will. I trust her. She's not wrong . . . that I know of, ever. So, I kind of have that to hang onto..." She shook her head. "Look, I'm rambling. Let me just tell you what I need to do, and you tell *me* if you're up for it, because I can promise you, it is gonna be a helluva lot harder on you than me. Okay?"

"'Kay."

"I get inside your head. All the way in, which means you don't get to hide anything. This is like, whoa, way more intimate than most people can handle, so you really, really *need* to want to try this. Then I trigger the first traumatic memory. I will be in there *with* you for it. This is the full empathic version of desensitization treatment, what the nurse tried. We get through that one, then next session we handle the next memory. I'll be doing a...healing treatment as I desensitize you, to rewire the neural pathways so that it stops being a trauma trigger and just becomes a shitty memory. That make sense?"

Mel nodded slowly. "How far back do you go? Just to what caused things, or..." She fidgeted and took a deep breath. "Never mind. You did Vegas; I'm sure there's not much that would turn you colors."

Bella laughed. "Paramedic on the Strip and off it. Oh, honey, you would not believe the things we removed from places they shouldn't have been."

"I 'tended in the Quarter. Wouldn't be surprised much, although you probably missed the Cajun flavor." She laughed as well, tension broken for the moment. "So, is there another room, machines, cranky bald men in white coats..."

"You lay back. I turn the lights down. We aren't going in chronological order. We're going from 'worst memory' and working our way up." She paused. "And don't worry about the projections, because I won't see them. I'll be with you, holding your hand, and we'll fight it out together. That's the difference. Every other time, you've been alone."

She did as Bella instructed, although she gripped the edge of the couch cushion in anticipation.

Bella fingered the lighting controls, and took things down to just short of dark, then scooted her chair closer to the couch and took Mel's tense hand in hers. "Touch telepath. Just don't break my fingers." Then she closed her eyes and insinuated herself into Mel's mind, found the spot that radiated the most pain...and poked it.

It was dark and impossibly humid, with the heavy scent of burnt hair and broken electronics. The others in the "box" had clothes, one even had a light blanket, but Mel had curled herself into the furthest corner. Hands cupped over her mouth, she breathed in the sweat and dust on her hands rather than the decay that had taken over the others. Outside, she could hear the screams—it was the kid, the one who had spent the ride out talking about his girlfriend—and she waited for the gunshots.

There were never any gunshots. Gunshots would have meant some end to the torture, but that never happened.

She felt something like...a presence? As if someone was holding her hand, only not. *It's a memory, kiddo. It's just a memory. I'm right here. I'm with you.*

The door—the hatch on the top—flipped open and a rough voice barked at her as several guns pointed to the corner where they knew she would hide. A bucket of foul-smelling water emptied into the "box" to wake her up and further the stench of rot. The three with her had been there for weeks; she could taste death if she moved her hands. The kid tumbled into the box, partially clothed and shaking. There was a flare of hope at the first sign of life, and it took control to wait until the hatch closed before she could crawl over to him.

Guilt, yeah, I know, already you're feeling guilty that there's nothing you can do. Not just compassion, there was *been there too.* Shared empathy. Sisterhood. Closer than blood. *We know. Only we know this, who share it.*

He was facedown, the blood pooling around his face and neck. "Rev? Rev, they said you were alive here. They said you knew how to make it stop." He lifted his head, and Mel choked back a sob as the kid tried to look at her with sightless eyes. He'd been cut from ear to ear, his young face methodically marked to cause the most pain without allowing him to die immediately. She held him by his shoulders and turned him over on his back, blood from the wounds on his neck pooling around her bare legs and feet. "Revvie? Say something, I can't see nothing in here. It's too dark."

"I'm here. The...the others are here, they're just sleeping." It hurt to keep her voice calm, the bile rising in her throat as he tried to look at her. "I'm in here with you."

"Can you make it stop?" Even as he spoke, the bit of life left in him trickled out over her skin. "They said you knew how to make them stop, but you wouldn't tell them. You could've tricked them, right?"

It wasn't that easy, but she couldn't tell the kid that. She tried to say something, but he gripped at her arm with burned fingers. "Can you make it stop, Rev? Just for a little while?"

Stop. The moment froze. She stood somehow outside herself, looking down at herself, with the blue gal—Bella—standing with her. *I've shut off all the emotional loading for a second, Mel. Now, this is what you couldn't do at the time, look at everything logically and dispassionately. Like I am right now. Look. Analyze. Is there one single thing you could have done to change anything?*

Standing outside herself, Mel could see the room, the bodies, the blood. She could draw upon the fragments of what she remembered about the area around the box, the numbers of people, and the resources they possessed. *No. They were going to go through the group one by one. They wouldn't touch a female meta, and they knew enough to not give me the chance to retaliate. They'd have done everything else, even if we'd told them what they wanted to hear.*

That was the moment when . . . something changed inside her. She actually *felt* it. Subtle. Like . . . exactly like what Bella had described. Rewiring. A new circuit opened. One tiny little change.

Go. The moment unfroze in time. She was back inside herself, but the watchful presence was still there.

"I can give you a good dream and make it go away for a little while," she was teling the boy, but the guilt didn't carry the same heavy hurt as before. "Can you let me do that?"

He nodded, his head against her leg as she tried to piece together what he'd told her about his girl back home; tried to replace the dark rot of the box with an Alabama springtime, and tried to make him believe that he was taking a summer nap in the sunshine.

Then the memory faded out. She felt . . . well, it was exactly like waking out of the nightmares, except . . . except she wasn't alone. She felt the couch under her first, then the tears on her face, then her hand being held. She heard sniffles. "Uh, mind if I let go of your hand? We both need some Kleenex."

She still had the iron grip on Bella's fingers. With no small sense of embarrassment, Mel dropped the thin blue hand and pushed herself up to a sitting position, arms hugging her knees as she rubbed her eyes with her sleeve. "Sorry," she mumbled. "Hope I didn't break your fingers."

"Nothing to be sorry about." The lights came up to about half normal, and Bella shoved a wad of Kleenex at her. "Oh kiddo, you did good. Then *and* now. Goddamn, you are strong." Bella mopped at her eyes and blew her nose.

"That was three weeks in. Wasn't my first tour, so I'd seen people done worse, just not..." She dabbed at her nose and folded the tissue into a tiny neat square between her forefinger and thumb. "Not for that long. Not that close. It was the smell that broke it after so long. You can shut your eyes and plug your ears, but the air..."

"Yeah."

Mel took a deep breath. "It takes everything I have to go that far. After weeks, I didn't have it." She swiped at her nose again. "So, what happens next?"

"Well...I have good news and bad news. The good news is, that is the worst we'll have to go through together. The bad news is that we'll be hitting that same memory path a couple more times to groove the new path in. Then we'll go on to the next worst. Can you handle this?"

"Will it put me on patrol faster if I say yes?" The question was immediate and sincere.

"Oh shit, yes. This is doable, I can fix you. I can do it without taking the memories. Kiddo, never, ever let them do that—it's what will make you what you are." It was Bella's turn to fix Mel with that direct and sincere stare. "One survivor to another. We need that guilt. We don't need it to cripple us, but we need it to keep us human and...yeah, humble, I guess. Metas..."—she waved a hand full of Kleenex vaguely—"...we have these godlike powers, we need this shit to remind us we're not gods. We're just people who can do things. And when the excrement hits the rotating blades...it gets on us, too." She took a deep breath. "Huh, now I sound like...never mind. If you're up for this, I'm all in for it too. We can go round two right now, if you can take it."

"Now." It was neither question nor demand, but more Mel contemplating the offer aloud. She ran a fingernail over the dark fabric that covered her knees and gnawed on her lip, eyes darting back and forth. "So, I wouldn't have to take my meds in a week? I could request assignment after that?" She lifted her head and offered an apologetic shrug. "I haven't been on duty in years. I just want to be useful, that's all. Blame the Army."

Bella laughed shakily. "Bad Army. No cookie. Yeah, this is going to take about the same amount out of both of us, but I'm going to guess that three sessions a day, for a week, should do it. And it is never going to get worse than it just was. It will always be a little better each time." Then, softly, "And . . . thanks. I just want to be useful too. Without having to kill someone to do it."

This time, Mel reached out for Bella's hand and gave it a reassuring pat. With the touch came a rush of what might have been feedback, if it hadn't been offered as a sort of explanation and example rather than an accidental release. She saw and felt a shadow of what had transpired with the Rebs, including the combination of emotion from Bella as the ganger crumpled under her mental bludgeon.

"With what you've got, you have to know the difference between 'want' and 'need.' You did what needed to be done. You didn't head out there *wanting* to have that be the end result."

"But I *need* to get the control so I know, beyond a doubt, that isn't the only option open to me. I *need* to be a laser, not a sledgehammer." Bella nodded, swiping at her eyes again. "Fixing you will help me get that control. So this is for both of us." She straightened. "Okay. Round two?"

Mel smiled and unfolded herself to lie on the couch once more. "Round two."

It was the same space, dark and rotting, but the four bodies had been pushed against the earthen wall. Mel hugged the kid's jacket around her tightly, the tags from her comrades kept safe in an inside pocket. Six days had passed since the last time the hatch had opened, and the noises she had heard hadn't involved any bits of broken English. She breathed through her hands and rocked herself back and forth, her own illusions letting her see the four men as simply asleep in their bedrolls as a calm summer sky stretched beyond them.

Gunfire rattled the space above her, bullets piercing the wooden hatch on the box. The noise broke the false dream and Mel crouched in the corner. There was more gunfire and shouting, and she tensed as something heavy slammed against the wood.

By this time the feeling of having Bella with her was familiar and comforting. The ghost in the back of her head that was *not* an illusion.

They knew where she would be if they opened the hatch. It wasn't unusual for these sorts of cells to change leadership and give up on their "prizes," which meant that Mel was no longer of worth to whoever had taken charge. Struggling to breathe through the dust and the smell, she crawled on her belly to where her comrades lay and positioned herself between the wall and the bodies. They had expected her to die anyway, but to confirm that . . .

They'll have to find me first.

The hatch opened and bullets showered the space where she had cowered and cringed for the past weeks. One of the cell's flunkies dropped into the space, semiautomatic at the ready as he surveyed the corner. Mel fought the urge to retch as she waited for him to turn. *Eye contact. I just need to see his eyes*, she thought. And when he turned to face her, she counted three and got up, and to the flunkie it was as if the entire pile of bodies had risen up to retaliate.

He screamed, and a second flunkie dropped into the box. The second saw not only the bodies of the soldiers as vengeful undead but also the man who was screaming. To make it even more authentic, Mel gave the first man the face and hollowed-out eyes of the kid they'd tortured. Panic ensued, with the pair babbling as she scrambled out of the box, pushing the same horrifying image on anyone she saw. To anyone outside, it would have looked as if the cell members had gone mad, shooting at each other or screaming in fright and fleeing. To everyone there, including Mel, all they could see were copies of the same empty face, the same tattered fatigues; all they could hear was the same wailing cry, and the smell of death and rot grew and filled the compound until it choked the air.

She tried to run, but the illusion was so vivid, so utterly real to even her, Mel froze just outside the door. Another group wearing combat fatigues and heavy gear came down the hallway, rifles trained on her as they approached. She threw the same sights, sounds, and smells at them in desperation, the projected nightmare coming to a crashing halt when the twin leads of a stun gun hit her damp skin and brought her to the ground.

Stop.

It was the familiar routine, and welcome now. The memory

froze even as she started to fall and she stood outside herself, looking at the scene.

The healer's presence was warm and supportive. *You know the drill.*

Mel felt herself nod, felt the same cool detachment from the scene. *It was a fight-or-flight scenario. I had to get out, even if it meant leaving them in the box. I used what I did as a resource to survive. And the ones here...* The focus went to the group in combat fatigues, the small patches identifying them as members of the United States Marine Corps, something easy to recognize as the memory stood still but difficult to see through fear and panic. *They should have brought a meta with them. Lack of preparation on their part does not mean that I'm responsible for my actions... right?*

Absolutely. And give them credit; they might not have had a mental meta available. But they recognized immediately what you were doing and took appropriate action given that they didn't have a power to take you out. One more thing. Your fellow soldiers were there for you as well as you for them. They would have been proud to give you that chance to escape. Would? Were.

Guilt rose up, followed by a tidal wave of shame. *But to use them the way I did... I know they never moved. I know that the team was able to get them out and lift them home for their families. And still, it feels like I crossed a line... like I disrespected them.*

Did they, or did they not, all carry organ donor on their tags?

It was a coolly logical question, one that Mel had never considered. *Did. We all did.*

How is that different? You give even after death so others may live. There was implied consent. There was no disrespect intended, right?

She managed another nod. *Right.*

It would have been one thing if you'd been, hell, doing that as some kind of juvenile hazing prank. Scaring the hell out of a gym full of teenagers. This was fighting for your life. In a way, you gave them one last chance to fight with you.

Mel looked down at herself in the memory. The kid's jacket hung on her, the inside pocket flipped back enough to show the chains from the four sets of tags she carried. *Yeah,* she finally admitted. *I guess you're right.*

She felt the warmth of Bella's comfort, and once again, that sense of something subtle changing. Now she knew what it was. A new neural pathway had just formed. By coming to that conclusion herself, and accepting it, she had formed it. Now Bella was making sure it was wired in hard, growing a couple new neurons in her brain. That was the physical reality. The emotional, the spiritual reality?

Saving her sanity, and maybe her soul.

Go.

Mel faded into the fuzzy sensation as the Marines rushed forward, two in front as a third hefted her over a shoulder. She felt herself swing around, and a pair of gloved hands touched her face. There were short crisp words that identified the speaker as someone she should trust, and he asked about the other members of her team. She shook her head "no," and the reminder triggered the same rush of illusions. The man in front of her fell back, eyes screwed shut as he tried to bark out an order to the others.

Almost simultaneously, a dark cloth was wrapped around Mel's eyes and a needle hit the skin behind her ear. She dropped into a blissful state of nothing as she changed hands and the rescue team made their way out of the compound.

The memory dissolved as the first one had, the same waking sensation moving over Mel as she came out. Without thinking, she sniffed the air expecting that the same illusions had manifested during the session. She slipped her hand from Bella's and sat up, rubbing her face and pushing her hair back.

"We've gotta stop meeting like this," Bella drawled. "People are starting to talk."

Mel gave a rough laugh as she passed the box of tissues to Bella. "Really? From the gossip I heard coming over here, you were cozy with the Ruskies. Something about how red and blue made purple." She blew her nose and tried to smile. "They really have a guy who talks to squirrels?"

"They do. He's got the mind of a six-year-old. A sweet six-year-old. Before his accident he was a leading scientist. Now he looks like a half-finished statue; he can eat anything, and he talks to squirrels. His name is Chug, and everyone over there loves him." She sighed. "Anytime I start doubting the wisdom of trying to save humanity I take him for a walk in the park."

"Sounds like good mutual therapy." She glanced to the clock on the wall. "You might have time for one before it gets late. I mean, if you think I'm okay for the day." Mel fidgeted with the sleeve of her Echo uniform. A week's worth of sessions with the blue touch-telepath had done wonders for her bruised psyche; in the same amount of time, Echo hadn't been able to find her a shirt that fit properly. "How many more weeks before I get to head out?"

"We're about to find out."

Bella moved her hand—and suddenly the office was flooded with the stench of rotting bodies. Mel jumped from the couch in a cold sweat, her body shaking as she fought with the knowledge that the smell couldn't be from actual decay and the memories of the box. For a moment, she visibly warred with the want to retreat into the couch. She appeared as if she might vomit. Then, slowly and controlled, the office around them shifted to worn water-stained walls, peeling linoleum, and a polished bartop. Cigarette smoke and cheap whiskey replaced the smell of death, and the blonde's shoulders and back untensed in a methodical fashion.

She took in a deep breath, then let it out, and the bar in New Orleans vanished, leaving Bella in the comfy chair.

"Awesome." Bella pushed another button. "Purge the office before I puke, Frank, this one's certified for duty."

CHAPTER FOURTEEN

Sleeping with the Enemy

MERCEDES LACKEY AND DENNIS LEE

Oh, all the things that we did not know.

I had tried to plug that hole. I had built a wild-hare system on a very old and outmoded PC with a bunch of outside-the-box spells on it. Now, magic as we have come to understand it in this century is hugely linked with math and physics, even if most mages can't work with the modern tools of math and physics. So I tended to have a lot of success with computer shamanism.

But this was right outside anything I had tried before. I was tired of being blindsided, and worse, I knew that we, Echo, could not afford to be blindsided much more. So I put together what I called my "Magic 8-Ball." Much like the toy, it gave you very simple answers. Generally the question I asked it—which I did, every time something big happened—was "who was behind this?" I did that with the Mumbai Incident, and the answer had come up "Dominic Verdigris III."

I knew about him already, of course, both the public face of the benevolent billionaire and the rumored face of the shadowy criminal mastermind. I'm paranoid, so I believed in the criminal mastermind part.

But I sure didn't see this coming, and unfortunately, the 8-Ball couldn't tell me.

Khanjar, bodyguard and sometime lover to Dominic Verdigris III, frowned with impatience at her—well, call him what he was—her meal ticket. She knew he didn't actually love her; he was constitutionally incapable of loving anyone but himself.

On the other hand, she was no different, so they made a matching set. He certainly paid well. And she was on occasion fond of him.

Not today, however.

Her posture on the white leather chaise lounge in his office was deceptively relaxed. The room was recognizable as an office only because of the computers on the round, polished hardwood dais. It had a stunning view of the infinity pool and the ocean beyond, and of his yacht, anchored in that ocean. He had his back to the view, and to her. "I fail to see the point of this exercise," she said, masking her impatience with a cool professionalism. "What do you need with Blacksnake?"

Verdigris was engaged in doing something he very rarely did. He was visibly working. He sat in the middle of his suite of computers like some starship captain on his bridge, and scooted around from one to the other on a chair of his own design, feverishly buying, selling, manipulating.... She reflected that he would be happier right now if he had four arms, like that Echo Op, Shakti. When had his shoulders acquired that stoop? And should she mention his hair was beginning to thin? He'd probably invent something to fix that better than Rogaine. It would make a lot of money.

"For one thing, this will stop them sending assassins after me," he said, absently. "I thought you'd be pleased about that. It would mean a little less work for you."

Khanjar crossed her long, elegant legs, sheathed in perfectly form-fitting, white silk jersey slacks, and frowned, because he was much smarter than that remark, even when preoccupied with six computer consoles. "Then those who wish you dead will simply hire someone else," she replied. "So—"

And then it dawned on her. "This has something to do with the Deva, does it not? The—Seraphym?"

Verdigris flinched. Aha, she had struck a nerve. In the shock following the Seraphym's visit to him, he had blurted out to Khanjar everything the creature had told him. If he'd had an hour to get over that shock, he probably would have kept this secret as he had so many others. But he had not; she had stepped out of the shower to find him shivering uncontrollably on the bed; the Seraphym had departed mere moments before.

Some might have thought she was a hallucination. Not Khanjar.

Khanjar knew; this was a Deva. Within moments of hearing Verdigris stammer out his story, she had been calculating how long, and what it would take her to balance her karma. One of her bank accounts was utterly depleted now, and there were exactly one thousand, seven hundred and fifty-four orphans across the world who had been taken from the most appalling conditions of child slavery, poverty, disease or all three and would be raised in good and loving families, given every opportunity to thrive. One for every life she personally had taken. And from now on, every time she killed, another child would be saved. Perfect karmic balance. Khanjar was not looking to improve her karma; she was actually quite satisfied with her life as it was, and would not in the least mind repeating it when something came along to end this one. But she had no wish to be reborn to the same circumstances as those orphans she was saving.

"She's not a Deva. She's just a metahuman." A little sweat that had nothing to do with how hard he was working stood out on his brow. Aha, again. No matter what he *said,* he believed as well. He would try to convince himself otherwise, but deep inside, he believed.

"A metahuman who showed you the future." Khanjar probed a little deeper, cruelly. It was rare when she could get Verdigris to show anything but a flippant disregard for anything much outside himself and his comfort zone, an attitude that was at once curiously childlike and curiously chilling. She got a certain enjoyment out of this. "A future in which you were a—'brain in a box,' I think you said?"

"That doesn't make her an angel. Matthew March saw pretty much the same future, it just didn't have me specifically in it." He operated two keyboards at once, one with each hand. "Probably because he didn't know me. I ran an analysis on his work for Echo. All the indications are he couldn't see anything in the future that wasn't somehow connected with people he knew."

"And now you are buying Blacksnake—why?" That bewildered her. What did he need with a small mercenary army—all right, one that did have a sizable number of metahumans, but still *small*—when he could, with the same effort, get the use of any one of a dozen national armies? If he tried hard enough, he could probably get the use of even the United States Army for an hour or two.

"I'm buying Blacksnake so I can get Echo. Ha!" He pushed away from the keyboards, face radiating triumph. "Got you, you bastards. You are mine now!"

"Ahhh." This, she understood. Echo, which had, more or less, cornered the market on metahumans, was the only organization that stood a chance of stopping the Thulians. Verdigris was going to make sure they did so—by somehow using Blacksnake and taking it over, so that he could be absolutely certain that all of their focus was on finding the Thulians and destroying them. None of this business about negotiation, making peace, or "keeping some for study." Verdigris had *written* some of the Evil Overlord lists; he thought they were hilarious. No, he would reduce the Thulians to ashes, and then shoot the ashes into the heart of the sun.

How he would do this, she had no idea. It didn't matter. This was Verdigris. He had made up his mind and it would be done.

But he was standing up and gesturing to her. "Come on, we're going to go pay a visit to my new headquarters before they figure out who owns them now and make it harder on everyone for me to move in."

She nodded, and swung her long legs over the side of the white chaise lounge, reaching for her white silk jacket. This was more like it. "Anything I should bring?"

He grinned, looking not unlike one of his pet sharks. "Your skills, my pretty. I suspect that the previous commander is not going to retire quietly."

She sighed as she followed him. Her bank account was going to suffer for this.

Khanjar wiped her hands on the general's jacket with distaste. "It's always a pleasure to watch a professional at work," Verdigris said. "How do I look?"

"Perfect, I suppose," Khanjar replied, eying the holographic disguise critically. "So long as you don't move too much. You tend to blur a little when you do." She seized the general's collar and pulled the dead body out of the chair. "Where do you want this?"

"I kind of like the idea of forcing them to walk over him as they come in, don't you?" Verdigris said cheerfully.

Khanjar sighed. "Your sense of the dramatic is going to get you into trouble, one day."

Verdigris took his place in the chair at the head of the table while Khanjar dragged the body over to the door. Sitting down would disguise the difference in height, later.

Verdigris buzzed the receptionist. "All right, Miss Francher. You can send the board members in now."

It might have been the shortest meeting in Blacksnake history. Verdigris informed the members of the board of directors that Blacksnake was in new hands. He regretted the unfortunate demise of the general—"He really should have been more careful about his health, my assistant did her best to save him, but the stroke killed him instantly." He then dissolved the board, and sent them all away with enormous bonus checks, which Khanjar handed to them on their way out, making sure that each of them looked directly into her cold, dark eyes as they took what was essentially blood money.

They were in quite a hurry to leave. Anyone who might be tempted to divulge what had happened here would find his temptation murdered as abruptly as the general by the information on the minidisk that was in each envelope with the check. Men did not rise in Blacksnake without leaving a lot of skeletons in closets, and those disks had enough information on them to rattle any number of bones. And the severance checks were outstandingly generous.

When the door had closed again, and Khanjar had locked it, Verdigris shut down the holographic generator. "I have to work on that," he said, hitting the side of his head with the heel of his hand. "Running it's almost like having a migraine. The kind with no pain, just all sorts of visual effects. You can come out now, Rancor."

At the end of the long conference table, a short man with enormous forearms materialized into view. He sat sprawled on one of the ultra-plush conference chairs, sporting a tan duster and a look of disdain, and calmly set the remote to his chameleon suit down on the table. Verdigris beamed at him. The man glared back, then removed a fresh cigar from his pocket and lit up. He took a few deep drags, his eyes never leaving Verdigris.

"Ranc, Ranc, Ranc, those things will kill you, you know." Verdigris shook his head.

"It's Jack now," the man said. "I haven't been Rancor in a long while."

"They'll still kill you." Verd steepled his fingers and tried to look concerned. He didn't succeed. Khanjar sighed to herself. This was going to be tedious. Dominic was going to try and be charming, Jack was . . . going to do what Jack would do. Men.

Jack continued to puff on his cigar and glare at Verdigris.

"So I think I've got it figured out," Jack said finally. "Correct me if I'm wrong."

Verdigris nodded, still beaming.

"Earlier today, you managed to buy up controlling shares of Blacksnake through your many dummy corporations. Your one obstacle was the current head, General Landover, the most successful leader Blacksnake has ever known, and the most popular, given his recent motions towards increased profit-sharing for all staff ranging from the field ops to the lowly secretarial pool..."

"I'm sorry," Verdigris said. "Was he a friend?"

"He was an ass," Jack answered promptly. "An ass with good luck, given that he fell into the crapper that the Kriegers generated and came out of the pit with his hands full of diamonds. But still, an ass." Jack stood up and strolled over to look down at Landover. He snorted and spit on the body. "Nice work, Khanjy."

"I consider her an artist," Verdigris replied happily. Khanjar said nothing. She didn't care for Jack. She didn't *hate* him; she just didn't care for him. He reminded her of the crude bullies that served the warlords back in her home province. Something she didn't much like to be reminded of.

"And so," Jack continued, pausing only to strike his heel across Landover's temple, "you decide to expedite the transfer of power by coming here personally and removing the general from his seat, pay off the current board to walk away, all the while wearing *my* face, which leads me to the conclusion that you have work for me."

"Work?" Verdigris snorted, his tone indignant. "A *promotion*, Jack! One must always look out for one's friends."

"Friends, are we?" Jack said, seating himself next to Verdigris. He paused to consider that. "Well, I suppose I've tried to have friends killed at one time or another."

Verdigris coughed into his hand. "Now, Jack, we should let bygones be bygones. It's a whole new world full of opportunity out there! You need me, now that the board thinks you're the coup master. And I need *you*. What could be a better basis for friendship?"

Khanjar did not roll her eyes. She had an excellent poker face; most assassins did.

"Keep talking," Jack said. "Be convincing."

"You get to collect El Generalissimo's salary, perks, and whatever you care to skim off the top. I'm serious, Jack. I did not buy Black-snake to make a profit. I bought it for two reasons." He held up one finger. "I got tired of watching Khanjar kill the morons they sent after me." He held up the second finger. "I want Echo. To get Echo, I need Blacksnake. But I can't be the head of Blacksnake, or I'll never get Echo. QED: You become head of Blacksnake."

"Uh huh," Jack muttered. "And why me?"

"You were the most trustworthy of the current roster that I could discern."

"Trustworthy in general or to you?"

"In general," Verdigris admitted. "My only trepidation in this whole affair is that you might still have some issues with..."

"With the way you ended our last arrangement?" Jack offered.

"Oh really, Jack, if you can't overlook a *small* matter of betrayal in the face of glorious immortality..."

"You tried to blow me up, Verd. Forty pounds of C-4 isn't what I would call 'small.'"

"Well, it is when you consider I overruled Khanjar and gave you a sporting chance." Khanjar noted the gleam in Verdigris' eyes. It was not entirely sane.

"Did it occur to you to ask me if I wanted in before adopting my identity and perforating the leader of a major coordinated force of mercenaries and metahumans?"

"And what would be the fun in that?" Verdigris grinned with aplomb. "Besides, I have a line on an old prize that might inter-est you. And this time, Jack, I'm not above sharing it. So? Are we BFFs now?"

"That depends," Jack said as he reached down and extinguished his cigar on Landover's exposed teeth.

"On what?"

"On what you can give that assures me I can trust you this time."

"Proximity, my dear Jack, proximity. You will have the prize before I do, and while you do not trust *me*, I trust *you*. You do have an impeccable reputation for delivery." Verdigris continued to grin. "And meanwhile, look at the lifestyle you get to enjoy! I really don't care if you clean out every offshore account as long as you can keep the company running long enough for me to get Echo."

Jack nodded, bowing his head in thought.

"The real deal this time?" he asked.

Verdigris nodded. "You do this right, we'll both live forever. And not 'continuing to age until we turn into wrinkled little raisins' live forever, either."

"Who's the mark?"

Verdigris smiled. It looked like a shark. "I need you to get into Tesla's office. A very little package I want planted."

Jack gave him a quizzical lift of his brow. "Tesla guards the secret to immortality?"

Verdigris chuckled. "Tell me, Jack. Have you ever heard of Metis?"

CHAPTER FIFTEEN

Thunder in Heaven

MERCEDES LACKEY AND CODY MARTIN

This story is the reason why I started raiding every resource I could get my hands on to build a system that would let me play Overwatch to more than one group at a time. After this was over, I swore that never again would my people be left without their eyes in the sky, if I had to wire myself into the computers and hook myself up to IVs and never leave my chair again.

John had really fallen in with his newest "comrades." They were certainly a motley bunch, comprised of metahumans from the USSR who were either decades past their prime or too green to reasonably be fielded. Still, each and every one of them had a "closeness" that John hadn't experienced in years. They were on the ragged edge, working with a shoestring budget and not nearly enough people...but they were still getting their jobs done, making do where they had to. There was the oddball Great Patriotic War vet who would push the Stalinist line pretty hard, but for the most part John's standing as a "sturdy worker" was enough to save him from most of the rhetoric.

Since joining the CCCP, the days had flashed by; there was always too much that needed to be done, so he was constantly busy. And it was a good feeling, much like what he had been doing in the neighborhood but with a bit more...was it legitimacy? The weight of the world wasn't on John's shoulders alone, anymore; he had backup, now. He spent most of his time patrolling and acting as a liaison between the CCCP and its Area of Operation. Odd-job construction bits around the HQ, taking breaks with Chug in the park or Pavel at the only working watering hole in the neighborhood, or filling out the ever-present reams of paperwork took up the rest of his time. John had finally got his stride back; if he could just shake the recurring chest cold and fatigue he seemed to have a run of, he'd have been better than ever.

For those seldom-quiet moments, he took his time to seek out Sera or Bella for conversation. Bella was the only American with CCCP ties that John associated with; there was that odd Vickie Victrix gal and Mamona, but John never saw much of them. Vickie was rumored to be somewhat of a recluse, and Mamona just had a different patrol schedule than John. And Sera...well, that was another matter. She'd virtually been with John since he'd entered Atlanta, in one form or another. He generally felt quite a bit better after meeting with her; the last time, he had attempted to introduce her to the concept of "ice cream" with mixed results.

Today there was a "simple" little task that needed doing in the upgraded infirmary, but of course with anything involving the CCCP, nothing was simple. What should have been freestanding, lockable supply cabinets needed to be shock-mounted to the wall, similar to what one would see in nuclear missile silos. Jadwiga was adamant about that. "More poundings on roof by *Fashisti* and all my bottles of medicines go flying? *Nyet!*" John had the free pair of hands and he kind of felt he owed Jadwiga at this point.

The base still didn't have reliably working AC—except in the computer room—so pretty much everyone but Upyr stripped as far down as decency permitted while within the walls. For some reason Upyr never seemed to feel the heat. So John was down to a wife-beater and shorts as he sweated through the installation to Jadwiga's specified cabinets. "Hotter than Hell on the 4th of July," he muttered. It was one of his father's favorite phrases, and had stuck with John.

"Lawsy may, it's raining men," drawled Bella. "You trying out for the Chippendales?"

John shrugged, tightening a bolt as he spoke. "Isn't there a play bein' put on for Smurfs somewhere in town? I hear they still need Smurfette." John flashed a smile over his shoulder. "If you're lookin' for a gig, I think they might just let ya audition."

John playfully swatted away a sponge that Bella had sent flying for the back of his head. "You should be grateful we're out of 'Souvenirs of the War of Northern Aggression.'" she mock-snarled.

"Saviour already bash 'em all? I know Old Bear made her go through at least a crate when he put in a requisition form for 'Going-Postal Notes.' Me an' Unter had a chuckle 'bout it in the rec room." He set down his wrench, turning and standing to face Bella. "What can I do for ya, Blueberry? Or'd ya just come to harass a hard-workin' comrade?"

She gave him a thoughtful once-over. "Oh...came in here to resupply." She put down her box of medical supplies. "By the way, there's a wrecked warehouse at what used to be South Peachtree Place that was a med supply house. I got hold of them, they told me they've written everything off but no one's looted it and we're welcome to what we can scavenge." Her eyes rested on the tattoo on the back of his hand. "And this is the point where if I wasn't an empath I'd ask you about the ink and the scars."

He frowned, ruffling his hair with his fingers. Bella noticed that he did so with his tattooed hand, specifically. "Well, gee, Bella. Here I thought we were friends."

"That doesn't mean I snooped. It means I know you don't want to talk about it...but I also know you need to. To someone, anyway. You've gotten mental ulcers over it." She turned her back to him and began stowing away little glass bottles in the infirmary fridge. "If you don't do something about it soon, it's going to blow up in your face."

"Yeah, well, it ain't exactly something that y'talk to anyone that you want to see breathin' for the forseeable future. Y'know what I'm saying?"

"Actually, no. Why don't you enlighten me?" She studied the labels on the bottles very carefully.

John looked around the room, his eyes staying fixed on the doorway for a few extra moments. Bella took that as her cue to close the door, and make sure it was locked. He sighed heavily, sitting down on a small wooden crate. "Well, shit. Whaddya know from what I told ya before?"

"Not much. And most of that is reading between the lines. You've got implants and the work is too good for it to be anything other than a program, presumably a government program, presumably the US government."

"Wasn't just *any* program. That's what they called it; 'The Program.' I'm gettin' ahead of myself, though." He shifted forward, resting his forearms on his thighs. "Grew up in Virginia with my folks, only child of theirs. Went through the motions in high school, then enlisted in the Army once I was graduated; kinda a forgone conclusion, since my old man had served for his career. Went '11-bang-bang,'—11b; Infantry. Passed all of what I needed to to get into Rangers, and went on to the 75th. Did this and that here and there. I loved military life. After I had gotten up in years and experience, I got a once-in-a-lifetime chance; tried out for 1st Special Forces Operational Detachment-Delta, y'know, the 'Delta Force' that Hollywood makes all of those retarded movies about. Counterterrorism; real bad boys that *knew* their stuff. Won't say with any small amount of pride that we were the absolute best at our mission profile, which was pretty damned versatile. Are you following me so far?"

"You sound like a recruiting brochure," she said dryly. "Go on."

"Yeah, yeah. Anyways. Did some things with Delta. There was a fairly big hiccup during one of 'em." John went silent for a few moments, looking past Bella before snapping to ever so subtly.

"I'm an empath, Johnny. That felt like more than a 'hiccup.'"

John continued to talk, not making eye contact with her. "After that, I got 'recruited.' There was a very hushed-up gig going on, and they needed the best and the brightest for it. Being a bit younger and a whole lot dumber, I went along with it. Program was as such: government had a couple of research stations where they were tryin' to develop the next sort of mass-produced, cyber-enhanced soldier." He held up an arm, displaying the symmetric scars running along the entire length. "It was a combination of surgical and cybernetic stuff. Overall it got called 'enhancements'— musculature, reflexes, hardened bones, an' so on. *Six Million Dollar Man* type of stuff; stronger, faster, tougher. We were the test batch for it, and it showed; we had over forty-five percent of our folks die from the trials for it."

Anger made her eyes glow for a moment. "There is a special place in hell for whatever MDs were overseeing that."

"We had all sorts; top of their fields, all of 'em. Just like us." John chuckled mirthlessly. "After the surgeries and procedures were done, those of us that were left went through physical therapy to get our bodies used to the enhancements, and recover from gettin' torn up. It was kinda like relearning to walk. Not too fun. Durin' the retraining period, I exhibited something that the docs didn't exactly expect." He snapped the fingers on his right hand, producing a lighter-sized flame. "I had natural metahuman ability. Y'see, the docs and project heads wanted to make every soldier be on par with some of the mid-level metahumans via the enhancements. For the few of us that they found with powers already, they had special plans. I got shuffled into a side program, where they tried to figure out more about how our powers worked, if they were replicable, and how best to utilize them for Black Ops."

"How...charming."

"While I was in the Program—and trust me, I was still going along with it at this point, since I figured this is what we all signed up for—some more things happened." Another very long pause on his part. The angry glow in Bella's eyes went out. Her brow furrowed and it looked as if she was going to try and reach out to touch his arm, but stopped herself at the last moment.

"That's—that's what they call 'collateral damage' where you come from, I guess."

"Yeah, well...after that, I became 'uncooperative.' Head researcher ordered me up for 'termination'; gettin' a lethal shot and then opened up on a cadaver table. I didn't exactly cotton to that. I...I lost my head, there." John smiled again, lopsidedly, staring past Bella for a moment before meeting her eyes. "Y'know what temperature steel melts at?" The lighter-sized flame on his finger intensified and grew to encompass his hand; the temperature in the room ramped up considerably as the flames became hotter and hotter before John suddenly extinguished them. "When I woke up, everything in the place was burned. Everything and everybody, you understand? So I ran, and had been runnin' up until I came to y'all here at the CCCP." He looked at her soberly. "You wanted to know. And there it is."

Bella's eyes widened, then narrowed again. Her frown deepened, and one fist clenched. John's experience told him she was in fight-or-flight mode from something she had read from him, and was working hard to stay on top of her gut reactions.

And that was when her comm went off.

She jumped, and slapped her hand to the unit on her hip. "Belladonna Blue, go."

"*We have an incident at the edge of a destruction corridor,* coordinates 123.45.3. Please meet with your team at that 20. Your team is Corbie, Granny Aiken, Little Dolly, and Leader of the Pack."

"Roger, on the way." She glanced over at John. "We'll talk more later. And...keep a heads-up around here. That's a lot of firepower for an 'incident.' Granny Aiken is a Psychokinetic OpThree, and Dolly is a walking arsenal."

"Keep it real, an' safe journies, Blueberry."

She gave him a penetrating look. "You too." She hesitated a moment more, then turned, flipped the lock, and pelted out the door. John gave an exasperated sigh. *That sucked. Only way it could've gone worse would've been if she had slugged me.* He had lived with his past every day, every time he used his enhancements or his flames. Getting flak from a friend didn't help things much. And to top it all off, he still had to secure these damned cabinets!

Bella wondered how Little Dolly could stand upright. She was something like 5 foot 6, but she had a rack that must have been 48 DDs.

She'd have gotten hit on a lot more if it wasn't for the fact that Little Dolly—whose metahuman abilities had manifested in the middle of the Invasion, like so many—was always packing. Never less than a pair of 9 millimeter pistols and a Mossberg slung on her back. Generally a lot more than that. She'd been a stripper in one of the Atlanta gentlemen's clubs that was right on what was going to become one of the destruction corridors. When Nazi troopers came crashing through the place she'd somehow gotten her hands on the bouncer's sawed-off and actually had done enough kinetic damage with it to allow the customers to escape. Once she got her hands on something more precise from a dead SWAT officer and found out about the joint weakness...

Her metapower was as an intuitive marksman. She never needed a scope, and she generally shot from the hip.

Granny Aiken was another WWII vet. She'd been Pretty Sally back in the day, and she threw things with her mind. Her body might be a good bit more frail now, but she made up for it with mental strength.

Corbie smirked at all of them. "So, I'll go scout from above, Dolly'll go in there and stun the blokes—"

Granny *tsked*, and Dolly scowled. Corbie rolled his eyes. "Blimey, you packin' stun grenades or not, Doll?"

"Oh." Dolly looked mollified. "Yeah, I am."

"Bad idea," Leader of the Pack said. He jerked a thumb at his dogs. "Let them. You make a hella big target in the air, birdbrain."

"Boy has a point," Granny agreed. Corbie made a face, but nodded.

They left their van at the edge of the corridor, and began working their way in. Bella was keeping mental track of the dogs, although it wasn't as easy as it was with a human—animals were on a different "frequency" or something. Leader had told her that the dogs couldn't exactly communicate directly with him as such; he could tell them what to do, and if they ran into something, they'd come back to him and by their behavior he could get a general idea of what they'd seen. Mostly.

Bella actually had the notion that he *was* telepathic with them, but telepathy scared him, so he consciously repressed what he was getting and reread it as behavior. Whatever worked.

"Don't you usually work with Handsome Devil, Shakti and Einhorn?" Bella asked Corbie as they moved cautiously though the wreckage—admittedly with more caution for what they might fall over or have fall on them than for cover.

"Conrad's havin' a bad-luck day, Shakti's makin' sure it doesn't go as far as havin' a Nazi show up at the door, an' Einhorn's with another team." He shrugged. "This lot isn't a team so much as who answered the comm."

He stopped, and frowned, holding up a finger in the age-old gesture for "listen."

They'd been hearing distant gunfire for some time. Bella had gotten pretty used to distant gunfire by now. But... wait. This wasn't just gunfire. It wasn't even just the bursts of an AK-47 or something else on full auto.

This was... a lot.

That was when she picked up a burst of fear from all of Leader's dogs, and they came dashing back so fast she didn't even have time to say something.

They exchanged startled looks. "Lots of full autos," Leader said slowly, as his dogs danced around him in a fandango of anxiety. "Grenade launchers. Bowser says a missile launcher, but I'm not sure I believe that—"

He was interrupted by an explosion. A big one.

"... or maybe I do."

They exchanged glances again. Leader reached for his comm. "I'm calling in help."

Bella slowly reached into her pocket and pulled out the slightly larger and far less sleek and high-tech unit that Sovie had given her.

"So am I," she said, and put the unit up to her mouth. "Gamayun, this is Bella Blue. I'm with an Echo team at what used to be the corner of Lee and Tate. We have a problem."

John was just about finished installing Jadwiga's cabinet when a small group of CCCPers caught his attention. They were running full-tilt down the corridor, coming from the barracks and heading to the garage, most likely. It wasn't terribly unusual; whenever the nigh-prescient Gamayun spotted trouble brewing, a patrol was sent out or a group of already patrolling CCCPers were redirected to see what was going on. Less than ten minutes later, however, he was startled to hear the base's klaxons go off. The Commissar had insisted on her personnel running a number of drills, even before the base was finished with its renovations. Fire drills, practice sessions for what to do in order to repel intruders, and the "all-hands" drill for when every able-bodied CCCPer was required to suit up and head out to deal with a threat. This specific alarm indicated that it was the lattermost, and that very fact gave John pause. Despite the CCCP being a ragtag, thrown-together lot, they were a capable bunch. What could possibly be so bad that it needed all of them to handle? Immediately an image of a renewed Nazi invasion thrust into the fore of his mind, and a cold, empty feeling gripped him. A rapid burst of something in Russian—in Gayamun's voice—blatted out over the intercom. John was still haltingly learning Russian, but he did recognize two words: "Echo" and "Rebs."

Before John could properly react, he saw Soviet Bear's head poking into the doorway. "*Davay,* comrade! We are to be rocking the Casbah!"

John stood up, perplexed. "The hell are you talkin' about, Pavel? What's goin' on?" Bear sometimes mangled his English terribly, mispronouncing phrases or butchering euphemisms.

Bear stepped fully into the doorway, his submachine gun in hand. "It is American for kicking donkeys or something, *da?* Bah! Never mind. *Davay!* Mount up!" Without another word, he trotted away, his clunky metal feet stomping through the hallway.

Before John could react to *that,* Upyr ran towards him from the other direction, laden with two AK-47s and her shotgun. She stopped just long enough to toss one AK and a magazine carrier to him before following in Bear's wake. "This is not being nonlethal, Chonny," she called over her shoulder. "They are having missile launcher." She sped off, and from her direction, he reckoned she was heading for the garage. Evidently, in her case, leather pants, jacket and armored pads counted as being "suited up."

John slung the rifle and the magazine carrier over his shoulder, running out of the room and down to the locker room next door. A number of other CCCPers were already there, changing into their patrol uniforms and body armor. John quickly unlocked his locker and changed with practiced precision. Less than a minute later, he was being shuffled and shoved into one of the CCCP's pool of vans; a couple of others, Untermensch and Red Saviour included, had already revved up motorcycles and were preparing to ride escort. Inside of his van were a few that he already knew; Bear and Upyr, along with the American psionicist Mamona. The other two were Russians: Perun, one of the veterans and an electricity-based meta; and then Zmey in his hydrocephalic flame-producing helmet. Everyone in the van was silent, checking their firearms and gear except for Bear, who was chanting a garbled version of "We Will Rock You."

Finally, as Mamona, who was driving, gunned the engine, Upyr leaned forward and stared into Bear's face and said something in Russian. Whatever it was, Pavel looked stunned and stopped. Upyr settled back with a smile on her pale face.

John leaned forward, satisfied after function-checking his rifle. "What'd ya say to him?"

"That I would be giving him shotgun enema if he did not cease with the racket music. Then Unter would to be doing buckshot extraction."

He smirked. "You're a mean one."

With a lurch and a grinding of gears, the van started forward out of the garage. Several very bumpy minutes later, the van screeched to a halt. Mamona called over her shoulder for everyone to pile out. John jumped down onto broken cinderblocks, the remains of a building demolished in the Nazi attack. He could clearly hear what sounded like all of the gunfire in the world going off in the distance. A block away, at most. The rest of the riders had piled out when Perun, his shaggy white hair blowing in the humid breeze, spoke up. "We are on foot from this point, *tovarischii*. There is a squad of Echo immediately to our southeast; they are being pinned down by an unknown number of Rebs in an abandoned building. A patrol is on scene, and requested backup. Due to the amount of firepower," he said, his words punctuated by a large explosion, "that the Rebs are using, we are weapons free. Lethal force if necessary, *tovarischii*." With a curt nod, he sprinted off towards the gunfire. The rest of the squad followed him, keeping a few meters between each of them.

Their comms crackled to life. "... *spasibo, Gamayun*. CCCP, Belladonna Blue, here. Mamona, Johnny, I'm with the Echo squad. I'll be doing this in Russian and Murkan for your benefit." A brief sentence in Russian followed. "Follow your leader, guys, I gave him the route for the safe corridor in to as close as you can get to us."

After a short run, with John behind Bear in their lineup in order to keep their rear secure, they arrived at their destination. Red Saviour and the rest of the CCCP, save for the squad on site with Bella, were assembled near a corner. Red Saviour was busy talking urgently with Molotok when she noticed John's squad arrive. "Comrades, gather. Blue girl managed to get out, rest of squad is pinned down. Echo was being called also, but all of their personnel are otherwise engaged." She shook her head. "Am not liking sound of this, but this is being on our back turf, so we will be taking standard urban advance to building across from the one we are here behind. Perun—you take squad and provide covering fire for our advance. Once we are in place, we will cover Echo retreat to our position. Then we unite and make the frontal assault."

"I'll do my best to baffle their brains, but there's a lot of them, and it's at a distance," Bella said, repeating it in Russian. "So don't count too much on it. They're mostly not good marksmen, but they have grenade launchers and at least one shoulder-fired missile launcher. You know what they say about 'close only counts'—and these ain't horseshoes."

With that, Natalya spoke in rapid-fire Russian to Perun. He pointed at John, Bear and Zmey. "Take position to lay down suppressive fire for the Commissar's squad, comrades." Without another word, Perun ducked around the corner. It felt as if every hair on John's body stood up on end a half second before the old veteran began sending hundred-yard-long bolts of electricity across to the building where the Rebs were holed up. John crouched low and took up a prone position about five yards from Perun. Unslinging his rifle and charging it with a fresh round, he took aim. Bear and Zmey did the same, keeping an adequate amount of space between them.

The Commissar sounded out the command. "Now!" John, Bear, and Zmey all poured small arms fire into the building in measured bursts—well, Bear fired with abandon from his PPSh, laughing raucously—while Perun loosed a flurry of electrical bursts. Red Saviour and her squad of CCCPers dashed to a building across from their position, making sure they weren't clumped together. The return fire from the Rebs was sporadic, thanks to the amount of lead that was being shot into their cover. A handful of heartbeats later, the Commissar and her squad were in position. She gave a command over the comms, and the CCCPers' positions exploded into a hail of fire again; more covering fire for the Echo patrol and CCCP squad pinned down by the Rebs. John could see that they had been crouched behind an overturned van and some rubble; one of the Echo metas had been invisibly uprooting huge chunks of rubble to intercept the Rebs' weapons' fire, chucking away each piece as it crumbled under the hail of bullets and explosives.

Both the Echo folks and the CCCP squad with them made a break for Saviour's position; very few of the Rebs dared to poke their heads out to try to take potshots under the combined fire from the Commissar's and Perun's squads. A few of the rescued were looking bloodied, but no one was incapacitated, so there was that much to be thankful for. With all of their forces regrouped, it took about a minute for Saviour to communicate with the Echo and CCCP personnel that had been under fire; once she was done, she signaled to Perun. "On my mark, comrades, fire and advance by bounds. We are to be assaulting the building. Perun's squad will be the lead element, and will take the first floor. We shall take the second."

Bella was already making her rounds of the wounded, as was Sovie. Between the two of them, it wasn't more than a few minutes before the injured were back in fighting form, injuries closed, if not healed. John hadn't seen a meta-medic in action before. Truth to tell, it kind of made the hair on the back of his neck stand up. People shouldn't be able to do that. Amped up on adrenaline, John had one of the moments of surreal clarity that some people experienced as a combat stress reaction; he wondered whether the world would be a better or worse place without metahumans.

Before he could ponder it any more, Perun shouted, "Now!" John brought himself up into a kneeling position, firing at all of the windows of the building in front of him. He fired until the magazine for his rifle went dry, and then reloaded it with a fresh one. Finally, after several other CCCPers had rushed past him, it was his turn to make the dash to the building. The stuff you heard and saw in movies about zigzagging when you're under fire was complete BS; he ran in a straight line, and hard, for the front wall of the building. Thanks to his enhancements, he crossed the distance in an instant, slamming into the wall, shoulder first, with enough force to crack the brick. He was at the end of the "stack," the line his squad had made on the wall. The Commissar's stack was opposite them; without a word, one of the CCCPers from her squad kicked in the door. Several flashbangs and fragmentation grenades were thrown inside of the doorway, their explosions barely muffled by the walls. The team was inside in an instant, with Chug leading the way as a stumpy shield; lots of gunfire and the varied sounds of metahuman powers being used rang out from inside.

Perun used a hand signal to indicate that it was his squad's turn. They all streamed through the doorway, following his lead. John caught sight of several Rebs' bodies in his peripheral vision as he followed Upyr, who was in front of him. They assaulted towards the stairway, guns trained upwards. The too-loud crackle and boom of Perun's electricity echoed, along with more rifle fire from the rest of the squad. Since John was rear security for this portion, he kept his attention split between following the others and making sure that there weren't any hidden Reb stragglers popping out to cause them trouble.

Past the first landing, the team lined up outside of the first door. Perun had positioned himself opposite the team on the doorway. With a plasma-charged fist, Bear knocked the door off of its hinges, stepping aside so that the rest of the team could enter. More gunfire, and John was stuck outside keeping security. Someone inside, it sounded like Mamona, called out, "Clear!"

Since John had been at the rear of the team, it was his turn to be at the front of the stack. There was only one more door on this floor; this was the one at the front of the building, facing the street where the Echo team had been pinned down. Bear made his way to the other side of the door, nodding to John; again, he keyed his gauntlets to allow plasma to flow from the conduits connected to his heart and into his fists. The door shattered, and John was through the entrance. A Reb was immediately in front of him, turning to swing some sort of rifle; John dropped him with two shots to the center of mass and one shot to his head before immediately turning right to clear the corner. The rest of his squad followed behind him, gunning down the remaining Rebs in the room in less than a second.

John shouted, "Clear!" echoing his comrades as they did the same.

The comm came to life again. Russian first, then English. "Comrades, regroup downstairs. Have not found grenade and missile launcher." Perun motioned for his team to exit the room. The squad jogged down the stairs, meeting up with Saviour and her group of CCCPers. Among them were the first squad along with the Echo patrol; Bella was in the process of grabbing one of them for another of her treatments. It looked as if they'd had more of a fight than John's group; a couple had been winged, all of them were sporting cuts and bruises from shrapnel. One of the CCCPers was limping from a bullet right through the thigh— the hole was visible in his trousers, but there was no bleeding now. Bella arched an eyebrow at John. "Gotta liberate us some nanoweave pants for you lot."

Before Natalya could raise a complaint, two Rebs burst from a storage closet, running as fast as they could for the back door. They shouldered their way through it, busting the door wide open. John couldn't get a bead on them with his rifle before they were outside, but he did notice that one of them was carrying the unaccounted-for "rocket launcher." It was an RPG-7, he guessed; widely available on the black market if you had the cash.

"*Davay, davay!* After them!" The Commissar propelled herself out through the door on a plume of her own strange metahuman energy. The congregation of CCCPers and Echo ran after her, a jostle of firearms and gear harnesses. They came out into another destruction corridor; the building the Rebs had holed up in had apparently been right on the edge. The two fleeing Rebs were almost across the entire expanse, as wide as a football field. John's group was about to give chase when they almost simultaneously noticed what was wrong with the scene.

On the other side of the destruction corridor were close to two hundred jeering, armed and very angry Rebs, led by Rebel Yell himself.

Holy Hell. It was all that John could think as he slung his rifle, shifting it behind his back and out of the way of his hands. The CCCPers had spread out and formed a line, everyone preparing in their own way. This was an ambush, and they'd taken the bait. There were less than thirty CCCPers and Echo, and at the very least two hundred Rebs; they were all armed with shotguns, pipes, chains, and knives. This was insane; the Rebs had a small army, and they were ready and willing to kill. The smart thing to do would've been to retreat under covering fire, and take the gang out at a distance, with rifles while behind cover. But none of the CCCPers ever got the chance to voice that option.

Rebel Yell strode out from the middle of the ranks of the jeering and shouting Rebs. His chest was puffed out and his chin was up; he was savoring every moment of this. Finally, he spoke, his voice carrying over the noise his compatriots were making. "You commies wanted a war? Well, you got a *war!*" The last word was deafening; John felt his equilibrium nearly go as he stumbled backwards, flailing to stay standing, the same as the rest of his friends and team. It was almost as an afterthought that he noticed that the building they had just left began to collapse, brought down by Yell's voice alone. *This is going to suck. A lot.* John didn't like to play fair; when it came to fighting, he cheated if he could. Life-and-death situations never had the luxury of allowing you to hold back; it was literally you or the other guy. Because of that, he absolutely hated fighting other metahumans. They could be as unpredictable as he could be, since there was a laundry list of abilities that any single meta could possess, with some of them being blatant and others insidious.

John hazarded a look down the CCCP lines; everyone's faces were set, their expressions stony. Bear was chomping at the bit, his fists already glowing with plasma. Untermensch and Molotok traded a glance before settling into fighting stances. Diminutive

Fei Li had her exquisite sword an inch out of its scabbard, coolly regarding the scene.

Saviour stood straight up from out of cover. "War?" she shouted back contemptuously. "You bring pipes and chains and call it war?" She spat. *"Nasrat.* You are less than *babushkas* at food riot. Comrades, disperse thugs! We are being late for dinner. *Davay, davay!"* Without another word the Commissar, unbelievably, literally flew straight for the Rebs' lines, beelining for Rebel Yell. The rest of the CCCP and Bella's Echo team launched after her. The Rebs, hungry looks pasted on their dirty faces, surged forward, whooping and hollering.

"Why does she *always* do this?" Molotok groaned.

"Spoilt, foolhardy *devushka,* comrade!" Unter hit Molotok in the shoulder as they ran, sprinting towards their enemy.

John took several quick, deep breaths; his enhancements keyed up, and he shot forward in a burst of unnatural speed. The world seemed to slow down for him; it wasn't exactly slow motion, because how he experienced the world didn't change that much. It was more like the world went on, but...deliberately. As if there were extra seconds between the seconds that were his alone, so that he had all the time he needed to see what had to be done and do it before the world caught up with him again. Instantly, he spotted his targets; a small bundle of four Rebs directly in front of him. One of them was armed with a ratty-looking shotgun, and the others had handheld weapons. *Piece of cake.* He met the line of Rebs at the same time as the Commissar; another half-look revealed that she had a wolfish grin on her face, her fist already cocked and burning with malevolent energies.

John calculated that in order to pull his weight in this fight, he'd have to take out at least eight of the Rebs. Probably more, just to be on the safe side. With the rest of his comrades just getting into the thick of it, he couldn't very well lose control and just fry all of the Rebs in a wave of plasma. This fight would take a little bit more controlled fury, some awful and deadly precision. John juked to his left, right before he reached his selected targets, hoping to throw them off. He chose the shotgun-wielding Reb for his first; a single too-hot beam of plasma shot through him, decapitating the thug. John swung around, ducking low and bringing his trailing leg out to sweep two of his would-be ambushers. They both tumbled to the ground facefirst, impacting with the sickening meat-packing thud that the human body makes when it hits something too hard. He immediately engulfed both of them with plumes of fire from his hands. Switching his attention back to the furthest Reb, John leapt from his crouch, jumping higher than the biker expected. He raised his fist up, bringing it down with sickening force into the Reb's face; John felt cartilage and bone break, watching as blood instantly erupted from the ruins.

The rest of the CCCP were being equally efficient in removing the opposition, with few exceptions. The Commissar was simultaneously fighting five Rebs, striking at them with energy-charged fists, kicking off of one Reb only to launch herself in a lunge for another. The twin pair of Sirin and Alkonost were working together; Alkonost was dazing her targets with her ear-piercing shrieks, while Sirin erupted the ground beneath them with subsonic rumbles. Untermensch and Molotok were fighting as a pair as well, working over a dozen Rebs with a flurry of incredible hand-to-hand strikes. Perun was electrocuting three Rebs, walking purposefully forward as he assaulted them with strike after strike of his metahuman-generated lightning. Bear was the center of a melee, chortling and shouting insults about how their mothers were *kulaks* as he blasted Rebs with alternate bursts of his concussive plasma and submachine-gun fire; sparks skittered off of his titanium body as several shots from a Reb ricocheted, hitting another biker.

Their Echo allies were putting up more of a fight than John thought they would. Bella was directing Chug; the rocky creature, frightening as he was to look at, was surprisingly gentle and didn't like to hurt anything. At Bella's direction, he would rush Rebs that had tried to dig in under cover; when they found their bullets spattering against his hide and saw him still coming, they would panic and scatter. He would bellow, panicking them further, leaving them open to his comrades. Then Bella would find another knot and send him after them. Corbie had struggled to lift up Dolly, the perfect marksman, onto a nearby rooftop to shoot at the Rebs from elevation. Granny Aiken, the Echo team's psycho-kineticist, was dueling with her opposite on the Rebs' side; they were throwing monstrously huge pieces of rubble at each other, mentally swatting them aside at the last moment or redirecting them at each other. Leader of the Pack was situated behind one of the ever-present ruined and abandoned cars; he fired his Echo sidearm while directing his dogs to knock down Rebs, rushing their legs at the knees.

While they were all holding their own for the most part, some of the metahumans were having trouble. Zmey and Upyr had been rushed by what appeared to be a berserker pair of Rebs; they were screaming, and didn't seem to feel pain from the shotgun blasts from Upyr nor the fire from Zmey's helmet. They bowled into the two CCCPers, trying to split them up. Stribog, gifted with the power to create huge gusts of wind, was being plagued by a Reb that could teleport short distances. Every time that Stribog attempted to power a gust at the Reb, he would teleport behind the Russian meta, slamming a rusty pipe into him.

Seemingly out of nowhere, tiny Fei Li leaped into a crowd of Rebs, her sword flashing between them. Heads rolled and limbs were separated from their owners with such ease that if John had any time to ponder it, it would've probably made him sick to his stomach. Snapping his right hand up, he hit a running biker with a huge jet of fire, sending the man sprawling to the ground. One had tried to sneak up behind him, but John's hearing had recovered since Rebel Yell's initial shout; he spun around to catch the Reb by the wrist. He was holding a knife that he would've skewered John with; twisting the man's arm behind his back, he planted it in the Reb's own back before throwing him to the ground and stomping on his throat once as hard as his enhanced strength would allow. Satisfied that he didn't have any threats immediately near him, he surveyed the scene. Nearly all of the Rebs were dead or incapacitated; the only one left standing was Rebel Yell himself, squaring off with the Commissar.

"You just wait, commie. You ain't seen nothing yet." The Reb leader inhaled, readying himself to loose another sonic barrage.

"*Da, svinya.*" In one cool motion, the Commissar unholstered a pistol from her hip and shot Rebel Yell in the throat. Surprise shocked through his face as blood gurgled from his mouth and the new hole in his throat. He teetered for a moment before falling backwards, clawing at his wound. Red Saviour walked up to him, her face expressionless as she sent a blast into his body that would have crumpled a car. It crushed the life out of him, ending the career of Rebel Yell messily among the wreckage of Atlanta. "And I am seeing nothing now."

All of their comms came to life again. "*INCOMING! Six o'clock high!"* screamed a female voice. Those who understood were just looking up, startled, when the rooftop where Dolly had been firing from exploded into a cloud of rubble and actinic energy. *No. No, no, nonono.* There was only one group that had weapons capable of producing energy beams like that, so far as John knew. Nazis. From the smoking rubble—all that was left of where the Echo Op Dolly had been positioned—three Nazi war machines floated into view, propelled by their awful orange energy. Each was bristling with ten Nazi armored troopers. John could make out what looked like a man standing on top of the center war machine.

He was huge, big even for a meta, and although he was armored, this was clearly not the outsized "suit" the troopers used, powered by hydraulics and who knew what kind of servomotors. No, whatever was inside that armor was all muscle, bone and sinew. His golden helmet had been made in the shape of an eagle's head, an extremely stylized, art deco sort of eagle's head, with two equally stylized wings sweeping back from either side. The eagle theme was carried out on the breastplate, where another eagle was incised into the metal, a double lightning-bolt "SS" in one claw, a stylized skull in the other. Waffen SS. And you could see all this clearly because the man was so damned *big*.

He lifted one gauntleted hand to the helmet, and raised the beak-visor, revealing a face that looked like it had been taken straight off of an old Third Reich statue. He pointed a sword straight down at Saviour.

"Weak scion of Red Saviour," the voice boomed in accentless, sterile-sounding English. *"The heir to Ubermensch greets you with death."* Without another word, the man actually *jumped* from the Death Machine, impacting with the ground in a crouch hard enough to pulverize the rubble beneath him. As he landed, all of the troopers attached to the Death Machines detached, crunching down behind him.

The remaining Rebs that hadn't been taken out had used the opportunity provided by the shock of the new arrivals to regroup. But without a leader, they milled about for a moment, uncertain. Saviour had not lost a milligram of her confidence, at least outwardly.

"Squad *Dva*, Echo, on the Rebs! Squad *Odin*, *Tre*, to me! *Davay, davay, davay!"* With the Echo team, the numbers were almost matched, save for the remaining Rebs. The thing that was going to kill them were the Death Machines; with their cannons and mechanical tentacles, coupled with the ability to fly, they were almost untouchable for most of the CCCPers. Molotok gestured to Zmey and John. "You two! You are firebombs; weaken their armor for us!" Zmey, looking somewhat shaken, managed to nod; he began adjusting the controls on his helmet. John could see several of the LED gauges redline as the meta ran after his squad commander. The Commissar had already engaged the leader, Ubermensch, flying around him and relentlessly blasting him with energy; the Nazi didn't seem to notice any of it. His armor wasn't deflecting it like the troopers'. It seemed as if he was actually taking all of the punishment that Saviour could dish out . . . and wasn't being fazed by it.

All of the troopers had finally coordinated after their rough landing. Arm cannons began to track targets as the CCCPers and Echo personnel peppered them with small-arms fire and ran to engage. Zmey, on the other hand, had run at a slant to the Nazis, flanking them and lining himself up with their formation. He inhaled sharply, static sounding over the comm as he did so; in the next second, he exhaled. His helmet was of his own unique design, and granted him the capability to turn his exhalation into massive amounts of fire. Now John knew why he had tuned his helmet to perform at the height of its power; a truly gigantic cloud of flame billowed forth from his helmet's emitter, belching out and engulfing the Nazi troopers. It looked as if someone had called in an air strike to drop napalm. His attack didn't escape the Nazis' notice; several bolts of blue energy arced towards him, sending him flying as the ground around him exploded. But their armor was glowing a faint, dull orange, the signal that it had overheated. The Nazis' armor, weakened by fire, was now vulnerable to the rest of his comrades. They raced forward, fighting by squad; those without powers that couldn't compete with the armor used their rifles to blast at the armored joints, crippling several of the troopers so that other CCCPers could dispatch them. Chug, in particular, seemed to have gone mad. Maybe he recognized the creatures that had killed so many of his friends. He hurled enormous chunks of rubble at them, tears streaming down his rocky cheeks.

John knew what he had to target; his fires might be able to take out the Death Machines, if he concentrated them enough and was able to keep the attack sustained on one spot for long enough. He wouldn't be able to move and do that, however; it'd almost certainly result in him getting targeted and killed, blasted to death by whichever two machines he wasn't firing at. Perun ran up to where John had positioned himself behind cover, a highway divider that had somehow gotten hurled or brought to this part of the city. "Murdock! You are able to use your fire to produce plasma, *nyet*?" John nodded curtly, not taking his eyes off of the Death Machines, which were quickly closing into range. "I see your targets. We will combine efforts to strike them. I will support you, *tovarisch*." John glanced back to his squad leader; Perun knew that what he was agreeing to would probably be the death of them both, but he didn't care. His comrades were in imminent danger, and that's all that mattered.

They both ran, breaking from cover. John found what he was looking for: a slightly elevated pile of rubble that would cover most of his lower body from view. It wouldn't do much to stop an energy beam, but hopefully it would conceal him and Perun from the troopers long enough so that they'd be able to take out a couple of the Death Machines. John took a few deep breaths, readying himself as Perun came bounding to his side. "Attack them, *tovarisch*!" He released his concentration, letting his fires well up and spring to his hands. Vaguely, he felt Perun's hand rest on his shoulder. John thrust an arm out, pointing it directly at the rightmost Death Machine. A solid, intense shaft of plasma flew directly towards the Nazi craft, connecting with its viewports almost instantly. A breath later, Perun had somehow used his powers to electrify the beam; it was startlingly beautiful, and awesomely destructive. Plasma was extremely conductive; what this meant was that John's fire was able to transmit all of the energy from Perun's lightning directly into the Nazi Death Machine. They had become an arc welder on a continental scale. The Nazi vessel lurched to the side as the plasma jet shot straight through it. It hung there, looking as if it was perfectly suspended before it exploded brilliantly, shearing into two fiery halves.

The blast was dazzling; those closest to the blast were pushed to the ground by the pressure wave, which was strong enough to knock even the Nazi troopers down to their knees. Recovering his composure and seizing the moment, Ubermensch hefted a huge fist, slamming it into the building that he and the Commissar had been fighting next to. John could see the glazed-over look in his eyes, the gleam of insanity and zeal. Fei Li, dragging herself to her feet and sword still in hand, cried out. *"Sestra!"* With a triumphant laugh, the Nazi leader sliced his sword—its blade was covered in an rainbow pattern of energy—through the weakened corner support of that building; the energy seemed to carry itself all the way through the building along the arc he had cut. Natalya, who was still on her back from the blast, didn't have time to react. Red Saviour was crushed underneath the falling building, not even given the dignity of seeing what had killed her.

Almost everyone was nearly stunned into inaction. Red Saviour II, Natalya Shostakovich and Commissar of the CCCP, was dead.

The fighting resumed almost immediately; several of the CCCPers had flown into rages, attacking the troopers with renewed ferocity. John knew that, even if they took out all of the troopers, it would be for naught unless those Death Machines were out of the picture. He looked to make sure that Perun was still in the fight; the WWII veteran had blood streaming from his mouth and his eyes, and he was breathing very raggedly. "Are you hit?" John shouted to him.

His squad leader punched him in the shoulder, pointing to two remaining Nazi vessels. "Finish the fight!" John turned back, taking aim at the center craft. Once more his fires leapt out, blazing towards their target. Perun screamed, electrifying the plasma stream once more. The lance of fire destroyed its target, sending it careening wildly to the left. It crashed into its sister craft, sending sparks and shards of metal flying. The disabled Death Machine plummeted to the ground, bursting into flames before its engines detonated. The third vessel limped away, clearly out of the fight. *We've done it! We've got a chance!* John, grinning broadly, spun to face Perun; his smile evaporated just as quickly as it had appeared, though. Perun was dead at his feet, his eyes wide and fixed in the direction of the enemy. John crouched down and checked for a pulse out of habit bred in training; he knew that there was nothing before he even reached down. Suddenly he felt very, very old. *Get back in the game; you can worry about funerals later, idiot.* John stood up again, looking for a target he could safely engage without hurting a friend.

He was so preoccupied with the death of Perun that he almost missed completely the droning sound that had slowly been filling the air for the past few seconds, slowly climbing over the din of the fighting. In a flash of metal and smoke, something shot out of an alley to the west. It was huge, and looked like some sort of car from a hell tailored specifically for vehicles. John bathed his hands in fire, ready to light up whatever this new menace was, until he saw it run over two Nazis, crushing them under wickedly spiked treads that looked more like chainsaws than they did as a means of traction. The vehicle wove through the melee, narrowly missing several of John's comrades, before skidding to a halt next to him. The treads melded into the machine, and were replaced by very thick tires. The vehicle, upon closer inspection, resembled a Mad Max, junkyard version of a salt-flat racer. A very familiar face that John couldn't place peeked out over the edge of it. "Echo OpOne, Speed Fiend, reporting for action! A mutual friend told me you could use a hand out here."

John was too stunned for words, at first. Finally, he jumped onto the back of the vehicle, then surveyed the fight. The troopers' numbers were diminishing, but their leader Ubermensch was still putting up one hell of a fight. He must've been somewhere close to as strong and resilient as Chug, and he was also fighting with that nasty energy-sheathed sword. "Start strafin' that guy; we've gotta get his attention. Think y'can do that?"

Speed Fiend smiled over his shoulder; he couldn't turn that much in place, since it appeared that he was actually hooked into his vehicle from the waist down. "Hang on; this puppy has some giddyup." With a squeal of tires and a spray of crunched rubble, the pair flew towards Ubermensch.

It was exactly like being in the middle of a nightmare. Bella saw the building fall on Nat; felt her—for lack of a better word—lifeline plunge. Watched as Ubermensch laughed and turned away.

She grabbed Chug's arm; the telepathic/empathic link she'd managed to establish with him surged with what was less words and more feelings and images. The rocky creature whirled with astonishing speed, eyes focused on the pile of rubble. He howled. And then he wrenched out of Bella's grip and lurched for the pile, and when he reached it, began ripping into it like a beagle in pursuit of a rabbit down a burrow, a plume of debris cascading behind him as he dug.

By the time Bella stumbled up to him, he'd half uncovered Saviour. Bella went to her knees beside the Commissar and clamped both hands around her head.

There was a point between "dying" and "dead" where, if you tried hard enough, and had enough energy, you could bring someone back. Saviour was just a hairbreadth on the right side of that, and with a gasp, Bella began pouring everything she had into the woman she was coming to think of as a friend. And pouring. And pouring...

And it was like pouring water down a drain...it was running out faster than she could pour, even if she drained herself to save Natalya.

This "Speed Fiend," or whatever he called himself, really knew how to drive. John had managed to strap himself to the vehicle with a harness that seemed to have been affixed as an afterthought for whatever passengers this insane contraption would carry. They were moving at blazing speed, the car sliding and dodging through the fighting; barely missing a CCCPer or Echo team member here, sideswiping a Nazi there. John couldn't focus on that, though; he still had a job to do if he wanted to really help his friends. Despite the jolting movement from the vehicle's shocks as it sped over rubble and wreckage, John was able to accurately target Ubermensch. It helped that he was one friggin' *big* Nazi, nearly as big as the powered trooper armor all on his own. John fired off bursts of flame, aiming for the Nazi leader's face and chest, as fast as he could; he guessed that he wouldn't be able to kill him or even injure him, but he could at least distract him, keep the bastard from going after someone like Upyr or Soviette.

Ubermensch was cursing, swatting at the flames as they splattered against his face. He swiped his sword at random, trying to swing it in whatever direction he thought John was firing from. Arcs of the sword's energy cut into the ground or flew harmlessly into the air before dissipating; one of them even bisected a Nazi trooper that Unter was fighting. The Russian looked up puzzledly as his opponent split into two halves, falling to the ground.

"Insect! What do you think you can accomplish with your little buzzing?" Ubermensch peered angrily through the flames.

The Nazi leader was able to see for a moment between John's shots; he oriented himself, setting his feet, before he charged ahead. He had guessed, correctly, where Speed Fiend was going to be driving through. Ubermensch lowered his shoulder, intercepting the vehicle. Its entire frame shook violently as he collided with them; the Nazi moved almost as fast as John could at his top speed. The impact destroyed the entire front end of Speed Fiend's racer, crunched metal and engine components squealing pitifully as smoke poured from under what passed for a hood. "That's not good!" shouted the Echo Op. The front end burst into flame, bathing both of them in greasy smoke. "That's really not good!" Putting the vehicle into a suicide slide, Speed Fiend brought them to a halt, crashing the side into a wrecked school bus. "You better get outta here, pal. I'll deal with the fire. Go kick that guy's ass!" John unbuckled himself, leaping from the ruined vehicle.

Ubermensch was wearing the same smug smile that he'd had when he killed the Commissar. "Well, communist pig. I slaughtered your sow, shall I make bacon from her piglet? Shall I smoke you over your own pitiful flames?"

John started to advance on the Nazi. "Make your last words a prayer, sucker. There ain't gonna be enough of you to bury once I'm done." John dropped down to kneel, bracing his right hand with his left. Just as Ubermensch began to raise his sword, John amped up his flames almost the highest he could before he risked losing control. With a sharp gasp, he released the fire; the rubble underneath the beam, which was the size of a man, exploded as any residual moisture instantly vaporized. Trash combusted, and the air took on the same ozone tang that happened after lightning struck. The blast hit Ubermensch dead-on, and actually bowled him over onto his back. One Nazi trooper nearly one hundred feet behind him was hit with part of the strike, exploding as the atmosphere inside of his suit superheated and combusted in an instant.

Ubermensch struggled to his feet. He looked genuinely surprised, and even a little bit . . . scared? His sword was sputtering uselessly in his hand, and his entire chestplate had been melted off, leaving his bare chest marred by the impact of the blast. He stood staring at John for a very long moment, and then locked eyes with him. His eyes were very cold, and in that moment, the hatred that filled them rocked John with an all-too-familiar feeling.

But neither of them had a chance to act further. The remaining crippled war machine lurched up over the building behind

Ubermensch, and an ear-shattering squeal filled the air. The few remaining troopers, the dead, and Ubermensch all flew upwards, attracted by whatever force the machines exerted to recall their men. And as soon as the sphere was covered, bristling like a dandelion from hell with its dead and living, it shot straight up and was out of sight in a moment.

The battle was over. At a great cost, they'd won an ambush designed to decimate them. And John could only manage to feel very weary.

"*Sestra*—" Soviette was tugging at Bella's arm. "*Sestra*, you cannot help her, she is gone—"

There was a buzzing in Bella's ears; she could barely hear Sovie. She couldn't see. She knew she was in trouble, but damned if she was going to give up. Nat wasn't gone. Not yet. And Bella wasn't going to let her go.

Not without going with her.

Gray faded to black . . . and just like they always said, there was a light.

But instead of Bella going towards the light, the light came to her.

You would give your life to save her? Bella knew that voice. Her wordless assent made the light bloom around her with warmth and a new level of energy.

The willingness is enough. And it is permitted. Take what you need, little sister.

Abruptly, Bella could see and hear again, and as had happened before with John Murdock, she found herself connected with a life-force that left her gasping. But she was not so overwhelmed that she wasn't able to think, and act, and siphon off enough to plug that energy-sucking "hole" that was Red Saviour, enough to stimulate every cell in her metahuman body into overdrive, enough to heal her, and enough to jolt heart and brain into action again.

Beneath her hands, Red Saviour began to cough and sputter, and gasp for air.

Soviette fainted.

As the war machine sped upwards, Ubermensch kept his eyes fixed on the American swine that had struck him. He would have remained to destroy the dog, if he'd been able. If he'd had the means of detaching himself, he'd leap down from half a mile up to land on him at this very moment.

He had thought his one great enemy would be that woman, that daughter of *his* namesake's nemesis. But no. She was nothing. He had crushed her like a fly, and the victory had had no lasting savor.

But this . . . man. Whoever he was. How *dared* he challenge Ubermensch and the Fourth Reich?

His hatred burned, burned like the man's own plasma fires, burned like the heart of hell. And Ubermensch made a vow to himself.

Whatever the cost—he would find out who this man was. He would make it his life's task to destroy everything he cared for, everything he was connected to, everything he wanted.

Then, and only then—Ubermensch would destroy *him*.

John had extinguished his fires as soon as the Nazis were out of sight, retreating with their dead and wounded. He felt horrible, spread thin and raggedy; despite that, he kept his eyes fixed on the sky for a few extra moments. It was chance that he was looking up at the right moment to notice the flash; he almost reignited his fires out of reflex, before he recognized the light. Flames and feathers. *Seraphym*. His eyes immediately shot to the patch of ruined building where Bella and Soviette were crouched over their dead Commissar. Saw Bella's eyes go wide, Saviour's body lurch and begin coughing as the life flooded back into it, and then Jadwiga fainting at their side.

Just as quickly as it had started, it was over. A single feather floated down from the heavens, carried by the wind. Another miracle had been performed. John surveyed the area; it was a battleground, a charnel pit a few moments before. Blood still spattered and pooled on the ground, on the piles of debris, with what was left of the bodies of the Rebs dotting it at odd intervals. Unter and a few other CCCPers had policed the very few survivors, binding their wrists with oversized zip ties. Another squad of his comrades had already begun the task of laying out the bodies of the Rebs in a line, their weapons disassembled and thrown into a pile. *Gotta make things all nice and tidy for when the cops an' Echo show up*, he thought with a tinge of bitterness. This was definitely going to stir up a hornet's nest; Nazis working in league with the Rebs, and making a concerted assault on a section of Atlanta. Lots of paperwork and wringing of hands, to be sure.

Paperwork. John walked stiffly over to where he had left Perun's body. The war veteran's hair was matted with dust and sweat, and his eyes were still gazing lifelessly toward where the enemy had been moments ago. John knelt down, brushing his hand over the dead man's face to close his eyes. In a testament to the skill and teamwork of the CCCP, and no small amount of luck, Perun was the only one on their side killed; if you didn't count the Commissar, that is. Several people were injured, some of them severely; Stribog and Zmey were both in need of immediate attention, and would have to be evacuated to the CCCP HQ as soon as possible. The rest of their force was a collection of cuts, scrapes, fractures and gunshot wounds. Bella and a revived Soviette were already making their rounds, tending to the most serious wounds first.

John coughed into his hand, wracking his body with pain. He walked towards his comrades in order to help with the clean-up effort, dismissing the specks of blood that he had coughed into his glove.

Over the course of the next three hours, the CCCP finished accounting for the Rebs and weapons. A contingent of Echo personnel arrived in their fancy cars, taking reports and helping to add to the organized chaos involved with cleaning up a large amount of death and destruction. Molotok had taken charge, given the Commissar's condition, and was making sure that everything was taken care of. When it was finally time to head back to HQ, John was operating on automatic; he was just too damn *tired* to get too worked up, to muster anything more than the necessary energy to walk and nod when addressed. Things were generally back to normal at the HQ in short order; those with wounds had them tended to, and everyone else went back to their assigned duties. Beneath it all was an undercurrent of anxious concern; his comrades whispered to each other about what had happened to the Commissar, her death and miraculous resurrection. John ignored it as best he could, stripping out of his patrol uniform and into one of the CCCP's issue coveralls. He was given a leave on his paperwork by Untermensch. "It can wait for later, comrade. Get rest, first."

John wasted no time signing out and leaving the compound. He knew that he was suffering a stress reaction to the entire incident, and knew how to deal with it. He just didn't care enough to bother. Not wanting to head back to his squat to be alone with his thoughts, he started walking aimlessly. He avoided the more heavily populated parts of his neighborhood. After about an hour, he'd recovered enough to start really thinking again. *How come we didn't see 'em coming? What's the connection between the Rebs and the Nazis? Who was the big sucker in charge of 'em? Why'd Perun die, and Nat get a second chance?* It was that last thought that stuck in his mind like a burning ember, stirring up his emotions. First, there was grief and guilt over the death of his squad commander, a man he hardly had time to know. Then there was anger. At the Nazis, the Rebs, and surprisingly... at Sera. John's feet had purpose now, and he started walking faster. Then he broke into a jog, then a run, and finally he was sprinting as fast as his enhanced body could carry him.

Hardly registering it, he was back at his squat. He vaulted up the stairway, through his apartment, finally bursting through the roof access hard enough to shake the frame.

The Seraphym knelt on the tar-and-gravel roof, her fires dim, her head bent so that a cascade of flame-hair covered her face. She was as still as a statue, and apparently so turned inward that she didn't even hear him, nor hear the roof door slam open.

Or did she? Was she just ignoring him? Blowing him off? John spoke, his voice even and low. "Sera."

Slowly she turned her head to face him. As always, her expression was serene, her eyes that unreadable, blank gold. But there were tears on those too-perfect cheeks.

Only for a moment, however. A graceful hand passed over her face, and they were gone, erased as if they had never fallen.

"John Murdock," she said, with no hint of emotion in her voice. "You surprised me." Then, with just a touch of irony, she added, "I hope you approved of the taxi I sent for you."

Seeing Sera crying stirred something in John, and he felt some of the anger leave him. Still, he was far too stubborn to get completely over it, so he walked up to her. "'Speed Fiend,' right? Where do I know him from?"

"The first time we met."

John shook his head, uncomprehending, when it dawned on him. *The truck driver.* The fella he had saved, or tried to, when he first showed up in Atlanta. The driver had been ambushed by a gang of looters, and John had killed them. He still remembered the look of fear on the driver's face when he first tried to approach him to help him get to a hospital. "I take it y'got him some help. With Echo, from the way he looked."

"He will only join Echo in the next hour. His . . . talent . . . emerged after he healed, and he has been learning it on his own." A pause. "I sent you what help I was permitted. I came and told him it was time, and where."

"And what of Nat? Isn't that a bit of a bigger job than you're allowed?" John set his jaw; he could feel the anger creeping up on him again, but was doing his best to keep it in check.

"*I* did not heal her." She looked directly into his eyes, and blinked once. "This is difficult to explain."

"Try."

"Perhaps . . . if you regard it as conservation of energy. Miracles, like energy, do not come from nothing. They must be paid for. For every miracle, something miraculous must in turn be sacrificed. Only in this way can the Law of Free Will not be subverted." Another slow blink. "In this case, it was not so big a miracle as you think. A very, very small one, in fact. Natalya Shostakovich is a metahuman, and a very resilient one."

John crossed his arms. "An' what about Perun? He was too, an' now he's just a very dead man."

"There . . ." She shook her head. "It is complicated. He was an old, old man. He had outlived most of his comrades and friends and all of his lovers. Part of him was ready to move onwards. Part of him *wanted* to do so long ago. But the rest of him did not want to do so in . . . in a manner unbefitting a warrior. He knew what he was doing and that it would probably kill him. And . . . there was no one willing to make that sacrifice for the miracle, for him."

"You're so sure 'bout that? What about me?" His jaw tightened, and he consciously tried to relax with very little effect.

One eyebrow rose. "So. Will you give me your life? Not your death, John Murdock. Your *life*."

He shook his head. "I don't follow."

"Then you would not do so. Belladonna knew what I asked of her and gave it without my need to ask for it."

He turned from her, spinning away quickly. "Goddamn it, it isn't friggin' *right*."

✧   ✧   ✧

John Murdock was awash with pain. Seraphym felt it; oh, she felt the pain of every mortal she was near, but somehow, his pain was more immediate, harder to bear. Guilt, anger, more guilt, mourning... the uncertainty, the sheer inability to understand what had happened. The agony of having no faith, nothing to believe in. And in this terrible grief and guilt she read the lacerations of guilt still present, but from his past, the soul-deep wounds of having survived—

She did not physically reel back from the impact, but it was the equivalent of being struck by a tidal wave of pain. The Program. Jessica...

Fire jumped into her mind. Images of the woman John had only known as Jessica... sterile rooms, training areas... an operation table... his fires manifesting for the first time... a man with cruel eyes... a chair with straps, used for executions...

Now she read it clearly. And her tears fell again, for him. She reached out to him, trying to offer him wordless comfort. He could not know, he did not *believe* that death was hardly an ending... so he needed that comfort all the more. *Be at peace, all will be well...*

John recoiled from her touch, whirling around to face her. "What're you doing?

She winced back from his anger, which lashed her like a whip across the face. "I... only meant... to ease your pain..."

His face contorted with indignation. "Damn it, Sera. People are supposed to feel horrible sometimes! We ain't supposed to be happy an' content all the time, with everything that happens." He shook his head. His anger faded to nothing just as quickly as it had flared up. He suddenly looked... hollow. "I'm sorry. I shouldn't have snapped like that. But... I don't know." He turned away from her again, facing the edge of the roof.

"I should not treat you as an unknowing child, incapable of understanding anything more complicated than 'I need' and 'I want,'" she said, after a moment. "But... it is hard. Because to me, you *are* a child. You are so very, very young..." She sighed, her mind filled with the memory of the moment when the Infinite said *I am* and everything began. She and her Siblings had been born in that moment. "And I am so very, very old." She groped for words. "John Murdock, there is one great Law that governs all that is—"

"Y'know," he said, interrupting her. "Y'can just call me John. I feel like I'm in school when y'call me by my whole name." He graced her with a shaky grin.

She felt... warmth. Human warmth, and felt her lips curving in a return smile. "John. You above all should appreciate this. The Law of the Universe is a simple one. All that is mortal has Free Will. Please think about that for a moment, and consider what that means to the Infinite, and to those of us that serve the Infinite." She paused for a long breath. "The Infinite itself knows all and is all, of course. And thus, It cannot act, because that would violate Free Will. Only those who cannot know and see all, can. And the more one can see, the less one is allowed to act. I... am allowed, comparatively, only little, little things. Things that will not cause unbalance. Advice, mostly, rarely intervention."

"Seems like since the war started, you've been intervening quite a bit."

Pain, this time her own, almost made her cry out. "How many have died, John? Not just combatants. Innocents. So many, many I was not permitted to save. Or *could not* more often than 'was not permitted.' I cannot be everywhere, at all times. Most often... I have to choose, choose only *one,* one who is needed, will be needed. And the rest..." She was weeping again. "The sparrow falls, and I cannot keep it from falling. But that does not mean I do not see it and mourn its passing."

He sighed. "It's triage. While y'say you're part of somethin' all-powerful, you aren't all-powerful, Sera."

She sensed a calm in him that had not been there when he confronted her. That calm resonated in her... and oddly, gave her comfort back. She had been wrong, as she had suspected, in treating him as a child who needed solace. Perhaps merely talking had been all he needed. Or... could it be that it was not "just talking." Could it be that he had needed to talk with her? To listen to her? To have her explain, treat him as he deserved to be treated? To begin to get answers indeed, but not just from "any" source—but from her?

And... there was no doubt. He, in his turn, was comforting her, though he could not know it.

"Thank you, John," she said, softly. "It is hard. It is good to... be forgiven."

"Don't fret." He shifted uncomfortably. "Y'know, I was wrong to jet outta HQ so fast. There's no doubt plenty that still needs doin', 'cause of the attack."

"Ubermensch," she told him, answering the unspoken question in his mind.

"How bad is he?"

She considered what she should tell him, and finally settled on something he could have found for himself. "Consider the past," she said. "When did they first appear? How did they first appear? The metas as a whole. Consider the pattern. Your answer will be there. Also . . . consider what he called himself. He is not the first of that name." The futures were shifting again, and she scanned through them, each word charting a change as she spoke. "Ask Natalya. Ask her father."

He nodded, turning to leave. "I'll talk with you again, soon?"

Warmth—happiness—lifted her spirit again. "I would like that, John. I would like that very much."

He smiled, and then left, closing the battered roof access door behind him.

She felt her mouth smiling again. This was nothing like the *joy* of the Siblings, and yet it was as intense in its own way, this happiness. And very mortal. Oh, she knew *about* the pains and joys of mortals, in the same way as one of them, landlocked all his life, knew *about* the ocean from reading, viewing, hearing recordings. But knowing *about* something, and experiencing it, were two very, very different things. It made her curious. It made her want to experience more. But not with just anyone.

Have I a . . . friend? she thought, suddenly startled by the idea.

There was no answer.

But then, she didn't expect one. The Infinite was still keeping Its secrets about John Murdock from her. She would have to discover them herself.

CHAPTER SIXTEEN

Total Eclipse of the Heart

MERCEDES LACKEY AND VERONICA GIGUERE

Watching Tesla slowly disintegrate—and I did watch it—was painful and infuriating. Painful because I could empathize with him. Infuriating because he had so many people around him who were willing to do whatever it took to make sure that the future he wouldn't reveal would never happen. Maybe it was the CEO in him that kept it secret. Heaven knows that if he'd broken open the Ides of March, he would have found dozens, if not hundreds, of people who could have proved to him that there actually was hope.

As Pogo said, "We have met the enemy, and he is us."

For the second time in as many weeks, the sight of the Le Parkour course on the Echo campus caused Ramona Ferrari to break down in tears. Never mind the fact that she was in the car, driving to the building that held her crummy hole of an office, or the fact that she was fully dressed in the dark frumpy suit that she wore as an Echo detective. She had simply turned the corner, blinked at the broken concrete and crumbling walls, and had thought for a moment that she had seen Bill.

And that was impossible. The last she had seen of the Mountain was from high above in Corbie's arms, Bill's stony figure sinking into the Atlantic. He might have been made of rock, but he needed air like most other living creatures. When satellites didn't pick up any movement near the Marianas Trench, the report came back that the meta was dead with an explanation of suicide.

Ramona sniffled and reached for a tissue, then thought better of it and just pulled over to the side of the Echo access road. She had the right tags and decals, so security wouldn't bother her. She just needed to sit and cry it out before she started another day at Echo.

Her eyes deep in a wad of tissues, she started at the tap on her passenger's side window. She looked up, ready to tell whatever officious security goon who was interrupting her private break-down to go take a hike.

But it wasn't an officious security goon. It was that blue DCO—Bella—peering in at her with a concerned expression on her face. When she saw that Ramona was looking at her, she made a little cranking motion.

Ramona sighed and punched the button for the automatic win-dow. "I'm fine," she lied, even as she crumpled tissues. "Allergies. You know, that with all that mold in those buildings, it flares up. Just wanted to take care of it before I got to the office."

"Bullshit," the blue woman said, with a knowing look. "A little bird told me you could use a shoulder. Well, okay, not a bird. But she has wings. Come on, Detective, I worked LVFD. *And* I'm an empath. *And* I have a friend that knows these things. Crying's better when there's somebody else to lean on and it sure as hell won't be the first time that I was a towel. You don't have to talk about it. Just have a good low-down bawl."

"I already watched *Steel Magnolias* for that. Twice." Ramona slumped in her seat and stabbed at the button to unlock the doors. She let a long sigh rush out as Bella slid into the seat next to her. "This whole place, they're slowly giving up on people. Sure, they'll take in any meta flake who can spit ice or sneeze acid, but they'd rather just cycle them through than do something with them. And if someone dies on their watch? It's not *their* fault, no," she sneered, waving a tissue for emphasis. "It's the someone's fault, for not being strong enough or stable enough. And that right there is bullshit. They want to fix this place? They can stop being so damned self-centered and lazy and start building the place back up instead of hiding in some DOUBLE-WIDE TRAILER!"

The last few words were shouted towards the center of the Echo campus, the effort seeming to take the last bit of energy from her. Ramona reached for a foil packet on the console and popped out two pieces of gum. "Damn Tesla," she muttered. "He's a weasel. A little weasel with a roomful of toys who's too

scared to do anything else but hide in his little weaselly corner."
She popped the gum in her mouth and made a face, but kept
chewing anyway.

"Actually . . . Tesla's a CEO. *Only* a CEO. That's all he's ever
been. Then all that"—Bella waved her hand at the mess that
was Atlanta—"got dumped in his lap. Ain't nothing in the management handbooks to cover the End of the World. So . . . he's
reacting like any CEO would, and not like the guy you'd think
would be in charge of a hefty percentage of the metas of the
world—paralyzed. Much as I loathe and despise the fact that he
hasn't cowboyed up and turned the reins over to someone who'll
act like a commander-in-chief and not a terrified little girl, I
understand what's going on in his head. He's not his father, who
handled the job in the war, and he's sure as hell not his great-
uncle, who probably would have reacted to the Ides with—uh . . .
did anyone show you the Ides of March?" She handed Ramona
another sealed packet of tissues.

"The Ides . . . no. You're not talking Julius Caesar, I take it?"
Ramona took the tissues but didn't open them.

"Nope." Bella took a deep breath. "Up in Chicago they had a
bedridden precog named Matthew March. Now, normally the only
way they got anything out of him was with a telepath. It took
special psions just to deal with all the crap in his head. Day of
the Invasion he got out of the bed he hadn't left since he was
a child, wrote about twenty pages of stuff in a notebook, threw
it as far away from himself as he could and set himself on fire.
What was in that notebook is what's being called the 'Ides of
March.' Reads a little like Nostradamus, but with more sense."
She took out her PDA and tapped at it. "And *that* is what has
Tesla so spooked. I don't think anyone is supposed to know about
this but Yank, Fata Morgana who had it transcribed, and maybe
that rat bastard from the Defense Department masquerading as a
janitor." She handed the PDA to Ramona. "I have clever friends
who can do impossible things. And one with wings that thinks
you should see this."

Ramona's fingers twitched as she took the PDA. She went
through the text slowly, pausing every so often to zoom in on
parts of the report. Her lips moved once or twice, but she read
through the report in near silence. Unable to sob and analyze at
the same time, she chose to analyze what the DCO had put in

front of her. When she had finished reading the report, she went back to the top and tried to access the attachments. Scanned images of the handwritten pages appeared, and Ramona examined those as she dabbed at her face. If this was authentic and even half of this had come true between the time that the precog had scribbled it down and yesterday, then the very existence of such a document would be trouble for all of Echo.

"That's a suicide note for Echo," Ramona muttered.

"That's what Tesla thinks."

"It's a suicide note now is what I mean. Maybe we couldn't predict the first few, but having this document could have helped move people, allocate resources, do some preventative action. And instead, Tesla keeps it to himself and does the cover-up dance while more people die. Brilliant leadership." Ramona's sarcasm edged out her tears for the moment.

"And why do you think CCCP has been so successful in being Johnny-on-the-spot the last couple weeks?" Bella asked. "Wish there were more of them, but hey, you do what you can with what you've got. And when you can't get there and someone clever can jinx the civil defense sirens to go off in time..." She shrugged. "Something else I need to point out about this thing. There is *no* mention of CCCP in it. But there"—she stabbed her finger at a set of terse notations—"and there, and there—those are incidents Saviour sent squads to intercept before they happened. And hey, they busted some buildings up, and a couple people got hurt, but nothing like the fiery catastrophe that the next sentence fragment describes. That friend of mine—the one with the wings—says that precogs generally can only see things surrounding stuff and people they already know about. The clever one says that looking into the future other ways works the same. March never knew the CCCP existed, much less that they were going to get dumped here. Read into that what you will, but there are *some* of us who are not going to curl up like an armadillo because the end of the world is predicted."

"Us is right." Ramona handed the PDA back and sat up a little straighter. "So, the Reds know about this to this degree, or have you just been feeding them the right bits of information? And this friend of yours, is she someone inside Echo or is she one of those post-event metas?" Her brain had started to click forward with names and associations and the spread of information among the various networks. If Pride knew, then Ramona was sure that the information stopped there. Of all of that upper tier, he walked and talked the absolute American heroic bit as much as breathing.

"Saviour knows the whole shebang. I think she's probably passed it all on to Molo and Unter—that's Molotok and Untermensch. Molo's her fellow Commissar, Unter was Spetsnaz, so both of them know how to keep their lips buttoned. *Maybe* she passed it to her old man, Saviour the First, and Worker's Champion, but I kinda bet not. There's not much you can apply to Russia in these ramblings, and she's not happy with Papa Boryets and Papa Saviour. *They* were holding out on her, and she doesn't just cherish grudges, she feeds and waters them and calls them pet names. And . . . I actually have two reclusive friends. The clever one, and the winged one. The winged one—" Her lips twitched with the hint of a smile. "The winged one informed certain parties that they could tell Tesla she answered to a higher boss than he was. And *I* wouldn't call her a meta at all, though your mileage may vary."

"Fair enough. At least your friends are doing something with the information, rather than shoving it into a drawer and pretending like it doesn't exist." Ramona folded her arms across her chest and cracked her gum. "I'm hauling Pride out to the Cracker Barn and we're going to have a moment over biscuits, I can promise you that. I can't fault him for keeping stuff close, because that's just the way he is, but I know he's not a puppet. He just needs a better reason to break a few rules."

Bella sucked on her lower lip a moment. "Okay. Anyone tell you about Project Overwatch?"

"The DNA database in case the buildings collapse again and we need to identify people by strands of hair? Between you and me, I think it's a lousy excuse to get more information by making dumb people feel better." Ramona snorted. "What about it?"

"That's the cover for the allocations and the equipment we've been using." She tapped something over her breast pocket. "Vic, I'm bringing in Detective Ramona Ferrari, like we talked about."

She handed Ramona an earpiece, a button cam, and a button throat-mic, all standard Echo issue. "Tesla actually knows about this one too. What he doesn't know is that half the stuff is going to CCCP. Go ahead, put those on."

Ramona obliged, fastening the mic such that her collar concealed the piece of electronics. When she had secured the earpiece, she gave Bella a "now what?" shrug.

"Good morning, Detective," said the voice in her ear. "I'm Echo OpTwo Victoria Victrix, callsign VickieVee. You are sitting in your car, driver's side, fifty feet south-southeast of the south corner of the Le Parkour course. Your heart rate and respiration indicate that you are distressed but under control. Your car will need an oil change in another thousand miles, and your favorite radio station is KBEZ and why anyone would listen to that is beyond me. Your GPS needs recalibration, it's off by twenty feet. There is an Echo security guard just behind the corner of the construction trailer directly ahead of you. He will come around that corner in three...two...mark."

True to Vickie's count, the security guard came around the corner and frowned at the car. He approached Ramona's side and bent down. "You lost, ma'am?"

"His name is Justin Blake, and he's a new hire," said the apparently all-knowing voice in her ear.

"Justin, honey. Fred up at the main guardhouse said you'd be out here. Detective Ferrari, good to meet you." Ramona showed him her badge and offered a smile. "Just doing a debrief with one of our DCOs. How's your first week going?"

Bella wiggled her fingers at him. The effect of hearing his own name combined with a pretty blue thing with the face of a supermodel waving at him had the desired effect. He stammered a "fine, thanks" and tipped his hat to the two of them before going back to the trailer.

"You need to pick up bread before you go home, the loaf you have is turning blue and green at one end. Also, the milk in your fridge is going bad. You should check the setting, you probably knocked it back accidentally and it's a tad too warm in there. And the way I know all this is because I am not your standard ordinary meta. I have a cyber-packet with your hair in it attached to the Overwatch computers, and I am a techno-mage. *Rara avis*, me. Don't know of too many in the world and I am the only one in Echo."

Mage. Magic. Ramona's eyes widened a bit, but her surprise ebbed and she shrugged her shoulders. "Okay." There was a pause, as if she was supposed to explain her nonchalant acceptance of things. "Look, I'm not like most civilians. When you've got to use everyday things like bandages and cell phones because you can't heal stuff or talk between somebody's ears like half of your coworkers, you just sort of accept what people can do and go on, regardless of where it comes from. Makes things easier."

"Fair enough. Here's my gig. I can make magic talk to computers and other things, and I use a suite of computers to talk back to me and my magic. Because of how magic works, I can hack into virtually anything if a certain set of parameters is satisfied. There are rules. It's not like Twitch Your Nose and you can do anything. But that is what Overwatch is about; I am the kind of all-seeing eyes and ears for special teams to give them that extra edge that gets them out alive." There was a pause. "For instance, I've hacked into all the security cams on the Echo campus to see you and Bell right now. I can do the same for just about any traffic cam, security cam, or ATM cam on the planet. Haven't managed intel satellites yet, but they're not really useful in keeping my teams breathing."

Ramona settled back in her seat and passed a hand over her eyes. "Breathing is good. And you're one of the revolutionaries who want to hold my boss accountable, in spite of his sudden spine-ectomy? We can totally be friends."

"That's good, since I hacked his desktop a long time ago. I'm the one who leaked the Ides. Despite the Commissar coming to administer detente with her typical iron fist, he still hasn't come totally clean with her. So . . . I'm seeing he keeps his promise whether he likes it or not." There was a polite little cough. "I'm not completely a loose cannon. My folks are FBI. Ever hear of Section 39?"

Ramona did a quick check of her own memory from the past year's worth of research that had involved the FBI's files on metahumans and didn't come up with a matching number. "Not recent enough to remember, no."

"Maybe not. You'd have dealt with Section 26, the metahuman division. Thirty-nine dates back to World War I. It's all magicians and . . . well . . . uh . . . mythological critters that aren't. My mom is a witch and my dad is a werewolf. They're two of the current three section heads. The third is a Navaho shaman. The number was kind of an inside joke, when they merged the original organization with the FBI. Three heads for an organization they called Agency 13 back when it was founded, so . . . three times thirteen, it became FBI Section 39."

"I can see how that would work, as well as how all of that would make Tesla shakier than a Chihuahua. I guess the jerk with the mop isn't with Section 39 then?" Ramona shifted in her seat, her mouth twisted in a frown. "He's the one who should have had the broom closet for an office, not me. Honestly, I'm one red stapler from a revolution."

"Tesla thinks I'm doing this all by some new metahuman mutation; he doesn't believe in magic," came the laconic answer. "And hold that thought about revolution. Bell, floor's yours again."

Bella cleared her throat. "Well, as you already know, I'm not the sort to follow the rules when the rules are getting people killed. As for Saviour..." She half grinned. "I guess I'm sort of a kinder, gentler version of the Commissar. She's been just about ready to storm Tesla's office and take over herself, and if she hadn't been so busy putting out fires, she probably would have by now." Then the grin faded. "The problem is, my winged fr—ah hell, why am I being coy? The Seraphym talks to me. A lot." She shook her head. "She says that *Tesla* is irrelevant to the futures. Not exactly sure what that means except that I don't think he's going to be in the driver's seat for much longer—assuming he still is now. So, maybe we might need a revolution, and taking the cue from my hippie parents, I'm looking for fellow travelers." She massaged a spot between her eyebrows. "And that is where things get really interesting. See, Tesla hasn't ever been exactly the one at the top of the food chain. That's elsewhere. Some place called 'Metis.' Which is where Merc is right now. Is any of this familiar to you?"

"Merc...wait, Mercurye? You mean Rick Poitier?" The words were out before Ramona realized how dumb it sounded. In the wake of the destruction, rebuilding and possible revolution, the non-meta had to ask about the whereabouts of the hot shirtless guy with the washboard abs.

"Tall, blond and built, the same. Got literally carried off to some Super Science Lala Land, which is where all of Echo's spiffy keen gadgets really come from." The blue woman swiftly unloaded an infodump that sounded like the craziest of B-movie scripts, right down to the science-fiction dingus rising out of Alex Tesla's desk in front of her and the Commissar just in time for them to see a frantic Mercurye telling them that "Metis won't help" before dashing off with someone in hot pursuit.

"So Tesla authorized a kidnapping, we don't actually own our technology, and the man who can't believe in magic is trusting a bunch of aliens who, for all intents and purposes, talk to him inside his desk." Ramona reached forward and gripped the steering wheel of her car, her knuckles slowly going white as she clenched her jaw. "I think I can rest easy losing my job over cracking him once in the mouth. Blue, can you regenerate teeth or is that beyond your ability?"

"Whoa there, Detective," said the voice in her ear. "Breathe, you're going to pop a vein. I did some very discreet research. This Metis place has been rumored for decades; what I found in bits and pieces in Alex's files just confirms what all the rumors had claimed. It's not aliens or magic, just people with big brains in their own cozy little science commune. Tesla the First and his buddy Marconi decided way back when that they were going to put together an early think tank for scientists. By the twenties, roughly, they'd transplanted the think tank to somewhere in South America. When metahumans showed up in the Second World War, some of them got the Brain-the-Size-of-a-Planet superpower, and Metis recruited them, then set up Alex's old man as the one to organize as many of the rest of the metas as he could after WWII was over. Now, where it gets funky is that from everything we can tell...Tesla the First and his buddy Marconi are still alive. Somehow. Not sure how. For all I know, at this point they could be brains in boxes. Point is, up until *now*, Senior has really been the one calling the ultimate shots. But with Merc saying that Metis isn't going to help, I'm guessing Alex got his safety net pulled out from under him and Great-Uncle isn't entirely in charge anymore, prolly because these eggheads insist on a pure democracy and he got outvoted. Hence, nervous breakdown."

The news had the desired effect, as Ramona sat back, deflated and confused. "They've been doing this for years, then. We all have to stick to regulation and to hell with any sort of reason because we have to do what the voices in the desk tell Tesla to do. Right now, there's nothing I can do."

"*Yet*," said the voice in her ear and Bella at the same time. "And not exactly," Bella added. "You're in the perfect position to get Yank to see reason instead of regulations. You're also in the perfect position to actually use the Ides right now. You have a copy, Vic can help you interpret. CCCP can't do a helluva lot outside of Atlanta, but you can leak warnings elsewhere and be believed. Say...oh, tell them one of the precogs got a flash. Actually, you know, that's entirely the truth, March was a precog." She sucked on her lower lip. "And...how well do you know Rick? Merc? Would you say he's, well, a really *good* guy?"

"Yes." The answer came immediately, and Ramona hoped this was her gut instinct after working with him and not some fascination fueled by that crummy knight-in-shining-armor fantasy. Sitting in the car with a healer meant that some of her girl-squeal could be picked up at any given time. "He's got a conscience, if that's what you're asking."

"Not...exactly." Bella was smiling a little. "But yeah, you know him, and you know he's got a good, solidly good heart. Trust that. He may not be a Science Big Brain, but you know what? I can't think of anyone who's ever been recruited into a fight by logic. If anybody can change their minds, I'd put my money on him."

"Bottom line is, Bell doesn't want us to just sit here and wait for things to happen to us. So *we* are putting together a safety net here," said Vickie. "Look, I am the world's biggest paranoid, and I believe in safety nets. Alex might get it together. Pride might take over. Metis might decide to saddle up their robot horses and ride in with white hats on and guns blazing. But if none of that happens, we'll have our little revolution, comrade, and keep right on punching, 'cause we planned for it in advance. Green?"

"Green." The gum had turned sour in her mouth, so Ramona spat it into a tissue and crumpled it in her hand. Suddenly, things had gone from mopey and depressing to confused and only slightly less depressing. At least she wasn't alone in thinking that her boss had lost his ability to lead. "So, what now?"

"Right now, we report for our shifts," the DCO replied. "And I refrain from punching Djinni in the jaw again. All that does is hurt my hand and turn him on. Pervert."

Twenty-four hours later, a dark-suited Echo detective and one of the commanding metas of the organization stood outside of Tesla's office. Ramona popped a piece of gum into her mouth and grimaced, but tucked the packet into her jacket pocket. Yankee Pride glanced over at her and raised an eyebrow.

"Y'know, unless that was your last piece, Echo regulations would demand that you at least offer me one." He tried to soften the joke with a charming smile.

Ramona rolled her eyes in reply. "You really want a square of junkie gum? This Nico-Quit stuff isn't exactly minty fresh."

His grimace mirrored the one she'd made a few seconds earlier. "Never mind, then. But good on you for trying."

"Yeah, well...not all of us have amazing abilities that let us abuse ourselves in the name of saving the world. Some of us are just salaried." She shifted the manila folder under her arm and checked her watch. Their appointment with Tesla was supposed to be a debrief on the Mountain situation, which she was all too happy to describe to the bossman in every single painful detail. A copy of the report would be sent to Bill's ex-wife if Tesla wasn't going to play nice. Wrongful death and all that wouldn't be such a stretch, especially with the miles and miles of paper trail on psychiatric evaluations.

For all of the bitching people did about the system, it was rather useful when you knew how to work it.

A dark sedan rolled up on the gravel road next to the trailer office. Tesla sat in the passenger seat, with the so-called janitor doing the driving. They both got out, Tesla clutching a bottle of antacid tablets. He popped two when he saw the pair waiting at his door. "Yankee Pride and Detective Ferrari. Was the appointment today?"

"Today, ten minutes ago," Pride drawled. "Sir, that can't be good for your stomach. I think Einhorn's on the campus today, if you'd like something a little more permanent—"

"No. No, this is fine. I'm fine." He gave them a shaky smile and motioned to the door. Ramona said nothing but strolled inside, taking a seat in the chair furthest from the door. The "janitor" scowled, silent as Pride followed and opted to stand behind the detective.

When the man followed Tesla inside, Pride drew himself up and folded his arms across his chest. "I'm sorry, but this is a private matter that concerns a debrief on the Mountain situation. I don't believe that you were part of that operation. What did you say your name was?"

The man's eyes narrowed. "I'll be outside. Right outside," he added to Tesla.

When the door clicked shut, Alex Tesla popped three more tablets and loosened his tie. Slumped in his chair, he looked more like a mangled middle manager than a CEO to Ramona. She felt a fleeting moment of pity for the man, but that died when he opened a desk drawer to put away the worry candy. This was professional and personal, and he wasn't some metahuman who could will her into a smoking heap of ash and polyester. This was a lousy boss, and she was an informed yet disgruntled employee. She could manage this.

"Debrief report on the Mountain situation, sir." Ramona slapped the half-inch-thick folder on the table and flipped it open. Full-color glossies from the satellite showed Bill sinking into the Atlantic, the path of destruction evident miles behind him. "There's the accompanying psychiatric evaluation, coupled with summaries of the wrongful death suits that will be brought against Echo by seven of the twelve Americco Construction employees before the end of the month. I'm pretty sure that you've already seen the suits filed by the city concerning the destruction of property and misallocation of resources to support that death march."

"If we're nice to our senators, Spin Doctor thinks we can get the lot dismissed under the Wartime Powers Act," Pride said, but with an edge of disapproval. "He doesn't like the idea. Says it's better to pay 'em off now, generously. Actually, not 'better.' His exact phrase, if I recall correctly, was 'it's the honorable thing to do.' Reckon our mop-bearing friend wouldn't agree though." Pride narrowed his eyes. "He still calling the shots?"

"Echo is still a private organization, according to the charter issued in 1947. We do not have any government sponsorship, as dictated by my uncle and his associates." The words came wearily even as he slumped further into his chair. "He's here as a military liaison on behalf of the US government. He's here to help contain the damage."

"Contain it?" Pride repeated. "Seems to me like he caused a lot of it. The Mountain was one of ours, Alex. He wasn't hurting anything sitting in the corner of the Le Parkour course. He coulda stayed there a while. Hell, the Djinni had just about worked himself up t'usin' Bill as a new challenge course. You coulda sold tickets to that. Put it on pay-per-view."

"Especially if Bill had started swatting at him," Ramona muttered. She stood up and leaned against the desk, making it a priority to look directly at Bill's picture. "You see that, boss? That was one of your team. One of my coworkers. Hell, Tesla, that was one of my friends, and your policies and your so-called janitor's priorities put him in a situation that led him to suicide. On your watch."

Tesla made the mistake of looking away. In a few quick steps, Ramona was around the desk with a hand on the back of Tesla's chair. She grabbed the picture and shoved it in his face, her voice strangely calm. She had already cried herself out and shouted irrationally to anyone who would listen. Now, it was time for the old "good cop, bad cop" routine, and Pride was comfortable being the good guy. That left Ramona to attack. "Look. At. The. Picture. That's the picture of one of your employees pushed to the limit because someone told you he was disposable. How many more of those do you have, boss? Two? Ten? Twenty? We can go through the new recruits' records and cross-check with a good number of databases, and so can any news organization."

"That was the result of the mutation, not from his employment with Echo. After everything that happened on Echo campuses, everyone's got some diagnosis of post-traumatic stress syndrome. It's an epidemic." Tesla jerked away from the photo and stood up, shaking. In his rumpled state, he bore a closer resemblance to his scientist father. Nikola Tesla would have been appalled at his nephew's appearance. He ran a hand through his hair. "I'm sorry that it happened, and I'm sorry that it happened to one of your partners. We're doing the best that we can."

"Oh, bullshit." That came from Pride, and Ramona blinked at the meta in surprise. "You're covering your ass and kowtowing to every suit that comes in here. You know what that janitor has done? He's been authorizing OpOnes to go out with impressment gangs to shanghai anything that looks like a meta, claiming some kind of phony government authority over 'unregistered metahumans.' Which is in direct violation of the US Constitution. If you were doing the best you could, you'd have strapped a steak to his scrawny behind and let Pack's dogs have some fun." The gauntlets kept Pride from being able to crack his knuckles, but the way he was grinding one fist into the palm of his other hand was conveying what Ramona considered to be the right impression.

Tesla winced at the gesture, his focus on the desk in front of him. "And what do you want me to do about it? Since the Invasion, every Echo campus has been in the same situation, and the government's got us in a choke hold. The fact that we haven't been closed down and our operatives haven't been relocated to some secure test facility is the proof that we're still in control."

The chair next to Yankee Pride fell apart as one fist slammed into the back of it. Ramona jumped at the sound even as Tesla covered his head with his hands. The meta straightened up and squared his shoulders, taking a deep breath. "As I'm not the sort of gentleman who deals well with repeated falsehoods, I must remove myself from this meeting." Northern in name and Southern in manners, Pride offered a half-bow in apology to Ramona. "Excuse me, Detective."

"Ferrari," said a quiet voice in her ear, startling her. She had forgotten she was still "wired" to Overwatch. "How much dirt do you want me to find on this janitor? I can tell you already he's deep in something that's Mil Black Budget."

"Mountains," Ramona muttered. Tesla hadn't heard, as he sat shaking, his hands over his face.

"Roger that. I got a suspicion he's planning on skimming Echo Ops and making them disappear into some military meta program or other, but that's just me, and I'm paranoid."

"He's no janitor, that's for sure." Ramona sighed and looked over at her boss, who had heard the last comment and simply nodded in agreement.

"Uh, 'cleaner' is agent-speak for someone who makes things go away. Just saying."

This time she hummed what she hoped sounded like an affirmative. "Boss, when's the last time you had breakfast?"

Tesla frowned at her, puzzled. "Breakfast? But I thought—"

It took every ounce of control that she had not to scream in frustration. Instead, she pinched the bridge of her nose and took a long breath. "According to you, mop-man works for the government and we know he's not on the up-and-up. How about we take a page from my book and go off-campus so we get a head start and have a chat? No spooks, no metas, just you and me having a professional discussion. You can't tell me that you like staying in this box."

"You, him, and the blue canary." A fragment of music played before Ramona could react to that nonsensical sentence. "*Blue canary in the outlet by the light switch/ Who watches over you. Make a little birdhouse in your soul...*"

"Well, no. But I thought—"

"When you scare the crap out of someone by bringing in the heavy, you usually follow up by offering them food. Standard Echo detective protocol." She smirked, hoping that he wouldn't ask for a policy number. "Besides, I'm hungry and I'm going to bet that you don't have a functional coffeemaker in this box."

"He does, but it's hidden behind a few boxes, and he only has decaf. Proof positive he's a sick man."

That sealed it. Ramona gathered up her files and tucked them under her arm. "Let's go, boss. Before the janitor comes back and tries to take out the trash."

With the help of Overwatch, Ramona had found a little family-owned diner located a few miles away from the destruction corridor. The diner served breakfast all day and advertised a bottomless cup of coffee. They sat in a back booth with Ramona facing the door, an insulated pot of coffee between them.

"I've never understood the logic in calling it a bottomless cup of coffee," Vickie said in her ear. "If it was bottomless, you wouldn't get any coffee at all."

Ramona smiled at the comment. Alex glanced up, then quickly looked behind him to see what she had found amusing. "What? Did you see something? What's so funny?"

"Bottomless cups. Nobody's after us, boss. Pride was kind enough to engage the janitor in a routine assessment of the dumpster outside of your office so we could leave." She pushed her folder to the side and poured each of them a cup of coffee.

Vickie's analysis had clearly raced ahead. "I'm thinking that if Pride is going to stop acting like a rules jockey and start acting like his old man, I need to get him wired in too. I mean, come on! Interracial romance? In 1942? Rebel, dude! If Pride can just get some of that moxie going, I want him on our team."

The detective nodded and reached for her coffee. "Pride's a good man, boss. There aren't many of them left in Echo. If I were you, I'd be using that resource a lot more often."

Tesla drew his shoulders up, hands around his coffee mug as he bowed his head. "There isn't much that's left of Echo, I'm afraid. The government wants a bigger part of our research, calling it a question of national security. And with all of the lawsuits following the Invasion, getting that involvement may be the only thing that keeps us functioning."

"And *this* is what he pays expensive lawyers to tell him?" Vickie made a rude noise. "Betcha with twenty-four hours of searches I can find enough precedents to get all those cases tossed out of court. Well, the frivolous ones anyway. It's not like Echo *asked* the Kriegers to come calling."

Ramona kept her voice as even as possible. She hadn't brought the man here to skewer him with logic and reason. She needed to keep him talking to figure out just what was going on. "So, if the government wants a bigger part of the research—"

He waved his hand, almost knocking over the fake flowers on the table. "No government. My uncle would rather see Echo destroyed than fall under government control. Would have rather," he quickly corrected.

"Ohmigod," Vickie said, suddenly. "Moles. Sleepers. Look, no matter what the storm troopers look like, they didn't just beam down from outer space, not with the Nazi connection. They've got to have plants, sleepers, moles all over. Like, in the military, in the government. They're trying to get at Echo and get their hands on that Metis connection!"

"Right now, I've got a few others in the organization who are seeking out private investors. Forward-thinking progressives who would want to invest in the technology and the humanitarian side of things." He lifted his head, and Ramona could see the dark circles under his eyes. "But you can imagine that's hard to find these days."

Vickie snorted. "He's better off asking the Twins about how to get out from under the lawsuits. They're better at that than I am. Also faster."

Ramona sipped her coffee, digesting both conversations as naturally as she could. "Well, what about the Twins? That's a great resource you've got, completely separate from any government influence."

"The Twins?" he repeated, looking puzzled. "What would I use them for?"

"Bitch-slap him for being a moron, would you?"

She did the next best thing and rolled her eyes. "Research. Problem-solving. Figuring out how to haul your ass out of the fire so that this doesn't become a government operation or someone else's pet project." She set her coffee down and leaned forward on her elbows. "Honestly, you've got people that you've barely tapped. The life preserver is next to you in the water, and you're saying that you can't reach over and get it. You're in charge of a worldwide organization of metahumans, Mr. Tesla. Think about it."

He shook his head and looked away. His hands slipped away from his coffee mug, and Ramona could see them shaking as they moved to his lap. "There's no organization. It's closer to a network, with people and information being pooled and shared and stretched too thin. When those war machines opened up on us, they opened up on everyone. You can't begin to understand the sort of loss that Echo incurred, Detective."

"I can't?" She gritted her teeth. "Let me remind you that I was on the campus the day things happened, and that most of my civilian coworkers were buried in the rubble. Don't you dare get all high and mighty about loss, Tesla." Ramona stood up and took a deep breath. "Now, before I do something I'll regret, I'm going to the little detective's room. And when I come back, we're going to keep talking about this 'private investor' idea you mentioned."

He slumped in the corner of the booth and Ramona quick-stepped to the bathroom before she could say something even more scathing. She shut the door, locked it, and pushed the heel of her hand to her forehead. "It's like dealing with a teenager," she muttered.

"An emo teenager," Vickie said sourly. "I swear to all the gods there are, I never thought I would say that it's easier handling the Commissar than Tesla."

"I don't like this private investor bit, but the government alternative is worse. They'd have him boxed and buried in hours, and probably blame one of ours for it." Ramona moved to the sink and stared at her reflection in the mirror. Like Tesla, she had her own dark patches under her eyes, but at least she still had some fight left in her. The man she'd left in the booth was a shadow of the legend who had carried on the Echo legacy once Nikola Tesla had died. "Shit. Seriously, what's the likelihood of a private investor buying out Echo?"

"Dunno. Haven't researched it. Been busy doing little things like finding the Goldman Catacombs. I'd say that's a problem for the Twins. I'm not real good at weaving my way through offshore accounts and shell companies."

"Then I'll find a way to tag them. I don't think they're on Tesla's radar these days. Of course," she added, shaking her head, "I don't think he's able to do much at all."

Ramona's reflection nodded wisely back at her.

"If you're asking me, rather than telling me, I have to say he spends more time staring at his computer than he does actually accomplishing anything. My keystroke logger is dying of boredom."

"Can you tell what he's staring at?"

"Is the bear Catholic? I bloody well *own* his computer," Vickie said with confidence. "Apocalypse websites. He's got his mind firmly grooved in that this is the end of the world and nothing we can do will change it. I'd suggest a Prozac enema, but who'd administer it?"

"And to think, I'd have been happy if you'd said porn." Ramona moved to unlock the door, but the metal hummed under her fingers. In fact, the entire building seemed to shiver, as if someone had decided it was a tuning fork and they wanted the proper tone. "Hey, that's not—"

"HOLY CRAP! INCOMING!"

For once, Bella was not having to go toe-to-toe with Yankee Pride about another rule she'd broken. In fact, all he really seemed to want to talk to her about was . . . Tesla.

Okay. It's not the first time. Even before Seraphym started with me, people seemed to think I was Counselor Parker of Starship Las Vegas. So she put on her interested and sympathetic face and listened until he ran out of mad.

"I never thought I would ever say this, but damn it, YP, it's easier dealing with the Commissar than it is the boss right now. At least with the Commissar she's all about *doing* something rather than sitting around." Bella made a face. "Even if her idea of doing something is to go out and smash things until an answer falls out."

"But she's *doing* something, Parker. The lady acts like a leader, and her people still respect her in that position, from what you've said. I simply can't respect a coward who hides behind a computer at his desk while telling us that his hands are tied." Pride looked angry, frustrated and defeated. And now that he wasn't yelling at her . . . she was really getting to like him.

Should she? Should she tell him how much she knew? If she did, would he flip into Captain by the Book? "He acts like someone who knows something horrible that he's not telling the rest of us," she offered tentatively. "Less coward and more broken. I mean, look, this is a guy who has never had anything bad happen to him in his life, and this gets dropped on him. And money won't fix it, favors won't fix it, and there's nothing in the management handbook that's telling him a way out of it. He's drowning, YP. He's just a CEO, and he's gotten dropped into quicksand full of alligators and piranhas."

"Then he should be asking someone to throw him a rope, instead of giving up." Pride looked pointedly at Bella. "The least he could do is ask for some help."

Bella was about to reply when her PDA shrilled an alarm, and Vickie broke in. "All hands on deck! Anyone wired in and listening, we have Kriegers, I repeat, we have Kriegers and they're targeting Tesla. One Death Sphere, six troopers. Four Points, 405 Catalpa, Mama Lou's Diner, your nav is up and running, go, go, *GO!*" There was a slightly muffled burst of Russian, then Vickie came back on channel. "Sound off so I can coordinate you!"

"Scope here!" "Acrobat, I'm with Scope, we grabbed a bike and we're accelerating down Foster."

"Bella Blue," Bella said. "I have Yankee Pride, I'll brief him on the way. He's not wired."

"Wired for what?" Pride shot Bella a frown. "Just what exactly is going on here, Parker? And what unofficial channels are you using to communicate?"

"Is being Upyr. Have commandeered Ural, and am being half-way there."

Bella grabbed Pride's shoulder. "Project Overwatch. What we were using in the Catacombs. There's Kriegers at Four Points and they're homing in on Ramona and Tesla. Oh shite, Ramona—"

"Got her on a separate channel for now, Bell; she's too busy yelling at Tesla. Can Pride fly?"

"I dunno—" She shook Yankee Pride's shoulder. "Can you fly? Can you carry me? Otherwise we've got to get something that's fast."

Pride shook his head. "Can't fly, but our janitor's parked behind that trailer and has been watching us. I think it's time to use Echo protocol Yankee two-zero-niner and commandeer his vehicle."

"Get a move on!" Vickie said tensely. "I'm throwing up rock barriers but I can't keep it up forever."

The meta broke into a run towards the trailer, badge out as he nearly tore the door off the hinges. Bella couldn't hear the janitor's protest, but Pride's rumble invited no argument. In seconds, the car pulled up next to her and the back door to the sedan opened. "I'll have you know, there is no record of an Echo protocol for stealing a government-issued vehicle," the janitor sneered from the passenger seat.

"Bell, lean over the seat and touch his GPS quick!"

Bella did so, bracing against the acceleration as Pride threw the car towards Peachtree-Dunwoody. Then she yelped as a spark jumped from her finger into the screen, which suddenly lit up with the nav already plotted for them.

"Goddamn, I wish JM was wired up today," Vickie muttered. "We need a fire power...or JM or Zmey, even."

Now Bella's PDA gave the Echo alert warble, as did Yankee Pride's.

"We'll do what we have to with what we've got, Vic," Bella replied. "If I can get close enough, I can scramble their fascist brains." She clutched Pride's shoulder. "I'm pretty much wired into Overwatch 24/7. We also passed out some sets to our allies; one is wired up and on the way. Acrobat and Scope had theirs on for whatever reason. So your first response team is me, Acrobat, Scope and Upyr."

Whatever was under the hood of this beast, it was big, and it was powerful. And Yankee Pride was driving it like he was Mario Andretti, and it was a rental someone else had paid for. The car dodged in and out of traffic, tearing through the midmorning rush. The closer they got to the coordinates, the fewer cars they encountered. From a half mile away, the Sphere rose above the buildings and plowed through the parking lot. Pride pulled up across the street in time to see the asphalt rise in front of them and provide some well-needed cover.

The two metas piled out of the car. As the dark-suited man moved to join them, Pride pointed a finger at him that was soon surrounded by a gold-tinged aura. Both of his gauntlets flared to life as he leaned over the seat. "Stay in the car. I wouldn't recommend trying to follow."

The front of the diner had collapsed under the troopers' feet. While Vickie had put out the call, Ramona had run out of the bathroom and pulled Tesla from under their table and into the kitchen. She had heard most of Vickie's alerts and had recognized some of the names for their first response team, but she couldn't say any of that to Tesla. Besides, as he cowered against the side of a refrigerator, he wouldn't have been too responsive anyway.

"Ramona, get in the walk-in freezer. We think they have some IR vision and, besides the armoring of the freezer itself, that'll foil it."

She looked around wildly. The door to her left looked like the same sort of freezer she'd seen during her summers working burger joints in her youth, so she wrenched it open. Ramona pulled Tesla inside, grabbing the heavy jackets on the hook next to the door and throwing them inside before she closed the door.

"Can I put you on team freq?" Vickie was panting, as if she'd been running.

"Yeah," Ramona wheezed. "And we're inside."

"Roger. Bell, tell Pride he's Team Lead. I have Jamaican Blaze confirmed and en route *fast*—she's got an Echo jet pack. She'll be there any second. There's your fire power you asked for."

Ramona felt for the light switch. It should be just inside the door.

"Upyr on scene," came the crisp Russian voice. "Am being to pass Scope and Acrobat, will to being no more than thirty seconds out."

There it was. Ramona flipped it on.

"Ramona Ferrari and Tesla are in the walk-in freezer in the kitchen, safe for now. Anybody got a spare headset for Pride?" Vickie asked.

"Jamaican Blaze just touched down," Bella reported.

Tesla was huddled on the floor, looking freaked out. She stuffed him into a jacket then pulled one on herself; her breath emerged in clouds of fog. The coat, amazingly, was too big, which was fine with her; she kept her hands inside the sleeves and sat down on a cardboard box marked MIXVEG.

"Well, get her out of that pack before you let her—*DAMN IT*—in combat," Vickie warned. "If the energy beams hit those things, they go up like a bomb."

"I grabbed Bull's Overwatch gear from the rack at the door!" Acrobat said in triumph.

"Good job, Bruno," Bella told him warmly. "Pass it over to Pride when you get there, let's get him wired in."

Ramona heard someone saying something; it sounded like Pride. "Okay, Tesla briefed you on Overwatch, yeah?" Bella said. "Upyr! By the dumpster! Vic Victrix runs it; it's part cybermonitoring and part magic. She's got all of us tagged magically so she can loc us on a map, and we're wired with button cams, throat mics and earpieces, all the standard Echo tech you're used to. There! See, she can do her geomancy remotely as long as we're on something like ground or it's a place she already knows. I stay wired all the time now, pretty much. We wired Ramona less than an hour ago. And—uh—I took the responsibility of wiring some of CCCP. They were really receptive to the idea." Before Pride could say anything, Bella then shouted "Yo! Bruno! Here!"

There was a very brief moment of relative silence—relative because Ramona could hear the Nazis tearing through the diner, looking for them.

"Yankee Pride. Testing."

"Reading you five by five, Team Leader," Vickie said formally. "You know everyone but Upyr. She drains energy from living things but it has to be bare skin to bare skin."

"Which is why am having brought SMG, with incendiary loads," Upyr said. "Also incendiary grenade launcher. Special *fashista* loads from Zmey's tinkering. Very hot, he says, but may be too dangerous here? May be to starting fires we cannot put out. With SMG I can to be heating up knees, so you others can be chopping off at."

Terrified screams coupled with the sounds of wood splintering and the telltale whine of energy cannons. Tesla crouched on the floor, rocking back and forth slightly. The chilly air was a mixed blessing; Ramona knew it would be uncomfortable, but it would probably keep him from getting sick from nerves. She touched his shoulder, and he flinched violently.

"This is how it ends. They're coming to finish what they started. They won't be satisfied until every last one of us is dead." Tesla's voice rose at the end, his eyes going wide. "I've seen things, Detective. The only way this ends is with everyone dead. All of Echo, all of Atlanta, me, you, every—"

Ramona reared back and slapped her boss as hard as she could across his cheek. He fell back and stared up at her, stunned.

"Good jo—*DAMN IT, PRIDE, DUCK!*—Ferrari. Tell hi—*Incoming, Blaze!*—that this is just a frickin' hit squad same as they sent after Saviour a couple weeks ago. *Yank, I'm running out of steam, here.*" There was more chatter, much of it from Bella, who seemed to know this neighborhood like the back of her hand, and was telling people the safe corridors to evacuate the civilians by. Yankee Pride's comments were a few tactical, the rest backing up Bella.

Ramona addressed her boss. "You can sit there and suck it up, maybe grow a pair while you sit in here. This is a hit squad, same as the last one that popped up a few blocks over." Ramona folded her arms across her chest as she glowered at Tesla. "But don't you pull that 'we're all gonna die' bullshit in here, because I *will* smack you again. Your people are out there, doing the best they can, to save you and the rest of us in here. The least you can do is act like they have a chance."

Because, she thought as she sat back down on the box of frozen veggies, *there's not much else to do while we wait in the freezer.*

Somehow, Bella had managed to direct the rest of the patrons and diner staff through the back streets and alleys to get away from the attack. Now she considered her job as DCO to be done with. She cast a significant glance at Upyr, who gave her that Mona Lisa smile. "Is to be second SMG on Ural, blue girl," the Russian said. Upyr looked at Yankee Pride.

"If you dare to tell me that healers don't hit..." she warned.

"Healer?" He looked directly at her, the gold aura coming to life about both gauntlets. "I don't see a 'healer' anywhere. Sort of a backwards designation anyway, if you ask me. Load up, Parker."

That was all Bella needed. Crouched over, she sprinted to the Ural and got the second SMG that had been strapped to the saddlebags, and loaded up on ammo. Untermensch had been drilling her on the care and feeding of Soviet arms ever since she started moonlighting with CCCP. This felt like an old friend in her hands now.

Hard to believe no more than five minutes had passed since the first response team arrived. The front of the diner had erupted in flames, the Kriegers' plasma cannons superheating the foundation and supports. Scope and Acrobat were on one side of the parking lot, with Bruno zipping over the still-intact cars and the stone barriers that Vickie had thrown up in the first assault. He taunted the machine, bringing it closer to one of the smoking cars. The other Echo Op, Jamaican Blaze, watched Acrobat pull the Krieger into the fire. Soon, it was knee-deep in flames. The meta brought her hand up, and the fires intensified around the joints. When they were glowing white-hot, Bella put a good long burst into the right knee, while Upyr concentrated fire on the left. The Krieger collapsed, and the flames intensified until parts of the metal sagged. Then Scope put two rounds in the head. The whole suit spasmed and was still.

"Nice shootin', Tex," drawled Bella.

"You too. Looks good on you," Scope called back. She motioned to Blaze, who was now pulling the fires down to manageable flicker-flames. "Same as before, your nine o'clock. Follow Acrobat!"

Pride moved next to Bella. "That's Bulwark's team, is it?"

She nodded. "Half of it. Red Djinni and Harmony are the other half; Djinni and Harm are still on med leave. I'm their off-again, on-again DCO. Overwatch is wired to all of us. I can only assume the reason Bull didn't have his set on—"

"Shower," Scope said briefly. "Butt naked and covered with soap when Vic scrambled us."

"I gotta figure out a way to implant that stuff," Vickie said on the common channel.

"I'm not sure if I'd be entirely comfortable with you in my ear twenty-four/seven, Miss Victrix. But I certainly can appreciate the thought." Pride motioned to the area where the Sphere had regrouped with two of the other metal men. "What's the damage ratio they'll take before they retreat?"

Vickie's tone turned grim. "The ones that went after Saviour were a suicide squad. They didn't stop coming until everything was paste."

"Thank you, Overwatch." If the news fazed Yankee Pride, it didn't show. "What's the construction on the diner, including the specific area in question?"

"Plans to your PDA, Team Lead." Pride's PDA chirped. "The freezer is dual-purpose, they just installed it after the Invasion. Intended to serve as a hardened safe room. I think I have enough in me to give it a layer of rock and dirt as well and I can make sure the electrics going into it are protected."

"Sounds like a lovely plan, Overwatch. Go ahead with that, and we'll join the program in progress with Bulwark's operatives. Scope, Acrobat and Blaze, you'll need to move away from the building to allow Overwatch to work." He flashed Bella a warm smile and took off at a jog toward the Sphere.

The ground around the diner began to shake and erupt. Vickie was doing a bit more than just protect the freezer; Bella saw some additional activity going on that would make it appear to the Kriegers that she was erecting a wall between the two with the

Sphere and the two still engaged with Scope, Blaze, and Acrobat. *Good, she's not creating an obvious target for them.*

"This is not authorized! Kidnapping, wanton destruction of property, involvement of illegal and undocumented workers in highly sensitive operations!" The janitor ran towards Pride, badge in one hand as he reached for his sidearm. "I order you to cease all operations until assistance from a regulated agency can arrive!"

The asphalt split less than twenty feet from where Yankee Pride stood, and the rising ground prompted the man to slow to a fast walk. "Or what? You'll report me and the rest of this team?"

"Yes! You and that healer with the cannon on her shoulder!" He thrust a hand in Bella's direction as she and Upyr targeted the crumbling joints of a second Krieger. "Order your team to stand down!"

Vickie sounded breathless and exhausted. "Team Leader, he knows Tesla is in there. It's in his interest to see he doesn't come out except in a bag. I have him linked to a military black budget program. If you tell him to stick it, he can't do anything without exposing that interest."

Yankee Pride stared at the man, even as shots rang out from Scope's rifle and the Krieger gave a final mighty shudder. "I'll politely decline your request that I acquiesce to your formal command, sir. And in the patriotic words of my own father... go stuff yourself."

The man stared as Pride punctuated his father's words with one of his mother's favorite hand gestures and took off towards the Sphere.

The walls of earth and stone held as a third Krieger collapsed. Acrobat bounced on his toes, giddy with success, as Scope reloaded. "This is amazing! This is the real thing, y'know! That's frickin' *Yankee Pride* out there with us!"

"What, and the Catacombs were a walk in the park?" Vickie reminded him, panting hard. "You're in the bigtime, kid, and rightly so. And... that's it." A forlorn little mushroom of dirt pushed up and sagged back. "No more juice."

"You've done great work, Miss Vickie." Pride's voice was warm. "Before I forget, I must say that it's an honor to work with someone of your caliber."

"You say the sweetest things, but my heart belongs to my cat." There was a pause. "Heads up. The Sphere is powering up. Now things are going to get ugly. And Gamayun says your backup is at least five more minutes out."

Scope peeked over the edge of the stone barrier. "Looks like it. What's the first target?"

"We'll need to hit the Sphere. The sooner we get that down, the sooner we get our people out of what's left there." Pride paused. "Miss Vickie, I don't suppose..."

Regret and exhaustion made her voice ragged. "I'm dry. I could fling pebbles, maybe. Uh...huh, wait a sec. There might be something I can do cybernetically. I'll tell you when I know if it's feasible."

"She is so *cool*," Acrobat whispered in fanboy fashion. Scope let out a laugh even as she tapped the back of his head out of reflex.

"Bruno, hon?" Vickie said quietly. "Outside of my safe room, I am a freaking basket case. But you, kiddo, are a real hero."

"I'm a spaz, in or out of a room," he answered with a goofy grin. "Scope'll tell you just as much."

"And he makes great bait," Scope added. "If we're going to bring down that Sphere, then we've got to pull it away from the building. That's going to be all him."

"Aha. That was what I needed. Okay, Bruno. You and I are going to play tag team with the Beach Ball. You're going to have to plot your path very carefully. I want you to touch down on your Le Parkour jumps behind stuff I can overload electrically. Transformers, streetlights, anything I can make a flashbang out of. We'll have to time this really well. I am pretty sure based on all the data that we can temporarily blind whatever they use as sensors and cameras with a flashbang, and that will keep them from being able to target you. *Capiche?*"

"Totally. Man, this is gonna be fun." He rubbed his hands together and turned to focus on the lot and the surrounding businesses. "Yeah, this should work. You want me to call it?"

"You're wired, so, yeah, you cue me when you want the flash— unless I happen to see something zeroing in on you first. I've got the schematics for everything cued up on my compie and I have control of a five-block-square area of the electrical grid now." She sighed. "Some people are gonna be very unhappy until the power company gets here. On the other hand, beats being toasted."

The subsonic whine of the Sphere filled the air and it swiveled toward the remnants of the diner. Bruno took the motion as a cue to get moving, darting into the mess of broken concrete and overturned cars. He let fly a small hook and line to get the Sphere's attention, the thin cable wrapping around one of the arms. It snapped as the Sphere turned, and Bruno lobbed a small flash grenade at the machine to secure its attention. The taunting worked, and the kid laughed as he took off over a broken stone barricade towards the first set of power lines.

"Hey, Scope? Remember, there are sensors in the ends of the tentacles and they are vulnerable, not armored. Your target, Annie Oakley."

"Okay, first target is the pole at my two o'clock, but there's the second behind and to the right of it. After that, there's the neon sign at the car dealership." Acrobat leapt to the top of a dumpster as he spoke, then flung himself toward the pole and grabbed onto one of the utility handles. He barely had enough time to get a foothold on another handle when a metal tentacle cut through the wood. The force flung him forward to a taller concrete piece that held a second transformer.

Bella held her breath. Vickie swore and blew the streetlight before the wires had a chance to snap and she lost the power. "Bruno! You okay?"

"Yeah! Forward momentum like that lets me bridge a gap up to thirty-six percent wider than I could do with a regular jump. Only with the wood, though. Concrete and metal don't have the same 'oomph,' y'know?" His arms went slack for a split second before he launched himself toward the neon sign. Behind him, the Sphere lurched to one side and steadied itself with a tentacle on the ground. It reached out for where Bruno had been, the claw scraping the side of the concrete pillar.

Vickie blew the transformer. It went up in a satisfying white flash and a shower of sparks. The Sphere drew back the tentacle that had been closest, the others flailing wildly to compensate for the explosion. It regrouped quickly, moving towards Bruno with a renewed vengeance.

"Ranger doesn't like that, Yogi," said Vickie. "Get clear, neon signs make shrapnel."

Acrobat scrambled up to a window ledge. "Cool! Okay, alley, another sign, and then the box on the corner. That'll get him across the street."

Vickie hadn't been lying. Bella winced as the neon sign blew.

The pop and flare of light happened as Bruno leapt to the ground and bounced through the alley. With a clumsy groan and the sound of metal scraping against asphalt, the Sphere tried to follow Acrobat's path as he crossed the street.

"Boss," Bella said quietly to Yankee Pride, "what's our move when Bruno gets the thing downrange?"

Pride glanced at the assembled metas, then focused on Upyr. "What's your ammunition, ma'am? Anything more than just standard issue?"

"Is being standard incendiary rounds in SMGs, but *bolshoi* special loads in grenade launcher," she said with pride. "Zmey is being to make them. Like napalm, only hotter and very sticky. Only problem is only one in four work. Three in four being duds." She shrugged. "Is being in beta, *nyet?*"

He nodded, frowning. "One in four. Not great, but not bad. You said it's like napalm, though. Are those pieces live before they fire?"

"Is being two stage. Zmey is to tell me duds do not mix properly. Launcher goes boom, is to shatter barrier inside grenade. Then grenade is to hit, small impact charge goes boom, liquid is to spread, proper mixture ignites when contacts air." She eyed Scope speculatively. "I am to being think rifle *devushka* should be to handle launcher. One of these on house would be very bad."

"Yeah, very bad indeed. Scope, you get the grenade launcher and we'll move downrange. That Kreiger looks like it'll follow us, since Acrobat and Miss Vickie are giving that Sphere hell." Pride motioned with a gauntlet across the street. "If you'll be so kind as to remind it that we're here, then we can start to wrap this up and get our folks home."

Upyr offered that same Mona Lisa smile as she took careful aim at the Kreiger's knee joints with her SMG. The hit and explosion caused it to wobble before it changed direction and charged at the group. As Pride turned to follow the rest of the group, a nasal officious voice cut through the air.

"That's it, Pride! You, Tesla, that blue commie mole, all of you! You're ordered to stand down and wait for proper backup to assist!" The janitor walked toward them, this time with a small bullhorn.

"He can't issue orders," Vickie said, blowing the next sign behind Acrobat. "Not without authorization from higher up. He's bluffing. Only reason he could order Echo around about the Mountain was because he'd gotten that authorization for that specific circumstance.... Oh, he should have gotten some plastic surgery. You would be amazed what my face recognition software is turning up."

Pride drew himself up to stand in front of the man. "And I ordered you to get back in the damn car, you sniveling rat. This is not your command."

The janitor stopped, walked back a few steps, then took off in a run towards the remains of the diner. "I'm authorized to speak with Alex Tesla, which is what I'm going to do right now while the rest of you play with the toy soldiers." The words came through the bullhorn. They sounded canned and tinny in the air.

"Ramona, if he comes busting in there somehow, shoot him," Vickie said instantly. "He's armed, he's clearly irrational, and you have no way of knowing he's not with the Kriegers."

"You don't have to tell me twice." Ramona's voice was dry and strangely calm on the channel.

The man climbed on top of the stone fortress that surrounded what was left of the diner and began kicking at the layers of rock and earth. Dull thuds could be heard through Ramona's headset as he tried to get in. "Which one of you made this happen? Was it the commie Goth? Is she the one helping you protect Tesla? Is she the one enabling all of you to commit *treason*?"

As he continued to pound on the stone, the Krieger slowed in his pursuit of the Echo ground team. The body swiveled toward the mound of debris and the "head" cocked to the side, as if analyzing the frenzied actions of the tiny irrational creature. At almost the same time, the Sphere slowed its pursuit of Bruno and spun to focus on the same area.

"Oh shit," said Bella in a small voice.

Both machines charged toward what was left of the diner. Yankee Pride took off in the same direction, but it wasn't soon enough to keep the Krieger from confirming what they all knew. The ground shook as the machines turned their full attention on the janitor and his attempts to unearth the diner. Pride reached the man first, grabbing him by the jacket and flinging him to the ground several feet from Upyr. He landed in an obviously uncomfortable position and looked up to see her frowning at him.

"Is being a very bad decision on your part." She pulled off a glove and placed her hand against the man's cheek for a few seconds, just long enough to ensure that he wasn't going to meddle in anything critical for the time being. He sagged to the ground, the bullhorn next to him.

The Krieger pounded a metal fist into the stone barrier that Vickie had thrown up around the walk-in freezer. There was another crack and pop of electricity as the diner sign blew out and the freezer hum through Ramona's headpiece went dead.

"That's not a good sign," said Bella. "Silence bad." She bit her lip and felt the blood drain from her face as she saw the Sphere bearing down on the wreck of the diner.

Then Ramona reported, "We've lost power in here. Advise?"

To his credit, Yankee Pride answered in a calm and collected drawl. "Sit tight, ma'am. Keep the boss safe, and we'll get you out."

Yankee Pride had spent the better part of his time following the Invasion behind a desk or in front of a podium, part strategist and part figurehead. During the actual hits on Echo, he'd been charged to take care of Tesla as a sort of bodyguard, someone for Spin Doctor to put in front of a camera to show the public that the metahumans of Echo were invincible in the face of this new threat. "Too valuable" to be on fighting teams, they said. Now he knew what Yuri Gagarin and Alan Shephard had felt like when they were sidelined for the same specious reason.

Leaders didn't sit behind desks and throw other people at a problem without regard for health and safety. Or if they did send folks into harm's way, they did it from the front lines, like that Commissar over in the slums. He was really beginning to like that woman. Alex Tesla could have taken a page from her little red command book, that was certain.

"What next?" Scope hoisted the grenade launcher and nodded in the direction of the diner. The Krieger stood with its metal hands clasped in a giant fist, and it brought them down upon the rock fortress with the force of a pile driver.

"They're in a commercial freezer, it's hardened as a safe room, and it's full of rock hard food," Bella said, as if she was thinking aloud. "It'll be a cold battery for a while..."

"Ain't nothin' going to actually burn with all that dirt and rock on top of it, and heat tends to go up rather than down," Vickie pointed out in their ears. "At least, I don't *think* that Zmey's *Supra-Sovietski Molotov* formula is going to burn rock."

Bella turned to Pride. "Boss, you need to make a decision and make it fast, because the Molotov juice might not get through rock, but that Death Sphere can."

He held up a hand. "Noted, Parker. Acrobat, you keep doing what you've been doing, and concentrate on the bigger of the uglies. I'd like to think that if we take that down, the other might turn tail. And Parker, you and Miss Upyr work on keeping Bruno from getting caught too quickly." Pride assessed the space between them and the diner. "Miss Scope and Miss Blaze, you stay here and wait for my signal. We'll move on my mark."

"Bruno, hold still a minute," Bella said, and put a hand on either shoulder, closing her eyes for a moment. She wilted a little; Bruno's eyes widened.

"What did you just do?" he exclaimed.

"Cleaned all the fatigue poisons out. You should be feeling like you just got out of bed after a good night's sleep." She pulled her hands away. "I don't do that often, it's usually a waste of energy I would need to fix wounds, but you'll need the edge."

Bruno grinned and watched Pride expectantly; if he'd had a tail, it would have been wagging a mile a minute. "We go now?"

Pride waited for the next downswing from the Krieger. "Now! If you trap that Sphere, get a shot on it, understood?"

Acrobat was off like a shot, with the other three racing after him. Pride moved toward the Krieger, gauntlets glowing. Bella followed him, unable to keep up with the rest of the squad. When he was on the edge of the debris field, he knelt to the asphalt and brought one fist up. At the same moment that the Krieger's fists slammed into the rock surrounding the freezer, Pride's fist hit the asphalt. The parking lot split with the impact, but nothing else moved. Again, he hit the pavement in time with the trooper's steady assault, weakening the foundation and causing more of the debris to slide. The fifth and sixth hits allowed the rock to crumble enough that the Krieger paused mid-swing—

—and looked directly at Pride.

It paused, the massive metal head focused on the mound of rock that covered Tesla's hiding spot. With a whine and whir of gears, it moved purposefully toward the meta whose fists continued to glow. Each step the Krieger took scattered rock and debris. Yankee Pride's likeness covered billboards in Atlanta, the image of Echo for the new millennium designed to instill hope and make metahumans relevant to the younger generations. Tesla was a figurehead, but this man with the glowing fists in red, white, and blue was a symbol of everything that needed to be broken and cleansed in this miserable city.

A subsonic whine filled the air as the cannon rose to target Yankee Pride. "Wait for it," Vickie muttered, even though she knew that Jamaican Blaze couldn't hear her. Scope could, though, and Scope had Blaze in sight. She gave Blaze the "hold it" hand signal. The younger woman nodded once to show she understood.

"Good one, Sure Shot. Boss, say when. Fresh fries on your call."

Pride stood calmly, the gold aura around his gauntlets glowing brighter as the cannon ramped up. There was a soft pulse as it prepared to fire, and Scope could hear it even as Pride called the mark. A CCCP special-issue grenade impacted on the muzzle of the arm cannon, the charge lodged dead-center.

"That's how it's done!" Scope crowed before spinning and ducking behind the rocky barrier. "I hope this one's a dud; otherwise, this is gonna be spectacular."

"And by spectacular, you mean shrapnel everywhere." Pride motioned to Blaze to have her move forward. "Let's heat this up a bit, if you'd be so kind."

She nodded once, her hands coming up to her waist as she pulled the heat from the still-smoldering debris to form a brilliant fire. At first, orange-yellow flames licked the concrete and dirt. In moments, the flames darkened and grew light again, white-blue as they leapt to life and concentrated around the legs and knees of the Krieger. The soldier smashed the side of the arm cannon against the rubble in frustration, trying to dislodge the grenade. As he did so, the casing broke and Zmey's custom cocktail leaked out all over his right arm and side. The flames leapt higher, igniting the stuff so that one half of the Krieger was enveloped in red and blue flame.

Pride crouched, one hand splayed on the ground as he gave the count. "Drop it in three, two, one—" With a muffled pop of air, the fires rushed back into the debris and left the Krieger glowing white-hot. Yankee Pride charged, gauntlets a brilliant gold as he readied his punch. The fiery compound dripped down from the soldier onto Pride's own Echo armor, leaving holes where it cut through the armor and found the nanoweave underlayer. The meta let out a yell as he slammed one fist in the back of the Krieger's weakened knee.

A weak wave of dust enveloped Pride. It was enough to smother the fire on him. He coughed and followed with a left uppercut to the inside of the leg joint, moving the hip from the socket. The Krieger tottered dangerously, liquid fire still leaking out the arm cannon. Pride swung both hands around in a two-fisted punch to the other leg, the impact into superheated metal leaving some of the molten residue on his own gauntlets. As he staggered back, the Krieger toppled to the rubble.

"Bring those fires back up and take cover!" Holding his left hand, Pride ran for where Scope had hidden herself. Blaze moved up as far as she could in order to see her handiwork, and the flames roared around the Krieger to ensure that it was finally down.

Bella sprinted for the same spot as Scope and Pride, diving into cover between them. Since the only part of Pride that wasn't covered in armor was his face, she slapped her bare hand over his mouth and concentrated on healing the burns. "Stop squirming!" she ordered. "Burns keep burning unless you do something about them right away!" That wasn't exactly what happened, but it was close enough for a layman.

She had her eyes closed, so she missed the slag-down of the Krieger. She did, however, hear Blaze slam to the ground next to Scope and the muffled warning before the crack and boom of exploding metal filled the air. As Pride and Scope had predicted, shrapnel went flying in all directions, and the massive arm cannon rocketed over their heads and through the car that had held Tesla's janitor. The heat and pressure from the exploding sedan whipped back at the four, bits of rock and glass catching any bit of skin that wasn't immediately covered.

Scope lifted her face from her arm; blood dripped from several gashes behind her ears and along her neck. "It might be uncharitable of me to say so, but good damn riddance. Asshole."

Bella clamped her free hand on Scope's neck; the bleeding stopped and the gashes started to close visibly. "Amen."

"I'll see if that janitor has any family," Vickie said in their ears. "If he does, I'll report he died heroically trying to rescue Alex. If he doesn't, I'll let his bosses figure out what happened. But we still have that Death Sphere to deal with—"

Belatedly Bella remembered Pride couldn't talk with her hand still clamped over his mouth, and let go.

"Thank you, Miss Parker." He coughed and flexed the fingers of his left hand. "Bruno, how're you holding up over there?"

Acrobat was panting and gulping air. "It's getting sticky, sir. It really wants to get back to find Mr. Tesla." There was a crash from the other side of the parking lot, followed by a yelp from Bruno over the comm. "Like, really-really."

"Noted. Miss Scope, how many of those commie rounds do you have left?"

"Four, sir." Scope paused. "So we have good odds of one right."

Upyr's voice came through the channel. "Is not being so simple. Zmey has twenty-eight of them, we were to be having five. Could all be, as you say, duds."

Pride got to his feet and motioned for the rest to follow him. "To be fair, math was never my best subject. I was more of a history and literature sort of man. Let's work with the assumption that they're all duds and we'll have to do something extra to break the casings. Understood?"

Any bit of assent was lost in the explosion of the last neon sign on the block bursting into a shower of glass and metal. Vickie broke in. "I've run out of flashes to blind the eyes. Bruno, make with the traveling music."

Acrobat scrambled to what remained of a bus stop and launched himself to the top of the one wall left standing from the three-story building. On the ground, Upyr darted toward the smoldering wreckage of the janitor's car, positioning herself directly across from the rest of the Echo team. From where they were, they could see one of the Sphere's tentacles smash the remaining wall; Bruno went flying forward, managing to tuck into a roll as his hands and feet met the pavement. He landed a few feet from Scope and gave her a wide grin, in spite of the lacerations on his arms and face. Bella grabbed him and went to work. "Jeebus, people, give a gal a chance to breathe, why don't you," she muttered.

"That was awesome, wasn't it?" Bruno was saying to Scope. "You've gotta tell Bull about that one, it was totally choice."

She shook her head and turned to Pride. "All right, boss. Where do we move?"

"What kind of ground do you want?" Vickie asked. "I'm out of juice but I have great sat-maps."

The Sphere, however, had other plans. Acrobat was out of the picture, and it zeroed in on the mound of rubble and dirt that hid the freezer where Tesla and Ramona were hidden. And nothing was going to keep it away.

There was only one functioning energy cannon on it, but the cannon was bigger than both of the arm cannons that the trooper had sported. As soon as it got within range, it started blasting away at the mound.

That was the bad part. But the good part—it was having trouble "seeing," missing at least half its shots. It moved in close enough to be right on top of the mound and the blazing, melting Krieger trooper.

That was the good part. The bad part was that in order for any heat to reach up where it hovered, Jamaican Blaze was going to have to stoke those fires very high indeed.

Ramona shoved boxes of frozen vegetables and ground meat to the far side of the freezer, building a strange sort of igloo out of them. She used the tubes of hamburger like logs to make walls, reinforcing them with bags of frozen peas and corn, and stacking the boxes around the outside. A metal shelf made the roof, with more bags of frozen stuff—berries and other fruit this time—on top of it. Her boss sat on the floor, still muttering to himself. She had dismissed him as useless the moment that Vickie had enveloped the freezer in earth and stone, and she hoped that he wasn't going to do something stupid that would endanger them both. She pushed the last of the cases of frozen tater tots to the wall and shed the down jacket. "That's the last of what we've got in here. Looks like we missed delivery day."

"It's gonna get very hot in there, Ferrari," said a worried Vickie in her ear. "I know that heat goes up, but Jamaican Blaze is going to have to stoke the fire above you to the point where the brick is vitrifying if we're going to weaken the Sphere. Some of that is going to go down. Is there anything else you can use for insulation?"

The detective looked around the small room. "That's a negative. I've stacked all that I can against the wall, and it looks like they used the freezer just for food."

"Okay. Get in under it, and yell if it feels like you're edging past 'sauna' and into 'oven' territory."

"On the bright side, this could be a helluva victory barbecue if it works," Ramona muttered, pulling Tesla with her. She jammed the coats into the spaces above them and sat with her back to a box of tater tots.

"I can't think of a quip," Vickie replied. Her voice sounded exhausted. "Stay safe in there."

The dead Krieger was white-hot now, and to Bella's fascinated horror, the bricks of what had been the diner were actually burning. She'd read about that—how during the Dresden firebombing in WWII the brick buildings had burned long after anything conventionally flammable was gone—but reading it and seeing it were two different things. Visible heat made the air ripple all the way up to the Sphere, which was now clawing at the rubble with a couple of tentacles as well as trying to shoot its way in.

"Bella, darlin'," Pride said, the tense sound of his voice at odds with his gentle drawl. "There any way ya can juice Scope like Harmony can?"

"I can sure give it the old college try," she replied, and put both hands on Scope's shoulders, willing steadiness and energy into her.

"It's not Harm, but it's helping, Blue," Scope said, sighting along the bazooka. "Keep it up."

No one said the obvious; that they had one chance to make this shot. Scope had already spent three of the four "special loads." It wasn't that she had missed, it was that the damn things had bounced off rather than lodging, where Scope could have shot at them with armor-piercing rounds to vent the casing, or exploding the way they were supposed to. This was it. There hadn't been a murmur from inside the freezer. Bella had been afraid to say anything, for fear that there wouldn't be an answer if she called out to Ramona.

"If you can give me a hair more . . . You're boosting my vision, Blue. I think there's a spot I can make this thing wedge into."

Bella closed her eyes and concentrated with every fiber. She sagged, and Pride moved to brace her. Scope's back tensed, but her arms relaxed, her lip curling into a sneer as she found the sweet spot along the top of the Sphere, right where one of the tentacles seemed to have jammed at an odd angle. The bazooka went off with a satisfying *whump*, the hot gasses blowing right past Pride's shoulder and ear. He didn't turn a hair.

The grenade hit; it exploded quite as if it was unaware it could have been a dud. Runnels of fire trickled down the top of the Sphere. From here, it looked like nothing, mere driblets. There was no way to tell that the stuff was so hot that right now it was eating its way into every crack and crevice it could find, weakening the Sphere—critically, they hoped....

"One of four," Upyr remarked calmly. "Was good odds."

"Let's bring those fires up on top, if you'd be so kind," Pride drawled, one arm holding Bella up. Jamaican Blaze nodded, sweat running down her face and arms as she moved to control both the fires in the diner and the smoldering metal atop the Sphere. "Miss Scope, you do what you do best."

Scope tossed the bazooka aside and picked up the sniper rifle, loading it with incendiary and armor-piercing rounds. "Way ahead of you, boss."

Upyr put one hand up to an ear. "I will to return," she said, stripped off her gloves, and dashed off. A moment later, she *did* return. She looked strangely—pink. She clamped one bare hand on Bella and one on Scope. Bella felt a rush of strangely frenetic energy—apparently Scope did too. "Daughter of Rasputin is to being find me looters," she said with satisfaction. "They are to being need to sit down now."

"You should bottle that," said Scope absently, and began firing steadily into the top of the Sphere. The weakened outer shell showed signs of damage, the rounds cutting through the outer casing. She cut a methodical pattern through the top of the Sphere, allowing Blaze's flames to cut a path that circumscribed the topmost piece. The fires beneath shifted and rose on one side, and the Sphere began to cant over sideways. The tentacles waved wildly. Scope switched to stitching a line across the now-exposed and glowing belly of the thing. It started to split open along the line like a melon under pressure.

Then everything went south for it. With a hideous howl, it actually turned turtle, inverting. Bella *thought* that the pilot might have mistaken his direction—but the propulsion unit underneath suddenly gave a *blat* and it accelerated straight down. It crashed into the mound of burning brick less than a foot away from where Vickie had buried the freezer. The impact of the Sphere could be heard through the channels, and Tesla's frantic screaming filled their ears. The feed abruptly ceased, soon replaced by a soft buzz.

"Channel's gone," Vickie said tensely. "Get those fires out! CCCP is almost here—" Plumes of dust spat up and settled down on the edges of the fire to the sound of muttered curses.

Pride looked around frantically for anything to use to smother the flames. Blaze had brought them down as much as she could, but she was unable to actually extinguish them. A broken piece of a Sphere claw lay on top of the rock. Pride grabbed the claw and began to use it as a makeshift shovel, pushing the burning pieces away from the freezer and covering the remaining flames with dirt.

A battered van with a motor that was screaming protest tore into the parking lot where they'd left the "janitor's" car. Three more people piled out, all in CCCP uniforms. One broke off a fire hydrant with his bare hands. The second made waving motions at it—and the stream of water shooting straight up suddenly bent over as if it was inside a flexible tube, to spray itself on top of the diner. The third person was Nat—Commissar Red Saviour— who proceeded to blast the debris off the top of the freezer with energy-augmented punches a lot like Yankee Pride's.

Pride set the claw aside, climbing to the top of the freezer. Precisely as Vickie had described, the unit had been designed to serve as a shelter, with a secondary access hatch at the top. He broke the lock with a solid punch and peeled back the dented door. The smell of burnt cardboard and cooked meat wafted up from the inside. Through the burnt remnants of a down jacket, half buried in soggy peas, he could see the detective crouched next to Alex Tesla, who held a wet pack of tater tots to a startling black eye.

"I'm going on a diet," Ramona Ferrari announced, looking up at Pride. "I never, ever want to see food again."

CHAPTER SEVENTEEN

Precipice

DENNIS LEE

I have to say here, I was just about ready to take Alex Tesla over my knee, or better still, haul him up in front of my mom for a good talking-to. Now I wish I had. Maybe with the mom-voice ringing in his ears, he'd have grown a spine.

Or maybe not.

Or maybe it wouldn't have mattered anyway. The road that brought us to where we are now was one I don't think any of us foresaw. Not even the Seraphym.

Jack wasn't the sort to have a lot of regrets. His had been a long and remarkable life, and one he planned to keep going for a good while longer. Possessing a meticulous nature and driven by a healthy dose of anxiety, Jack usually found himself ahead of the game; or at the very worst, when everything went to hell, surviving it. This was his *modus operandi;* to stay on top of things, to keep his options fluid, and to always, *always* have an exit strategy. Such characteristics lent themselves well to staying focused on the tasks at hand; they also tended to quiet the din of past transgressions. Still, any man had regrets, even if just a few.

The first he never spoke about. Hell, he made it a point to never even think about *her.* Whatever recompense was due on that one, he had paid it in full. That's what he did; it just wouldn't do to let regrets fester. Unfinished business could haunt a man 'til the end of time, if he let it. And so, this one driven by pride, he had hunted her killers down, had let them appreciate her suffering, and had ended them. It was an early lesson, and a hard one, and he had never sought love again.

There were things one needed in life, and for most, love ranked right up there with wealth, with family and friends. Jack had scorned most of these; his needs were rooted in survival now. Wealth came and went, family was nothing but leeches, and friends? Friends were an uncertainty even in the best of times.

Still, unless you were a hermit living on the edge of civilization, friends were inevitable. And there it was, another regret. Gunning someone down was often part of the job, but he had never, ever hesitated like he'd done with Red. He had felt something almost alien with that act. He was so unfamiliar with guilt, so untouched by remorse, that with each slug he had driven into Red's chest he had fought down a sharp pang of fear. He knew, he *felt* he was destroying something dear to him, and for what? To survive, of course. The way of the world, of his world, demanded this sacrifice.

Then, like a bad joke, the world had changed, within seconds, with the arrival of metal giants bent on destruction. Old enemies were forced to band together and when the Djinni had reappeared, apparently risen from the dead, Jack's assessment of the new world was lit with new possibilities and dangers. Amidst this new chaos, the Djinni could be allowed to live after all. The Invasion would leave a void, a need for individuals such as himself. Such as both of them.

Possibilities. He could name his price, even one as exorbitantly high as the assassination of one of America's most elusive crime lords. This new world didn't have a place for someone like Tonda anyway. There was a new threat, one that would require the attention and focus of all the major players, and suddenly something as impervious as Tonda's mighty underworld seemed as significant as last year's reality television. Goodbye Tonda, goodbye kill order, and welcome back Red. Perhaps it could be business as usual, even in the bleak landscape of a world perched on the edge of Armageddon.

It was wishful thinking. Jack had not considered the notion that Red could partner himself with an organization like Echo. His actions to spring the Djinni from his Echo prison cell had backfired. Red, it seemed, didn't want to leave after all, and Jack's regret remained unresolved. He had done wrong by the Djinni and he was determined to make it right. This time, his need was driven by friendship. Save the Djinni, Jack didn't have any friends now, none who were still breathing in any case. He hadn't given it much thought, until he had seen Red with his own eyes, collapsing unceremoniously between him and Amethist in the Vault and flashing her a grin from beneath that crappy scarf of his. Red Djinni, oozing blood from a dozen holes in his chest, yet still up, still laughing, still fighting. Jack had felt a moment of wonder, of delight, yet more foreign emotions, and might have laughed in spite of himself if he had been able. He never could laugh. It never felt or sounded right, like some demented hyena choking over a metallic voice box. Red could appreciate that. Red was his friend, after all.

He kept that firmly in mind as he watched Bulwark's trainees trip over themselves on the Echo practice grounds. True friends were judgmental—they owed their friends that much—and by Jack's estimation Red Djinni was being an ass.

"Rhythm, Bruno!" Red taunted from his perch high above the Le Parkour course. "Keep up the pace! You're one stumble from being brain food!"

Below, Acrobat cursed as he weaved through the shambling mass of automatons. The androids were first generation, able to do little more than home in on their targets, their movements stiff and artificial. No one used these anymore, and there were hundreds packed away in storage bunkers far beneath the main Echo complex. With the sudden influx of raw recruits, the training facilities that had somehow survived the Invasion were in high demand these days and these antique robots were all Bulwark had been able to procure. Djinni's solution for using crap no one else would bother with had been simple. He had dressed the androids in worn and faded clothes scrounged from the donation bins in the main hangar, dipped their hands in a yellow, viscous slime used to temporarily seal waterlines and with a little creative reprogramming of their voice units had set them loose on the Le Parkour course. The result was a dense corral of makeshift zombies, or "Zombie Paintball" as Red called it. The goal was to elude being slimed as the mob closed in on you, for as long as you could.

The Misfits had mixed reactions to this new exercise.

"This is so AWESOME!" Bruno howled as he vaulted over a pack of zombies, ignoring their sluggish attempts to tag him with goop, their hungry moans strangely melodic when heard in unison.

"This is so *stupid*," Scope mumbled. She sat next to Djinni and Bulwark on the observation deck. Her clothes and body were splattered with patches of yellow. She grunted as she leaned forward to watch, in part from the humiliation of being "killed" so early in the exercise, but mostly from the pain. Red had neglected to disable the original programming of the killbots. When they tagged you, they didn't hold back. The bruises were still fresh, and she wasn't looking forward to the sting of healing flesh in the days to come. This wasn't what she *did*. She stood off, aloof, and struck from afar. She wasn't supposed to mix it up down and dirty.

Red shook his head, disappointed. "You tried to shoot bulletproof robots twice your size, five times your weight, thinking that would stop them, much less slow them down. And then you let them flank and corner you. Don't blame the exercise, Scope. You still have a lot to learn."

"Like *what*?" she snapped. She was shaking with anger.

"Like how guns don't solve every problem," Bulwark said, his eyes still intent on the action below.

Scope shrank back from the reprimand and turned to watch the others. Her eyes glistened as her hands crept up to rest on her holstered pistols.

Beneath them, oblivious to their teammate's humiliation, Acrobat and Harmony continued to elude capture by the mindless horde. Bruno was carried by his momentum, by his talent to duck and weave and fly over his opponents. The sheer exhilaration of his flight made it clear that the boy was having far too much fun. There was no strategy to his actions and the flailing of his arms betrayed the complete and utter joy of a child running haphazardly through a busy playground. It was stimulus-response, rinse and repeat, as he dodged through swinging arms that kept him constantly in motion. In a way, he was as mindless as the androids that chased him. In contrast to Acrobat's wild dervish dance, Harmony had kept low and in the shadows. She crept along the walls and parapets of the course, seeking moments of opportunity when the horde's attention was drawn by her teammate to silently sprint between concealing structures. She had only been seen a couple of times. Emerging from a squat concrete tunnel, she had found herself trapped between two zombies. As they stumbled towards her she froze, gauging their acceleration, and at the last moment dove forward. The lumbering giants crashed together and toppled over, their arms locked in a grotesque embrace and she sped away into the shadows once more. Like Acrobat she was constantly on the move, but carefully, methodically, and on the few occasions she became cornered was quick to use the environment to her advantage. Bulwark nodded in approval. Harmony was the clear star of the day.

"Okay!" Acrobat shouted. "I think... I'm tired now..."

Bruno had come to rest atop a short scaling wall, beyond the reach of the robots, and had slumped over, his breathing heavy and labored. The horde clambered about him, their moans synchronized in an eerie song, their hands banging on the wall beneath him. He managed a weak laugh.

"Can't slime what you can't reach, morons!" he wheezed. "Guess I'm just too smart for—"

His taunt was cut short as the wall broke in half. The zombies had rallied, their blows hammering through the dense wood, and Acrobat fell amongst them. The androids were suddenly upon him with heavy blows.

Bulwark shook his head and pressed the flashing safety switch on his touchscreen tablet. Below, the zombies stopped their assault and became still, their groans ebbing away as the light faded from their eyes.

"And then there was one," Red laughed. "Harm takes the prize today."

"She did good," Bulwark said, and Scope sank further in her despair. Bull glanced at her, and told her to sit up straight.

"A little help down here?"

They peered over the edge, and saw Acrobat groaning as he struggled in a mess of broken lumber and mud. Harmony came over and extended her hand, pulling him awkwardly to his feet.

"It was a good run, Bruno," she said shyly, favoring him with a timid smile.

"Thanks, Harm," Acrobat said. "It was fun, wasn't it? Except for that last part. Jeez, those things hit hard..."

"It was pathetic," Bulwark barked from above. "That was sloppy and childish, Acrobat, racing off like that at the start. You left your teammates to fend for themselves."

Bruno winced, bowed his head and scratched absently at his neck.

"Scope," Bulwark said, turning to his lieutenant. "What were you trying to prove, racing after him? This exercise wasn't a contest pitting you against each other. This was a test to see how well you three worked as a team—a team *you* are supposed to lead, I might add. You still haven't tempered your ambition, girl. I am at my wits' end with you, I am so disappointed."

Scope also bowed her head, and nodded. "Yessir," she said, her dead voice a transparent mask to her shame.

Bulwark looked away, and down at Harm. "Together, you three might have lasted a very long time. Harmony, you had the right idea. You even tried to rally these two idiots to your plan at the beginning before they chose to tear off on their own; I heard it. Alone, without their abilities, you managed to survive the longest. Well done."

Harmony blushed, and muttered a weak thanks.

"Aw, c'mon, Bull, you're being too hard on them," Red Djinni said. "Yeah, Harm rocked the joint, but you have to admit, Bruno totally Gene Kelly'd his way around the field for twenty minutes."

Acrobat beamed up at Red. Scope also glanced at Red, her eyes questioning.

"Not you, Scope," the Djinni said. "You sucked ass. The point is, part of this test was to keep a clear feel for your surroundings. Harm somehow kept tabs on the whole playing field, even when she was hiding. Bruno managed to snake his way through every opening he could find. That was key, man, to stay alert, to stay completely aware of your—"

Red gave a shrill cry as a thin line flew about his neck and locked into place. Far below, Jack tightened his grip and drove down with his enormous arms, tearing the Djinni from his perch. Though the ground was soft and giving, Red fell hard on his back and gasped for breath.

Jack stood over him, and sighed. "I used to tell you the same thing," he grunted. "You always were my worst student."

"You would be well advised to step away from him."

Jack looked up, and felt the wry smirk creep across his face. Despite their poor showing on the training field, it occurred to him that he was, in fact, facing a well-trained team. There had been no hesitation. In a heartbeat they had positioned themselves, and now he faced four Echo operatives, spread out around him, each with a firearm aimed right at his heart—two, in Scope's case.

Jack let the line drop, held his hands up and backed away from Red.

"Sorry," Jack said. "Wasn't my intention to start it this way. I just always found it best to put Red in his place once he gets his condescension on."

Bulwark watched him for a moment, looked down at Red, and then back again, his gun never wavering. "Harmony, check Red. Scope, Acrobat, drop him if he so much as takes a step forward. And you—" Bull thumbed the power setting on his pistol to maximum "—you start talking. Your name, and why you're here."

"His name's Jack," Red coughed, motioning to Harmony that he was fine, and came softly to his feet. "As to why he's here, you'll never get it out of him unless he wants you to know."

"How did you get in here?" Bull demanded. "Our security perimeter..."

"Needs work," Jack interrupted. "A little sloppy. Timed a few patrols, and I breezed right in. Wasn't hard."

"Don't let him fool you," Red muttered. "Our security here is tight, but that wouldn't stop him. Speaking of sloppy, it's not like you to just step out in the light like this, not before the work is done. What's your move here?"

"To talk," Jack said, shrugging. "I figured showing up was the best way to do that."

"Ever hear of a phone?" Red asked.

"Would you have taken a call from *me*?" Jack countered. "Besides, you're not the only person I'm here to see. I want to talk to Alex Tesla."

Red laughed. "I doubt he'd clear his schedule for a Blacksnake agent."

"This guy is *Blacksnake*?" Acrobat blurted.

Jack ignored him. "He probably wouldn't, under normal circumstances, but I'm here to talk business. Oh, and I'm not just an agent."

Red waited for it.

"I'm the new chief, the Grand Poobah himself."

"Chief?" Djinni said, his tone incredulous. "The top dog? How'd you manage that?"

"Internal office politics, childish pranks, name calling..." Jack said, waving it off as inconsequential. "I wouldn't want to bore you with the details. The point is, this is legit. I'm here to talk about an alliance. We've got bigger troubles than this stupid feud between our organizations, and Tesla knows it. He'll want to talk.

I'm talking redirection of our precious remaining resources at the common threat and not wasting it on each other."

"You don't need me for that," Djinni said, his eyes narrowing. "Hell, I have no pull with the top brass here. You could have gone through official channels..."

"We don't have time for that," Jack said. "Do you know all the crap involved in setting up a meeting like that? It would have taken weeks just to convince Tesla's toadies this wasn't just a crank call."

"All right then," Red conceded. "You could have gone straight to him. I know you. You would've found a way to get into the man's own bedroom and had a private chat without security being the wiser. Why reveal yourself to us, why now?"

"That would've taken time to plan as well," Jack sighed. "The outer perimeter is one thing, but the heart of Echo itself? Besides, I have other unfinished business to take care of first."

"And what's that?"

"You, Djinni," Jack said. "I'm here to make things right with you."

Red stared Jack down. There was no outward look of surprise or suspicion, but Jack knew better. Red's mind was racing now with questions and for his part Jack would try to answer them all. There would be a sweet satisfaction to all of this. It was an elegant and neat solution to his problems. He would do right by the Djinni— hell, for both Echo and Blacksnake, by negotiating a deal to bring the two organizations together. And best of all, he would begin to scratch a terrible itch that had been gnawing its way deep inside of him for years. He suspected an alliance would counter Verd's true intentions for Echo and Blacksnake, whatever they were, and that would do for a start. Verdigris thought of him as a professional, as a cold mercenary who could be bought off in any situation. Verd had never grasped just how much he had taken from Jack. In the wake of Khanjar's bomb, so close to the prize of being an eternal, Jack had instead tasted death. Stripped of anything but pain, Jack had become an animal for a time. The extent of his wounds were so severe that as much as his body needed time to heal, his mind needed more to knit together the pieces of his sanity. Today, he would take his first steps in repaying that old insult. Immortality, a long-sought-after-prize, was a luxury that could wait. This was about need, a need to fix another regret.

This was a need driven by *revenge*.

✧   ✧   ✧

"Bull, can we trust this guy?"

Bulwark acknowledged Acrobat with a look, but didn't answer. He watched as Red and Jack stood apart from the group, speaking quietly. At times, Red looked as if he were about to make some sort of outburst. Each time, Jack held up his hands and spoke quickly, talking the Djinni down with calming gestures. And Bull continued to watch.

"No," he said finally. "I don't think he's the trustworthy sort. Helluva thing, though. I can't shake the feeling he's telling the truth."

"How do you know?" Scope asked.

"No sure way of telling," Bull grunted. "He's got the walk, he's got the weight, this old boy's been around for a while. He knows how to play, but something tells me he's on the level with this one. Got nothing to say it's one way or the other, really. Just instinct."

"We trust your instincts, Bull." Harmony said with a soft smile. "They've carried us this far."

"Mmhm," Bull answered.

They watched as, after a strained moment of silence, Red reached out, shook Jack's hand and caught him in a rough embrace.

"Gosh," Scope muttered. "Guess this means we're all friends now."

Bulwark nodded. "Looks like. By now, you all know as well as I do that Red's a reader. When you watch him. When you look past his bluster and bravado, past the wit and bad humour, when you watch his eyes. He's always watching, even when he's ranting, he's watching you. He sees tells, he picks up on the most subtle body language, and his intuition is pretty solid... where people are concerned, anyway."

Scope considered that, and nodded. "That it is."

"And it looks like Jack's got Red believing," Bulwark said. "So the only question is, has Red made the grade?"

The Misfits shared a look of confusion.

"Bull...?" Harmony started.

"Do you all trust him yet?" Bulwark asked.

He regarded them each in turn. They looked to each other again, their eyes probing for a consensus. Finally, they met his gaze, and nodded.

Red sauntered up, and flinched as he caught their attention.

"What's with you guys?" he asked. "You all look like you want to hug me or something. Especially you, Bruno. Quit it."

"So what's your verdict?" Bulwark asked him.

Red glanced back at Jack, who had lit another cigar and stood under a canopy of trees. It was Jack's turn to watch them.

"I think he's all right," the Djinni said. "He's just here to talk."

"You're sure?" Scope asked.

"He's not armed, for one thing," Red answered. "He usually has a few guns tucked here and there on him, and a blade at the small of his back. I didn't sense anything on him, not even a pocketknife. I figure he knew we wouldn't let him anywhere near the boss with his usual hardware. As for the rest of it... I've known him a long time. Call it intuition."

"All right then," Bulwark said. "Harmony, call it in. If Tesla's willing, you and I will escort our visitor to him."

"Wait, what?" Red objected. "Just you two? Hey, this is still the head of our main competition here..."

"I'm sure Harmony and I can handle ferrying one unarmed non-meta to Tesla's office. After that, he'll have to go through us as well as Tesla's squad of armed guards. We'll be fine."

"What about us?" Scope asked, pointing to herself and Acrobat.

"You two get to the infirmary," Bulwark said. "I want you both checked out."

Scope and Acrobat immediately started to protest, but Bull cut them off. "Forget it. I saw the hits you both took. Once the adrenaline wears off, you'll feel it. Plus, you could be sporting some bad bone bruises, hairline fractures, even breaks. You know the drill. You get tagged on the field, you get checked by the docs."

"And me?" Red asked.

"You know Tesla's banned you from his presence, Red. He doesn't want you anywhere near him, not since the last meeting you two had."

"Oh, come on," Red protested. "I only roughed him up a *little*..."

"You nearly broke his nose, Djinni. Stay here, we'll fill you all in later. Besides, someone needs to clean all this up." Bulwark gestured to the course, parts of which were completely destroyed, and interspersed throughout, the androids stood patiently, dripping their viscous payloads of goop. Red glanced at the wreckage and winced.

"I mean it, Bull," Red warned. "I think Jack's on the level here, but he never has just one item on his agenda. Just because I've got these dumb issues with him about second chances doesn't mean you owe him a thing. Don't let down your guard, not for a second. Double the guard. Hell, triple it. Always keep a few guns trained on him. You won't believe how fast he can move."

Harmony was speaking quietly on her comm unit. "Understood. We'll meet squad four by the east gate. That's right, load them up, full battle gear." She turned to Bull and nodded.

Bulwark grunted. "I guess Jack was right. Tesla must want to speak to him pretty badly. I can't remember the last time someone gained an audience so fast."

"Bull..." Red sighed, his tone a warning.

"I got it," Bulwark said. "No chances, Djinni, I heard you. When was the last time I took a chance on anything? Or anyone?"

The Misfits looked at each other, at Red, then back at Bulwark, and broke into helpless gales of laughter.

Alex Tesla sat alone in his office. He had expressed his desire to be left undisturbed to his assistants, had dimmed the lights and collapsed with a groan into his chair. He let his head fall back against the plush rest and drifted away, if only for a moment.

He thought of a time, not so long ago, when his life consisted of board meetings, policy meetings, project meetings, departmental meetings, PR meetings, meetings to discuss and organize conferences, a gathering of individuals to attend even *larger* meetings. In hindsight, the ennui of that life had been near enough to drive him to the madhouse. Despite the tenacity of their rivals, the promotional nightmare of convincing Joe Everyman to trust superpowered Echo agents able to level entire city blocks, not to mention the daunting obstacles in reining in said mavericks to be the backbone of a well-oiled peacekeeping institution, Echo had grown into the preeminent meta organization on the planet. Alex had much to be proud of, but at times he wondered if he had done too good a job. There seemed no crisis that Echo couldn't handle. But then, had there really been anything on the scale of the last World War to really test Echo's mettle? And so, he had settled down to run his highly trained band of action figures and law enforcement personnel in a sort of mindless haze to maintain peace in a stagnant time. The challenges of the past were forgotten as he fell into a complacent routine that consisted mostly of deciding which new technology Echo would introduce next to the world, how the patents might further add to their stock options,

and what color socks to wear to the office that day. And fighting the never-ending battle to get Nikola Tesla's broadcast power
finally accepted for everyday use, and not just for the vehicles and
gadgets Echo used exclusively. That fight was so slow, so drawn
out, and so glacial, it hardly seemed like a fight at all. There
were moments, usually during proposals from other men in suits
droning on and on, fueled by their own self-importance, when
he had caught himself wishing for an apocalypse, some enemy of
worth to pit Echo against. An excuse for Echo to shine.

Alex stood up, his shoulders weary, and staggered to the window. He laid a hand on the glass, and the optical blinds faded to
let the harsh light in. He gasped, wincing at the sudden light, yet
forced himself to look upon the center of his beloved enterprise.
He took in the view—broken complexes held together with ugly
scaffolding, mounds of displaced gear, supplies and sundries tied
down by mud-splattered tarp and canvas, hastily erected tents
of drab green and gray, and amongst them were people, milling
about seemingly without direction or purpose. They each had
their own job, of course, a reason to be out there, but what was
once a beautiful, sprawling esplanade had become, in the stroke
of one massive assault, the combined offices, storage and housing
for most of the personnel here at Echo HQ. The crowded conditions demanded a certain chaotic appearance, no matter how
organized the stream of human traffic actually was. And for each
soul he observed from his aerie, Alex saw his own despair and
defeat mirrored back at him.

This, he thought, *is Echo. This is how we shine.*

No, he realized. He couldn't put any of this on them. They had
withstood the assault. They had rallied and now worked tirelessly
to mount their defenses against the coming storm. This wasn't
anyone's fault but his. For years he had dismissed all proposals to
strengthen what forces they had. He had been far more interested
in sustainable growth, in market shares, hell, even in the political
machine, than to fortify what he believed was an indestructible
vanguard. His arrogance had brought about an air of complacency,
and complacency had left them open to this.

A cheerful chime from his desk interrupted his descent into
self-loathing, alerting him to an incoming message. Ignoring it,
he found his seat and brought up his command screen. He stared
at the numbers again, and shook his head in disbelief. Someone

out there could smell the blood in the water and was buying up shares in Echo like it was going out of style. He was steadily losing the voting majority. Even here, in his area of expertise, he was losing the fight.

Some of his advisors had been optimistic. It was encouraging, they claimed, and a sign of public confidence that Echo would, again, emerge on top. The market being what it was after the Invasion, everything was thrown into chaos. It didn't make sense. The buyers seemed too varied to be a united front, but something about this just screamed "hostile takeover." Over the last few months, Echo had taken massive losses in personnel, infrastructure and, of course, in capital. Aided by the fervent efforts of men like Spin Doctor, Alex had spent a good portion of that time building up as much stockholder confidence as he could, and over the last month the precipitous drop in share values had leveled off, and even climbed to a modest plateau. Still, the dismal quarterly numbers would be released soon, and it was fully expected that the market prices would drop again, and hard. This was a piss-poor time to buy into Echo. The numbers just didn't add up. Which meant someone out there was looking to force themselves in.

Ding! His screen blinked as a new alert appeared. Echo shares had just dropped, heavily.

What?

Alex stared in horror as he watched the ticker. Blacksnake stock had just jumped 20 points...30...40...

Oh. Wait...what?

Frantic, Alex brought up the lights and activated his wall of monitors, jabbing at the touchscreens for his preset channels. Scanning the business news, he fell back a step with a gasp. Blacksnake and Echo were everywhere, in dozens of headlines, all proclaiming a heavy downturn for Echo in light of Blacksnake's new push for international contracts. He brought up the *Bear and Bull* site and read...

> *...breaking news on the sudden reemergence of Blacksnake. The Blacksnake Corporation is most known for its unprejudiced solicitation of services, offering full security contracts manned with metahuman personnel available to the highest bidder. Operating on an international scale for over a decade,*

Blacksnake has faced opposition from both members of the United Nations and independents for suspected trafficking of human slaves, for black market drug and munitions trading, and has faced allegations of breaking nearly every edict sanctioned by the Geneva Convention. These accusations have often undermined market confidence resulting in widely fluctuating indices since the mercenary corporation went public ten years ago. Today, rumors of recent negotiations with high profile interest groups have been confirmed, and Blacksnake is poised to hold sole possession of security contracts spanning entire cities in Dubai, Singapore, South Korea and Japan. Additionally, insider buzz persists of top secret negotiations with the United States military. Blacksnake's main competitor, the US-based metahuman security giant Echo, whose shares have only in recent weeks begun a slow arduous climb from the bear market left in the wake of the worldwide invasion, found its options tumbling today in light of these events...

Alex Tesla stared at the feed in disbelief. He quickly gleaned over his monitors, skimming through all the major news feeds, and, sure enough, they all reported the same thing. He felt the knot in his stomach tighten as he staggered back to his desk and cast a pained look at his command screen. Sure enough, Echo stocks were being gobbled up by hungry investors. It was done. His majority vote was gone. With a roar, he lunged forward and sent his command screen flying. It flew across the room and crashed hard into the marble floor with a harsh flash of light and then, darkness. He stared at it, his lips trembling with rage, and smashed a fist down on his desk. The thick glass gave with a crunch, and he was dimly aware that his knuckles were now bloodied.

In response, his desk sounded off with another cheerful chime. Alex jabbed at his intercom, like swatting at a pesky mosquito.

"WHAT?" he barked. "I TOLD YOU ALL I AM NOT TO BE DISTURBED!"

There came a nervous titter, then a timid voice. "I'm...I'm sorry, sir, but I was informed this couldn't wait. It seems the new head of Blacksnake is here to see you."

"New head of Blacksnake?" Alex hissed, taken aback. "Here? Now? Where, at the gate?"

"No, sir, it seems he is on the grounds. Operative Bulwark has him under heavy guard. He is requesting an audience."

Alex fell back into his chair. What were they playing at? Whatever those bastards had planned, surely there was more to come. Echo was down, but far from out, and it was far too premature to come swaggering through the front gates like victors claiming the spoils of war. Besides, a meeting of the heads of Echo and Blacksnake was unheard of. It was too risky; it promised bloody violence to just show up in the lion's den...

Bloody violence...

Alex looked at his hand and grimaced. He reached for his handkerchief and wrapped it around his knuckles.

"Have him brought up," Alex said. "I want to talk to this man."

"Yessir."

They want a fight, then I'll give them one, and I'll be damned before I lose any more ground.

And so, for the very first time, the leaders of Echo and Blacksnake met, face to face.

They sat and watched each other from opposite ends of the long conference table. It was a historic event, though far removed from the pomp and circumstance that would normally be associated with such a gathering.

There were no freshly pressed suits, no gratuitous medals on display and no assumed smiles to mask otherwise discernible signs of contempt. Alex had not slept in days. His hair was dishevelled, his eyes red and his clothes were wrinkled and unkempt. His smile was absent and his contempt was palpable. Jack lounged in his seat, his duster pushed forward and shading his eyes, his hands resting comfortably, folded together on his stomach. Dirt and oily patches clung to his ragged vest and khaki pants and his combat boots were caked with mud.

There were no dignitaries, no celebrities, no waiters moving through crowds of breathless guests awaiting the first exchange of pleasantries between the two chiefs. There was hardly anyone in attendance at all, save for two Echo operatives and six impressively armored guards who surrounded Jack with six equally impressive energy cannons, each trained on Jack's heart. Bulwark stood behind Alex at a respectful distance, yet close enough to capture Tesla in his protective field at a moment's notice. Harmony patrolled the room, slowly moving about with her scanners at the ready. Bulwark had heeded the Djinni's warning. It just wouldn't do to be caught off guard.

At a formal event, the tension might have been heightened by the nervous tittering of a crowd, anxious for something of a political play to unfold. Here, Jack and Tesla sat in quiet contemplation of each other, the drawn-out silence unhindered by the lack of spectators and the absence of cameras. Alex didn't allow surveillance devices in his own office. Besides, he wasn't sure he wanted this particular exchange on the record. If things went badly, a recording of Blacksnake's new and unarmed director being gunned down by Echo sentinels would prove embarrassing, to say the least.

"You're not exactly what I pictured," Alex said finally.

"Yeah?" Jack grunted. "Gotta say, I'm a little surprised too. From your rep, never thought you'd let yourself go to seed. You had a few minutes 'til I got escorted up here. I don't rate even a quick shave?"

Alex bit back an angry retort. Instead, he sniffed and leaned back in his chair.

"What is it you want, Mr...?"

"Jack. Just call me Jack."

"What is it you want, *Jack*?"

"It's very simple," Jack said. He glanced at the guards and their guns, and as he shifted his weight he was careful to keep his hands clearly in view. "I want you to trust me, Alex."

Tesla ignored Jack's overt gesture of familiarity. He was being baited, provoked. He wouldn't consider the possibility that Jack was, in fact, trying to be friendly.

"Trust you?" Alex scoffed. "I can barely trust you're even who you say you are."

Alex brought up the overhead holo-projectors, which flashed moving screens from the day's media feeds. "See there? The latest press release from your Blacksnake. That's clearly you, identified as their new CEO, but you don't even have an official name. You're simply the Blacksnake Commander. And here..."

Alex brought up a fresh screen with Jack's profile.

"From our own records—alias Jack, real name unknown. Very little in the way of history, as if you sprang into existence only a decade ago. Some charges, none proven, only one clear documentation of a street brawl with one of our own Echo Ops teams some years ago. You took on Operative Amethist's team, alongside..."

"Red Djinni," Bulwark supplied, his eyes fixed with a fierce intensity on Jack's profile. In one corner, a blurred and slightly out-of-focus snapshot revealed Amethist dodging gunfire as jets of ice flew from her hands.

"Red Djinni," Alex sighed. "Why am I not surprised? You realize the fact that you and the Djinni are old acquaintances does little to help your case."

"Red runs a little hot sometimes," Jack agreed. "I wouldn't discount him, though, especially as Echo material. The boy's got it in him. He might surprise you."

"He already has," Alex said, massaging his nose. "Regardless, you can't possibly have thought you could just stroll in here and that we'd take you at your word."

"No, I didn't," Jack said. "I didn't bother with the nice stuff or the usual games you gotta play when you pick a new best bud. That would have taken too long, and we don't have the time. We've got a lot to do, Alex, and we need to get started. We all got caught with our pants down the last time..."

"We?" Alex asked, surprised.

"Yes, 'we'!" Jack barked, ignoring the synchronized hum as the guards ramped up their guns. "You think Echo's the only meta group out there? Forget the company profiles, the publicity stunts, it's all a cover-up! Blacksnake was hit *hard* that day. We're in no position to take any of those big-ass contracts we've got lined up! Hell, we didn't even set those up! It was..." Jack paused, and retreated into his seat. Silently, he berated himself for a moment's weakness. He wasn't ready to give up Verdigris. Not just yet. It was the last card to play, when he knew he had Tesla half-convinced.

"Yes? Who?" Alex urged him. His eyes narrowed, puzzled by Jack's sudden outburst.

It makes no sense. Why tell me this? Why tell me the recent surge in Blacksnake options is all based on deception? Why give up your hand so early?

"I told you," Jack said finally, reading the thoughts play themselves out on Alex's face. "It's about trust. I need you to trust me or we're not gonna get a single thing done."

"How am I supposed to trust you?" Alex asked, finally.

"We gotta start small," Jack admitted. "We don't have time for it, but I don't see we got much of a choice. So we share some secrets, even small ones, and that'll get things moving. Here, I'll start. I'm sure you have an agent or two planted in Blacksnake."

Tesla gave him a puzzled look.

"Save it," Jack said. "You'd be an idiot not to. Our plant here is Emily Schoedel..."

"I'm not familiar with..." Alex began, but Bulwark was already drawing his guns.

"...callsign: Harmony."

"Hands where I can see them, Harmony!" Bulwark barked, as his pistols hummed to life.

Harmony froze and dropped her scanner, her arms rising in the air. She looked at Jack with a rueful expression.

"Two years, Jack!" Harmony moaned. "Two years I've been in the deep, in the deep with Bulwark and now the *Djinni*, and they never made me! I could've gone the stretch, why would you...?"

"Don't worry, kiddo," Jack grunted. "You'll still get your comp for the full five. This is important. Game's changing. It's time to start working with Echo."

Harmony bit her lip and glanced at Bulwark. Bull's expression remained cold, but his eyes burned with fury. He kept his guns trained on her.

"Guard," Bulwark said. "Relieve Operative Harmony of her firearms."

"Bulwark," Alex said, "shouldn't you be the one who...?"

"It's fine, sir," Bulwark answered. "Her ability is to ramp up meta abilities. She has nothing offensive on her own."

Harmony rolled her eyes as a guard removed the pistols from her holsters and motioned her to take a seat next to Jack. She gave Jack a withering look as she collapsed into the chair and folded her arms, defeated.

Jack ignored her, and gestured to Alex.

"What?" Alex asked, confused.

"Your turn," Jack said as he leaned forward. He rested his elbows on the conference table and brought his hands together, his fingertips pressed together as if in prayer.

Alex gave him a weary look. "Do I have to remind you that you're not the one here that needs convincing?"

Jack looked disappointed. "Trust has to start somewhere, don't it? And trust is a two-way street; you gotta give a little to get a little. Fine, since I'm the one at gunpoint here..." He shrugged and reached into his mouth. With a loud crack, he snapped out a tooth.

"Christ!" Alex yelped, scrambling to his feet.

"No, no," Jack said, his tone soothing. He wiped the tooth on his vest, leaving a smear of blood, and laid it gently on the table. "Nothing so big as that—far from it. Just a bug, really. You see, Alex, the reason I was sent here was to drop this in your office."

"Your...tooth?" Alex asked, puzzled, as he sank slowly back into his chair.

"Not mine," Jack said. "Just a filler, a falsey, engineered to bypass detection. Once activated, it'll stick to any surface, pick up conversation and transmit out undetected on the back of your own broadcast energy signals."

"You were sent here to bug my office?" Alex asked. "By who...?"

"Not yet," Jack said. "We're not quite there yet."

"All right," Alex said. "Can you tell me why then?"

Jack nodded. "Immortality, Alex. You are the gateway, the key to the one place on Earth where the secrets of immortality are kept."

Alex stared at Jack, his bewilderment giving way to dawning comprehension.

"You...you want..."

"Metis," Jack answered. "I was sent here to find out the location of Metis."

Alex fell back in his chair while a myriad of emotions played across his face. Jack had hit him hard with blunt truth.

He's starting to believe, Jack thought. *Or at least he's considering the possibility that I'm on the level.*

"That's not something I can possibly tell you—" Alex began.

"And I'm not asking," Jack said. "I told you, that's the reason I was sent here, but I'm not sticking to the plan. Proposing an alliance between Echo and Blacksnake was a cover, but I'm making it the mission. We've got some common problems, Alex. I think it's time we dealt with them. Immortality can wait."

Alex shook his head. "I don't think it's what you had in mind, anyway."

"What do you mean?" Jack said.

"I mean, you probably think it's something you drink," Alex

said, shrugging. "Some magical elixir that will keep you young and strong forever. Or some operation, radiation bombardment, something out of the realms of science fiction. You'd be sort of right, I suppose."

"How's that?" Jack asked. He was beginning to feel alarmed.

"The science fiction part," Alex said. "I can tell you this—it's not what you think. You wouldn't have a body. You would be conscious, caught in an electrical matrix that would sustain your brain patterns, and you could conceivably live forever, but not as you are now. You could communicate with the physical world, but that's about it. You would essentially be a ghost."

"That doesn't make sense," Jack mused. "He would have known that..."

"Who?" Alex asked. "Who sent you?"

Jack ignored him; it was his turn to be puzzled. This wasn't the sort of eternity Jack and Verd had ever pursued, not together at any rate. As far as Jack knew, Verdigris had already determined the logistics involved with housing one's brain in an artificial system. So why was he here? There was no reason to plant a bug to get something you already had. What other information was Verdigris so desperate to overhear?

"Jack," Alex said. "You said it yourself, Jack. We have things to do, and we need to start trusting each other. From the look on your face, I'd guess we just uncovered another enemy we have in common. So who is it, Jack? You want my trust? Start with this. Who sent you?"

Their eyes met, and Jack relived his last conversation with Verd, struggling to make the connections amongst the scattered bits of truth Verd had peppered throughout his animated pitch for everlasting life. Like the Djinni, Jack had a talent for reading people, and Verdigris knew it. Verd hadn't lied, but had artfully concealed the truth. It was the curse of an eidetic memory. Jack could only recollect the conversation in a linear fashion. He was missing something... something...

"Jack?" Alex said. Tesla's tone betrayed his impatience. It occurred to Jack how much he needed this man's trust, now more than ever.

"It was..." Jack began, then stopped.

He had just figured it out.

I did not buy Blacksnake to make a profit... I want Echo... to get Echo, I need Blacksnake... you become head of Blacksnake...

if you can't overlook a small matter of betrayal...proximity, my dear Jack, proximity...I need you to get into Tesla's office...very little package I want planted...

Jack turned to Harmony, who favored him with a pitying look. She leaned forward with a sympathetic smile and laid a hand softly on his shoulder.

"It's okay, Jack," she said sweetly. "I'll take it from here."

Jack stared at her, then shuddered as his eyes rolled back into his head. He slumped forward on the table like a poleaxed cow.

Harmony gasped, her hand still on Jack's shoulder, and let out a long wavering sigh.

"Jack!" Harmony squealed. "Oh, Jack! You never told me you were a meta too..."

"What is this?" Alex cried, rising from his seat. "What did you do to him?"

Harmony glanced at Alex in contempt. She released Jack and was on her feet in an instant. As one, the guards opened fire, but Harmony was already on the move. She reached out, snatched up Jack's false tooth and dove beneath the conference table. The guards began to yell at each other to surround her, and stopped, confused, as their guns powered down. Harmony emerged from concealment, smirking as she held up Jack's tooth, which was now blinking.

"Not a bug, gentlemen," she told them with a grave expression. "Localized inhibitor, keyed to Echo's broadcast energy frequencies. Your guns are cut off from their power source. Now then, let's see how you fare without your toys..."

They didn't have time to answer. Harmony darted towards the nearest guard and jabbed at his eyes. The guard howled and staggered back as she slammed her palm against his face. Like Jack, he fell, his body limp and lifeless as Harmony bounded to her next target. The guards flailed about, helpless against her frenzied assault as she ran amongst them, dodging slow and clumsy blows and felling the guards with just a touch. Her body seemed to hum and vibrate with excess energy. Bulwark blinked, unable to focus on her. She had never been this fast, this strong. She was a blur, like a ghost skirting the edge of reality, her skill and speed abruptly off the charts. Somehow, the real Harmony had been hidden all this time—from the recruiters, from the lab techs, from *him*. He cursed as he stepped in front of Alex and summoned his shield to surround them both.

"That's enough!" Bull shouted.

Harmony came to a full halt, absolutely still, having pounced on the last guard, and at rest her resonating limbs seemed to snap back into focus. Her hand at the guard's neck, her thin frame draped across his fallen form, she raised her head slowly to meet Bulwark's stare.

"I'm sorry about this, Bull, really," she said. She rose and strolled over to him, laying her hands gently on his shield, pressing herself to it, as if she meant to embrace him. "I'd ask you to say goodbye to Scope and Bruno for me, but this didn't go down as I'd planned it, and I can't have you telling people what happened here. Not everything, anyway."

"What are you talking about?" Bull demanded. He stared at her through the distorted field of his force bubble. She seemed genuinely sad, and more. She looked older, lacking the soft innocence and impish naivete she normally carried. Even the color of her skin seemed muted, though it may have been a trick of the light softly reflecting off his shield. Still, her face seemed wiser, grayer, as if the unblemished shine of youth had simply been a false image maintained by sheer force of will. For all he knew, it had been. Sheer will, for two years...

There was steel there, somewhere within the raw talent and uncertainty when she first came to us, I could feel it. She used it and made us think we could hone her skills when she was already at the top of her game. She can act with the best of them, she played all of us, no one ever could have suspected. How long has she been at this? Who are you, Harmony?

Harmony shook her head in wonder. "You see it, don't you? Yes, I can tell. You do have a way of sizing a person up, Bull. I had to be extra careful around you. I had to learn everything about you, just to be safe. Yes, I've been around for a long, long while. Longer than any of you could have dreamed. You have no idea what I've seen. And yes, I'm a Blacksnake agent. I was to be rewarded handsomely for infiltrating Echo. Well, Blacksnake's under new management and the plan's changed, and the terms of my contract with it."

"A change of plans..." Bulwark said, his eyes narrowing. "You're here to end it, aren't you? You're here to end Echo."

"No," Harmony said, and looked at Alex. "I'm here to open the door for the new boss."

"This is as close as you're going to get," Bull said, defiantly. "You can't get past me, and sooner or later this room will be buzzing with metas. It's over, Harmony."

"Oh, Bull," Harmony sighed, disappointed. "Haven't you figured it out yet? I don't just ramp people up..."

She slid her hands over the shield, caressing it, and dug her fingers in, piercing the bubble.

"I break them apart too."

Bull gasped as Harmony clenched her hands into fists, and he felt his shield dissipating in her grip. Instinctively, he doubled his efforts to sustain it. Too late, he realized all he was doing was feeding her his energy. With an awful sound, like sheet metal being ripped apart, Harmony tore the shield wide open, drawing Bull's energy into her. She lunged forward, clutched Bull and Alex by their necks and drove them down to the ground. Alex grappled with her hand, an immovable vise around his throat, but his efforts grew feeble as she siphoned away his strength and used it against him. Bulwark, already spent, lay motionless. He couldn't speak, much less move, and only his eyes betrayed his fury. They were fixed on Harmony, who could only offer a tender look in return.

"I wish it could be different, Bull," she said softly. "I almost wish things could have stayed the same, for at least a while longer. I think I loved you, as much as I could anyone. It's so rare that I meet a good man, a truly good man...."

She paused and turned to Alex, who was still struggling weakly beneath her grip. She gave his throat a sharp squeeze, jerked her thumb against his jaw, and snapped his neck.

"...But I couldn't pass this up," she continued. "Got offered something I've been looking for, for a long, long time. I'm going to have to leave you now, and I don't think we'll be seeing each other again."

"No..." Bull coughed, fighting to speak. Harmony laughed in pleasant surprise.

"Goodness, Bull, you *are* a marvel! Just when I think I've taken it all, you show me up by giving me more!"

She released Alex and gripped Bulwark's neck with both hands as she continued to siphon away his energy. Bull moaned and glared at her. His lips trembling, teeth clenched, he continued to struggle and even managed to lift his head closer to hers.

"No..." he vowed. "I'll see you...again..."

"No, love," she disagreed, and brought his head even closer. "This time, you won't be getting back up. I need to leave you with just enough; just enough to tell my story, but you won't ever rise up again. You see, Bull..."

Harmony leaned in, and brushed her lips against his.

"This is the part where I break your spirit."

She kissed him, delving into the whole of him, sifting through recent memories and neatly excising the truth. She was careful. To even a trained telepath, the loss of short term memory would seem the result of trauma. She left him one mental image—her and Jack, seated together, being interrogated together, the new Blacksnake chief and his double-agent flunky. She continued to drain him, leaving just enough to keep him breathing, a fragile tether to life.

She rose, touched his face once more and closed his eyes. Moving quickly, she doubled back to the fallen guards and snapped their necks. With ease, she picked up Jack's still form, threw him over her shoulder and carried him from the room.

It was time to see Verdigris and collect her payment.

CHAPTER EIGHTEEN

Boulevard of Broken Dreams

MERCEDES LACKEY AND CODY MARTIN

We never saw it coming. Harmony had been so meticulous about never allowing a psion near enough to read her.

Well, we *never saw it coming*. Matthew March had, but we knew that only in retrospect, a passage that no one had been able to interpret until after the fact:

> Double agent, double-named Balance and Betrayal, Light and Pain. The end of the heir, the end of the era. The echo dies. And the wild card wins.

That was the problem, you see. March didn't know the callsigns or the names of the people in question. Harmony—Balance and Light; Harm—Betrayal and Pain. And Jack, of course, though usually it's the Joker that's wild. And with the death of Alex Tesla, the end of the line, and the end of Echo as we all knew it.

Of course, the office alarms went off when the guns went offline and the inhibitor field went up. And the whole complex lit up when Tesla's heartbeat stopped. Einhorn was the first in, and since Bulwark was the only one still alive, he was the one she went to. She tried to stabilize him, and pulled back, damn near passing out. But she got the slideshow of images—Harmony and Jack, together, Jack pulling out his tooth, Harmony triggering it, Harmony killing Tesla. She gasped out what she saw, for once her inability to put a governor on her mouth doing us a favor. Bull was medevaced to the new sickbay and the best state-of-the-art bed Echo had.

Acrobat and Scope were in the mob that followed her, and when *the milling around stopped, they were AWOL. Some people thought they had been part of the plot—but not me, and not Bella.*

But I'm getting ahead of myself. One story at a time.

Bella was in the shower, when she heard someone rattling keys in her locks. Since there was only one person who *had* keys to her locks—Vickie—she didn't think anything of it until she heard the door literally slam open.

And then the bathroom door slam open. "Bell, hose off, *now*," Vickie ordered from the other side of the shower curtain, her voice tight and frightened. "We have to get out of here. Tesla's been murdered."

At first, the words didn't make any sense. But Vickie was radiating and close enough for Bella to get images along with the fear. Images of the Echo campus in chaos, of Bull on the floor surrounded by bodies, of Einhorn babbling something out, framed in—a monitor? She must have somehow gotten her link to Tesla's desk working within moments of the disaster.

Einhorn, hysterical, but what she said was clear enough, things she had inadvertently picked up from Bulwark. The assassins were Jack—Jack Something, the new head of Blacksnake, who was supposed to be making nice with Echo—and...*Harmony*?

No wonder she never wanted me touching her...That was all Bella could think, numbly, as Vickie shoved the shower curtain aside and reached for her wet arm. Bulwark was hurt; Vickie didn't know how badly.

"Come *on*, we have to get out of here," Vickie urged. "He knows where we are! We need to get out, get somewhere that no one can get to us while we figure out what to do!"

"What? Who? Blacksnake?" She was baffled; they were way too low on the foodchain for Blacksnake to be interested in *them*. And she needed to get to Echo to help Bull—

"No!" Vickie hissed. "Verdigris! Dominic Verdigris!"

Bella stood there with water pouring over her head and wondered if Vickie had finally snapped. "Who? Why? Wh—"

"Come *on!*" Vickie said, pulling her out of the shower in a surprising show of strength and throwing a towel over her. "He's head of Echo! That psychotic sociopath is head of Echo! We have got to get somewhere he can't find us until we can figure out what to do!"

Completely confused now, Bella just toweled off and scrambled into clothing while Vickie blurted out the entire story in tense, terrified, and short sentences. By the time she was dressed, Bella was also convinced. Echo was now in the hands of someone who was not locked up in an Echo high-security prison only because he was *so* good at hiding his tracks he had never been caught. She couldn't do anything to help Bulwark that others couldn't do as well. *First rule of firefighting: you can't help others if you're dead.*

"JM," she said, finally. "No one knows where JM lives but Saviour and me. He's barely on the grid and sure not on the radar."

"My car's in the lot and I've thrown everything I need in it," Vickie replied. "Let's get out of here. Leave your Echo stuff behind. Nothing they can use to find you."

Vickie didn't have to tell her twice.

It had been an overly long day for John. The Commissar had a particular liking for twelve-hours-on, twelve-hours-off shifts. John made it a priority to check in with the neighborhood after his assigned duties. Tonight, that took up about three hours; there were a lot of wrecked cars that weren't serving any purpose, so he helped to cut them into scrap with his fire. He had about another hour before he needed to pass out, to help stave off exhaustion; he wasn't in the mood for yammering television, and he surely wasn't in the mood for anything less than a screaming emergency. He left the little TV off, and turned his comm to "off duty" so nothing less than a full alert would get him. Right now a book and a beer sounded about right. Something by Heinlein, maybe.

John had finally settled down on his battered mattress, cold beer and worn-out book in his hand when the knock came on his door. *The front door downstairs is shut up tighter than Fort Knox. Sera doesn't use doors. There shouldn't be* anyone *knocking on that door.* In an instant, John was up, his distractions forgotten. He had his old 1911 .45 pistol in his hand, and was off to the side from the door.

"*Who in the hell is it?*"

"Bella and Vic, and it's an emergency, Johnny. Turn your frickin' TV on."

John hesitated for a heartbeat, then opened the door. He only stayed long enough to verify that it really was Bella Blue and Vickie, then stuck the pistol in his waistband. "Come on in, gals."

He marched towards his TV set, turning the power on. "What am I supposed t'be seein'—"

The frantic yammering of the talking heads and the graphic images of Alec Tesla's corpse and the frantic search for the killers answered that question.

John looked to Bella first. "Talk. What's the sitch, kiddo?" *What in all the nine hells has jumped into my lap now?*

It was Vickie who answered, so wound up she didn't even slump or try to make herself look invisible. "Look, I can tell you how I know all this later. Tesla was murdered by Blacksnake, but Blacksnake was ordered by Dominic Verdigris. And now Verdigris is in charge of Echo. *Not* Yankee Pride. He engineered it all, and what direct evidence I don't have yet, I *will* have and I don't know how much he knows already about us, our little conspiracy to get Tesla a spine and a pair or at least dance around him, or about Overwatch."

"Stop there. Blacksnake killed Tesla. Orders were from some dude named Verdigris. This fella is now in charge of Echo. Correct me if I'm wrong?"

"Dominic Verdigris III, overt owner of Verdigris Dynamics, multibillionaire, and covert owner of more shadow companies than I can count off in five minutes. Psychopath, sociopath and a guy who poisoned all the water sources in Bombay post-Invasion so he could sell them water purifiers, then arranged for those to fail so he could 'save' them with 'good' water purifiers, and arranged for the contact that bought the bad ones to have a fatal accident..." Vickie paused briefly for a breath, but it looked as if she was about to launch into more.

"Spare me the details, Vic. What's important right now is that you an' Blue here potentially have Blacksnake *an'* Echo on your tails. Which means, we've gotta split from this spot immediately." John was up and moving, walking towards the door. Vickie noticed that there was a bag set to the right side near the hinge; a "go bag," obviously, with everything he'd need. He snatched it up. "If anyone knows you're here, then they know me. If anyone knows me, they know you might be here. We're on the move."

"My car's downstairs." She held out her hands; they were shaking. "Can you drive?"

"Haven't had a license in a number of years, but I figure that won't stop me, will it?"

"You're with CCCP," Bella said. "You have metahuman ally and diplomatic immunity for traffic stops. Where are we going?"

"Easy. CCCP HQ, and not because they have diplomatic immunity; Blacksnake doesn't give a shit 'bout that sorta thing. Bullets an' bombs don't stop killing because you're 'diplomatically immune.' What the CCCP does have, however, are a bunch of commies that are more trigger happy than I am, and would love to perforate some mercs, given the chance." John grinned. "Sound good to y'all?"

"Better than good," Bella replied. "What else do you need?"

John slung the bag on his shoulder, then started towards a closet. He paused, turning to face Bella and Vickie. "Before we go on; how the hell did y'two get up here?"

"I magicked the front door," Vickie said. Her voice was starting to shake. "Locked it behind us."

"Make me a promise? Once all of this settles an' I can actually come back here, make sure that no one can do what you did. Roger?"

"Wilco."

He nodded, opening the closet door. From it, he pulled three rifles: one M4 carbine and two AKMs. He kept the M4, while holding out the AKMs to Bella and Vic. "JIC, comrades." *Just in case.*

They nodded. Both of them took the rifles with body language that said they were comfortable with firearms. Bella examined hers; Vickie acted as if she was familiar already. "Variation on the AK-47, Bell," Vickie said. "Soviet. Works the same."

Bella nodded. "Okay. Got a chance to play with those at that over-the-top range in Lost Wages." She didn't ask how Vickie got her obvious knowledge. "Point and hose, roger."

"Negative, comrade. You point, you squeeze, an' you make 'em count. I don't anticipate it, but if we get into trouble, you shoot 'em dead." John shrugged as he loaded his cargo pockets with spare magazines. "Don't matter much; if it's a halfway decent ambush, we're dead." He nodded. "Ready, comrades?"

Bella looked at Vickie, about to protest that it wasn't possible for Blacksnake or anyone else to know what they were doing this soon. Then she snapped her mouth shut on the words. Vickie looked grim and terrified. John and Vickie were both convinced. She'd protest later. Maybe. "Ready."

Vickie nodded.

"Rock an' roll. Follow me, stay at the door on the ground floor. Wait for my commands. An', above all, keep your eyes open. That's important." Without another word, he was out the door, his rifle at a low ready position. Bella followed. Vickie followed her, but was walking crabwise, semi-backwards, keeping her rifle in the same position but pointed back the way they had come—after securing the door to John's squat. It was unnerving. Bella was used to combat now...but not this sort. Not where they might be the quarry of assassins.

John moved quickly and confidently, scanning everything as he went. When they came to the front door, he motioned for them to stay put. *Well, if someone's gonna get shot right now, it's gonna be me.* John stepped to the door, keeping his rifle pressed against his right leg. He nodded at Bella, using the fingers on his off hand to indicate that he wanted her to keep an eye out. Vickie made as if to toss him the keys, but he held his hand up to stop her. "You're gonna start it from the passenger side, Vic. I'll drive, but I'll be providin' security until then."

They both nodded back. He unlocked, then kicked open the front door, Vickie took the opposite side of the doorframe from Bella without direction, her eyes going everywhere. John was on the ground, checking under the car, checking under the hood, in the tire rims, the trunk, anywhere something could have been messed with in the brief time the women had been upstairs. After two minutes, he was done. He motioned with his free hand for them to come up; immediately, his rifle was up from his side, and he was scanning every angle, looking for anything amiss.

Vickie was out the door first, wrenched open the back car door, then the front, and went back-to-back with John and brought her own rifle up while Bella grabbed John's bag and dove with it into the back seat, feeling as if the world had turned upside down as much as the day of the Invasion. Vickie kicked the door shut behind her, then popped into the front passenger seat, slammed her door and started the car. Then she brought her weapon up to cover the front while Bella did her best to cover the rear. John was in before the engine had fully turned over, slamming his door shut, putting the car into gear, and gunning the engine.

"Keep watchin' outside, an' remember; this thing isn't hardened. Bullets can come in an' they can go out. Remember that, if y'need to fire."

"Try and keep the engine block betwixt us and harm, Johnny," Vickie said.

"If it's a decent ambush, it'll either be comin' from one side, or from the front an' the side. Our only options are to fight through, in any case. Let's hope there ain't any ambushes set up." John was taking a long route to the CCCP HQ; he never walked this route, and certainly never rode it when he was on one of the issued Urals. Any patterns may have been noticed, and patterns made it easier for enemies to plot against a convoy or patrol.

John fished the CCCP communicator from one of his pockets, keying the frequency for the base. "Gamayun, this is Unit 05, come in, over."

"*Da*, comrade. Was being to monitor your approach. Commissar has been giving permission to enter on arrival."

"Got two packages with me, high priority, how copy?"

"*Da*, copy, and confirmed. Permission granted."

"Roger, they'll be comin' in first. Gotta get rid of somethin' 'fore I make my grand entrance. Unit 05, over an' out, comrade." John glanced over his shoulder. "Y'all are gettin' a fine welcome."

Vickie smiled weakly. "I alerted them. Gamayun probably knew we were heading here."

It took the trio twice as long as it normally should if they were traveling regularly to get to the back door of the HQ, but they arrived unmolested.

"Sit tight. After I have the door open to the HQ, get in fast. I'll drive the car off somewhere safe, an' meet y'all back here."

"Johnny, I have a kit in the trunk. I *need* it," Vickie said urgently.

"I'll bring it to the door, an' drop it on the right once I'm inside. Roger?"

"That'll work. Don't want you lugging anything on the way back."

"I have your go bag, JM," Bella said from the rear seat.

"Y'all are too kind." John grinned again, and was out of the car. In a flash, he was at the rear entrance with Vickie's kit, punching a code in. The door swung open; one of the CCCPers was there with another AKM, warily looking at the street. John placed Vic's duffle bag and heavy backpack inside, then motioned for the two Echo operatives to come to him.

Once again, Vickie was out first, bracing the AKM on the roof of the car while Bella scooted in the door with John's bag, feeling entirely unnerved. Once she was inside, Vickie kicked the doors shut, dropped off of the car, bent over, and ran for the safe haven of the open door.

"Best hook up with the Commissar, kids. I'll take care of the car. Wish me luck." Without waiting for an answer, John was back in the car. With a squeal of tires on gravel and asphalt, he was off and driving away into the destruction corridor.

John drove fast, but carefully; between the rubble and the potential dangers of an ambush, he had to. Something still tugged at his mind, however. Victrix seemed particularly knowledgeable about what to do in the situation they had found themselves in. *That sort of knowledge doesn't come cheap, or easily. Or out of books. That's training to the point where it's reflex, and not necessarily Echo training. And that's . . . interesting.* He snapped back into the moment, scanning everything as he drove. *Stash the car, exfil back to HQ, don't get killed. Sounds like a plan.*

Red Saviour stared at both of them, face impassive. Bella sat numbly in the hard office chair, still trying to process what had just happened. Vickie, however, was pacing, gesturing, talking passionately.

". . . Verdigris has been on the FBI 'want' list for decades, which is why I've always kept track of him, but he uses so many shadow companies it's next to impossible to even get hints of what he's doing," Vickie was saying. "So I started experimenting, and when I put Overwatch together I used an old, outdated machine for what I call my 'Magic 8-Ball' program. It doesn't tell me a lot, and it doesn't predict *anything*. What it does do, is sometimes gives me really simple answers to the question of 'who did this, who is responsible' for stuff that's going on in the rest of the system. It doesn't give me the proof, because it's more than half magic, but it tells me an answer. Now the 'who is responsible' is limited to a set number of known troublemakers that I put in the 8-Ball. For instance, I didn't bother with the Thulians in general, that wouldn't be useful; I've got Doppelgaenger, Ubermensch, Valkyria in there, and if we get any other biggies, they'll go in it too. Verd's in there, so are some other high-profile types, and I didn't limit them to who's not in jail, because jail might not stop them from operating. It's not consistent, and I don't get a lot of hits, because it's still an experiment, but the answers are reliable. And the second Tesla died, it popped up with Verdigris."

She ran both hands through hair that was damp and clumping with nervous sweat. "Commissar, I swear to you on my life, I *know* he did this. I don't know if I'll ever find the way to prove it, not with the kind of forensic evidence that would pass muster in a court case, but I *know* he did it. As for how he got Echo—Tesla said something a while back about 'independent investors.' I haven't gotten a chance to snoop in the Echo financial records, but I should still have a couple back doors in there and I bet I'll find two to three of Verd's shadow companies that bought up enough stock to take over. I also bet I'll find something in the company organization that screws up the succession, so the majority stockholder gets the CEO chair, and not Yankee Pride."

Finally she ran down, and slumped into a chair. And rather than answering, Saviour got up from hers. She went to one of the old-fashioned filing cabinets that lined the wall, unlocked and opened a drawer, and brought out a slim folder. Taking her seat again, she opened it.

Someone rapped on the door. They all looked up. Untermensch poked his head in. "Murdock is returned. Vehicle is safe, no problems."

Saviour nodded, and Unter closed the door. Both Bella and Vickie sighed with relief. Bella would have hugged Unter if he'd stuck around. Guilt. She'd dragged Johnny into this.

"On last trip from Moscow, I am having Molo bring me old case records from CCCP office," she said, and her lip curled into a little sneer. "My father and Boryets are not seeing value of my old paper records, and let them go. Are forgetting lesson of Stasi and NKVD. Paper records cannot be, how you say, 'jiggled with.' And ... *da*, Dominic Verdigris, this name I know." Her face darkened. "And we, too, have had much suspicion and no proofs. Not even so much proof that I could be giving him boot to face to encourage talk, should he ever enter Russian border." She looked down at the file, and Bella could feel the tension in her. "I believe you, Daughter of Rasputin. I believe you." She shut the file. "First, you must be finding if he has even slightest of suspicion of you and *sestra* Blue, even hint he knows of Overwatch. You can do that?"

Vickie nodded, slowly, and Bella heaved a sigh of relief. "It'll be slower without the computer suite in my apartment, but yes, I can do that with what I have with me."

"We consider worst case first. If *da,* I offer you sanctuary, here." Saviour spread her hands wide. "We do not know why Verdigris wishes Echo under thumb. It may be he has turned over new plant."

"Leaf," Vickie corrected automatically. "Neither of us believes that, given *how* he did it."

"Truth. So...if he knows of you and Overwatch, we find out why he wants Echo, what he would do with you and Overwatch. You both will be welcome with us. If he does not know of you and Overwatch..." She paused. "You still will be welcome with us. Even cat."

Bella felt a tremendous weight of fear leave her. "Nat—"

"Bah, you are both useful," Saviour said, waving it off. "To be doing things first. Collect intelligence. Gamayun may be of help. Meanwhile..." she smiled slyly. "In light of current tragedy, CCCP is understandably on lockdown. And you, who were *just visiting,* are also understandably...not available. CCCP regrets, and you are in good health, but no one comes in, no one goes out, until crisis is resolved."

The smile turned wolfish. Bella returned it.

In three days, they had learned a few things. Jack—whoever he was—was gone. So was Harmony. They hadn't resurfaced, nor had they been dug out, and that argued for a very well-laid plan. Acrobat and Scope were gone; knowing them, Bella and Vickie were sure they were trying to track Harmony. The betrayal would have cut them to the heart. Bulwark would live—probably—but he was in the intensive care unit and still wasn't conscious. He had every resource that Echo could muster. One more healer wouldn't make a difference. She couldn't dismiss him from her mind, but there was no point in obsessing over him when there were other things that she needed to concentrate on.

Verdigris did not know of Vickie's back doors into the Echo system, nor did he know about Overwatch. Now, this particular piece of intel came not from Vickie's hacking, or not entirely, but from Vickie's magic. Bella didn't know a lot about hacking and even less about how Vic's magic worked, but Saviour seemed satisfied and Bella was inclined to follow her lead.

Last...Bella and Vickie were very, very far down on Verdigris' list of interests. Echo hadn't even inquired about them until today, and had appeared satisfied with Saviour's answer that they had been making a casual visit and got caught in the lockdown. There hadn't even been a demand that Bella join the medical team on Bull's case, nor that Vickie track down Harmony, Scope or Acrobat.

The question was . . . would they stay "invisible" if they left CCCP territory? Well, Bella was considering that anyway, though she was pretty sure Vickie would follow her lead. Wouldn't it be safer, wouldn't they be able to do more, with CCCP?

She wasn't going to ask Saviour; much as she liked Nat, the Commissar was very much inclined to "requisition" every resource that came within grabbing distance, and the two of them were definitely resources. No . . . no, she had someone else in mind.

She lurked around the recreation room until that "someone else" put in an appearance after his shift. By way of a bribe, she had a six of Guinness.

"Hey, tall, dark and waterproof," she said, swinging the six-pack suggestively. "Got a minute or three?"

John looked over to her instantly, already grinning. "Someone been tellin' ya stories 'bout me, Bells?"

"Aw come on, who doesn't like Guinness?" She winked.

"I'll have some of the dark stuff. Pull up a milk crate, comrade; I wouldn't trust that couch. Already eaten 'bout three remotes; might graduate to blueberries or somethin'."

Bella laughed, and handed him the six. There were a lot of mismatched cushions from deceased couches and chairs stacked in a corner; she grabbed one and sat on the floor.

John pulled up one of the aforementioned milk crates, gingerly sitting down on it while he cracked open the first beer. "Y'got the look of someone with a lotta things on their mind. What's up, kiddo?"

She took a bottle and opened it, sipping to give her a moment to phrase things. "Well, we know some stuff now. Not nearly as much as we'd like, and Vickie is still working on that, but we have enough to make a decision. Vic'll probably do what I do, so it's pretty much on me. Stay with Echo, or defect?" She took another sip. "We are pretty sure that Verd doesn't know about Overwatch, and that so far as he is concerned we are among the herd of faceless powered flunkies. Which means . . . if we stayed, potentially . . . potentially we could run a revolution via the Overwatch system. But should we? Because if Verd does find out about it, he's not going to be offering severance pay, unless you're talking about heads on silver platters."

John had already finished his first beer while he listened, and was starting on his second. "So, what you're askin' is, should y'stay with Echo, or defect to the CCCP, right? Weighing the risks an' whatnot."

"That'd be a ten-four."

"Easy, then. Stay with Echo. Wanna hear the not-so-easy reasons for it?"

She spread her hands wide. "You have my undivided attention."

"I'm good like that. Let's look at this big-picture-like. One, you're already on the books with Echo. You've got access to stuff via Echo that we don't necessarily have here at the ol' CCCP. Echo, even under this Dominic guy's control, still has resources out the ass, an' then some." John took a swig of beer. "We can use that here. You two've already passed us a bunch."

"And Vickie can get into the inventory and make sure that anything we swipe for you never existed." Bella paused. "But if we weren't still with Echo, we'd never be able to swipe it in the first place."

"I, personally, like the path of least resistance. So, point two. While y'all are with Echo, you're small fish, like y'already said. You defect to the CCCP . . . you might just show up on radar, and make our signature bigger. Way things are, with y'two friendly an' cooperatin' with us under the table, it serves everyone's interests best. You can help us, we can help you, an' so long as we're careful, no one is the wiser. If things get too hot over at Echo, we can pull y'all out an' go from there."

"But once we're out, it's not going to be easy to get us back in." She nodded, and sipped. "Third reason?"

He finished his beer. "Third reason: I don't think you'd look as good as I do in this uniform. Just doesn't go with your eyes, Blue."

She mimed a blow at his head. "You know, somewhere out there, a village is missing its idiot."

"Might wanna skedaddle home then, kiddo; someone's bound t'be keepin' your seat warm." Another grin. He always seemed to smile so easily. About half the time . . . she didn't believe the smile. Maybe more than half. It was certainly charming, even disarming, but to her there was always some pain, and it seemed forced. More like a weapon, a tool or a defense he used so habitually he wasn't even aware of doing so. "So, what're your thoughts on . . . well, my thoughts? Remember, most people askin' for advice are only really lookin' to get their own opinions confirmed."

She sobered and finished her beer in one long swallow, putting the empty down beside her. "Should I run a revolution? Am I totally insane? I mean, yeah, look, the blood of my hippie ancestors is running around in my veins, chanting and waving signs, but this is *Dominic Frickin' Verdigris* we're talking about. Supergenius. You must have talked to Vic, or even just listened to her muttering to herself lately. This guy pulls off stuff most crime lords wouldn't even dare to dream about, and for him, it's only Tuesday. He took over Echo, for god's sake."

"Does he got any sorta special abilities, aside from havin' a big brain? Immune to damage, can phase out of reality, or fart out showtune lyrics?"

"He doesn't need anything but that big brain. The big brain makes him money, and the money buys him everything he could possibly need or want."

"Sounds like he can take a bullet just as easy as the next guy, then."

"Wait—" Bella said. "Let's go talk to Vickie."

"You don't have to go talk to her; she's standing behind you," said Vickie's voice from the door. "A little cat told me you were having a discussion I needed to contribute to. There had better still be a beer left."

She listened without comment while Bella outlined the conversation, and nodded when Bella was done.

"She had been listenin' for a minute an' a half before ya noticed her, but damn if the little blonde ain't sneaky." John held a fresh beer out to her. "We'll have to start breakin' into the vodka, soonish."

"I could go for that. Even Comrade's Choice. Okay, Johnny, let me tell you what I've winkled out so far, and bear in mind that Dominic Frickin' Verdigris probably has a lot more layers around him than I have been able to find." Vickie looked beyond tired, like she hadn't slept in the last three days, and thinner than when he'd last seen her. "So. When he's at home, which is mostly, he has a primary defense system running on an AI that's not hackable without being on the premises and within that primary perimeter. Rumor hath it that he has a lot of . . . how to put this... *demented* pieces to this system. Like a shark tank. No lie. This is a system that runs traps and kill zones *only* and it probably costs the GNP of a small country. He has a secondary system that runs the alarms. He has guards, perimeter guards and bodyguards, and his *personal* bodyguard, who never leaves him and probably sleeps with him, is a metahuman named Khanjar who has never, not once, missed." She drank half the beer. "That is what I know about. Which is probably no more than half of what he actually has."

"Y'done, comrade? An' where's the part that I'm supposed to be impressed?" John put his hands up in defense. "I'm not tryin' to be an asshole, honestly, though it's hard for me. I'm just sayin'; where there's a will, there's a way. This guy has security, okay. You just listed off a lot of major stuff. The best sort of security is the sort that no one knows 'bout til it's bitin' them in the ass. Sure, there's definitely more, no 'likely' about it. But we got a chunk of it. Here's the thing with runnin' security on a VIP. If you're part of the hired help, you have to be right every time, all the time. The bad guys? They only have to be right once. That makes security a losin' game, in the long run. Eventually, the 'bad guys'—us, in this instance—get lucky or get it right. An' we're not a bunch of preschoolers around here, if'n ya hadn't noticed." John finished his fourth beer, reaching into a small refrigerator for a fifth. "So, are we talkin' about killin' this guy, or what?"

Bella held up a hand. "Just a second." It shocked her, and she didn't want to show it, that Murdock was that ready to go, that fast. That he either could justify an assassination that quickly, or just figured it was in order as long as *she* thought it was justified. She'd known he was hard...she just hadn't quite known how hard.

"Let me think out loud here. Now, you're saying *we,* and while I am sure that Nat would be perfectly happy to put one between the man's eyes, Nat doesn't have an infinite number of people to send after him. Limited resources, and I think after she thought about it, she'd have to say that one target is not worth what it would take. Which would pretty much leave the *we* being the three of us here."

"I'd say it depends on the target. Is this guy enough of a threat to warrant the risk? From the sound of things, he very well could be. If he screws over Echo, that's a major roadblock that has been removed for the Nazis. In the position he's in, he could screw over the CCCP. Neither of these things are things that we can abide, correct?" John shrugged. "I trust you, Bella, an' I trust Vic. She says that he killed Tesla in a power play. That seems t'make him fair game, in my book."

"That's the thing. We don't know what he wants Echo *for* yet. It's not likely, but it's possible that he got a scare tossed into him by one of those Thulian pop-ups. Or something else. He might be on our side."

"By killin' the leader of the largest metahuman organization in the world, covertly." John cocked an eyebrow, taking another swig of his beer.

"Whose leader was spending most of his time hiding under his desk and the rest of his time letting petty bureaucrats boss him around and hamstring his organization to the point of casualties." Bella frowned. "Case in point, the suicide of the Mountain and the collateral casualties among the civilians."

"There's lots of reasons to kill folks, an' I've explored quite a few of 'em. Incompetence takes more than a bit to get my blood or fires up, kids." He sighed. "Listen, I know y'all are playin' devil's advocate here. An' I get it. But, honestly; y'all think this guy is workin' with us? I want your honest opinions on it. He is a guy that we figured might have somethin' set up to kill all three of us; I've had my troubles with both Echo and Blacksnake, mind you. Call me biased."

"I think he's working his own game," Vickie piped up, clearly too tired to have energy to spare for her usual nerves. "I don't think it's currently incompatible with Echo's, even though it's not going to be in Echo's best interests down the road. Look, Johnny, one of the things I try and do is get inside peoples' heads, and I think the reason Verd grabbed both Blacksnake and Echo is to put *them* solidly between him and the Thulians. Because I suspect if they know about *him,* they'll try and put the snatch on him, and I *think* that he finds the idea of working for them revolting. Not because of what they are or do, but because he refuses to work for anyone but himself. He's a sociopath. No one matters to him, but him. But conversely, that means the idea of anyone exerting authority *over* him would make him furious."

"Part that grabbed me there the most was 'put Blacksnake and Echo between himself an' the Thulians'. Doesn't sound like Echo an' Blacksnake are on the winnin' side of that equation. A shield is made to get chewed up in battle."

Again Bella raised her hand. "I get that." She pinched the bridge of her nose just between her eyes to stave off a headache. "Look. Two things. One, we can't, and I mean, can't, start acting like the bad guys. We do, they win, because we become them. Two, this isn't answering the question I asked."

"Y'have my answer, Blues. Stay with Echo, until the moment comes when y'can't. Y'can do more good there, for all of us. Plus, it'd make it easier to eliminate this guy with y'all on the inside, anyways." He shrugged easily, finishing his beer.

"But—look, there are only four people who *might* run a revolt from inside. Bulwark, Ramona Ferrari and Yankee Pride. And me. Of the three, I think I am going to be the one least watched, and the one...the one with the most *will* to do it. Bulwark is out for now. Ramona and Pride are in shock. Once *I* get the ball rolling, I am pretty sure the others will follow. But am I the right person for the job?"

"So, the matter is settled for ya? Of course you're the right one for the job, kiddo. Ain't necessarily 'bout bein' the 'right one' so much as it is bein' the one that's there an' willin'. Roger?" John stood up, discarding his empty bottle in the trash bin with a toss.

Slowly, Bella nodded. "I guess...talking about it out loud... yeah. Kind of solidified things. And...I think the way to do this with the least number of casualties is to topple him. Not kill him, just get him out."

John nodded in response, placing his fists on his hips. "Then it's settled. Just remember; we're at war. Folks get killed; some 'cause they need to, some just 'cause."

"But no one wins a war fought on two fronts much less three," Bella retorted. "We can't fight Verd *and* Blacksnake *and* the Thulians." She turned to Vickie. "Vic, first thing. We need that desk. Got me? Get in touch with Ferrari, find out where it went, because we can't let Verd get it, and we need it bad."

Vickie nodded. John raised an eyebrow and let the incomprehensible comments slide by.

"Funny y'say two fronts. Argument could be made that this guy bein' alive, period, might create that. *Nyet?*" John took his turn to hold up his hands. "Just sayin'. I'm good to go for whatever; I'm just a shooter, now. Not a planner anymore. 'Kay?"

She frowned. "No. That's not okay. If I'm going to be in charge, I refuse to be handicapped because someone who knows more than I do won't use his brains."

Another smile. "All right, but I already told ya; I can be a real asshole when I try."

"You can be a real asshole when you don't try, Johnny," Vickie said wearily. "It's part of your charm."

"I've got charm? Don't tell Ol' Man Bear, he'll get jealous."

Bella shook her head, then reached out and mussed his hair. "Moron. Look... thanks. For evacking us. For getting our backs. For helping me."

"No need t'thank me, ma'am. I'm just doin' my job." This time he really smiled, and it felt real for Bella. "Seriously, though, forget it. It's what we do, isn't it?"

She nodded, soberly. "Yes, it is." She looked him in the eyes. "And I think you know why."

He met her gaze for a few moments, purposefully, then shrugged. "We've all got our reasons, kiddo." John looked around, confused. "So... are we outta beer? If so, I think that's a tragedy in the makin'."

"I think I'm up to one beer run," Vickie replied. "As long as you ride shotgun and do the heavy lifting. Then I'm finally going home to my real bed."

"I'll go along on that," Bella replied. "I'm ready to see my own bed too. I'll even buy the beer."

"Ridin' shotgun means I get to bring a shotgun, right?"

Bella smiled. "I wouldn't have it any other way."

They dropped John off at CCCP with two cases of Guinness. A bottle of single malt came home with them. "We need a nightcap," Bella had declared.

Vickie raised an eyebrow. "Doesn't mix with my meds," she replied, quite seriously. Bella knew she had been medicated up the entire time they'd been at the HQ. Saviour had considerately put her in a little room all her own, then put Chug on guard at the door. For some reason, Vickie's people phobia didn't include Chug.

"All right, then, I need a nightcap. You can keep me company with tea."

They didn't talk much in the car, nor on the way up to the top floor in the battered old elevator. Bella half expected Vickie to beg off when they got to their floor, but instead, the little mage followed her in. When Vickie headed for the kitchen, Bella forestalled her. "You go sit," she said. "I'll make tea."

"Afraid I'll burn the water?" Vickie asked wryly, but didn't argue. She wasn't moving well today; probably a night on the CCCP cots hadn't done her much good.

"Where did you learn all that gun stuff?" Bella asked, deciding after due consideration that green chai was probably going to be all right. It was either that, or black chai, or chamomile, and she wasn't sure how the chamomile would go with whatever it was that Vickie was taking. "Green chai, sugar, cream?"

"Yes, one lump or spoon and no," Vickie replied. "Can I put something on your stereo?"

"Sure." A moment later, *Kindertotenlieder* was wafting through the apartment. Bella brought in a cup for Vickie and a single measured shot for herself.

She handed the cup to Vickie, who took it, carefully, her hand trembling just a little bit. "The school I went to—okay, you know the college system in England?"

"Every uni has a lot of colleges, that's where people live rather than dorms or frats, and the college is partially responsible for your education. I've read my Dorothy Sayers." Bella sipped the scotch, savoring the smoky bite.

"Well, there are two special colleges over there, one at Oxford, and one at Cambridge, that are—kind of invisible. Merlin at Oxford and Taliesin at Cambridge. You only get invites to join if you're a magician. You can only get into the building, literally, if you're a magician. At Oxford, the door into the magic college is in a hallway in Magdalene. Well, I went to Merlin. Before that, I went to another place called St. Rhiannon's for my high school years. Both of them are pretty hardcore about not turning out pasty-faced little bookworm mages. Merlin has the equivalent of ROTC, and I was in that." Vickie took a long draught of her tea. "But before that, and during it really, I worked unofficially with my parents for some of their FBI cases—unofficially, because even the FBI would have significant problems with a twelve-year-old helping Mommy and Daddy work a case. I learned most of my gun stuff with them. Sometimes C4 works better than a cantrip." She made a face. "Yeah, you'd never guess, would you? Bundle of nerves and phobias that I am. You know—"

But Bella never got a chance to hear the end of that sentence, because the room suddenly washed over with a bright, soft light, and...they weren't alone.

The Seraphym stood just inside the window and looked about her curiously, folding wings that were far too large for the apartment to hold, not in the sense that they brushed the apartment walls, but in the sense that they seemed to extend into some dimension outside the usual three.

Vickie made a small sound, and the almost-empty cup fell from her nerveless fingers. Bella swallowed down the usual reaction she had to the angel, the one that made her want to throw herself on the ground at Sera's feet. Instead she glanced at Vickie, whose eyes were so wide and pupils so dilated that they seemed to take up half her face.

"You see her," Bella said, flatly.

"Yes," squeaked Vickie.

"*I keep telling you, I am not an hallucination,*" the Seraphym said, amused. "*Though a goodly part of the time, John Murdock does not believe me either.*"

Wait—she talked to Johnny *too?* This was the first that Bella'd had any inkling that the Seraphym spoke to anyone except herself. *So... is there something the Seraphym wants out of him? I already knew he was important, or she wouldn't have helped me save his life, or insisted I get him into CCCP. But to speak directly to him—*

But before Bella could ask anything, the Seraphym spoke again.

"*You remember, I asked you for a promise,*" she continued. "*I come to ask you to fulfill that promise.*"

Oh no... oh no. Sera didn't want her to rock the boat. Sera wanted her to back off. Sera—

"*I wish for you to oppose the one called Verdigris,*" she said, and sighed. "*I showed him his future, if he did not oppose the Thulians, and this is his answer. I may, myself, not work against him. It is not permitted. But it is permitted that I ask you to do so, since you have already determined that someone must.*"

The flames that were Sera's hair stirred restlessly. Bella had noticed that they did so when Sera was—well, she never actually *showed* distress, but Bella sensed something like it from her.

"And just how far—" Bella began.

But Sera shook her head. "*You must make those choices for yourself. I must not interfere with your Free Will. I can only tell you that the one called Verdigris is making his and they lead to destruction. You had already decided to oppose him. I am only asking you to keep your resolve, and see that your choices are good* ones. Even when they lead you to places you would not otherwise have gone and you are not sure you are fit for where they take you."

Well, she was already not sure she was fit as the leader of a conspiracy... but Bulwark was going to be down for a good long time and you can't run a conspiracy from a hospital bed; Pride was too used to obeying authority to think of this himself until it was too late; and Ramona, while smart and capable, wasn't—

The Seraphym smiled. "*You are...*"

—sneaky enough—

Bella smiled wryly. "I guess I am."

The Seraphym nodded gravely. "*Then, if it helps strengthen you, know that this is a good choice, now that you have made it, younger sibling. Follow your plan. Consult with others. Choose well.*"

Bella thought she was about to do one of those vanishing acts, but instead, to her bemusement, she turned to Vickie. Vickie looked as if she was trying to vanish into the seat cushions.

"*For you, this. A wise man, a writer like you, once said, 'There will come a time when you believe everything is finished. That will be the beginning.'*"

"Louis L'Amour," Vickie gulped. "But—"

"*Remember that.*"

And now the room washed with warm, bright light; Bella shielded her eyes, and when the light cleared she was not at all surprised to see that the Seraphym was gone.

The stereo was still playing. Appropriately, Bell recognized Rautavaara, Angel of Light.

Vickie's eyes slowly went back to normal. "Does she do that often?" the little mage finally whispered.

"Talk to me? Uh...yeah."

Vickie shivered. "I do *not* envy you. I've only seen her that close once before. I'm surprised I don't need a change of clothing now."

"I guess I'm used to it. Sort of. As used as you can get to it." She didn't bother to tell Vickie that was a *muted* version of the Seraphym. Then again, Vickie probably knew that. She remembered the scotch still in her hand, and tossed the rest down. "All right, well," she said, in as normal a tone as she could manage. "Since we seem to have gotten a thumbs-up from on high...and since I think it's going to be a while before you can calm down enough to sleep...let's talk about getting Tesla's desk."

CHAPTER NINETEEN

Suffer

MERCEDES LACKEY AND DENNIS LEE

We both knew that we had to have that desk—the Metis communication device that was hidden inside it. We knew that Metis was on the fence. We knew they needed a big push to get off. But unless they heard the real story, the whole truth, and not whatever version they got from the media—assuming they even paid any attention to the media, or were not cut off in their never-never land—we knew that we could never use Tesla's murder as that push. And they had to hear it soon.

So we planned to pull off the biggest caper of the century. Rob Echo.

And for that . . . there was only one person we could turn to.

Yeah. Guess who.

Okay, I had come to a detente with Red Djinni. So, he had a thing about magic, but he'd put up with it now. I still didn't know why but—

—but I was about to find out, and it was going to irrevocably change both our lives.

It had been a very bad day.

Vickie had been out on the Le Parkour course this morning, because she was out on the course every morning, and to break that pattern could make someone—Verdigris—take notice. Right now, having Verd take notice would be a disaster. The conspirators had to make everything look normal. Normal. As if anything could be normal now. She tried not to think too hard about Bull;

she'd slipped into the Echo hospital unit to see him. What she could of him, under all the machines. He looked...like a special effect. And not a good one.

"Nervous" did not even begin to describe how tightly she was wound up. She didn't dare drug up this close to an op, but she was a hair away from a panic attack. Piled on top of raw nerves was worry over Bulwark. He was one of *hers,* the first to really believe in her in Echo, the first to give Overwatch a chance. And atop the nerves and the worry was guilt. If only he'd been wired...if only she'd found some way to get *some* sort of camera feed for the meeting. If only...

It had been hotter than the Mojave Desert and dripping humidity, and she, of course, was out there in long sleeves, long pants and gloves. She thought now she might have gotten a touch of heat exhaustion, but all she knew for sure was that there was one moment when she was jumping (or trying to) and reaching for a handhold, then there was a moment of blankness, and the next thing she knew, she was falling.

Okay, she fell all the time...except this time she'd been halfway up the wall, and the automatic reaction was to scramble wildly for handholds to save herself. Her brain knew what to do; her old reactions knew. The only way to make this suck less was to grab and let go, grab and let go, slowing your fall rather than stopping it. And every time she grabbed, she pulled and wrenched and strained things that really didn't want to be pulled, couldn't bear being wrenched, and tore under strain.

By the time she hit the ground and rolled, her body was screaming with pain. Her skin felt like it had been shredded, her muscles were sobbing, her tendons...she just lay there on the ground for a very long time, her whole body a symphony of agony. Nobody was going to come, of course. Ever since encountering Djinni one too many times on the course, she'd put a little spell in place to make people not see her when she was there. And this was how such things came back to bite you in the ass.

Finally she managed to move, but that was all she could take; no getting back on the horse today.

Maybe not ever.

She got herself off the course, dragged herself to her car, got home, fell on the couch and assessed the damage. Or assessed it as much as she could without undressing.

Then, she cried. Partly from the pain, and partly from defeat. She had been *trying* to make some kind of physical recovery, trying so hard. Bella encouraged her, said it would help with the panic. Said she needed to get out, join the field teams, that she could get back some of what she had been, once. That it was going to work.

But it wasn't, not when every time she went out, she seemed to do worse, not better. *This is impossible. I can't do this... I should just stick with what I'm capable of.* She hugged herself, rocking, shivering, crying, too sick with pain to even move to the bathroom.

She knew she couldn't afford to indulge herself like this. Not when her team was counting on her, and they would have to have her soon, at the top of her game. *Get yourself together. The team's ready. The Vault's as cleared as Pride can make it. Two hours, they'll need you and we have* got *to get the unit.* That precious, precious Metis communication unit.

Bella and Pride both agreed; getting that unit was key. Right now Metis might not know Tesla was dead; they certainly didn't know that there was someone very bad in charge. Bella was right; they had to get proactive. *We can't chance Verdigris getting it, and we have* got *to get in touch with Merc and Nikola Tesla, maybe help them knock some sense into Metis.*

That was the logical little voice in the back of her head; the rest of her just wanted to curl up around a bottle of pain pills and keep crying. She knew which part she'd listen to... eventually. Just... not right now. Not when it hurt so damn bad she was sick, and it was all she could do to keep from opening a vein to make it stop.

She heard the knock on her door.

It had been a very bad day.

But then, when was the last time he'd had a *good* one?

Try as he might, Red Djinni couldn't shake the voices. They threw their taunts, their jabs and sharp daggers of accusation his way. Despite years of finely honed reflexes, he had not been fast enough to save Amethist. For all his experience at reading people, for gauging their strengths, weaknesses and character, he had not been shrewd enough to see through Harmony's act. And Jack? He had been stupid enough to trust Jack. Again.

Yet the work continued. There was always more work to do. This time, he was determined to do it right. No more jobs on the fly, they had barely gotten out of the last one alive. Again, it had almost become a disaster because of him. Arrogance, self-preservation, even blind faith in his own stupid luck had placed not just him, but his entire team in danger. People he was responsible for.

He was not about to admit he cared for them, yet.

He shrugged it off and ascribed his determination to do things *right* this time to a professional code of conduct. *Watch their backs, they will watch yours, do the job and get out alive.* And he wanted to do this job, though he wasn't quite sure why. It wasn't for redemption, was it? Surely not. That never ended well. Pride? Faint glimmers of newly found heroic tendencies? Laughable.

Nevertheless, *they* needed to do this, and *he* needed to help them.

Of course, his first reaction had been far from positive.

"Another vault job? I thought the point of me joining this outfit was to *stop* being a criminal bastard!"

It was Victrix, of course, who explained it to him. The others had thrown up their hands and walked away, letting Victrix calmly lay out the logic. How they were very close to losing their way to any foothold they still had on their own destiny. The revelation of the existence of a genuine angel was a bit of a shock—though Red still had his doubts about that and had merely nodded to get Victrix to shut up about it. The legend of Metis though, that had definitely fired up his imagination. So it was clear, the first step was to reestablish contact with them. And to do that, they needed what Victrix called (with heavy irony) "The MacGuffin," neatly tucked away unbeknownst to Verdigris in Echo's own Vault. And for that, they needed to convince the thief.

Eventually, even Victrix lost her patience.

"Unless, of course, you'd rather see Echo under the control of the same guy that poisons water supplies so he can sell water purifiers to people who are dying of thirst. The same guy who planted Harmony on us, who trained someone so treacherous she could not only kill Tesla, but flawlessly convince Bulwark she was a wounded bird until she put him down for the count."

Then she showed him the evidence. It was enough to convince even him.

So they got to work, all of them. They planned it out, banging their heads together in secret every night for a solid week in Bella's cramped apartment. Victrix brought the floor plans and schematics, Yankee Pride the guard schedules and postings for the Vault, Djinni his considerable tactical know-how for circumventing countermeasures, and Bella the bodies, the members of a conspiracy he hadn't even known existed. A conspiracy that had somehow managed to rope in Yankee Pride and Ramona Ferrari.

A gal named Mel brought the booze and pizza and Chex mix. Red Saviour of the commies offered a safe place to stash the MacGuffin when they got it. Ramona found the exact Vault where the desk had gone, then mapped out a way to get to that Vault that would skirt them past any opposition until they reached the building. And Bella, unable to contribute anything to the planning, came and went, often returning with armloads of black mesh outfits, weaponry, ammo and other sundries. Unmarked, of course.

The plan was solid, with smaller windows of opportunity than he was normally comfortable with, but solid. The only flaw, as far as Red could see, was they were still one man short.

Or woman, rather.

He paused for just a moment, then knocked on her door.

Paranoia means you don't have a peephole in your door, you have a camera system. Paranoia means you don't even stand *near* the door to see who's there. Vickie stabbed at the camera control next to her with a shaking hand three times before she managed to turn it on, and the image of her visitor came up on her TV.

Fear lanced through her. It was the Red Djinni. Of all people, it was Djinni. How? Why?

Were they calling the raid off? Hope and despair battered her at the thought. Hope that they might have, and she'd have a little more time to get herself together—despair that they might have, and they'd never get another chance. She jabbed at the microphone switch.

"Djinni," she croaked, her voice a harsh rasp. Crying did that. She hadn't screamed, not even when she fell. She never screamed anymore. "What?"

"You sound terrible," he said, his voice clear over the intercom. "Open up, Victrix. Let's talk."

She didn't want to let him in. She didn't like letting anyone into her space, but she didn't want to let *him* in, especially. Not at any time, particularly not now.

"I'm . . . kinda sick," she said. "Look, I'm in no shape to . . . just tell me what you want. Is the op canceled?" That was safe enough to ask. They were Echo. It could be *any* op.

"No," he replied, his head turning to appraise the hallway. It was quiet. They *seemed* to be alone, but who could take chances? They had come too far. "Let me in, maybe we can talk face to face, y'know, for a change."

"I'm sick," she repeated, and then had to grab for a waste basket, because she *was*. Great. Just great. "Trust me, you don't want to be in here right..." *urp* "...now." And the heaving just made her whole chest and shoulders and stomach wail with pain.

"I can take it," he began. "I've seen—"

"No!" she cried as her teeth clamped shut, fighting to keep her breathing steady and unlabored. Steady breathing. Hyperventilating only made the panic attack worse. "Please, just...I'll be all right, I just have to...I need to get..."

Djinni swore and counted to ten. *Patience,* he told himself. *She doesn't want you to come in, fine. You don't need to go in there, but she sure as hell needs to come out.*

"Look, this op—" It was a clumsy way to go about it, arguing with strained words to avoid being overheard by the wrong sort of people, the sort who might go running to Echo's new boss. And through a microphone when she was just feet away, on the other side of the door. He wasn't as good when he couldn't see the mark in question. He needed body language, facial cues and...

She's not a mark, he sighed. *Stop thinking of her as a mark. You used to have friends, y'know. Not everyone is a mark. Wait... since when? Gah. Just talk to her, show some empathy for once in your godforsaken existence.*

He started again. "This op, it...it needs..."

Damn it, girl, he's a teammate. He might even be a friend. You used to have friends, you know. "I'm sorry," she said. "I...I'll be ready. Really I will. My word on it. I just...need time to..." She paused. "I need about an hour. Get this thing under control. Got to have that, can't afford to medicate on this one..."

"It's not that," he interrupted. "Okay, it's sorta that. It's about you being ready. But not in there. Out here."

"Wha and huh?"

"Out here," he repeated. "We were cut off last time. You've done the research, we're prepped, and there's precious little you're going to be able to do to help stuck in there this time. I want you out here, with us, when we go in."

"I can't run Overwatch from out there!" she yelped.

"We don't *need* Overwatch, not this time. Think! Think where..."
He paused. "Think where this op is! You have tried to probe it,
you said so. You can't. There's nothing down there you can hack.
And you hit a wall with remote magic. It'll be a black hole for
you, except for our feeds. No more mediums, Victrix. I know
what I said, but I'm not willing to mess with your magic when
there's a simpler option! You're not channelling through me again,
you hear me? We need you there. *You*. And..."

He paused. "And you need this too."

Her vision misted over gray. She tried to say something, but
all that came out of her mouth was a wail of pure panic. She
couldn't even shape it into words.

The door next to Djinni slammed open, and he was shouldered
aside by a dripping wet blue girl wearing only a towel. She had a key
ring in her hand and was methodically opening every other lock.

"You fricking moron, what the hell is wrong with you?" Bella
snarled. "Are you *trying* to push every panic button she has?"

She got the door open, squeezed through it, and slammed it
in his face.

God, she smells good, Djinni thought. He thought of knocking
again. He even raised his hand to rap on the door. And then
what? Give his god-given talent at making things worse a go,
while trying hard to ignore the surge in his blood every time
he even got in mild proximity of that hot smurf? And that was
assuming he could even get in the door.

Man down, and we haven't even started.

"Breathe," Bella commanded, her wet hair dripping all over
the couch. Vickie obeyed. Meanwhile the healer was doing that
"laying on of hands" thing and the pain was...ebbing. Not gone,
never gone, but it felt like she could move again without sobbing.
"Long slow breaths, like I showed you. What the hell happened?
Before Red showed up."

"Fell," Vickie said, unclenching her teeth. "Le Parkour course.
Up the wall halfway."

Bella nodded, her face a mask of concentration. "Gotcha. Look,
he's—"

"Right," Vickie interrupted, fighting the wave of panic again.
"He's right. But I can't, not today." *Maybe not ever,* she added to
herself. "Just...can you get me working?"

Bella snorted. "Baby, I can 'get you working' in my sleep. Sera gave me a jolt of angel juice. Good God, if I could bottle that, I could make half of Atlanta metahuman and we'd roll over the Kriegers without even stopping to notice. Close your eyes and breathe."

"Don't be mad at him," Vickie said quietly. "He just tried to do what a good tactician would."

Bella just snorted again. "Breathe."

They were in. It had been easy. Pride had done exactly what he said he would. His supplied codes had worked and they sped through various access points with no need for on-the-spot jamming. The guard schedule had shown a brief window of thirty minutes when a skeleton crew worked before the next major shift rotation. Victrix, sounding as if that wail of panic had never crossed her lips, examined the video cameras via Red's feed and read him back the instructions on hacking them with the electronic doodads that Mel had in her pack, putting them on a loop of an empty corridor. The one time they'd encountered a lone guard on his way out of the bathroom, Mel had stepped forward and met the guard's gaze. He saw a group of black-clad and masked mercenaries rush him, and in the lead, Mel charged, hidden beneath a carefully constructed illusion of the renegade Blacksnake head, Jack. The guard shrank back in fear. And from beneath her illusion, Mel struck, knocking his legs out from under him while Pride descended and knocked him out. Bella made sure he was going to stay out... and that there was no permanent damage. They left him in a stall, sitting on a stool, door locked.

They were in. They were undetected and most importantly, they had planted an image of their patsy. Their plan, up to this point, was going well.

I've said it on many occasions, Djinni thought. *The best job is an inside job.*

"What is this place anyway?" Bella asked, frowning. "You'd think Echo would be using all this office space. Or whatever it is."

"They were until two days ago," Vickie replied. "Verd cleared it out and hasn't moved his own peeps in yet. Even Verdigris can't get a bureaucracy moving, not even when it's his own."

"'Specially not when Miz Ferrari is runnin' the bureaucracy," Yankee Pride chuckled.

"Shut up, Pr...prick!" Ramona hissed. She pointed at her head, then Pride's and made a harsh gesture with her hands. Pride nodded in apology.

Right, use the code names, he thought, admonishing himself for his stupidity. *Can't be too careful.*

"Check for an audio pickup?" said Vickie, with a touch of urgency. "Anything, might be something in a phone. Fifty feet around you ought to do it. Gadgeteer has the bug detector."

"We've been clean since we got through the last checkpoint," Mel answered, pointing to a small device on her wrist. Various lights representing meters flickered across the surface, bobbing up and down in slow and steady waves. "And once more, for the record, I want to remind you all that I *hate* my code name."

"I wish Appollonius wasn't so literal," Vickie fretted.

"Whatsa Appledorius?" Mel wanted to know.

"Appollonius of Tyana. He was a blind seer, mystic and mage," Vickie said absently. "I hate doing this thing blind. Though Appollonius was also one of the greatest magicians of his time. He was—"

"Knock it off," Red said, pointing his camera to the Vault door. "We're here. Picking up on this, Appollonius?"

"That's your objective, Badger."

"I should never have told you that story," he muttered. "Or let you pick the code names."

"Payback, she is a bitch."

"Yeah, yeah. So *we're* in position, give me readings."

As Mel stepped forward and gave the Vault a scan, Vickie felt a stab of guilt. The others might not have heard the accusation in Red's tone, but she had. She should be there, she should have been standing next to Mel, feeling about for any sign of arcane traps or locks. There shouldn't *be* any; Echo didn't believe in magic. But that was what they had thought about the Goldman Catacombs, and besides, there was a new boss in town. It had been a major topic of contention during the planning stages. Try as she might, Vickie couldn't penetrate this Vault at a distance, it had been properly shielded against any and all of her scrying efforts. There might be more overlap between magic and psionics than she had thought; certainly the place was buzzing with psionic white-noise generators; Bella said it was like having a bee in your head. Or it might just be that there was nothing in the way of natural materials there for her to get an anchor on.

Inevitably, someone had brought up the idea of her tagging along, of dealing with any mystical protection of the Vault on-site. Ramona's question was met with a moment of terrified blankness from Vickie, a warning look from Bella and an impatient shrug from Red Djinni. The compromise came from a surprising source, though reluctantly, from the Djinni himself. Victrix didn't need to come along, she could use a medium, preferably someone she had operated through before. Of them all, curiously, the easiest link was made through Red.

Mel stepped back, and shook her head. "I'm not reading any unusual cavities in the surrounding walls or unexpected read-ings from the door itself, electrical or otherwise. I think you can blow it."

Red didn't move, as he was busy fighting his own demons. Just days ago, he had silenced the fruitless arguing and had suggested acting as Victrix's medium. They were running low on options, and time, and he had put it out there to get them back on track. He hadn't really let it sink in, until today, what he was agreeing to.

This never ends well... this never ends well...

And just hours before, hadn't he tried to talk Victrix into leaving her nest, the safety of her home? But had he done this because she needed to be brave, because it made the most sense to have her with them? Or was he simply afraid? Afraid of giv-ing up control, of letting someone else surge through him with chaotic forces? It hadn't been the first time. And no, it never did seem to end well.

Did I cave for her or for me? For her strength or my weakness?

Finally, he drew a deep breath and stepped forward. Grimacing, he laid his hands on the door. "You set, Appollonius?"

"Yes sir," Vickie replied. "I'll make this as unobtrusive as possible."

"Gee, thanks," he muttered. "Hit it."

Back in her room, she stirred a little, winced as her abused muscles whimpered, her skin pulled and rippled with sharp pains. She took deep breaths, waiting for the hurt to subside, then narrowed her concentration and whispered the words of the mnemonic.

This was actually the opposite of the spell that had called Herb; that one was going out, this one was to allow things to come *in*. Her hand moved the planchette-mouse on the drawing board, the mouse drew—

Nothing, except—"There's nothing on the door," she reported. "But the Vault has something surrounding the inside. 'Something' is as close as I can get. It's like an energy field? Or an internal skin..."

"A giant dry cleaning bag," Mel suggested.

"That's not a bad analogy." Vickie said.

"What's it do?" Red asked between clenched teeth. He fought panic and a terrible desire to simply wrench his hands free and leave. Instead, he leaned in and pressed against the barrier, his arms trembling with the effort.

"Keeps things out. Like the psionic jammer except it's a field. So it's keeping magic out too. I don't think that's on purpose, but I'm not sure." She sighed. "The difference that makes no difference is no difference. It's sealed for someone's protection."

"Can I blow this door or not?" Red grated.

"Yes," Mel and Vickie said simultaneously.

"There is nothing on the *door,*" Vickie added.

Red withdrew his hands immediately from the barrier.

"Then get out of me," he snarled.

Vickie cut the connection abruptly. "Right, sorry," she stammered.

Red motioned for Mel to hand him her backpack, rummaged quickly through it for the battery-sized explosives and the detonator, and went to work.

He didn't say another word.

The door supports had snapped with muffled pops as the suppressors on the encased explosives muffled the blast. The barrier started to fall, and was deftly caught by Pride who struggled under the weight. He was soon joined by the others. Slowly, they eased the door aside and cautiously entered the Vault. Beyond the portal was a large room, everything in it stored haphazardly, as if people had just shoved things in here they knew vaguely were valuable without knowing quite what anything was, or did. They saw the expected cache of weapons, sealed file cabinets, a couple of racks of armor, bottles and jars and boxes that could have come out of ancient tombs or been teleported from the future.

And there, finally, they saw Alex Tesla's sleek, futuristic desk. It had been dumped off to the side and shoved up against a wall, like a thing of no importance. Obviously the only reason it was here was because—

Ramona walked up to it and rattled a drawer. Or tried, the drawer was pretty solid. "Locked," she said. "Not something easily jimmied. That's probably why it got sent here. V—no one wanted to take the chance that it might have something important in it, but since no one took dynamite to it, they just don't know whether there is something important or just pencils, staplers and a bottle of acid reflux pills."

"Appollonius," Pride said. "Are you able to read this room now that the door has been blown? More importantly, can you do something to circumvent the lock?"

"No," Vickie answered in frustration, her hand extended in front of her as she pushed on the distant barrier. "That field is still keeping me out. I haven't found a way to crack through it yet. Which tells me it's psionic, and keeping me out is secondary. I don't know enough about psi to get leverage on this thing. It's like wrestling with a wet snake."

"Goddamn it," Bella muttered, shaking her head as if something was in her ears. "She's right, it's psi, it's like having a high-pitched whine in my head...getting louder..." Suddenly she froze. "Oh, shit— *Everybody out!*"

Too late.

An alarm sounded as a secondary barrier slammed down out of the ceiling, covering the hole where the Vault door had been. The air vents gushed clouds of pale white vapor. Pride's head snapped up, his eyes widening as he realized he was right under one of the ceiling vents. He got a faceful, and went down as if he'd been poleaxed.

Vickie slammed her hands down on her desk, her eyes frantically scanning all the feeds as one by one, her team fell limp, like a bunch of rag dolls. The telemetry said they weren't dead—of course not, this was an Echo vault, and Verd hadn't had a chance to go lethal with countermeasures. They were all down. All of them. Except...

Of course.

Djinni.

"Don't you breathe?" she screeched, her eyes fixed to his camera feed. He was darting about the room, his hands running along the walls. Meanwhile she was running a fast search through the Echo protocols for what the hell they might have as knockout gas in a vault.

"It's Urmayan—!" she shouted.

"It's Urmayan gas, yeah." Red grunted. "I'm somewhat resistant to it."

"You're *resistant* to . . . ?" she stopped, for once, totally without words. "Okay, look, there's stuff in Bella's medic pack that should wake them all up. Vials are coded red, premeasured doses in single-use hypos—"

"That's great," Red gasped, "but someone should have a talk with the techs who set this up. The dosage is too high! I'm starting to get a massive headache, and our friends here will have brain damage if they're exposed for much longer! I need to get this damned door open!"

Vickie swiveled in her chair to face a side monitor, which displayed a rapidly scrolling page of schematics.

"Left, about three feet!" she yelled. "Square metal control panel!"

Red leapt and tackled a stack of crates away from the wall, revealing the panel in question. He reached under his jacket and removed a sturdy blade. He jammed it behind the panel plate and threw his shoulder against the hilt. Slowly, the plate was dislodged and, finding a grip with his fingers, he wrenched it free. He stumbled back. He was getting groggy. He struck himself in the face, hard, and reeling forward, he speared his entire hand into the newly formed hole and closed his fist around a mess of wires.

No time to get fancy. . . .

With a shout he pulled, gasping from the strain, and managed to tear away a tangled mesh of rubber and metal, leaving an exposed clump of cable. He drove his blade into it and collapsed as he neatly electrocuted himself while shorting out the system. A moment passed, and then there was the sound of a *thunk* as the barrier locks released.

"Re—*Badger!* You have to raise it! It won't come up by itself!"

"Yeah . . ." Red stammered, his words beginning to slur. "I know . . . I . . . whoa . . . balance is a bitch—"

He stumbled forward, falling to his knees by the door. His arms fell as he reached forward, fumbling for any semblance of a grip on the smooth steel. He took a couple of deep breaths, and began to cough and hack and wheeze.

"*Burn something!*" she yelled. "You'll either set off the sprinklers and that will clear the air some or you'll clear some of the gas!"

"No . . . time . . ." Red coughed. It was time to break some rules.

No names, no powers, nothing to link them to the theft, that had been key. But they had been stopped in their tracks, and they were dying. It was worth the risk, and on the off chance *something* was watching them, Red prayed this was small enough to escape notice. Still, he had to be sure, he had to...

He glanced to his right, and saw Bella lying motionless on the ground.

"To hell with it!" he heard himself say, he heard himself *snarl*, as small, pointed and ultradense claws sprang from the tips of his gloves. He thrust his fingers under the door, heard the metal squeal in protest and he dug his fingertips beneath the bottom. He hopped to his feet, and with a low groan that slowly crescendoed into a scream, he pulled himself up, and with him came the door. He managed to bring it up, waist high, and prop it open with a toppled crate. He rolled out, coughing and shaking his head, on all fours, his chest heaving.

The gas, which had begun to saturate the room, flooded out into the hall. In moments, the haze of the room became clearer, though much of the faintly vanilla odor—and effect—of the Urmayan lingered in the air.

The alarm continued to blare.

"*Get up!*"

Red shook with a start, struggling to come to his feet.

"Time to move!" Vickie urged him, her voice sounding hoarse. "There's still gas in there, enough to keep everyone knocked out! The stim shots won't do the others any good till it's cleared out, and it's just building in the hallway now too! You don't see a fan in there, do you?"

"Gimme a time, Appie," he growled, shaking his head. "We're on the clock here."

"Ten minutes until the new guard shift, less for the current crew to rush your location. Can you drag the desk out into the hall so I can hack it?"

Red took a deep breath and ran into the Vault. He skidded to a halt by the desk, and shoved at it. He might as well have been shoving the SunTrust Building. "No can do."

"Blow it apart?"

"This isn't a door. We'll wreck your MacGuffin."

"Hack it apart?"

"With *what?*"

"Your *claws!*"

"It's solid *steel,* woman! Damn it, we need a mage, *here,* now! Get someone!"

"*Who?*" she shouted back. "Name me one! I don't know anybody nearer than Savannah!"

"*Then get your ass in here.* Wiggle your nose, teleport, whatever it is you do, but I—*we*—need you here, *now!*"

"And without the mystical landing pad I become a thin smear of pink goo on the floor. Good one, great solution." She'd try it anyway, she *would,* if she didn't already know what always happened. Send Herb? He'd never dig there in time.

"Okay..." Red panted, sinking to his knees, placing his face close to the ground, where the air was clearer. "Okay. Think... think... we need to get into this desk, and we need to clear this area of gas... and we need to do it ten minutes ago...."

Vickie cursed and lurched to her feet, too frantic to simply sit still in her chair. "Okay! You were right! I should be there! If I was in that room, I could clear it! And I could hack that damn desk!" She sobbed a little. "If I was only *there!*"

"If you... what?"

"If I was *there!* You were right! I was wrong! You moron! I—I—I—" The last words came out as a sad little squeak. "I'm just so damn scared...."

"I heard you," Red grunted, and he began to crawl towards the door. "What if you had no reason to be? What if you..." He paused as he rolled out in the hallway.

"No reason to be—what? Scared?" *Gee, that would be nice... maybe when pigs flew.* "No reason to be there?"

"—had nothing to lose?"

"What are you *talking* about?" Vickie demanded. It had to be the gas. It was making him babble.

"No risk... well, to you anyway." Djinni coughed and, startled, felt something wet splat against the inside of his hood. He pulled it up and felt about his mouth. Sticky. He drew his hand up, and saw the blood. So much for nonlethal. It looked like Verd *had* gotten in here. Easiest way to turn non into lethal? Pump up the dosage, no other change required. "Not a lot of time here, Appie, so tell it to me straight. Can you take me over?"

She felt as if she'd been sucker-punched. "You mean body-surf? Uh—that's really unethical—" *Except with consent.* "Uh—yes? But—"

<*Jeebus, Vic . . . that's dangerous.*> Grey hopped up onto the desk and stared at her with eyes the size of his food bowl. <*To you, I mean. He knows shit about the risk.*>

"It's easy enough," she lied. Well, it wasn't exactly a lie. The enchantment was easy. It was the fallout that was hard. "The spell is easy, fast. It's dangerous, though. Really dangerous."

No shit, Red thought. *Remember the last time? Remember . . . No. Don't think about it, don't . . . just . . . just . . .*

His head was spinning. He slapped himself hard, just enough for one more moment of clarity. There wasn't a choice. To hell with the consequences! He needed to let her do this, or they were dead. He swung his head to the side, and caught a blurred picture of his team lying there, helpless, and again, his eyes locked on the still form of Bella. She was dying. Bella was dying . . .

"*Do it!*" Red screamed.

The next thirty seconds or so went past in a blur. The spell required willpower, magic energy, and something physical from both parties, and the ability to twist your mind through the complex mathemagical calculations that flung one soul into another body.

Then came the spinning, disorientation of the thing taking hold. She already had the second spell to clear the gas out of him queued up; it fired as she took possession.

Then she was *there,* and with it her first clear thought . . .

Footsteps. Many of them. And moving fast.

She was up, riding a wave of adrenaline as she flung herself against the corner. There were people she needed to take out without killing them, and she acted on instinct and training, but with a body that responded *instantly* and didn't fight her or seize up without warning.

The first came around a corner and gaped at her. She got his baton off his belt before he even started to move.

Holy crap, Red's fast. . . .

Proper application of force to the right point on his head and he was down and she was on to the next, who didn't even know she was there when she hit him. The third did, but he was only human, no way he could counter her in time. Then the fourth who got a shot off that ricocheted off the wall behind her before she knocked him cold and then—

It was over. Twenty seconds, from start to finish.

That was when she doubled over, suddenly overwhelmed with sensory overload. It *hurt*, and she was struck by a wave of panic. No! It wasn't fair! Even now, even out of her scarred and broken body, she felt her skin flare up and bombard her with jagged needles...twisting mercilessly...

But it wasn't all pain, some of it was...

...*my god...my god...* it was like having skin radar, she was aware of *everything*...

It all piled on top of her and she almost passed out. *I'm...in his skin...why does it hurt?*

...*can't pass out now*...

She fought it. Sorted through it, just the same as when she had to sort through spellweaving or computer hacking or the combination of the two. Unraveled it. *This* was the radar and it could go over there and *this* was the heat sense and *this*...

This was the pain. His pain. Not unlike hers. Really the only difference was...

Was that his body still worked. Hers didn't. That was the only difference.

Jeebus, Red, she thought, with the force and direction that she needed to "talk" to the person whose body she was riding, *I had no idea.* She waited for his response.

There was no response.

The hell?

He had let the fog come, as he knew it would, as he had trained himself to so long ago. Granted, it was easier this time, what with the Urmayan doing its thing. But before, there had been another Red, a foolish, reckless boy who sought to peer behind the curtain of all of life's mysteries. Damn the torpedoes, pedal to the metal, it was about speed and near misses and the brass ring. Once upon a time, Red Djinni could give a shit about consequences.

He had gotten tired of the constant defeats at the hands of local heroes, even Amethist, and had decided that he needed to stop running solo. He began trying to recruit other young metas and individuals gifted with paranormal abilities; tried, but that wasn't what he got. A few of his recruits had...other talents.

To his astonishment, Red found himself surrounded by young men and women who practiced something he hadn't believed in at first. Magic. One had a feeble but growing ability to summon creatures, another could channel and control elements, and a third had the unnerving ability to project her consciousness into other bodies—animal at first, but then as she got better at it, human. Together, they experimented and came to an odd synergy, at times a real unity, defying the usual boundaries that delineated the realms of summoning, conjuration, elemental control and outright witchcraft. And Red, fascinated by the new world they showed him, became an enthusiastic participant. He was never actually good at it; he simply did not have the patience or aptitude for any of their disciplines. Though he was, they had to agree, the most remarkable medium they had ever come across.

It began simply enough. Why do the jobs themselves, when they could control others? They took risks, crossed some lines they probably shouldn't have, and defied the odds. And soon, they grew bored with petty larceny. They delved deeper, expanding the breadth of their experiments, heady with the excitement brought by power, by knowledge, until there was only hunger for more. It stopped being about the job. It turned into an addiction for *experience,* and each one had to be bigger, more risky than the last.

For Red, his rush came as a willing participant. He became all too familiar with the surge of power as he accepted another consciousness into himself, at the drive and burn of two distinct minds working in perfect unison. He fed from it, adored the synergy.

Right up until the day everything went horribly wrong.

Caught up in the fog of transition, he couldn't block the memory out. Though silent, he screamed as he felt her die, her own screams ringing out through the furthest recesses of his mind, falling away, as his will smothered hers. He had loved her and he had killed her. Even now, so many years later, he could still feel her final moments.

He wept as he opened his eyes, his hand moving instinctively to wipe away the tears.

The hell?

His hand *hurt.* Sharper, yet more diffuse, different—no, it wasn't just his hand, it was everywhere, there was nothing that didn't hurt.

So what? You're used to that . . .

No, this was different. Victrix was the rider, he was the submerged conciousness. He shouldn't be able to move at all, to breathe, to smell, or to control *anything!* And the pain, it overwhelmed him. There was nothing to temper it, no radial senses, nothing from his skin except pain. It was like being partly deaf, yet partly bludgeoned with sound until you bled out of every orifice.

He sat up in shock and quickly scanned the room. He was half-reclining, in some kind of chair, in the dark, a wall of flickering monitors in front of him. And the biggest cat he had ever seen was glaring down at him from a perch on a desk beside him.

Cat...monitors...

He looked down and tore the glove off his hand. He hissed through clenched teeth, horrified by what he saw.

Victrix...what have you done?

Shitshitshitshit. She knew what had happened. Her team, in the Goldman Catacombs, her watching Red hurtle deftly over obstacles, and that one unguarded moment, that one instant of *stupid, unthinking* loss of control. That one phrase.

"I wish I was you."

Magicians could not, *could not* lose control like that. *Especially* dared not use the fatal words "I wish." Words were power in the mouth of a mage. Words became spells when you said them with as much longing as she had. She had set in motion something that had only been waiting to pounce.

Moron. Idiot. Stupid bitch. Guilt hammered her.

She let it drive her. Guilt was a good substitute for strength and could put a needle-sharp point on will. First things first, a transmutation spell, Urmayan gas into its antidote. Fortunately she didn't need to know the chemical composition to make an antidote; she just had to "tell" the gas to become its opposite, using the laws of similarity, opposites and contagion. Quickly, before the stuff could start to make Red's body dizzy again, she concocted the right set of calculations, set her will at the beginning, and blazed through them to the end, as focused and controlled as her ill-considered phrase had been vague and reckless.

"Fiat mutacio," she whispered, and there was a faint flash of light and a little release of heat as the molecules of gas transmuted.

She braced herself as Red's knees buckled. That took...a chunk out of both of them. Nothing comes out of nothing, everything has a price. Transmutation costs in energy. Just a good thing this was a gas; not a lot of mass to transmute.

When she thought she could move, she stumbled over to Bella, and rooted in her medical kit for the stimulator shots in their preloaded syringes, then went from one to another of the team, giving them hits into the jugular. Bella first. The clock was ticking.

Red stared in morbid fascination at the corded, scarred thing that had been under Victrix's glove. It actually looked a lot more like the hand of something that had died and mummified in the desert than a human hand. It *worked* all right, but, *hell,* it hurt. In fact, his—her—whole body hurt like that. And everything was . . . damaged, damage that interfered with each movement. There was delay, there was hesitation, but more than anything else, there was a *hitch* when he tried to move, exactly like rusted machinery, catching and lurching instead of working smoothly, and each lurch causing more pain.

No wonder she couldn't run the Le Parkour course.

"The hell—" he muttered. "What does something like this?"

The cat stared down coldly at him from the desk. <*That's what happens when you lose a mage duel, asshat,*> it said, right into his head. He started. He'd had telepaths in his head before, but never this strong. <*You want to know what does something like that, leaves someone with third- and fourth-degree burns from neck to toes? That's what happens when you steal a very nasty magical artifact from your uncle and he comes after you and finds out you destroyed it. She's just "lucky" the family intervened and lucky they know a boatload of magical healers.*>

Red stared at the cat. "Family feud?" he ventured. *Third- and fourth-degree burns? How do you survive that?*

The cat snorted. <*Not that simple. The Nagys are hereditary vampire hunters. The thing made you and everyone with you invisible to vampires, so most of the family tried not to think too hard about where it came from. Her father Alex wouldn't have anything to do with it, but the Euro-trash branch wasn't so picky. They'd pass it around to whoever was currently on the Fangs' hit list. But it was created around the time that Rome fell by murdering ninety-nine children, and the power had to be renewed with the blood of another nine children every eighteen years. Year eighteen was coming up. Vickie stole and destroyed it.*>

The cat hesitated.

<*There's more to the story than that, but that part's not mine to*

tell. But this is why she's a wreck of a recluse, loathes herself and has panic attacks. And why she freaks when she thinks someone is going to see what's under all the clothing. This is why she breaks her heart and her neck on a Le Parkour course simpler than the ones she used to fly over as easily as you do. Everything hurts, and what doesn't hurt, doesn't work anymore.> The cat turned away, then abruptly turned back, glaring at him with icy yellow eyes. <And there is only one reason why I don't slit your throat right now and leave her the sole tenant of that very agile, healthy carcass of yours.>

"Why's that?" Red croaked.

<She'd never forgive me.>

The clock was ticking. When she was as sure as she could be that the rest of the team was going to be all right, Vickie went back to the desk. She toggled Red's private freq back to the Overwatch suite as she stared at the desk, drawing little arcane diagrams on it with her finger to see what answers came up. *Talk to me, my friend. Tell me what I need to know. Who can make you give up what I need, and what does he need to tell you to do it?* "Grey. Grey, damn it, grow some fingers and take over the comm freqs," she muttered, feeling the mic hidden under the skin of his throat vibrate. "We both know you can. Use the damn vocoder app and the keyboard."

"Keep your fur on, I was doing it," said the Stephen Hawking-like voice in her earpiece. *"You inflicted me with an unwelcome interloper in here."*

"I know, it was an accident, put me on speaker, please. Badger? I am sorry, sorry, this is all my fault, I'll ... I'll explain later." She drew a few more diagrams and read the crude answers. Law of Contagion: the desk "knew" exactly what it needed to release the unit. She just had to ask the right questions. "I'll reverse it, but I need to be with you to do it. If you can figure out the comms, go ahead and take over. I swear to you, I will recompense you whatever you demand for doing this to you. Aha."

The last was because she saw it; saw how to convince the desk to make the unit come out. She needed to give the desk power in a form it could use, the DNA of the next in succession, and code phrases. Fortunately she had the next in succession right here.

Pride was just beginning to stand up and move. She got him

and dragged him back to the desk, taking his right hand and and slapping it down onto the invisible—to everyone but her—DNA sampling and recognition scanner. She drew him closer and whispered in his ear. "Get your face close to your hand, whisper your name, Echo serial number, then say 'Protocol Open Sesame,'" she hissed in his ear, as she fed the desk broadcast energy from the portable unit Mel had in her pack to run their tools.

Pride looked at her blankly, but finally nodded and did as he was told.

The desk considered these things for a moment, then there was a little pop of locking mechanisms springing open, and as Pride took his hand away, a panel in the middle of the desk slid back, and something rose up.

It wasn't obviously the bizarre communication device Vickie had seen before—but she recognized parts of it, folded down flat, the whole of it making a transportable object about the size of the Oxford English Dictionary. The code words that the desk had revealed to her had made the desk prepare the communicator for transportation.

She hefted it; it didn't weigh too much. Ramona could pack it out. She stowed it in the backpack they'd brought for that purpose and dropped it next to the detective, then scooped up a second pack—because they were going to have to make this look like they'd come after something else. She made a dash into the shelves, scooping up small things that looked valuable or dangerous. And then she saw something that made her heart race.

She knew what they were; little self-contained camera units in spheres about the size of a golf ball. But they were in a box marked "Antigrav self-propelled camera/sensor units, Verdigris Dynamics" with a sticker slapped next to the label that said NOT YET WORKING AS DESIGNED. Of course they weren't. Only the Thulians had antigrav at the moment. But *she* had levitation.

She dumped the whole box in her pack and came sprinting back to the others.

They were all on their feet now, if a bit unsteady. "Come on, people," she said in an urgent growl. "Get with the looting! Guns, experimental ammo, armor, whatever you can carry without compromising maneuverability. Next wave will be here any minute."

Bella stared at her, slightly unfocused, then did a double take. "You're not—"

Vickie made a shushing motion. "Explain later, move now." She looked frantically around for a weapon. A nonlethal weapon.

And then she saw it. About the size and length of a broom handle, but Echo nanofiber. A little shorter than a quarterstaff, but that would make it easier to use in a corridor. And in her hands, lethal or nonlethal as she chose.

She seized it, and started herding the others out. *Well, this should help confuse things. Red Djinni's not a staff-fighting expert as far as I know...*

Red stared at the monitors, and watched his team scramble to fill their pockets with anything small and important-looking. Through Bella's cam, he saw Mel pause and pick up an energy rifle. From time to time, he glanced at the cat, Grey (as Victrix had called him), who stared back, his luminescent eyes fixed in an angry glare.

He had heard Vickie's apology. "It was my own damn stupid fault, and no excuses. I said I *wished I was you*. I know better, I *knew* better and I'm not going to say it just slipped out. I screwed up, but we both got bit in the ass. Whatever it takes to make this right with you, I *will* do." He had not answered.

The cat bared its fangs. *<In case you haven't figured it out, no magician with any sense or morals ever says "I wish." A mage uses words like tools. Saying the words makes a spell, that's where the term "en-chant-ment" comes from. She screwed up. That spell was just sitting there, lurking, waiting for her to do something that would make it come home. Now she's just created another spell, this time on purpose. She's just bound herself to do whatever it is you want, however much it costs her, to make this right with you. No term limits. No time limits. It doesn't end until you say "now I'm satisfied." I hope you appreciate that. Because if you don't...>* The cat showed a little more fang.

Red ignored him, and brought Vickie's hand up, forcing himself not to cringe as he painfully balled up her fingers into a fist.

"She's lived with this, for how long?" he asked.

<Four years. Almost five.>

"And this is what keeps her here, in this little room," Red mused. "Of course, only four years..."

<Not exactly. A lot of psychological damage too. Panic attacks, especially fear of crowds and strangers. Fear they'll see the scars.>

"Well, *yeah,* duh..."

Red reached down, picked up Vickie's glove, and put it on. "Jesus," he said, finally. "I had no idea."

<Nobody does but me. Hiding is something she's good at.>

"Yes, hiding, that *would* come first," Red mused, closing his eyes and leaning back. "But not forever. She ..." His eyes snapped open, and he turned to Grey. "Has she given up?"

<For a while. The Nazis changed that.> The cat licked its whiskers. *<Might have been the best thing to happen to her in four years. If you ask me.>*

"A wake-up call, yeah. Lot of that going around."

The cat turned its attention to the monitors. *<Oh, look at that. That's my girl. That's my little warrior.>*

The team had gathered up the loot and gotten their behinds in motion while he and the cat had been staring at each other. And they had just run into the second wave of Echo guards. Vickie—Red—had jumped right into the middle of them, and was laying out the guards with some very pretty quarterstaff work.

<The school she went to doesn't turn out pasty-faced Dungeons and Dragons wannabe mages. Mens sana in corpore sano. The St. Rhiannon School demands physical ability to support the magical ability—can be marksmanship, martial arts, Le Parkour, anything that works the body out. She always loved the physical side, especially the fighting, the weapons. Any martial art. Maybe because she's so short. You know, compensation.>

"Yeah, yeah," Red nodded, watching himself move on the monitors. "She's good, plenty of training ... experience ... I see it. It's all there. So why can't she do that all the time?"

<Try standing up and walking around, dipshit.>

Red obliged, and rose to his feet. He felt the muscles scrape across themselves, her skin scream in protest at the slightest movement. He took a tentative step, then another, noting the fire that seemed to erupt from every limb. He arched his back, then bent forward. More pain. It was considerable, he had to admit, but familiar.

<Now do something fast and see what happens.> The cat cocked its head to the side.

Red turned to look at Grey, his stance relaxed and still. The next moment, he held the cat by its throat. Vickie's body erupted in pain, but more than that, it didn't move as he would have expected, and he grunted from the shock.

Grey hissed, wriggled free and leapt away. *<Asshat. I'd have bit you if it hadn't been her body you're wearing. Did you feel that? Everything lurching sideways and twisted?>*

Red returned to his seat, deep in thought.

"Sure," he said, finally. "Nothing that can't be compensated for, eventually. It's still all there. She's got the goods. She needs to see that."

<Exactly. But she's never had anyone to show her how. You've got to be in there to understand what doesn't work right, what can be fixed by specific exercises, what you can stretch out and what you can't. She's a mage and a fighter and a computer wizard. A physical therapist, she ain't.>

Red pointed to the monitors. "Look at her. You can't see it, you walking set of fiddle strings, but she's still in pain. That's *my* skin she's wearing now, and it's not a picnic. But look at her..."

He motioned as Vickie delivered a devastating roundhouse kick, transitioning to a smooth leg sweep, felling two more guards.

"... She's still got it. It's not the body. There's something else in her way."

<Don't look at me. I'm a cat, not a shrink.>

Red glanced at Grey, then turned back to the monitors and watched.

CHAPTER TWENTY

Illusion

MERCEDES LACKEY AND DENNIS LEE

The rest of the team was at CCCP HQ in Sovie's medical bay, being checked up on. Obviously the last place any of them wanted to go was the Echo base hospital. They were all still showing the effects of a gas overdose. If Bell hadn't been loaded with a shot of power from the Seraphym, she probably would have died; as it was, they were tying her down to a bed, despite her protests.

Vickie managed to fob them off, aping Red's habitual rudeness, and escaped. She had to get back, give Red his body back. That was not an option.

The apartment looked strange through his eyes. Different angle, he was nearly twice her height. And his vision . . . she thought he might see a bit further into both ends of the spectrum than she did. She dropped the pack of camera spheres and other intriguing tech just inside the door, and Bella's med pack beside it, staggering with weariness. She could return Bella's pack later. Too much; too much for too long, and she was drained, not only of physical stamina but of magical energy. She had to go face Red, once she had stuffed this body full of fast-burn calories, and beg him for the time to recharge.

She stumbled over to the kitchen. Now that she wasn't fighting and running on adrenaline, control was a little more problematic, He was much, much taller than she was and had longer arms; she kept overshooting when she reached for things.

Magicians burn a lot of calories, and what with her stomach almost always being in nervous revolt, she stockpiled protein shakes and glucose drinks in the fridge. She reached for one of each, then pulled off his trademark scarf to drink them.

And caught a distorted glimpse of his face in the reflective glass door of the microwave.

She looked away, quickly. So that was the rest of it, besides the pain and the disorientation of his skin-sense. No wonder he kept his face hidden. He wasn't in this skin now, she was; she didn't know how to control it, and what she had just seen was the real Djinni. She brought his hands up to touch his face. He should have had a chiseled profile; the bones under the skin were good. Strong and, well, manly. But the skin hung off those bones like the jowels and sagging hide of a Shar-Pei. He was all scars and wrinkles and pendulous folds. Tight in places, bizarre and loose in others. He looked as if some sort of monstrous sfx makeup had been applied to him. It was as ugly as her own scarred body, enough to disgust anyone who might have caught a glimpse. But she knew, she understood, and again, like his pain, she was surprised at how familiar it all was. For all he could do in this powerful body, he was trapped in it. Just like she was. And like her, she knew damn well he would *never* show it to anyone... except, maybe...

Maybe that *other* Victoria.

She gulped down the shake and the glucose quickly, then picked up the scarf and carefully did not think about what to do when putting it back on. She relied on his muscle memory, so it would be tied correctly, and with luck he wouldn't know it had ever been off. Right. Time to face the music. She steeled herself, and walked his body into the Overwatch room.

Two sets of eyes glared at her; her own, and Grey's. She felt the glare as if it was a body blow; braced herself for anger. "I need ten more minutes, Red," she said quietly, and sat right down on the floor, bracing herself against the wall. "I'm not stalling. I actually have got to take a rest. I'm running on empty and I can't put you back right this second."

The truth was, she needed that ten minutes for something else as well. She had to convince herself that she wanted her own body back. That was harder than it sounded; despite the pain of his skin, the weirdness of being in a male body, the disorientation of his skin radar, she'd had, for the last hour or so, more physical freedom than she'd had in five years. She'd wanted the body to do something, and it *did* it, without hesitation.

She convinced herself—bone deep conviction—by the only means that worked. Keeping his body was *wrong*. It was his, not hers. And though she cried inside for losing it, that didn't matter. She was steeped in ethics, perhaps more so now than when she had been whole. What mattered, what always mattered, was doing the right thing.

The silence built for an awfully long time. Finally she broke it. "It would help if you'd say something. At least I would know whether I need to break out the radiation shield after I put you back. You know, for when you nuke me." More silence; she felt her spirits sinking. "Hello? Earth to Djinni?"

"Put us back," was all he said. Actually, he growled. Vickie ignored the oddity of his intonation and inflection overlaid on her light soprano.

She hauled herself to her feet. A quick internal check said she just—barely—had enough to pull it off. "This won't take long. Just let me check a few things first."

The swap back was mathemagically a lot more complicated than the swap out—because, as she said, she was an ethical mage and had to be sure she left nothing of herself behind. She went to the computer to double- and triple-check her computations and diagrams, ran a few simulations to make sure she had the best probability that Heisenberg wasn't going to kick in and Murphy was going to leave her alone. Then she knelt next to him. Herself. *Remember, that's me. I need to be in there. I need to be in there.* She looked herself in the eyes, stared into her own eyes and let the power build. When it felt as if it was going to explode, she powered through the calculations. "*Fiat reverto,*" she croaked, wanting with every fiber to be back where she belonged.

There came that feeling of falling through the universe, where there was no up or down. Then, with a mingled sense of triumph and bitter disappointment, she felt all the old pains, the old aches, the all-too-familiar tightness and cramping and she knew before she opened her eyes that she was back.

But she opened her eyes anyway to make sure that *he* was, too.

The glare alone told her. She swallowed. "Grey? Bugger off. I'm back."

The cat sniffed, stuck its tail and nose in the air, jumped down off the desk and stalked out the door.

"So should I get to my fallout shelter?" she asked in a small voice.

Red stood up and moved about the room, testing his limbs and stretching. He craned his neck and grunted as he felt his vertebrae strain and pop. He sank down, resting on the balls of his feet and bowed his head.

"It seems you can move after all," he said, finally.

She got up. Slowly. As usual, she had to catch herself a little and as usual, her right side tightened up in a cramp. "As long as I'm not piloting *this* thing," she said, trying to make it sound... well, less than bitter.

"It's more than that," he replied. "You might have noticed this body isn't much fun either."

"I'm sorry," she said. "If I'd known... but it was... amazing." She bit her lip. "It was so good. I mean—I haven't moved like that except in dreams for a long time. Your body... it moves right. No, more than that, it moves brilliantly. Like driving a perfectly balanced, perfectly tuned sportscar."

"Yours could too," Djinni said. His face shifted beneath his scarf, and she saw the hint of laugh lines creep into view around his eyes. "Just ask Grey."

"You're... you're not angry?" She could hardly believe it. He wasn't mad?

"I'm trying not to be," was all he could manage. "It was an accident, Victrix. You don't think I get that? Hell, if you knew the shit I've pulled... well. I was watching you, and you can move. Now you just have to move..."

He pointed to her body.

"... in *there*."

She bit back every angry reply she wanted to make, swallowed down a sob, and tried very, very hard to only say the truth. "I try. I... don't know how. Everything I try seems to make things worse."

"You're fighting yourself, you know. I was just in there. I think you can get past this."

She shook her head violently. "It's all been broken and put together wrong. It's like trying to hold water in a cup you glued back together."

"But it can be done. You can fix it. I'm not saying it won't take time, but as much as you need to heal here"—he leaned forward, and gently took her arm—"my guess is you've a lot more to deal with up here..."

He reached up, and laid his hand softly on her head.

This was, literally, the first time a man had touched her, physically, since the healers had finished with her and said there was nothing more they could do. And it wasn't—professional. It wasn't hesitant. Her eyes stung for a moment.

Then her mind raced after possibilities. If he was right... maybe... "Maybe I can figure out some sort of... if I could channel magic energy on a microlevel like I do with the tech..."

And then he was up, his hands withdrawn and his back turned angrily to her.

"For god's sake... *magic*? Again with the magic? When will you learn? Haven't you seen enough yet? Haven't you *felt* enough? Look at you! Your hands, your whole body... *Wake up! That's magic, Vickie!*"

She felt as if he had dumped a barrel of ice water on her. "You... you *saw*?" She froze, every muscle seizing up. "*You saw?*"

Then anger flooded her. "And... and how is that different from you? Okay, it wasn't magic that melted your face, it was your own damn powers! So haven't *you* seen enough, felt enough? How is that different?"

He turned, and she felt the heat blaze from his eyes. He came at her, but there was no gentleness this time. He was shaking with rage, and with rough hands he grabbed at her arms and brought her to her feet.

"*How DARE you!*" he shouted. "*How DARE you take off my...*"

"You took off my gloves too, and you had no reason to!" she squeaked. "I was down to zero, dehydrated, I needed to get a drink! I didn't—there's—" The words froze in her throat.

"*Goddamn it, woman!*" he screamed. "*I've killed people for this!*"

All she could do was stare at him. His grip on her arms was so excruciatingly painful, and she was so afraid, she couldn't even manage a single word. She desperately wanted to apologize for the inadvertent violation, and couldn't.

Red shuddered, fighting to control his anger. She was scared, and he was hurting her. He looked down incredulously at his hands, at the deep impressions they made on her arms, and he released her.

She collapsed to the ground and held herself, refusing to look at him. He backed away, shocked at—himself? At her? She couldn't tell.

Slowly, she looked up at him, so desperate to try and say something, and so unable to, that two tears of frustration burned their way down her cheeks. And there, she felt her strength growing again, founded in anger.

"We're both scarred," she said finally, her tone bleak and forced. "Inside and out. So tell me, Djinni... how is it different?"

He knelt again, his hands reaching for the knots of his scarf.

"Don't you get it?" he said, jerking the concealing fabric off. He brought his terrible face close to hers, his eyes crazed and his mouth drawn into a feral snarl. "I didn't have a say in this! This was years of neverending pain and total loss of control. I suffered, and not *once* could I figure out a reason *why*!"

He gestured wildly towards her. "This! This was a result of *your* actions! Even now, you keep messing with this crap! You keep defending it! Why? *Why?*"

Why? Because it was as much a part of her as his skin was a part of him! Because it was all she had! Because it was the only thing left that made her anything other than a pitiful cripple hiding in the dark!

Because it was the only thing she had that she could *fight* with!

"What do you want from me?" she cried, hands balled into painful fists. "What possible thing can I do to satisfy you?"

"I want you to stop doing magic!" he shouted.

Vickie gasped. She felt the geas close in around her like the jaws of a trap.

The Djinni had made his wish.

Red stormed out, so full of rage that if he had not already left her in a state of stunned shock, she would have been so completely terrified of that anger that she would have run and hidden in the closet, then curled up into a fetal ball as she had the day of the Invasion.

But now...she had felt his demand settle into the spell, eviscerating her, and as with anyone mortally wounded, she was too numb to feel anything yet. That would change. But...she could finish this before the shock wore off.

<*Vic? Vic? What'd he say? What's wrong?*> Grey came bounding back into the room, followed by Herb.

She had to get them out of here. No way she could do what she intended to with them still here. "Nothing. Nothing important. Look, I'm beat, would you two go get the mail for me?" That was easy, believable; Grey and Herb did that all the time.

<*Well...okay...*> Grey cast a doubtful look at her, but she kept her best poker face on.

And the moment they were outside the door, she slammed it. She threw all the locks and drove her hand across a heavy set of books perched upon a floating bookshelf, letting them tumble to the floor, and exposing a small numeric key panel. She punched in the code and blinked as several panels in the ceiling popped open, releasing a dormant spell and activating her emergency mage-shields. It was old magic, caged magic—she had not broken the terms of the geas.

Grey and Herb wouldn't be able to get to anyone in time. Bella and the rest were all the way across town. Grey could apport, but only through walls.

By the time he got anyone, it would be over.

She'd planned this a long time ago, against the day when it all became too much to bear. She made sure no one was aware how close to the edge she was, and was so careful how she got what she would need, hoarding the strongest pain pills, doing without antianxiety meds to stockpile her stash, that no one ever guessed. And once, deliberately catching influenza to get a scrip for antinausea drugs. She knew she would never get more than one chance, her parents would see to that. So there would be no throwing up the lethal dose.

Nothing would compound failure as much as a failed suicide.

The option of ending it all had, strangely enough, sometimes been all that had kept her going. Knowing she had the means, at hand, had kept despair just dulled enough that she would pull through another day. Then, of course, the Invasion had changed everything. But more than that, figuring out that she could put together Overwatch, that she could be *effective,* that she could contribute as much as any able-bodied member of a team—that had actually given her a reason to live.

Now that was gone.

She *was* a failure, and utterly useless now. Overwatch was as much magic as tech. Her hacking required magic. Any geek off the street could do what she could, and better.

Without magic, she was just a cripple, loaded down with phobias.

She knew what would happen next; Bella would waste time and effort trying to find something she could *do,* expending effort they should be putting elsewhere. She had been a military commander of sorts, even if it had only been of a tiny group, and she knew all about cutting losses. "No man left behind" was fine if you had infinite backing and infinite resources, but right now, Echo was on the verge of falling apart and in the hands of Verdigris, there were the Thulians, and things were only going to get worse.

She couldn't even hack the Metis communication unit. Not without magic.

In a strange way, what settled about her now was relief. No more responsibility, no more fighting through pain, no more living in a near constant state of fear. The tunnel had an end, even if there was no light in it.

The mage-shields kept everything out, including Grey and Herb's protests. She was utterly alone in the silence.

She put her "favorites" collection on the stereo on a random shuffle. She needed music, or she'd lose her nerve.

Quickly she wrote out a last letter, laying out everything; how much of a liability she was, and how she refused to let them waste what few resources they had on her. She left it on the coffee table for whoever found her. She had made it unemotional and logical, and had tried very hard to phrase things so all the blame fell on herself. She found herself second-guessing her own convictions even as she wrote it, until she began to wonder if, all this time, everything she had believed about herself and what defined her was completely wrong.

"Red Djinni may be right. Magic might be too uncertain, too dangerous to ever use. Gods know Saviour thinks so. If so... at least I stopped before I killed someone."

She'd taken so many pills in her life that four bottles' worth went down in minutes. She lay down on the couch, and closed her eyes, letting the music wash over her, and then the numbness of spirit wore off. She cried for all the mistakes, for the loss of everything that defined her, for the failure, cried and cried until she finally felt oblivion come on soft, dark wings.

Red didn't call for transport, he needed some air. He slammed the roof access behind him, and braced himself against the rooftop ledge, breathing hard. The sheer gall of that bitch! How *dared* she try and compare the two of them! What did she know of his past? Of his pain? Spend a night in the Djinni's body, and that gives her an excuse, the *right* to...

He dug his hand under the mask, and ran his fingers over the scarred flesh. All these years, adopting faces, tearing the skin away to grow new masks... and it was still the same. Left to its own devices, his own deformed and mutilated face always returned. A constant reminder.

All right then, so there were *some* similarities...

He collapsed on the concrete, resting his back against the ledge and his face in his hands. He felt his anger ebb away, as usual, to be replaced by remorse. Damn his temper.

But he *had* killed people for...

What was wrong with that woman? Why did she always have to goad him like that? What was it about her that always brought out the worst in him?

Magic. That was it, her and magic. You'd think she couldn't live without it. Like some damned crutch. It wasn't as if she didn't have plenty of other—

What if she doesn't?

The thought had not occurred to him before. For some, magic was as natural as breathing; he'd seen that with his own eyes. What if, for her, it was as *neccessary* as breathing? That damned cat of hers... it had more or less implied she'd been fooling around with magic since high school, or even earlier. Or... wait, not "fooling around" at all. Using it, seriously, to do... stuff for the FBI? Wasn't that something *she'd* said? Not exactly fooling around. Not like—

Red muttered something and came to his feet. *Enough. It'll keep for another day. Just another day in paradise for Djinni and Overwatch. I'm sure there will be some heartfelt apologies later. You're usually good at those. Just, not right now. I can still feel my hands on her, wanting to hurt her...*

He glanced around him. The rooftops seemed close enough together. He started at a quick run, and began flying from building to building. As usual, the speed and danger began to calm him.

The first inkling that Red had that something was horribly wrong was when the damn cat leapt on him from behind and bit and clawed the crap out of his calf and thigh. Red swore, landing awkwardly on a fire escape. He struck hard, and batted Grey off. The cat landed smoothly and hissed, his back arched and body shaking.

Grey was incoherent with anger, fear, and grief blasting babbling thoughts into his head. But the images that came with those thoughts were clear. Vickie locking the cat and the rock elemental out. Vickie gulping down handfuls of pills.

And finally, a few coherent "words." <*You took her magic, you fricking bastard! You stole the only thing she had left! You've killed her!*>

"Killed her? Took her magic? With what, a shouting match? The hell are you...?"

<*I fricking told you! She bound herself to your will! Open-ended, no time limit, no term limit, and you said—*> Grey couldn't even form the "words," he was so angry.

"Oh," Djinni said, blankly. "Oh...shit. Then she's..."

<*Yes.*>

"And so she decided to..."

<*Yes.*>

They stared at each other for a moment, and Red was off, racing back to Vickie's apartment, and Grey was hot on his heels. <*Faster, asshole!*>

Noise. The comforting, enveloping fog lifted for a moment. Was it Death? Death wasn't supposed to be noisy. It was supposed to come silently, creeping from the shadows, with sweet whispers of oblivion and eternal rest. But this was loud...thunderous...pounding...

Footsteps overhead on the flat roof of the apartment building...

Go away. Leave me alone.

With a terrible effort, she turned her head to look. Outside, the city seemed otherwise quiet. Trees rustled softly in a mild breeze, their leaves lit by a gorgeous full moon. She was touched by the serenity of it, a serenity broken as a masked figure landed unceremoniously on one of the branches outside her window. He cursed as he grappled with the branch, then hopped up and sprinted along the groaning limb towards...

Her window exploded inward as Djinni hurled himself through it, landing in a roll and colliding with her coffee table. He banged his forehead neatly on the edge, and he howled in pain.

"Oh hell...it's you..." she murmured. "Why is it always you...?" And dove back into nothingness, the ultimate dark place to hide. And this time, she would never have to come out.

Red scrambled to her, grabbing her by the shoulders and pulling her up. "Victrix! Damn you, this is not cool!" He shook her, and she hung limp in his arms. He scanned the area, and watched as four empty pill bottles rolled off the coffee table onto the floor, and they were not small bottles. He let her go and examined them. Three Percodan, one Valium. There was a fifth bottle, much smaller, something he didn't recognize. And she had gulped them down, all of them... he didn't have much time. Her breathing was already shallower.

He spotted Bella's med kit by the door.

He leapt over the couch and grabbed it, spilling its contents on the floor. He sifted through the gauze, bandages, syringes and a couple dozen vials of liquid. What he needed would be in a preloaded shot, because it wasn't always the trained DCO that had to use these kits. There! Epinephrine, with a long needle. He grabbed the syringe.

"C'mon, c'mon, stay with me, Vickie..."

He pulled off her glove, ignoring the sight of her gnarled flesh, and rolled up her sleeve. His heart sank as he examined her arm. The skin was too damaged to find a vein. Helplessly, he tore off both sleeves, but both arms were an equal mess. Not a vein in sight.

She wasn't breathing now—she was gasping, in between long, long intervals. He checked for a pulse under her chin.

Shit. It's weak... and falling...

His jaw clenched, his mind swimming in indecision. *Veins in her feet? Jam an artery? Red, old boy, you're losing her...*

The needle was just long and heavy enough. He drew a deep breath, and stabbed the needle into her chest between the ribs, right above the heart, ramming the plunger down.

The reaction was instantaneous. Her eyes flew open, she convulsed, and took a huge, gulping breath. And another. Her heart started hammering as he pulled out the needle.

"That's right!" Red shouted, scooping her up in his arms. "Keep breathing, Vickie! Keep awake! Keep..."

She shuddered, and cried out in protest.

"N-n-n-n-NO!" she sobbed. "G-g-go aw-w-way, you b-b-b-b—"

"Keep hating me!" Red said in encouragement, as he carried her to the bathroom. He held her to him with one arm as he opened her medicine cabinet. His hand flew over the shelves, knocking over bottles until he found the ipecac. He unscrewed the top with his thumb, leaned her back, and dumped the contents of the bottle down her throat. She struggled as he clamped his hand over her mouth and nose, forcing her to swallow the stuff.

Then he held her over the toilet while she emptied out everything she had swallowed down.

"Y-y-y-y-you... sonova..." But her tone wasn't angry. It was a desperate wail. She started to hyperventilate, and her head wobbled. He ignored her, turning the shower on full cold, and dragged her under the freezing stream of water. She collapsed against him.

"Hey!" he shouted, letting her head fall back under the falling water. He slapped her cheek, and was rewarded with a flutter of her eyelids. "Stay with me, damn it! *Vickie! I'm sorry, all right? I'm sorry I made you...that I said...FUCK! Wake UP!*"

He held her close and felt for a pulse. It was there, she was alive, but so limp, so *lifeless*. He brought her face under the water again, slapped her again, harder, and screamed her name over and over. At last, she opened her eyes, but what he saw...

There was nothing there but despair. Past all hope. The last time he'd seen eyes that looked like that—it'd been Howitzer's, and the boy had been begging for death to take away his pain.

I fricking told you! Grey had said. *She bound herself to your will! Open-ended, no time limit, no term limit, and you said—*

"I TAKE IT BACK!" Red screamed in panic. "YOU HEAR ME! I TAKE IT BACK! TAKE YOUR MAGIC BACK! BUT TAKE YOUR LIFE BACK TOO, DAMN IT! I JUST..."

He shuddered and held her close to him.

"I just want to help you come back..." He wept.

Every door in the apartment slammed open. A wave of— something—swept into the place, through Red, and into Vickie. Her eyes opened again, but now they were alive. She looked at him, she looked *through* him, for just a moment.

Then she laid her head on his shoulder and began to sob.

He let her cry herself out; then he bundled her up in a towel much too big for her, and tucked her under a couple of blankets. She fell asleep immediately, a healthy sleep of exhaustion.

He staggered out into the living room. The wind coming in through the broken window blew some papers against his leg. He picked them up and caught sight of his own name.

Red Djinni may be right. Magic might be too uncertain, too dangerous to ever use...

The letter was written in Vickie's flowing script. He sat down to read it. A few times. Finally, he tore up the letter and let his head fall into his hands. He had torn into her tonight. He had even been warned, and still he had done it. Uncertain and dangerous, he couldn't disagree, but it was a part of her. It was something she couldn't simply deny.

He would have to live with that, if he was going to help her.

CHAPTER TWENTY-ONE

Heroes and Thieves

CODY MARTIN AND MERCEDES LACKEY

In a sane world, we'd have spent at least a week recovering from . . . all that.

We didn't have a week. We didn't have days. We had hours.

I had minutes. Unlocking the desk and getting contact with Metis could not wait.

Red Saviour didn't like magic, but the *malenkaya vedma* had proved her usefulness and reliability enough by this point that she was disposed to allow Victoria to do whatever she wished to. Even within the confines of CCCP headquarters.

The woman had been spending most waking hours here ever since Belladonna had brought the communications unit from Tesla's desk here for safekeeping. Obviously, the last place the thing should be was anywhere near the dwelling places of any of the Echo Ops that had stolen it in the first place. It was safest here; Natalya could make certain no one got anywhere near it with very little effort.

The mage had been working on getting the thing to come to life ever since it had been brought in and hidden away. The only time that Vickie left was to return to her own apartment. To sleep, presumably, although given the dark circles beneath her eyes, the Commissar was not certain how much *sleep* she was getting. While Red Saviour found her drive commendable, she was troubled. Victoria seemed distant, even more skittish than usual. Saviour had seen this before, in those days following a sudden loss, when grief was desperately pushed aside and replaced with some distracting task to keep oneself preoccupied. She liked Victoria, and would have liked to question the girl about what troubled her. Yet a voice inside told her to keep out of it, that perhaps it was best for the girl if she behaved as if nothing was out of the ordinary, and for once, Saviour listened. So instead, she fumed and dropped agitated remarks on the interminable length of time the girl was taking. To her relief, she was rewarded with snappish and sometimes snarled requests to be patient. It was good, the girl still had fire in her.

Still, the work plodded on, and the Commissar *was* actually starting to lose her patience, when she looked up from her paperwork to see the little magician leaning against the doorframe, exhausted.

"I've got it," Vickie said. "I haven't woken the damn thing up yet, but since it's in your house, I figure you have the right to decide who's here when I do. Bella, of course. You. I need Yankee Pride to make it work. Got any more picks?"

Saviour considered this for a moment. On the one hand . . . the member of CCCP who was the greatest tactical expert alive was Fei Li. On the other hand . . . Fei Li—or the General—had been acting rather erratic of late. Vanishing from HQ, telling no one where she was going, saying nothing when she returned . . .

She pondered this. She needed someone with experience. Georgi was a good fighter but not so good tactically; "the best way out is through" was a maxim he took to heart. And his answer to most problems was to apply explosives, a rifle or fists to it. Bear? A disaster; he was best treated as a directed disaster with adequate supervision. Molo was back in Moscow and would not return for another week. Dare she trust—

Well . . . it would be a good test.

"Comrade Murdock. When can you do this thing?"

Vickie didn't voice any objections at all. Interesting. "As soon as I can get Bell and Pride here."

She nodded. *"Davay.* We have been delayed enough."

John had received the call from HQ shortly before his shift ended. It'd been a long and hot day, so he double-timed it back in order to have a shower and change. *Beer'll have to wait for later. Hope Jonas has something cold in stock.* Quickly ducking into the head facilities, John made himself presentable, throwing on the standard working jumpsuit. The call had requested that he show up at the Commissar's office; for what purpose, he didn't know. It seemed that the Commissar only called him in to assess an after-action report, or to chew him out, or both. Jogging through the hallways, he came to the door for her office. He braced himself, then knocked and waited.

"Come!" Saviour called impatiently. John opened the door and quickly stepped into the room. Saviour wasn't alone, as he'd expected. Bella was there, leaning over Saviour's desk as she examined something. Flanking her was Yankee Pride, one of the more visible faces for the metas of Echo. *Well, then. I wonder what these three've got brewing?*

"Reportin' in as requested, Commissar."

The Commissar looked uncharacteristically sober, with a poker face that was giving nothing away, so he relaxed a very little; he'd discovered that he personally needed to start worrying only when she smiled. "Comrade Murdock, Operative Blue has evidenced great confidence in you. Despite your destructive habits, you perform almost with the efficiency of a Soviet. What you are about to see is not to be discussed except among those in this room, and Daughter of Rasputin." *Vic. Saviour doesn't cotton to magic almost as much as me.*

"We good to go?" Bella asked.

Saviour nodded and got up from behind her desk. "Follow me."

John did so, holding the door open for the three of them before exiting himself. *This is getting more interesting by the minute. Blue is vouching for me . . . but for what?*

Saviour led them to the part of HQ that she hadn't made any plans for yet; these had probably been storage rooms once, since they were inside and had no windows. It was strangely quiet here, the only sounds were a few distant footfalls and the faint sound of the Soviet Bear shouting at the television. Saviour tapped on one of the closed doors.

Vickie cracked it—at least, the bright blue, bloodshot eye peering through the crack between door and jamb was at the right height to be Vickie's—

Then the door opened. The Commissar shooed them all in. Vickie closed the door behind them.

In the light from the single naked bulb in the ceiling fixture,

John saw that there was only one thing in this room. One of the ancient desks, and—some sort of techy thing on top of it along with a portable Echo broadcast power unit. It looked . . . odd. Simultaneously as if it had come from some time in the future, and as if it had been built in the 1930s. Incongruously, the little Echo broadcast power unit used to supply juice to tools that was sitting next to it looked far more high-tech.

"Okay, JM, this is what Vic and I were babbling about the other day," Bella said. "And I'd ask you to sit down, but . . . there aren't any chairs." Quickly she filled him in on just what it was he was looking at. And its background.

John held up a hand. "So, lemme get this straight. There's a super 'science city,' with all sorts of outstanding tech. The verifiable ghosts of Enrico Marconi and Nikola Tesla exist and direct this joint. They've got crazy shit that does things people have only dreamed of. Right?"

"Yep. And from what we saw the last time we saw this thing, they weren't going to help the rest of us," Bella said grimly.

"Good, good. Now that we're on the same page 'bout that, I have one other question. Commissar, permission to speak freely?"

"*Da, da,* I would not being have you here if I did not want to hear what you say," the Commissar said impatiently.

"Thank you. My question is, where the hell were these bastards when the Invasion happened? Why are they sitting on their asses now?" He wasn't making any effort to hide how pissed off this revelation made him. *Millions die, and these sons of bitches did nothing to help?*

Bella shrugged. "My impression is they got caught with their pants down by the Invasion too. The rest? Mercurye didn't have time to tell us, and if Alex knew, he never told anyone." She took a deep breath. "We're hoping to get some answers by getting this thing to work."

"It's a communication device of some sort, then? An' here I was hoping for a really high-tech scoop of ice cream."

"Boy thinks he's a wit and he's half right," Vickie muttered under her breath. Then she straightened—as much as she ever did, when she was hunched over and trying to stay invisible—and headed for the desk. "Yank, one of the things I need is you." She pointed to a chalk circle on the floor. "Stand there. This shouldn't take long. Now that I know what to do, anyway."

She licked her begloved finger, and "drew" in the air with it. A glowing trail followed the finger as she sketched signs. Each time she finished one, it disappeared; she moved so fast all he got was an impression of geometric shapes and strange "letters." But then—she "drew" a rectangle, and said, *"Fiat apparatus di Tesla."* And—

Something like a ghostly PC, only one that was just a kind of glowing drawing of a PC appeared floating in the air in front of her. Complete with keyboard, which she proceeded to type on. Somehow. John got the hair-standing-on-end feeling whenever Vickie did obvious shows of magery like this; it was worse than Bella's touch-healing, and something that he didn't think he'd ever fully get used to. Metahumans could do some amazing and oftentimes unbelievable things, but something about magic just bugged the hell out of him.

"I can't use my own computers; the comm will reject them. All I can do to talk to this thing is give it something it's convinced is Alex's computer," she said as she typed. "That's what had me so stymied. Hold still, Yank, it's going to scan you in a second."

Part of the apparatus suddenly unfolded and a beam of light transfixed Yankee Pride.

"Okay, now ID yourself and say 'Commence Inheritance Protocol.'"

"Yankee Pride. Commence Inheritance Protocol," Yank said obediently.

The response was immediate; the thing unfolded itself on top of the desk; unnervingly, it did so without a sound.

"Now say 'Initiate Emergency Contact Protocol.'"

Yank did so. There were two slender antennaelike things thrusting up from the object itself. A field sprang up between them; blue with little sparkles in it.

Vickie stopped typing. Bella held her breath.

After a long time, Saviour frowned. "Is working?"

"As far as I—"

And the blue field shimmered. "Alex?" said a strangely flat, yet accented voice. "Alex, my boy? Where have you been? What has been happening?"

Shitfire. Whoever this is doesn't know.

They all froze. Finally it was Bella who answered.

"I'm very sorry, sir. It was Yankee Pride that opened contact.

Alex was murdered two weeks ago." She took a long, shuddering breath. "And you are—?"

There was silence again. Then a strange, thin sound for a moment. It wasn't anything recognizable, but it sounded—like grief.

It stopped. "Forgive me. I assume that Yankee Pride must be with you or the quantator would not have responded to you. This is Nikola Tesla." John glanced at the others. Bella and Saviour nodded. Vickie just left the ghostly PC and sat down in a far corner on the floor, wrapping her arms around her knees. Yankee Pride looked stricken.

"What happened?" the voice asked.

Pride shook himself out of his fog and explained, belatedly introducing everyone in the room. When he had finished, there was silence again.

"You will not like what I am going to say," Tesla replied, the voice somehow conveying an impression of someone laboring through grief. "This changes nothing. Metis is governed by a pure democracy, and the majority have voted not to come to your aid or defense. If they knew about what has happened, and I have no reason to think they do not, they have not even had the decency to tell me, so their minds have not been changed."

Saviour and Bella looked as if they were about to explode. John beat them to it. "Bullshit."

"Pardon?" said the voice, sounding startled.

"You heard me. I said that that's utter bullshit." John walked forward a few paces, crossing his arms. "We're facin' the greatest threat that humanity has ever been exposed to, aside from itself. Space Nazis, Thulians, Kriegers—whatever y'wanna call 'em. They've got numbers, they have technology, and they have a ruthlessness that enables them to use both to burn down the world. The Invasion stopped only 'cause they wanted it to, not 'cause they were *losin'*." He paced back and forth, waiting for Tesla's response.

"And you, my impetuous young communist, are dealing with a city full of ivory-tower scientists, certain that they are the pinnacle of human evolution, and desperately frightened that the Thulians will destroy *them* if they get involved," said a new voice—also synthesized, but with a different accent. "Our citizens here believe that it is best that they simply wait this matter out, then assist the survivors. Personally, I think that they have been overly influenced by that Wells movie...what was it, Nikola?"

"*Shape of Things to Come,*" said the first voice, sounding broken.

"Who's the new guy?" John stopped to face the projection again.

"*Mi scusi,*" said the second voice. "Enrico Marconi. Allow Nikola his moment of grief. I will answer your questions."

"Well, my name's John Murdock. I'm not a communist, but I am with the CCCP. I'm with them because they're doin' somethin' to fight the Kriegers. You're still wrong, an' it's still bullshit that y'all aren't helping. Y'know, they say that history repeats itself, an' that's what it's doin' right now." He jabbed a finger at the projection, bulling ahead. "When the Nazis first tried to pull this shit, no one else wanted to try an' stop 'em. Everyone figured it was a European problem, that it'd sort itself out. An' then when the next country got swallowed up, they figured that it still wasn't their problem. An' so on, an' so on. These suckers aren't gonna stop until they get the whole world. Sittin' on the sidelines now doesn't mean jack, other than you'll be the last ones to get chewed up an' spit out."

"*Un moment,* my dear hothead," said the second voice. "We never said that we *agreed* with the majority. After all, we have the perspective of having lived through what you just described. Twice. Nikola and I will do our best, but unless and until your colleague Rick—Mercurye—manages to persuade the Metisians otherwise, what we can do is rather limited. It isn't as if we have bodies to go out and do things, after all, and this is our sole line of communication with the outside world."

Bella and Pride exchanged a look, and both of them glanced to the Commissar, who nodded and gave a little hand gesture indicating they should reply. It was Bella who spoke. "Well, you have more problems than just that. Echo is now in the hands of someone we are fairly sure engineered Alex Tesla's assassination."

That required more explanation. When it was over, there was silence again. Finally Marconi spoke.

"Can you keep this device secure?"

Saviour snorted. "Firstly, thanks only to good fortune, *svinya* Verdigris is not being aware it exists. Secondly, if he becomes aware, he would have to go through all of CCCP to get it."

Not to mention the near literal wall of lead the CCCP would throw in his way, John added mentally.

"Ah, good," Marconi replied. "One less thing to tell to self-destruct."

"Forgive me," Bella said, her voice gone very hard indeed. "But you seem to be taking this all a little too casually for my liking. The casualty rate out here is astronomical. It's only going to get worse. And all you're worried about—"

"Mi scusi, bella donna. Nikola and I—we have been electrons whirling in circuits for fifty years, and before that, we spent decades with parts of us being replaced by gizmos and gadgets. It is difficult to maintain one's humanity, and emotions become a thing of memory." The voice managed an inflection of genuine humility, and Bella's expression softened a little. "Nevertheless, we, at least, are with you. Insofar as we can feel grief, feel horror, we do feel them on your behalf. We do not mean for you to think we take all this lightly. These are perilous times and though our citizens would like to believe they are somehow *homo superior,* the fact is they are pure children of the human race, as you are. We will do our best to awaken them to that, you have my word as a gentleman. And I trust you will forgive me, if I seem to be as detached as they. I assure you, Nikola and I are not, and we are committed to aiding you."

"Well, what *can* you do?" Bella demanded.

"Since you have secured the quantator, what we can do is this. Nikola and I can send you plans for things you will find useful, without Metis being aware. They will be tricky to build, but I have confidence you can do so. We can also use Metis resources to do limited research for you. I say limited because we are going to be confined to using and transmitting information. We cannot do anything physical, for instance, such as metals analysis. But anything that can be done in the realm of the theoretical or mathematical—"

"I have something," Vickie suddenly piped up. She got to her feet. "Can you make that thing extrude a data port or something like one?"

In answer, another appendage unfolded from the contraption which appeared to end in a standard USB port.

Vickie scooted nervously across the room to behind them all. There was a laptop bag there; she fished a USB drive out and scuttled over to stick it into the port. "That's some of the intel we got thanks to the op in the Goldman Catacombs," she said. "I got what I could once my stuff came back online while the wolves and eagles were still active, there was a microtransmission my system managed to capture. I can't make head or tail of what looks to me like coded communications, and I don't have enough number-crunching ability to unravel it. I know they must be using their own stuff, their own means to communicate, because they aren't using our Internet or landlines."

"*Un momento,*" said Marconi. "Number crunching, we can do. And if you can give me access to several terrabytes of storage, I can transmit some plans to you now."

"Give me another port, and I'll give you access to my servers," Vickie replied. When another appendage unfolded, she stuck in a wifi dongle, then typed some more on the ghost-computer. She seemed very confident that Marconi—if, indeed, this really was Marconi—was not going to frag her system. John was disposed to leave that to her best judgment.

"And . . . there. And now we have their information decoded, I think. We will shortly have a full language base for you—for the nonhumans. There is enough duplicate communication in German and Thulian to give us a satisfactory lexicon."

"Well, that's good," Vickie sighed. "It'll make reading anything else a lot easier."

"And right now, I believe we have a location for you to investigate."

Now something appeared in the projection. A map, with a dot highlighted. "This seems to be where the orders for that staging zone were being issued from. I assume this is useful? It cannot be Ultima Thule, there was not enough, how you say, traffic. So, one assumes, some sort of command or relay post?"

John looked at the map. "Vic, can you extrapolate some more data from this? What the site is, the surrounding location, an' so on?"

"Oh, she does not need to," Marconi said. The map zoomed out. "It is an old missile silo in the middle of Kansas."

"Deactivated, I assume? An' which of the series was it?"

"Deactivated, yes. It was previously an ICBM staging platform for the American Titan I. And it is in private hands. Echo bought quite a few of them when we could. Useful staging and storage areas. This one never came up on the open market; presumably the Thulians felt the same and managed to get this one before it was offered openly for sale."

"What's the purpose of this site? It's secure, and secluded enough, an' presumably not on anyone's radar; the Thulians seem to like keeping their operations innocuous until they strike."

"From these communiques, I would say it is a command center for individual units, as well as larger forces in that area," Marconi replied. "I would expect this sort of thing. Their organization is probably pyramidal, based on cells. Each cell knows only about the command module above it, not each other. Well, my allies, are we satisfied with one another?"

This time it was Saviour who replied. "For now," she said. "You have yet to actually prove your worth."

"I am aware of that, Commissar. Shortly you will have your proof. I have instructed the quantator to respond to any of you, but I recommend that we keep our communications brief. The Metisian majority is perfectly capable of removing access from Nikola and myself if they suspect we are meddling."

"Understood," replied Pride. "We're grateful you're willing to risk it."

"It is only our duty, young man," Marconi answered. "To you, and to humanity. And now, I think we are about to exceed our safe time. Good luck, and *arrivederci*."

The field between the two antennae faded. Vickie retrieved her thumb-drive.

"Well?" asked Pride.

"We are having location to investigate," Saviour said. "Clearly, Echo cannot do this without alert of Verdigris, so it must be CCCP." She almost looked smug. "Shoe is being on other shelf."

"Foot," Vickie said automatically. "I think this had better be with Overwatch."

"An' I think this better be a one-man recon, Commissar," John put in. "If it turns out that the location is bogus or a trap, only leaves one dead comrade as opposed to a team. Forgive me if I'm in the minority here, but I still don't trust Metis."

"Agreed. And you are volunteering, Comrade Murdock." It was not a question.

John grinned lopsidedly. "Hell," he said, "Anythin' I destroy down there ain't gonna be CCCP property. An' Vick an' I work pretty well t'gether."

"True enough." Saviour raised an eyebrow at Pride and Bella. Pride shrugged.

"We can't do a move on that base without Verdigris finding out. It's yours, Commissar," Pride agreed.

"I can't see any other way," Bella seconded. "Ramona can sneak you on an Echo transport, in the jump seat, unlisted. If anybody asks, you're doing another CCCP parts run."

"*Horosho.* We are agreed. It remains for Murdock to pack." Saviour looked as satisfied as a wolf with a full belly.

"And me to get Ramona to siphon CCCP some cash," said Bella. "Maybe purloin a couple gadgets that might be useful."

"And me to cover your tracks in the systems and make things vanish from inventory," added Vickie.

"Then we have plan." Saviour raked them all with her startling blue eyes. "What are you waiting for? May Day parade? *Davay!*"

Davay they did.

CHAPTER TWENTY-TWO

Roll the Bones

MERCEDES LACKEY AND CODY MARTIN

Finally, a payday. Finally, what we had been working for, hoping for, praying for. Never mind that Dominick Verdigris had struck us a blow that would have been mortal—except that Echo wasn't alone. The faithful of Echo had an ally that, I suspected, Verdigris was dismissing just as Saviour's own father and Worker's Champion had dismissed them—the CCCP. They were wrong; they were all wrong. Nat and her crew had something to prove, and this was the chance to do it. She had been fretting at the bit, I knew, tired to death of always playing a defensive position, of being reactive instead of proactive.

And she was right. Oh boy, was she ever. Even Sun Tzu would have advised against such a strategy. The Thulians could whittle us down a little at a time until we were small enough to crush.

But now, now we had a chance to strike back. Finally, we were on the offensive rather than the defensive, acting rather than reacting.

And me? Now it was my time to really do my stuff.

"So. That's what I've got. That's *all* I've got," Vickie told John Murdock. Not that she was face to face with him; she was just a voice in his ear. She might have been a ghost, except for the stack of transmitted pages Saviour had handed to him before he boarded an Echo cargo plane headed for a small airstrip outside of Wichita. As the CCCP was an Echo ally he got access to empty seats on no notice and with no records—though Vickie, careful as ever, had a simple cover story that he was picking up more of the

401

antiquated equipment that was CCCP's standard. The flight had actually passed quickly, and in a way he hadn't expected. Vickie had piped music to him—asked for a basic playlist and played DJ for an audience of one. The cargo-master had given him a pitying look after a glance at the sheaf of equipment he was supposedly purchasing. John tried not to feel too much resentment.

After all, if Vickie and Bella were giving him the straight dope (and he had no reason to think that they weren't), Bella had already raided Echo for some of their best and newest gear during that raid on the Vault, and would continue to do so and pass the results on to CCCP under Verdigris' radar. That was enough to make the Support Op's smirk a little more palatable.

Before touching down, he had been able to have a Rental-Wreck truck arranged through Vickie: American-made and not all that new. It'd fit in with the usual traffic, which was important. John didn't want to stick out in the slightest for this assignment. Through some sleight of hand she'd been able to have it left at the airport in the long-term parking lot, though these guys normally didn't do delivery and pickup. Maybe it had been money. He hoped she was raiding Verdigris' petty cash.

After driving for about three hours and change, he was on the outskirts of Kansas City. He took the time to stop the truck on the side of the road and to get out to survey it, just take things in. He was still on schedule, but the few minutes it'd take him to orient himself would be worth it. A voice piped into his ear, interrupting his thoughts.

"If it's abandoned, my plans will be good. If the Thulians have it, I would bet that the underground plans are still good. Those things were built to withstand a direct nuke, and it's going to be hard to alter the basic layout or where the ventilation, plumbing and wiring goes."

"Hey, Vic?" John adjusted his baseball cap, waiting for a reply. "Roger?"

"You're ruining the moment."

"Bite me, monkey boy."

He grinned, then returned to his truck, starting it and driving towards Kansas City.

John didn't take long to find a fairly rundown motel to check into; he'd developed a keen eye for these sorts of places when he had first gone on the run six years ago, back when he still had enough cash to actually afford a place to stay. It was the kind of motel that had hourly, weekly and monthly rates. "No-Tell Mo-Tel." Using an assumed name and an extra few bills slipped to the night clerk, he checked in and received his key for the room. He had made sure to back his truck in to park it, with his room being on the ground floor; if he needed to split in a hurry, the extra few seconds both considerations would afford him would be worth it.

"You want anything besides the motel cable for entertainment?"

"Yeah. Brief me some more on the facility while I unpack."

"Turn on the TV, find an empty channel and tell me what it is. Make it one from the sat dish or cable." John did so. "Now take the remote and hit pound sign 4573. I have to send feed to the whole motel but that will unscramble it."

"Done." John threw the remote onto a recliner in the corner, then bent down to heft several large duffel bags onto his bed.

The first thing that came up was a map, side by side with a military satellite picture of the whole site, which was a couple hundred acres. Missile silos tended to not have neighbors, or at least not close ones.

John unzipped the duffel bags, and began unpacking them. An M4A1 assault rifle with an attached suppressor, his old Springfield .45 ACP pistol with its own suppressor, load bearing equipment, breaching charges, several different types of surveillance gadgets, AN/PVS-14 night vision device, a number of miscellaneous other gizmos that he'd either been given by Vickie or picked out himself.

"We are pretty sure this was a coordination center for the Invasion, maybe even temporary C and C. We're also pretty sure there's still function there. It's not big enough for a deployment base, and its very nature as an early sixties-era hardened facility gives it limited advantage as a communication center, but it's definitely still live and manned, which means we have a ninety-percent shot at extracting some intel from it, especially if we can sneak a line into their data-cloud. Here in the north you've got your best access. See the creek?" A cursor traced the path. "It crosses under Section Line Road NS 272 at the quarter-mile mark after EW 440." The map scrolled up a little. "This is a winter shot, so all the leaves are off the trees. If you pull in here"—the cursor pointed at a place just off the road—"you can pull the truck right under the bridge and it won't be seen from the road. Then you walk in on the creek. It's pretty well overgrown with trees the whole way."

"Right. Now, for once I get there; we got any intel about access to the base itself?"

The maps—clearly on computer windows—closed. A new map came up. "This is the old plan for the base. As you can imagine, the aboveground stuff can be penetrated from several places. The creek is the most obvious and so is the most likely to have old booby traps still there. Or new ones. Or both." The cursor moved around as Vickie identified which buildings used to have which functions. "Now...I don't want to tell you how to do your job..."

"Then don't, comrade. Are there any structures topside attached to the silo? As opposed to the service tunnel with the blast doors."

"Just the old guardhouse and ready room. There's just no good quiet way to get down there. One way in."

"If you say, 'ventilation duct,' I'll strangle you."

"Staircase."

"That'll work. All right, I'm gonna kit up and start out. I ought to be gettin' there right early in the morning; hopefully they'll be running a little sloppy that early."

"Oh, one other thing? If this is Thulians running the show, don't expect to plug that relay port I gave you into anything. This is not a movie. Aliens do not use Minisoft."

"I'll worry 'bout that when I get there. I'll feed ya some video 'fore I use the comp link on anything. Now, be useful and play me some CCR."

"Ten-four." The screen of the television filled with images from some random screensaver while the tinny speakers relayed his own private station.

John smirked as he readied his gear. "Y'know what this whole bit reminds me of, Vic?"

"I'm guessing it's not *The Sound of Music.*"

"Naw. It's the Doolittle Raid."

"As in the bomber strike on Tokyo. Huh. I can see that. The only disconnect is there was no real strategic reason to bomb Tokyo at that point in the war, and they did damn-all damage, but the psychological effect was *huge.*"

"Two things, girlie. One: Psychological effect is huge strategic effect. Never forget that. Make the bastards afraid to fight, they won't fight. Two: Well, this whole thing is making me grin like a bastard."

"What? 'Cause we're finally going to kick 'em in the knee instead of reacting?"

"Not just that," and John's grin did go even wider, "but because after this... we're gonna drop a couple of *real* bombs on these sons of bitches."

"Yeah... well... we gotta pull this off first. If we shoot craps here, we're never gonna get a second chance."

"If we shoot craps here, I'm dead. Either from Kriegers or the Commissar's wrath. So, lemme jam out while I get my guns ready. Roger, comrade?"

"You got it."

John had arrived on-site at about 1:30 in the morning, which was perfect for him. There was a light fog, and the chill clung to him. Kept him focused and awake. For the next hour, he took his time creeping along the creek that Vickie had described to him earlier. It was low; obviously there was a *lot* more water in it during the spring. Now there was barely enough to wet his boots. And there weren't any booby traps, thankfully. Still, he wasn't about to get lulled into a false sense of confidence, and he performed listening checks every few meters. All he heard were mourning doves and bobwhite quail. He reached the terminus for the creek just on the perimeter of the guardhouse, then stopped to observe. Less than a minute later, he saw what he'd been expecting: a roving guard, dressed in simple, nondescript fatigues.

John keyed his throat mic, whispering low. "Vickie, y'there?"

"Roger."

"Think y'can do some wizardry for me? I need you to scan for about the next half hour, check out if these guys are using their radios at all. Sendin' ya some vid now." Tapping a switch, the miniature camera on his shoulder came to life, transmitting live video.

"While you do that, put one bare hand on the dirt please."

He grumbled. "I already have; I'm flat on my stomach, here."

"Skin contact. This is the magic part, JM. If I work through you I have to work *through* you."

John peeled off the Nomex glove on his left hand, keeping his movements deliberate and slow. "Get on with it."

There was a pause. An ant decided that John's sock looked like a good place to make a home He hoped it wasn't a fire ant. "Okay. There are two guards topside. One you can see, one on the other side of the old barracks. There are three people in the old barracks, they're asleep. I can't magic-see inside the silo, it's too dense with man-made material." There was another pause, a longer one. "Okay. Coded check-ins. I think they're checking in with an automated system. Both guards used the same number sequence, typed in, one number off for the one at the barracks."

"Got it recorded? Can y'fake it?"

"Is the bear Catholic?"

"You're weird. Tell me when you're good to go." John slowly pulled his drag bag by its strap, bringing it up to his chest. He'd practiced stalking like this before, so the actions were nearly automatic. Keeping his eyes trained on the nearest guard, he pulled out his rifle and checked to make sure that it was both loaded and that the suppressor was attached properly. Finally, he shouldered the rifle, turned on the 4x scope, and *breathed.* His sight reticule found the guard's temple easily.

"Anytime."

G'night, Gracie. John squeezed the trigger of the M4, and was half-surprised when the rifle lightly kicked against his shoulder. He had sighted it in with the suppressor attached, so he was absolutely certain of where his rounds would strike. The single 5.56 projectile impacted with the guard's head; he dropped instantly, making nary a sound.

"Moving." John unhooked himself from his drag bag, and then loped towards the guard's body. He checked for a pulse with his off hand, and was satisfied to find none.

"Turn off his radio so I can fake it," Vickie requested. He performed as asked.

"Gimme a countdown for when the next guard will round the...NE corner of the barracks. Copy?"

"Ten-four."

John brought himself up into a half-crouch, leveling his rifle for where an average-sized man's chest would be. He waited patiently, settling into his stance and measuring his breaths.

"Approximately sixty seconds. Thirty. Ten. Five. Three, two, one. Mark." At that exact moment the guard rounded the corner. John fired three shots; two at the man's chest, and one at his face. All three found their target, and the guard crumpled with the slightest whimper.

"Same drill, get his radio. And update, someone in the barracks had to tap a kidney."

"Roger." John was already up and moving when Vickie started speaking; in no time at all, he had disabled the second guard's radio and dragged the body over to the first. "Is the fella that's awake facing away from me, with the door as a frame of reference?"

"No. Urinals are on the door side."

Screw it. "Going in." Without waiting for Vickie to protest, John opened the door to the barracks. He still had his NVGs on, and immediately spotted the sleeping forms of two of the Thulians. Taking a moment to gauge where their heads were, he let his rifle hang by its sling at his side, unholstering his .45. The pistol was quieter suppressed than the rifle, due to the rounds being naturally subsonic. Two more shots, two more bodies. John reoriented his sidearm on the bathroom entrance, the dim light coming through like sunlight to his night vision.

The Thulian appeared in the door, and there was something just slightly off about his appearance, things that, if you already knew he wasn't human, would have clued you in. The skin was slightly shiny, as if it didn't have any pores at all—which was, in fact, the case. The eyes were too far apart, the nose too flat and the nostrils were a pair of slits. The mouth was too wide and too thin, and almost lipless. The eyes widened for a moment in shock when the Thulian saw John, and the kidney-shaped pupils dilated. John's pistol jumped in his hand, and the life slipped out of the Thulian's eyes.

"I'm clear in the barracks. Heading for the stairwell." He hit a relay on a flat and squarish device on his left forearm; a series of three LEDs lit up, then went quiet. Toggling another switch, he tested to make sure the device was in working order. "Just checked your sniffer. If'n ya get any spikes with your superstitious mumbo-jumbo before this gizmo picks 'em up, lemme know."

The only reply was the sound of Vickie blowing a raspberry.

John holstered his pistol, bringing up his rifle again. With practiced calm, he entered the stairwell and began to descend into what he was sure to be a Thulian stronghold. It was a spiraling metal staircase; John had to take extra care in controlling his footfalls in order to minimize his sound signature. He reached the bottom without a single peep from the sniffer device on his arm. *So far, so good.*

"Any updates 'fore I venture on?"

"All I got is the old plans. And I need bare earth or something less man-made to be able to make like a witch doctor."

"Wonderful. Keep on those radio checks and the sniffer. I'm headin' in."

It was only midway through the facility that John started encountering problems. Up to that point, nearly every room had been cleaned out, and he had dropped little packages that Bell had given him in each one. There were scuff marks on the floors from heavy equipment being moved around; pieces of furniture and nonvaluable bits had been left behind, but for the most part there was nothing left in the rooms. He'd made sure to stop by what was the equivalent of a power control station for the silo; the two guards there hadn't posed as much of a threat as the security camera. After having Vickie tap the radios of the two guards and record a loop for the camera, he made sure to shoot out all three, thanking his lucky stars they were using human tech. Once his business was done in the power room, he quickly moved on towards what he hoped would be his main objective.

Now, he had a problem. He was at a juncture between several halls; at the end of the one he needed to get to was what appeared to be an automated sentry gun of some sort. And it *wasn't* human tech. It waited with the inhuman patience of the inanimate, a wicked-looking muzzle pointing in his direction. He'd used a fiber optic camera to peep around the corner in order to avoid being detected by it; from the fuzzy picture projected onto a built-in LCD screen, it looked like the entire juncture had been covered from all four ends at one point. Now, only the single sentry gun remained; whatever it was guarding had to be important.

"Well, that's ugly."

"It's mean. Got any suggestions?" John snaked the fiber optic camera back from the corner, coiling it and stowing it in a pouch.

"It's Thulian. So it's armored in their alloy and it's probably an energy gun. Get the reflector shield. There's no way you're getting past that quietly so just get past it alive."

John reached for his pack. He pulled out what initially resembled a small, polished silver bowl. Upon touching a button on the bottom of it, it unfolded to the size of a large kite. This was something new, "borrowed" from the Echo labs by Bella. It was designed to reflect the energy beams from one or two hits, but no more than that.

"This thing has been tested, right?" John whispered into the throat mic.

"So Bella says."

"Then here we go." John had started out around the corner, shield-first, when the blast came. It tore the upper right section entirely off of the shield, almost spinning John with the force. He quickly ducked back behind cover, forcing his back against the wall. "So much for that." The shield was smoking from where the sentry gun's cannon had shot away a portion of it.

"Odds are that thing is hooked up to an alarm. You're on the clock and it's ticking."

"Got any bright ideas?" John slung his rifle at his side, examining the smoking shield.

"Lemme check—"

"No time; gotta improvise." He threw the shield, *hard*, into the hallway, ricocheting it off of the wall. Almost instantly the sentry gun tracked to it and fired, finishing off the silvered partial disk. In the same instant, John ducked around the corner, concentrated, and released a controlled stream of plasma, impacting the Thulian machine dead-center. It exploded in a shower of sparks and acrid smoke, debris filling the hallway. "Time to move." He brought up his rifle again, centering it on the door ahead of him. He kicked it just left of the handle, sending it flying off of its hinges; his augmented strength served him very well in situations like this. Reverting back to his training, he checked the corners of the room, sweeping it for any targets, Thulian or otherwise. The room was clear of any threats.

"Still with me, Vickie?"

"Five by five."

"I think I'm at the objective."

"Gimme a sec...okay. At your three o'clock. Big wall panel. Under the thing that looks like a clock is a slot. You'll find the doohickey I gave you fits that. Let's hope my techno-shamanism speaks alien."

John fitted the palm-sized gadget—if you could call something that looked like Vickie had married half a science fiction gizmo to half of a voodoo doll a "gadget"—into the slot. Immediately a jury-rigged LED on it began flashing green. He could hear Vickie muttering under her breath, then—"Bingo. Human files." Then: "And it doesn't like me being there."

The clocklike dial lit up and began pulsing. "It's trying to self-destruct."

"Get what you can; I figure I'm gonna be getting company—"

"Shit, this is like being in a wrestling match with an anaconda—" He could hear the strain in her voice. Whatever it was she was doing...it was a *real* fight.

John's concentration was broken when he heard an almost imperceptible crunch of a boot stepping on glass. He immediately ducked and spun, bringing his rifle up and centering it on the doorway. Reflexively, John fired five rounds, all center of mass for the body that was standing there.

There was no way that anyone would mistake this creature for human. The eyes were so far apart they were almost on the sides of its head, the skin was shiny and gray-green, the mouth like a lizard's, the nose reduced to the nostril slits. It smelled; a bitter, musky smell with an overtone of grapefruit. *Thulian.* It was wearing body armor, and merely grunted and staggered back as John's rounds hit it.

"I got what I can! Grab the dingus and throw it at him!"

John did one better; he unslung his rifle, dropped it to the floor, and keyed his enhancements. In a flash, he was across the room and on top of the Thulian. The Nazi bastard was good; John led the attack with an elbow that should have killed the man, followed by a flurry of blows directed at his face, neck, and abdomen.

"Flashbang! Close your eyes NOW!"

"Shaddup! I'm in the middle of a fight, here—"

Too late. Vickie's "dingus" went off like a solar flare. John and the Thulian commander staggered, but John recovered first. Still half-blind, he struck at the commander; bones cracked and John could feel the distinctly wet feeling of blood soaking into his gloves. He hit something hard, maybe the Nazi's armor, and then his opponent was on the ground, dead or unconscious. John struggled back to retrieve his rifle, blinking rapidly to clear his vision. "Gimme a reading, here! What's going on?" He had already started out the door and back the way he had come, shouldering his rifle to a low ready.

"Corridor ahead is clear as far as the camera can see. Pickup is getting remote footfalls, running, other end of the complex. Getting one...two...three. No sound at the stair end."

"Got it. Moving." John ran as fast as his metahuman legs could carry him. As he worked his way up through the base, he came to a section of hallways and spotted a group of Thulians at the end of it. One was carrying a box, the others, weapons; he triggered and threw an HE grenade without a backwards glance, and was already at the entrance to the stairwell when the explosion rocked the corridor. His legs pumped up and down, slamming loudly against the circular stairs, finally carrying him up into the old barracks room.

Thankfully, the only Thulians there were the ones he'd dispatched earlier. He ran in a flat-out sprint, busting through the door and out into the morning. *It'll be just my luck if some straggler or someone I missed spots me and tags my dumb ass.* He couldn't spare a moment to pause and check; the entire base, or what was left of it, was on full alert and likely heading right for him.

"Far west end of the complex, patrol of five, must be in a vehicle or powered armor, they're coming your way about twenty klicks an hour—"

"Cut it; just lemme know when I'm clear of the facility." John didn't bother whispering now; his rifle was tucked away, and he was making a beeline for his vehicle.

He was well into the tree line when Vickie said, *"Now."* John mashed his fist into a toggle on a device he had removed from one of the pouches on his gear. There wasn't any sound, at first. But he felt what happened next, as clear as if he had seen it. The ground shook, jumped, and then fell down. He was in midstride when it happened, and was dumped hard into the ground at close to thirty-three miles per hour. He rolled, cutting himself against rocks and brush before coming to a rest.

"That'll leave a mark. You gonna make it back to the truck?"

John took a few moments to breathe, then slowly picked himself up off of the ground. "Yeah. I'm not gonna look pretty, but I'll make it."

"Mind telling me what you did?"

"Dug a pretty big hole, by the looks of things." He bothered to glance back at what used to be the Thulian-occupied missile silo; all that was left was a fifteen-foot-deep depression on the ground, black and oily smoke seeping from the center.

"Patrol still coming." Vickie's voice had gone sharp with alarm. "At least one power suit. No, two. Make that three. Coming in fast."

"What happened to the other two?" John did a quick inventory. He only had his rifle, his pistol, a few of the charges that Bella had supplied him with, and some grenades. Not much, in the scheme of things.

"I think the blast got them. You'll have visual in three...two... mark." It was just as Vic had said. Three powered armor suits, all tracking towards him, coming up over the edge of the crater he'd made. "I think they are very unhappy with us."

"Y'think?" They started to spread out; one was coming straight for John, while the other two veered off to his sides, flanking him. None of the Kriegers had fired, yet. *Looks like they want a prisoner. Mistake on their part.* The suits came to a rest about 50 yards around him. He gauged their distance, then looked to the lead Thulian in front of him. "Y'know, if it was me, I would've shot first." Without waiting a beat, John snapped his arm out, a bolt of superheated plasma arcing from it and impacting the helmet of the Thulian.

"Johnny, I got nothing to help with. Wrestling that intel out of the computer took everything I had." It sounded as if she was grinding her teeth. "Someone out there in Krieger land knows some rudimentary techno-magery, and he has a lot of power behind him."

John recognized and filed the information away as he heard it. He had already figured that he'd be alone for this fight. It was best to count on being alone for every fight, with whatever backup being a welcome bonus if it ever did come. The first Thulian's body had hardly thumped into the fertile Kansas soil before the other two charged. They were looking to catch him in a pincer move, attacking from both sides at once to incapacitate him. John decided to take their initiative away, and ran hard towards the one on his left. The distance between them closed quickly, and at the last minute John engulfed the Krieger in a jet of flame before juking around him. Pivoting to face the temporarily blinded Thulian, he simultaneously unslung his rifle and dropped into a crouch, flicking the selector to 'full-auto.' Two suppressed bursts cracked from the rifle, stitching the knee joints of the Thulian from behind and sending it crumpling to the ground.

The second one that had been following John finally caught

up—by jumping *over* its wounded comrade. *Well, shit. That's new.* It took John's mind less than a second to process several things about these Kriegers. They weren't wearing the normal power armor that everyone was used to seeing. These suits were more streamlined, not as bulky, and physically smaller than the terrors that fought in the Invasion. Closer to normal metahuman size. They also appeared to have a lighter-weight armor over heavier exoskeletons, as opposed to fully-hardened power armor. The camo job over the normally shiny silver coating completed the differences—what looked like a Wehrmacht camo pattern from the '40s, if John remembered correctly.

The second Thulian didn't waste any time; immediately upon clearing its downed comrade, it fired an actinic energy beam at John. The shot went wide, rending the ground to his left. John barely had time to react before the Thulian was upon him. These suits were definitely faster than their counterparts. The Krieger immediately tried to deliver a double overhanded blow to crush the life out of him, kicking up more earth when John snaked out of the way. Every time John tried to gain distance and use his fires, the Krieger would be right there with him. *Smarter than your buddies.* With his enhanced strength, John could probably keep pace with the suit; only problems were that it had a longer reach, and armor. He was still his usual squishy self; a good blow could lay him out, permanent-like. The enhancements were very good and all, but he'd have a hard time getting up with a broken back. *Gonna have to outmaneuver this bastard, outthink him.* John focused solely on deflecting blows, keeping himself out of the way of all the energy being directed his way. The weight behind the punches and strikes the Thulian was throwing was staggering; several hundred pounds of metal, controlled by flesh, all hurtling towards John.

"Y'call that fightin', *scheisskopf*? I've had a worse go in French whorehouses!" The Krieger certainly understood one word of what John said—one advantage of being at a US base in Ramstein was you picked up plenty of insults. He threw everything he had into a hard right hook; John leaned far out of the way, but still felt the air coming off of the punch. John reached down before the Krieger could react, and suddenly snapped the man's arm behind his back. John did his best to lean away while he jammed the Thulian's fist into his own spine. Then the blast came. The Thulian's arm cannon triggered, blowing viscera and metal fragments out the front of his power armor, ending the fight. John was thrown back several feet, but managed to land without bashing his head against the ground for once. He picked himself up and examined the scene. The second Krieger was on his back, with a hole the size of a basketball through his chest, obviously out of the fight. The first one that John had disabled, however, was looking to get back into things; he was shakily trying to raise his arm cannon in John's direction.

"No luck tonight, pal." John raised his own arm in response, sending a bolt of fire right into the Krieger's face. A few seconds later, there was nothing but a charred stump.

"Fourth Krieger, on the ground, unarmored, on your eight." Vickie's voice was harsh with fatigue.

"Did y'make sure to record that last bit? The suits these Kriegers are wearin' are different. Scout variant, maybe." John could appreciate that she was exhausted, but they both still had a job to perform.

"Ten-four. Saw that. Got the site tagged—explain later."

"Roger. Gonna do one more camera sweep over the bodies, close-up and detailed, for the record. Then we'll go talk with our survivin' friend." After John was done recording the bodies of the three dead troopers, he leisurely made his way over to where the sole survivor of the patrol was. An unarmored Krieger, human. He was struggling along the ground with what looked like a badly broken ankle—probably took a bad spill when the base exploded. John dragged the man bodily to his feet. "Can you understand me, pal?"

This one was fully human, or so much so that he didn't show any of the alien traits. The man glared at him with hate-filled eyes, eyes that looked at him as if he were looking at a particularly large and violent insect, and said nothing.

"Okay, that's fine." John nodded. "Overwatch, I'm gonna need ya to translate in a second. But, not for this part." John broke the man's right arm. First at the elbow, then at the wrist, and then between the two for spite.

"Jeezus, JM—"

"Shaddup an' translate. Green, comrade? You can have output on this headset, right?"

"Yeah." He heard her take a long and shuddering breath. "Pull

out the right earbud. I'll boost the output. Hold it at arm's length."
John did so. He took a moment to think on Vic's hesitation. But
only a moment.

"All right, pal. Here's how it is. You sons of bitches aren't going to
have your way with the world anymore. This is just a taste of what
you bastards got comin'. Y'dig?" John waited for Vickie to translate.

She did so. There was a pause, then she added more. From
the little German he had, it didn't sound anything like what he'd
said. *Personal touch? Good girl.*

That was when the Krieger's face went just a little greener.

"Glad we understand each other, Fritz. Be sure to tell your
bosses. We're comin' for ya, and next time? We won't be so nice."
John punched the man in the abdomen with his free hand, cracking three of his ribs, and then dropped him to the ground before
walking away. "We good here, comrade?"

"Put your ear back in. We're good." There was another pause
on her end. "My Gramps was in Theresientstadt."

"I didn't ask any questions, comrade. We're cool. I'm gonna
peel off the ninja suit and drive back to the hotel. Gonna take
me a while; gonna double back a few times and take some wrong
turns, make sure we're all right. You monitor on your end. Roger?"

"Ten-four. Bella and Saviour want to debrief ASAP. Do that on
the way, or at the roach-tel when you get there?"

"Let's wait till I'm back at the roach coach. I want my full
attention to make sure I don't have a tail stuck on my ass. Pin
the donkey ain't my favorite game when I'm the donkey."

"Ten-four. Take the way you came, go left instead of right at
the first turnoff. That'll take you into a little town with a good
distraction in it. There's what was supposed to be a development
that collapsed with the housing market, it's a maze, I'll guide
you through."

"Done. Good work, comrade."

"Try and be quieter next time, comrade. I think you woke up
Bear."

"Heaven help us all, and Chef Boyardee." John finished the
drive with a sense of self-satisfaction for a job well done. It was
a feeling he had missed for a long, long time.

The fuzzy picture in the TV screen looked like something on
public access; three people crowded together at a very small table.

Bella, sandwiched in between Red Saviour and Yankee Pride (who looked exceptionally uncomfortable out of his signature red, white and blue Echo armor and half-helmet).

"Okay, JM," came Vickie's voice, both out of the tinny TV speakers and through his earbuds. "I'm running the show from my laptop; we're in CCCP HQ for security. Your cam is live. We're ready for your debrief." The tiny camera he'd taped on top of the TV set had no light to show him it was on; but then it was meant for Vickie's use usually and was part of his shoulder-rig.

"Roger. Commissar, Bella, Pride." John nodded to each in turn, and then dived into his debrief; the lead-up to the assault on the Thulian base, his actions inside, how he gathered the intel, and the skirmish once he was outside. "The last bit, I took some personal initiative on. Vickie, care to queue the vid for that last livin' Krieger?"

"Rolling." A new window popped up on the TV, effectively obscuring Bella's head. The feed from his shoulder-cam ran. It paused as it got to the part where Vickie added something. "This was where I told him that they weren't facing the sort of people they'd been spying on via our television, they were facing people who'd fought the originals of which his crew was a rather inferior copy. And won."

Nat smirked. "I was catching 'Stalingrad,' I am thinking?"

"I might have mentioned it," Vickie replied.

Bella made a choking sound. "Did you have to—the guy was on the ground, for God's sake, JM!"

"Broken ankle is nothing!" Nat spat.

"He'll live. And it's a message that he'll take back to his masters, even past his words. Murderin', genocidal bastard lived. Can't ask for more than that. I didn't cut anythin' off."

Vickie started the footage rolling again. "Look, Bella, YP—JM had to get out of there, didn't have cuffs on him, and was running short of time. Ankle down, and he's crippled—until he can reach a stick, then he's ambulatory. Take out his arm, and he's gonna have to crawl until he can get to a comm that can reach out to wherever his masters are. When I figured that out, I was good with it."

"Uh, yeah. That was totally my reason, too." John did his best to suppress a smirk, and failed miserably.

On his private freq, Vickie blew a rasberry in his ear. "Damn it, bonehead, at least *try* and cover it up, will ya?"

"I tried," he whispered. "Just not very hard."

"I see the operational necessity," Pride said, gravely. But there was a touch of both a smirk and a little guilt at the same time.

Nat didn't even bother to cover her smirk, but as the footage finished, she sobered. "Comrade Murdock, this was being strong psychological blow against *svinya*. It was more than good that you sent message. Am seeing in behind-sight was necessary."

"Murdock mentioned Doolittle's Raid at the beginning of the op, in the planning phase, Commissar," Vickie said. "I think he should give us his thoughts."

"The old man told me a little about that," Pride said, his brow creasing. "The Aces kept Divine Wind busy while Doolittle's bunch got in, and I never could see the point. They didn't do that much damage."

John was silent for a few long moments, absorbed in his own thoughts. "Up until this point, we've been reactin' to these bastards. We've done well enough, now that we know how t'deal with them. But y'ask any general, down back to ancient times, and they'll all tell y'that reactin' to violence ain't any way to win a war. And we most certainly are at war." He paused, then continued, "This is different. We *found* them, instead of them findin' us. We went in there, and wrecked their toys. Not only that, we got the info needed to go and keep on ruinin' their day. That means somethin'. In the scheme of things, this hasn't hurt their ability to operate and make life difficult for us. But—" and John took the time to let a wide half-grin spread across his face, "this is the first time that we're gonna make life truly difficult for them. They're gonna start to think 'bout how we did this. And they're gonna fear about how much worse it'll be next time. Goddamn it, next time...we're gonna really make 'em bleed."

EPILOGUE

There it was, our first real victory, one where they knew it was us that hit them, hit them hard, and got away with it. And we hurt them. John was right about this being like Doolittle's Raid on Tokyo. An enemy that thought it had everything its own way had just discovered it could be hit, hit with planning and precision, and hit out of nowhere. The psychological value of this was immense, not only against them but for us. This had been a command and control center; though they had been in the process of moving out of it, it was still active, and more than anything else, the win here had given us that most precious of resources, intel. Those of us in the know got the word back out to the others we trusted and . . . and it gave us something, something that we had sorely needed.

Finally, we had hope.

Another freaking hot day, and the light gray gloves and track suit were only marginally better than the black. Vickie did her stretches methodically, remembering to breathe through them, instead of wincing and tensing up.

It still hurt like hell.

And as she started her run, it wasn't hurting any less.

That damned wall came up much too soon. *This* time, though, she got her timing right. Planted her right foot where it should go. Made the first jump and catch.

Plant, plant, hold on, swing, catch . . . The first ten feet went fine, but she could not help but be aware of how far away the ground was getting—and then she got to that bad spot, and she started sweating from nerves as well as exertion. All she could think about was how she'd missed that hold; her pace faltered, her arms and legs started to shake . . .

"Move your ass, Victrix! I haven't got all day!"

Red Djinni glared down at her from the top of the wall, jarring her out of her incipient panic.

"Breathe, blondie! Do I have to get you an MP3 player to tell you to do that too?" His tone mocked her. "Breathe in, breathe out. Breathe in, breathe out."

She *did* breathe to the rhythm he was setting, and matched her catches and holds to it. That got her over the bad spot.

"I could knit another scarf waiting for you up here."

Five more feet.

"Seriously, my mother can climb this faster than you."

Three. She paused.

"Giving up already?"

She snarled up at him, her breath harsh in her lungs, her side burning. "No."

One.

She threw an arm over the top of the wall and hauled herself up beside him.

"Your timing is lousy."

"That's because you've got no rhythm," she retorted. "Goddamn it, Djinni, why is it I'm supposed to like you again?"

"My endless charm? Because I'm suave and debonair? Pheromones—"

"Do *not* go there." Vickie swung her legs over to the other side of the wall. At least getting down was easier than going up.

"Stop a minute," Red told her. He gestured around him. "Catch your breath. Take in the view."

She did. The actual view was pretty mundane, and nothing she couldn't see from an office window.

The *metaphorical* view, however—she had never been up here before. Here she was, at the top of the climbing wall on the Le Parkour course, and the mere realization took her breath away. She found herself smiling, and glanced over at him.

The lines around his eyes were clear; the Red Djinni was smiling, too.

Doppelgaenger ran the entire sequence through replay, for the hundredth time, studying Red Djinni, looking for nuances he might have missed the first ninety-nine times. When he was done, he sat back.

So. With Bulwark down, the Red Djinni had taken over Bulwark's training duties...interesting. Very interesting.

Something, surely, could be made of this. And...of the Red Djinni too.